B

```
||| ||| || ||| ||| |||| ||| ||| ||| |||| |||
         D1014828
```

FATAL LEGACY

Also by Elizabeth Corley

Requiem Mass

FATAL LEGACY

A Detective Chief Inspector Andrew Fenwick Mystery

Elizabeth Corley

M
CORLEY
2001

Thomas Dunne Books
St. Martin's Minotaur
New York

THOMAS DUNNE BOOKS.
An imprint of St. Martin's Press.

www.minotaurbooks.com

ISBN 0-312-28381-4

First published in Great Britain by HEADLINE BOOK PUBLISHING
A Division of Hodder Headline Group

First U.S. Edition: October 2001

10 9 8 7 6 5 4 3 2 1

For Mike, with love

For I the Lord thy God am a jealous God,
visiting the iniquity of the fathers upon the children
unto the third and fourth generation of them that hate me.

Exodus 20:5

PROLOGUE

I have a rendezvous with Death.

Alan Seeger

It was the bitterest of nights, too cold for snow, with an easterly wind that tore at his throat and drew tears from his eyes. Frost outlined branches on which leaf buds had been withered by the unseasonable weather. In the distant sky, stars seemed to shrink and shine fearfully. The track was set in waves of iron-hard mud. Pools from the previous week's snows had frozen to thick black ice, but not thick enough to bear the weight of a heavy-set man.

The bulky figure stumbling along the starlit path lost his footing and landed heavily on his behind in a large puddle.

'Sod it!' His voice punctured the night like a gunshot.

The ice shattered and set him down ingloriously in freezing-cold water. Even his expensive trenchcoat couldn't protect him from the muddy liquid as it oozed through to his skin.

'Bloody stupid place to meet,' he muttered to himself as he lurched heavily to his feet again with the soft limbs and lack of coordination of a desk-bound middle-aged man who had let himself go.

He set off again at a determined trot, freezing now despite his heavy coat and good shooting suit. The wind shredded the racing clouds, allowing moonlight to guide him as he made his way deeper into Foxtail Wood. It was nearly two in the morning and no living thing stirred in the fury of the night.

Up ahead the man saw the first flicker of torchlight, and he hurried forward, relieved to have found his destination at last. A gentle voice called out to him.

'Over here, Alan. Mind that stump – oh, ouch. Are you all right?'

Swearing even more furiously, Alan rubbed his shins and finally made it to the small clearing where the torchlight steadily beckoned him.

'Bang on time as always.' The voice was calming, but he was in a foul mood and wasn't about to be pacified so easily.

'Bloody stupid time, if you ask me.'

'Yes, but there's a reason. I told you on the phone, we have to be very careful.'

'But why? What's happened? You said everything was fine when we last met.'

'Calm down. Here, have a drink, it'll warm you up.'

Alan took the Thermos flask and poured himself a large mug of whatever it contained. Fragrant steam wafted up to his appreciative nose – highly spiced mulled wine. Just what the doctor ordered for a night like this. He took a swig, swallowing half the contents in one mouthful. They'd used damned good claret for this; pity to spoil it, but he wasn't going to complain. Behind the rich fruitiness he could taste brandy, cloves, cinnamon, lemon, and something else . . . what was it? As he emptied the cup, a bitterness on the back of his tongue made him shudder.

'Still cold? Here, have another.'

He took the cup and started to drink without even thinking about it. The wine was certainly warming and he began to relax a little. As soon as he'd finished the second beakerful, he turned on his companion.

'What's so important, so urgent that we have to meet at this ungodly hour in this blasted spot? Why all this sk . . . sk . . . skulduggery?' He stumbled over his words. That wine had really gone to his head. He'd have to watch himself.

'I'll explain everything. Just come over here.'

Alan followed his companion across the moonlit clearing; all trace of cloud had gone now. It was treacherous underfoot and he slipped in a dark shadow of ice, landing heavily on his hip.

'Here, let me help you.' A surprisingly strong hand pulled him up by the elbow and guided him on as he tottered a few more yards. His legs felt very unsteady now and the trees swayed at crazy angles as he tried to stare at them and get his bearings. Everything seemed to be twisting and turning in the wind. He could barely stand up.

'I . . . I don't feel too good. Need to sit down for a moment.'

'No, not yet. Wait until we get to the car, then you can.'

'Car? You said not to bring my car.'

'I know, but I brought it for you, don't worry.'

He saw the bleary outline of his silver-grey Rolls up ahead.

'How . . . ? I don't understand.'

'No, you wouldn't. That'll be the effect of the pills – they were bound to act fast with all that alcohol.'

Alan felt the first shadow of fear as he looked up at the familiar face next to him. He recalled the bitter taste in the mulled wine.

'You've poisoned me?'

'No, not quite. Only enough to make you cooperate. Now relax, we're nearly there.' His gloves were pulled off his frozen fingers before he could prevent it. He could hardly focus now, but he knew the lines of his beloved car so well that even in his drugged state he could tell that there was something wrong. It had grown a snake-like tail that seemed to twist up and out in the wind. As he reached the car, he put his hand out to steady himself and his fingertips brushed the tail. It felt ridged and rubbery beneath his bare fingers.

'Good boy, now go on, touch it down here as well . . . and here. Good. Come on.'

He was pulled round to the driver's side. The door was open, engine running.

'Gosh, you're heavy. Here, give me your hand, you're a dead weight.'

Alan clung on, looking desperately for compassion in the face he knew so well. He was rewarded with a tight smile as he sat down obediently in the front seat. He reminded himself that he was with a friend. All he needed to do was explain how ill he felt and it would be all right.

4

The hand grabbed his arm and pushed him further in.

'Oops, not too tight! There mustn't be any bruises. Easy now, swing your legs up. Good boy.'

Alan sat befuddled, unable to move, his mind desperately trying to make sense of what was happening to him. He felt his bare hands pressed around a small plastic bottle, which was then thrown on to the seat beside him. Next, what felt like a wine bottle was placed between his thighs, wedged upright. His fingers brushed it loosely.

There was a cloying chemical smell in the car, which he recognised but couldn't name. The fear was back now, real, smothering fear that made him feel sick and caused his whole body to shake. He was so tired. He wanted to sleep, but more than that, he needed to understand. He struggled to form words.

'What's going on? Tell me, please!'

The well-known face turned towards him and stared him straight in the eye.

'It's simple. You're dying, Alan, right here and now. You're dying because you're old and useless, a liability that's outlived its purpose. Sleep tight.'

The door was slammed shut and locked from the outside. Alan struggled with the dead weight of his hand to try and reach the door handle, but it was too far away. His fingers brushed the rich leather padding of the armrest as he inched them higher, but the alcohol and drugs filled his head and limbs with a deadly weight. He relaxed back into the headrest with a sigh as sickly-sweet exhaust fumes thickened in the car.

Out of curiosity, the young policewoman picked up samples of the shotgun cases with a pencil and put them into evidence wallets, which she labelled quickly. They had been sheltered by leaf mould and there might still be prints. It would be interesting to see whether any were his.

The body had been discovered by a local gamekeeper, coming to check on the state of feed bins in the wood. He had recognised the car at once. He rarely visited the clearing, as it was only good for rough shooting, and it was vaguely ironic that the dead man had been one of the more regular guns. If he shot here it would explain how he knew about the concealed track to the clearing.

The young WDC had hesitated about whether to call out a SOCO team and photographer, but after talking to the duty sergeant she had done so. They'd be here soon; she only had to wait for them to arrive and the body to be removed and then she could leave. This was the worst part of the job, waiting around, sometimes for hours, with the only enemy boredom.

She walked carefully around the car, far enough away to avoid the worst of the smell, but the buzzing of the flies was still audible. A confusion of deep rutted tracks led to the clearing, and it was impossible for her to tell which ones belonged to the Rolls.

Once again she walked up to the car, her hand clamped hard over her nose and mouth, to stare at its single occupant and his buzzing entourage. It was grotesque what decay could do, yet she still found it fascinating. In the ten days that he had been missing, a sudden sunny spell had worked destruction on the body shut up tight in the car. Decomposition was well advanced, and she didn't begrudge the pathologist his job. Where the corpse's skin was exposed she could see green staining and some marbling of veins on the back of his hands.

She wondered where the flies came from in winter. For one terrible minute she imagined that everyone carried flies eggs within them, as seeds of their own decomposition, just waiting for the moment of death. She shuddered.

A length of hosepipe had been attached to the exhaust pipe and fed into the top of the window, where brown plastic parcel tape had been used to seal the inch-wide gap. The rest of the tape had been used on the other window cracks, and the empty cardboard spool lay in the left-hand footwell. She noticed all the taping had been done from the inside.

WDC Nightingale ran out of breath and withdrew from the car to breathe in lungfuls of fresh air. She gave one more glance at the decaying body sitting in the driving seat in its bundle of expensive clothes, and then firmly turned her back on the scene and its power to form lifelong memories.

PART ONE

To reign is worth ambition though in hell:
Better to reign in hell, than serve in heaven.

John Milton

CHAPTER ONE

It rapidly became common knowledge that Alan Wainwright had committed suicide one icy winter night, an action which delighted and appalled his family and acquaintances in equal measure. Apart from a mild heart condition, the sixty-three-year-old widower had been regarded as a man to envy. His difficult wife had died years before, allowing her energised husband a reprieve in which to enjoy a belated bachelor's life. And of course he was known to be a multimillionaire.

For over thirty years he had run Wainwright Enterprises, a sprawling conglomerate of local businesses that was one of the most successful in the county, and divided his leisure time between his estates in Scotland and the Caribbean. The family seat, Wainwright Hall, spread over hundreds of acres of the most productive agricultural and forestry land in Sussex. His sudden death was an unexpected blow to his business and created the potential for an extraordinary windfall for his expectant family. It made them less anxious than perhaps they should have been to question what could possibly have caused Alan Wainwright to take his own life without warning or explanation.

Two weeks after the discovery of the body, Alexander Wainwright-Smith, nephew of the deceased, and his new bride Sally were sitting unobtrusively in the solicitor's office waiting for Uncle Alan's will to be read. They had selected two upright chairs, tucked into the far corner, leaving those of comfortably upholstered leather for more important family posteriors. In the front row, facing the large walnut desk, sat the late Alan Wainwright's brother-in-law, Colin, with his wife Julia, Alexander's mother's sister. She sat in dignified silence, still beautiful despite her middle age, and perfectly turned out in the latest fashion.

Behind them their six grown-up daughters sat or lounged in a sprawling row, bored by the wait and impatient to learn what their rich uncle had left them. Of his six cousins, the only one Alexander liked even vaguely was Lucy, the youngest. He had endured a childhood of seemingly neverending humiliation at his uncle's house, and not one of them had ever befriended him.

The room became stuffy as they waited for the solicitor to join them. Jeremy Kemp had been the Wainwright family's legal adviser for many years and knew better than to start before the arrival of Alan Wainwright's only son, Graham. Always late, inevitably bohemian, despite having passed his fortieth birthday, Graham was the family black sheep. He had been spoilt almost to ruin by his overbearing mother, and his father had been so jealous of her attention that he had resented his son's presence. It was no wonder

Graham had left home and the family business behind him as soon as he was old enough.

At a quarter past three, exactly fifteen minutes late, Graham flowed into the office. He was not alone.

'Good God, Graham, what have you got with you this time?' Colin flushed brick red.

Graham smiled, obviously delighted that his gesture had not gone unnoticed.

'It's not a what, it's a whom, Uncle. This is Jenny, a friend of mine.'

Jenny was dressed in, well, very little. Despite the cool spring day, she was wearing a short skirt slit to her upper thigh, and a white halter-top. The materials of both made it absolutely clear to anyone who was interested that she had decided against underwear today. Alexander wondered that she wasn't cold. Colin tried unsuccessfully not to stare.

Jeremy Kemp had followed Graham into the office. He completed a rapid and unobtrusive assessment of the room and its occupants, pausing only briefly as he glanced at Sally, Alexander's wife, to give her a tight smile, then he ordered fresh tea and greeted each of his visitors by name. He knew them all well, as the Wainwright affairs, both family and business, accounted for most of his firm's revenues and all of its profit. Once the tea had arrived, he seated himself quietly behind his desk and brought the babbling group in front of him to order.

'Good afternoon, everyone. As you know, we are here to read the last will and testament of Alan Winston Wainwright.' He spread out the manila papers in front of him with slender manicured hands that looked as if they should have been holding a flute or a watercolour brush, not a dead man's words. The tension in the room was palpable. Alan Wainwright had been a wealthy man, but he had also been a secretive one, and no one knew how much he was really worth. Even the relatives he employed in his businesses were ignorant of the precise size of his entire fortune and had survived grudgingly for years on meagre incomes in anticipation of this moment. Julia was as anxious as the rest. Having six children and unfulfilled social ambitions was proving difficult to manage.

Jeremy Kemp looked at the expectant faces before him. Significant wealth and power was a corrupting mix – look what it had done to Alan Wainwright. He wondered what it would do to his heirs and suppressed a shudder.

'This is the last will and testament of Alan Winston Wainwright, executed on January the third of this year.'

There was a small gasp from somewhere in the room. He had changed his will less than two months before his death. Why?

'*I, Alan Winston Wainwright, being of sound mind and judgement . . .*' The solicitor's voice adopted a practised narrative tone as he read through the preamble. The whole family listened intently, waiting for the first mention of a bequest. '*. . . To Julia Wainwright-McAdam, my sister, an income of thirty thousand pounds per annum in due recognition of her moral support of my businesses over the past thirty years.*'

Julia had ignored the business, living off her mother's trust fund and devoting her life to fashionable good works until she had met and married Colin. She had lived in anticipation of becoming a serious participant in charity circles and now she looked furious. This was a pittance by her standards and would barely fund the costs of her wardrobe and beauty treatments. No one could meet her eye. They looked either nervous or expectant, depending on their conscience and natural optimism.

Only Alexander appeared unaffected. He could have no realistic expectations of an inheritance, given the unpopularity of his mother's elopement with a travelling salesman thirty-two years before. Even though she had once been his uncle's favourite sister, she had never been forgiven, and now that she was dead, even old memories would count for nothing.

'*To Colin Wainwright-McAdam, my brother-in-law, an income of ten thousand pounds whilst he lives, together with a lifetime interest in Manor Cottage, in recognition of his fondness for my Sussex estate.*'

Colin turned purple and Julia bone white. Her dreams of local patronage and committee chairmanships finally withered. At the very least they had expected the Sussex estate; enough hints had been dropped over the years. Julia couldn't even remember what Manor Cottage looked like. Colin could, and recognised it for the insult it was.

All eyes turned to Graham, who was lounging back casually, stroking Jenny's left thigh as she sat behind him. Jenny grinned at Alexander sitting next to her but otherwise appeared completely unaffected by it all.

'*To my son Graham, I leave half of the remainder of my estate as detailed in Annex I dated the thirty-first of December, and including the lodge in Scotland, half of the valuation of the Wainwright Family Trust and the works of art he chooses from Wainwright Hall to the value of thirty thousand pounds.*'

Graham scowled. He had expected the lot, however much it was, and he waited with barely contained anger to learn the name of whatever charity it was that he assumed would receive the rest of his father's legacy.

'How much is the Wainwright Family Trust worth?' he cut across Kemp. The solicitor merely pulled a computer printout from a file by his side.

'The valuation of half of the trust at the end of the last quarter was £7,567,308. I have estimated the total value of your portion of the estate to be just over fifteen million.'

The atmosphere in the room became frigid as Alan's brother-in-law and sister finally realised the enormity of the insult that had been handed down to them. There was silence for a moment, then a verbal storm erupted from Colin, Julia and their children.

'How could he do this?'

'He must have been mad.'

'The gall of the man!'

'This is just bloody stupid.'

'Don't swear, Colin, please. The least we can do is behave in a civilised manner. Anyway, we will need to consider contesting the will.' Julia's cool, carefully structured tones cut through the raised voices and there was a moment's calm as eight very angry people considered the potential revenge of a court battle.

Kemp spoke into the silence. 'There are further bequests, for the Wainwright-McAdam children.'

'You mean he's given the other half of his estate to them?' Colin sounded appalled, but his daughters were silent at once. 'Get on with it then, let's hear the worst.'

'Your brother-in-law left specific instructions as to the order in which the will was to be read.' Kemp cleared his throat and continued. '*For my nieces, the children of my sister Julia Wainwright-McAdam, thirty thousand pounds each and their choice of jewellery or furniture to the value of two thousand five hundred pounds each from Wainwright Hall.*'

'Then where's the other fifteen million gone?' Julia asked indignantly. 'Oh God, he hasn't gone and given it all to charity, has he? If he has, I tell you, he was not of sound mind! He never gave to charity in his life.'

Jeremy Kemp continued as if she hadn't spoken. '*And finally, I leave the remainder of my estate, goods and chattels as set out in Annex II attached, but explicitly including Wainwright Hall, its contents save those that have been bequeathed elsewhere, my estate in the Caribbean as set out in the deeds attached hereto, and the residual half of the value in the Wainwright Family Trust, to my nephew, Alexander Wainwright-Smith, and his wife Sally, as joint beneficiaries.*'

There was an awful silence. Alexander looked stunned. Sally had been sitting rigid throughout and now she just stared ahead, eyes glazed. No one in the room spoke. One by one his relatives turned and stared at Alexander, loathing, disgust, anger or simple jealousy in their expressions. It was impossible for them to believe what they had just heard. Alexander, of all people!

'How have you done that, you little weasel? You bastard, with your weekend visits and your phone calls and your bloody boring jobs working in the business. All the time you were plotting this. Who'd have thought you had the brains? Or perhaps you didn't.' Graham's apoplectic face turned to consider Sally. 'It was you, wasn't it? You cunning little—'

'Enough!' Kemp cut across him. 'There is absolutely no call for this personal invective; it will do no good. Some emotion is understandable at a time like this but there is no excuse for bad behaviour, and anger is a very unsound basis on which to reach decisions. I suggest that, unless there are any practical matters to be disposed of, I draw this meeting to a close, and that those of you who would like to discuss the matter with me further arrange individual appointments for tomorrow or Friday.'

But Graham hadn't finished.

'What about Dad's interest in the family firm? Wainwright Enterprises must be worth fifty million at least – it employs half the county, for Christ's sake.'

'Your father's main interests in Wainwright Enterprises were disposed of years ago. His small residual holding is part of the family trust you have been left.'

This was shock upon shock. They had all assumed that Alan Wainwright owned the whole of the business they had variously avoided or slaved in throughout their adult lives.

Colin's purple face glared at Kemp with something approaching hatred.

'You knew he'd changed his will, didn't you, and yet you said nothing. I bet you're going to get a nice fat juicy fee from this – and the more difficult it becomes, the more money you'll make.'

Kemp stared back calmly, meeting his eye with no difficulty. He was used to the man's rages.

'Colin, there is no point being angry with Mr Kemp when you know it's Alan who has done this.' Julia turned to the solicitor. 'I think your suggestion is a very sound one, Jeremy. We'll leave now, but please realise we *will* be back tomorrow.'

One by one the family left, until only Graham, Jenny, Alexander and Sally were sitting in the office. Sally still hadn't spoken. She looked from Alexander to Graham and then to Kemp, her hands clenched into a tight ball in her lap. Her smart but inexpensive skirt was starting to crease badly in the warmth of the office. Kemp decided to move matters along. He turned to Alexander.

'You obviously need to know that this firm is the sole executor of your uncle's will.'

'So old Colin was right then, you are going to benefit nicely from all of this.' Graham stood up as he spoke, trying to make himself more imposing by squaring rounded shoulders and thrusting out his bony chest. 'Well, there's one piece of business you won't be able to rely on in future, and that's mine. Come on, Jenny.'

Alexander struggled to find words for his cousin, but before he had them ready, Graham was gone, leaving him alone with his wife in the solicitor's office. Whilst he stared ahead, still in a daze, Sally spoke quietly with Kemp, then she took her husband's arm firmly and guided him outside.

'I think a nice cup of tea is called for,' she said, and Kemp smiled gently at her retreating back.

CHAPTER TWO

Jeremy Kemp had given his secretary strict instructions to keep a minimum of a half-hour gap between the Wainwright family meetings. The last thing he wanted was an impromptu gathering that might deteriorate into a brawl.

Colin and Julia arrived first, without their children. It was an uncomfortable meeting that overran, so that as they left, Julia, in Jaeger and pearls, was able to confront Sally, wearing a neat navy Marks and Spencer suit and pink blouse. As she tried gently to step to one side, the other woman moved to block her way.

'Just where do you think you're going, young woman? I want a word with you.'

Sally shook her head, unmoved by Julia's anger. She had been patronised by the older woman ever since she had married Alex, and she knew that the knowledge of their inheritance would be enough of a punishment.

'Please, Julia, this is hardly the time or place. Why don't we discuss this in private later over a nice cup of tea?'

'Cup of tea?! Dear God, who the hell do you think *you* are, inviting *me* for a cup of tea like Lady Bountiful. Frankly you're the last person I want to have tea with. I have my standards, you know.'

Alexander stepped forward and placed a firm hand on Julia's shoulder.

'Aunt Julia, please don't upset yourself. The last thing Uncle Alan would have wanted was for this to divide the family.'

Julia threw back her head and let out a blast of high-pitched laughter.

'You simpleton, that's *precisely* what he wanted. This is hardly the stuff of happy families. You're so stupid. Mind you, I shouldn't be surprised; your father was an idiot. What can one expect?'

'That's enough.' Alexander's tone was barely polite and carried the unmistakable weight of authority behind it. They all looked at him, held silent by surprised intakes of breath. Julia recovered first, but her voice was querulous and had lost much of its arrogant assurance.

'Don't think I don't know how all this has come about. You wait until I take you both to court. It'll all come out then, about you and your whore!'

'Enough, Julia!' Colin looked aghast at his wife. The new Alexander standing before him seemed quite capable of retaliating with an action for slander. He glanced sideways at the young couple. If his wife's outrageous insult had been intended to discomfort them, it had missed its mark completely. His niece by marriage regarded him with a cool, detached contempt; his nephew with impatience. Then, with absolute assurance, they stepped past his wife and greeted Jeremy Kemp with a warm handshake, leaving him to escort his unusually silent spouse outside.

Kemp settled Alexander and Sally into comfortable leather chairs and offered them a sherry. It was only eleven o'clock but he felt they all needed one. Sally sipped hers gratefully whilst Alexander, after touching the glass to his lips, ignored it. The meeting ran on past twelve, then to one o'clock. Kemp, engrossed in the detail, had forgotten about the appointment with Graham at quarter past, until he heard raised voices in the outer office. He looked apologetically at his clients.

'Graham was due to see me at one fifteen. For once he's early, and he's obviously objecting to being kept waiting.'

The door was flung back with such force that it rattled the windows, and Graham stalked in, smelling faintly of whisky. An apologetic Jenny stood behind him, dressed in extraordinary tight flared white hipsters and a cropped lime-green top that left her flat brown stomach and pierced navel bare.

'Typical. I should have known you two'd get in first.'

'We were just leaving. And as to what we discussed, none of it was confidential. We will very happily share it with you when you can spare us a moment.' Sally smiled, openly relaxed. Alexander took her arm and turned to Kemp.

'We'll leave you to it then, Jeremy. Come on, Sally.'

He opened his mouth to say something to Graham, but then closed it again and shook his head, as if unable to find the words. Graham stared in astonishment at the sudden change that had come over his cousin.

Alexander might have adjusted with unexpected ease to his unexpected wealth but his world was about to become even more complicated. He walked into Doggett and Hawes, Wainwright Enterprises' accountants, with a simple list of questions at three o'clock in the afternoon, and left at seven with a set of new responsibilities that would have intimidated even the most experienced of businessmen.

Doggett and Hawes' offices were the essence of anonymity and discretion on the outside, but once past the security-coded front door and card-controlled lift, the façade was swept aside, to be replaced by solid, tasteful luxury. As Alexander stepped out of the lift and walked towards the antique table that served as a reception desk, he was sure that he'd made a mistake and somehow ended up in a gentleman's club.

Faded Persian rugs covered a highly polished dark oak floor; a round inlaid rose- and satinwood table supported a massive willow-patterned bowl, planted with spring bulbs which perfumed the air with hints of an alpine meadow; an eighteenth-century grandfather clock ticked away steadily with a satisfactory 'ker-clunk', as it had done for the last two hundred and fifty years. The receptionist was a balding, portly little man dressed in a pristine white shirt, regimental tie and navy pinstriped three-piece suit.

He rose to his feet and said, before Alexander had gone three steps, 'Mr Alexander Wainwright? Mr Doggett is expecting you, sir. Would you like to leave your, er, anorak with me?'

The clock was chiming three as Alexander walked down the short corridor, past closed mahogany doors with brass fittings that had been polished to a smooth glow, to the last door on the left. The third chime sounded as the receptionist opened the outer door without knocking and then tapped firmly on the inner door immediately behind it.

'Mr Alexander Wainwright, sir.' He ushered Alexander in and closed both doors behind him.

Frederick Doggett sat behind an antique desk in an office more than double the size of Alexander's sitting room. It was better furnished, too. Despite the air-conditioning, a log and coal fire burned in a cast-iron grate set in a reproduction Adam marble fireplace. Walnut bookcases lined one wall and a collection of shooting prints covered the other three, while yet another grandfather clock measured out the time with a dry tick.

Alexander was so taken aback by the room that he missed the opportunity to study Doggett before the man was at his side, shaking his hand and simultaneously guiding him to a wing-backed chair in front of the fire.

'Alexander, how good to see you, but in such tragic circumstances. Please do allow me to extend my condolences to you and your family. A great loss and, I am sure, a great sadness.'

The man was so smooth that it was impossible to discern any double meaning behind his extravagant sympathy. Yet he must have known how little Uncle Alan had been loved. The sense that he was being laughed at, however cleverly, irritated Alexander and made him determined to dislike the accountant no matter what else the man said or did. As he took an A4 lined sheet of paper from his pocket, Doggett watched him in silence, a one-sided smile playing on his lips that changed infinitesimally, as Alexander looked up at him, into one of concerned enquiry.

'It's a list of questions my wife and I want to ask you concerning Wainwright Enterprises. I believe you already have a copy.'

'Of course, by all means. Would you like to go through them now or after you have had your uncle's directions concerning the future management of his companies?'

Alexander felt a fool, and that in turn made him annoyed. However, he said, mildly enough, 'Good point. Uncle Alan's instructions first, I think.'

As he sat in silence listening to his dead uncle's words, he realised with growing satisfaction that his working life would never be the same again. At its simplest, his uncle had recommended him as managing director of Wainwright Enterprises. He was to be given a seat on the main board and executive positions in the subsidiaries.

'I know that this must be a shock, and it is a considerable responsibility, but your uncle had the highest regard for your abilities. He felt very strongly that you should succeed him. You have spent time working in many of the company's businesses, and your uncle told me you have done well in them all. I know that he would have wanted you to step up to the mark, Alexander. It may be slightly earlier than any of us might have expected but nevertheless it was his wish.'

Alexander leant back in his chair and closed his eyes. From being the family underdog to controlling the whole firm was an intoxicating idea, yet Doggett clearly felt that he might need persuading. How they all misjudged him. After a suitable pause he nodded.

'Very well, I agree. Now you'd better tell me what it is that I'm responsible for.'

Doggett explained every aspect of the business – he had no choice under Alexander's relentless questioning. After over three hours, Doggett raised a weary hand as if he had had enough, but Alexander had one final question.

'As managing director I report to the shareholders. Tell me about them.'

Doggett's expression of helpful enquiry didn't change, but his whole body tightened slightly.

'Well, it's rather a complicated shareholder structure. The company has grown up in quite a . . . let's say higgledy-piggledy way over the past thirty-odd years. Wainwright Enterprises is eighty per cent owned by Wainwright Holdings; ten per cent was held personally by your uncle and has been bequeathed fifty-fifty to you and your cousin, Graham Wainwright; and ten per cent is owned by Councillor Ward.'

'George Ward? I voted for him.'

'Indeed.'

'And who owns Wainwright Holdings?'

Doggett shifted slightly in his seat.

'Would you like some more tea? Or a beer or whisky perhaps, given the hour?'

'No thanks. You were saying, about Wainwright Holdings.'

'This is where it becomes more complicated. For various reasons – predominantly tax, but I can assure you it is all legitimate – Wainwright Holdings is owned by a number of trusts on behalf of several local businessmen.'

'And they are?'

Three of the names he recognised immediately: Frederick Doggett, the man sitting opposite him; Jeremy Kemp, their solicitor; and James FitzGerald, his late uncle's financial adviser.

The clock chimed the quarter hour. Doggett glanced at it and stood up.

'This is a little bit awkward, Alexander, but I actually have a dinner engagement – I'm meant to be there now. Could we continue this some other time?'

'Of course. How about first thing tomorrow morning?'

'Diary's rather full, I'm afraid. I'll get my secretary to call yours and set up a time.'

Despite his urgent supper engagement, Doggett watched from the vantage point of his upper window as Alexander left the building, following the underdressed new managing director of Wainwright Enterprises with his eyes until he turned a corner and was out of sight. Then, all thoughts of dinner apparently gone, he sat down at his desk and picked up the phone. The number he dialled was answered at once, and he spoke without preamble.

'James, he just left. It didn't go quite as well as we expected. He's more assertive than we were led to believe . . . Bright? Well, yes, I'd say he was, surprisingly so, but I think it's more his persistence than any intelligence we'll have to worry about. There's more of the Wainwright blood in him than we'd all thought.'

There was a longer pause, in which Doggett shifted uncomfortably in his grand leather chair, beads of sweat forming on his forehead. When he spoke next it was with an effort to maintain his smoothness.

'Yes, of course, if you want to meet. I'll call Jeremy and wait for you here.'

Doggett replaced the receiver with a shaky hand and ran knobbly fingers nervously through his hair, disturbing its immaculate finish. He sat unmoving for several moments then, loosening his tie and undoing his top shirt button, he got up, walked over to the drinks tray and poured himself three fingers of whisky. The splash of soda he threw into it was so brief it was virtually all spray, but psychologically perhaps he could tell himself that he wasn't drinking neat spirits. Then he sat down heavily in a wing chair and stared vacantly into the dying embers of his fire.

James FitzGerald let himself into the rear entrance of the office block using his own key. Frederick Doggett and Jeremy Kemp were waiting for him in the ridiculously oversized office that Fred insisted on, and he gave them one of his smiles. He knew that it would unsettle them and the thought made him grin even more broadly.

'Evening, gents!' He had never bothered to change his working-class Sussex accent and he enjoyed watching their joint suppressed shudder at his tone. 'I'll have one of whatever it is Jeremy's drinking, thanks.'

Doggett handed him an iced gin and tonic and he took a swig.

'Lovely. Let's sit down then, no point standing around like spare pricks at a wedding.' He took the chair closest to the low fire and waited for the others to settle before asking, 'So what's your considered opinion, Fred?'

'Of Alexander Wainwright-Smith? He's very curious and far from the pushover Alan led us to believe.'

'He's a Wainwright; bound to be an awkward bastard. When we agreed to him becoming the next MD on Alan's retirement, we had assumed that the old man would replace George as chairman and be able to keep his nephew in check. Now he's dead you'll just have to do it yourselves. I'll get you both on the board.'

James watched their reaction as his shot went home. They were neither of them made of the same stuff as their fathers, and he missed his old contemporaries with a sudden yearning. With Alan's death he was the only survivor of the original team that had restructured Wainwright's to suit their own ends. Fred Doggett's father had died a grand old man at the age of ninety, leaving his wimp of a son to run the accountancy practice and play with young men in his spare time. Jeremy's father had died of a heart attack less than a month later.

'I'm not sure going on the board would be appropriate, James. I'm your auditor; it would cause raised eyebrows.'

'Fair enough. How about you then, Jeremy?'

The solicitor flushed and took a long swallow from his crystal glass.

'I, er, well . . . It's a very close connection, and I am Wainwright's legal adviser . . .'

'I see. No takers, then.' James hadn't expected either of them to want to be so closely associated with the firm, but he had tested them anyway. That was the problem with the second generation: they were poor copies of their fathers and couldn't be relied upon in a crisis. Not that this was a crisis, yet. They were watching him as a mouse watches a snake, waiting for the strike that might not come but wouldn't miss if it did. He let them wait and sipped slowly on his drink as he considered his options. After a long pause, during which the tension in the room had turned Doggett's baby face puce, he replaced his empty glass on the side table and stood up to leave.

'We'll do nothing for the moment; let's see how he settles in. Fred, make sure you stay close to him, and Jeremy, you keep in touch with his delightful wife. That shouldn't be too difficult, even for you!'

Without waiting for their replies, he turned and left them to their evening, which he knew would now be filled equally with a dread of ghosts from the past and a fear of the shadows cast by an uncertain future.

CHAPTER THREE

Graham pulled out an upholstered gilt chair and Julia backed into it graciously. Colin settled Jenny into a matching seat on the opposite side of the dining table and then sat down heavily in his own and raised his glass to drain his strongly ginned martini.

The restaurant was full, but the high level of background chatter, which guaranteed them privacy for their conversation, compensated for the long wait to be served.

Graham ordered champagne and smiled away his aunt's disapproval.

'In honour of Dad. He would have approved, and we need to do something for the poor old bugger after that memorial service.'

'It was very . . .' Julia searched for a word, 'understated. It took them months to arrange it after all. They could have handled it better.'

'Oh, the service itself was all right. I think Alexander was right to keep it low key. After all, the funeral was only three weeks ago. It was the awful funeral meats afterwards that got to me. Sparkling wine, for heaven's sake, and ham sandwiches!'

'Well, that would have been Sally, she's incredibly mean with money.' Julia's tone said it all.

'You really don't like her, do you, Aunt?'

'She's awful, a common little tart with ideas above her station.'

'Really, darling, there's no need to be so blunt.' Colin glanced at Jenny, hoping that she hadn't taken offence. She had dressed in black out of respect for Graham's father, but there was very little of it and an awful lot of Jenny on display. She appeared indifferent to Julia's remarks. Julia ignored her husband and pulled Graham closer so that she could speak more privately.

'I'm convinced that she . . . How can I say it politely?' Julia paused, clearly uncomfortable at what she had to say. 'Well, bluntly, Graham, I think she seduced your father into changing his will.'

'Interesting. And a number of his friends today were insistent that it couldn't have been suicide.'

'Well, it was hardly an accident!'

'Exactly.'

Unease about the coroner's verdict had been rife among Alan Wainwright's acquaintances, but initially they had found no answering concerns among his family, who had all been too eager to learn of their inheritance to allow room for doubt into their minds. But, with the will read and disappointments received, they were all too ready to share the concerns that remained over Alan's inexplicable suicide.

Julia gave Graham an appraising look, then leant even closer to whisper in his ear. 'If it wasn't suicide, then . . .?' She stopped quickly, realising that Graham had been one of the major beneficiaries of his father's death. He sensed her embarrassment and changed the subject.

'What do you know about Sally, Aunt?'

'What do any of us know? Very little. She turned up here in Harlden less than six months ago and married Alexander in January. There were no relatives or friends from her side at the wedding, and she insisted on a register office ceremony. Then, just over a month later, your father died. Are you suggesting . . .?'

'I'm not suggesting anything. I just think it's been very convenient, that's all.' Graham paused, and then continued with a look of calculation on his face. 'After the will was read, I hired a private investigator to dig into her background. He's not from around here, I found him in London. So far he's been a waste of money, but I've retained him for another week or so. One thing he is sure about, though: she changed her name or her date of birth at some stage. The maiden name on her marriage certificate is Price, but there's no record of a Sally Price being born on the date she gave as her date of birth.'

'Well, let me know what you find out.' Julia smiled unpleasantly. 'I'm very interested. It is unbelievable that your father could have left Alexander half his estate; he could hardly bear to look at him some days.'

Graham and Jenny had taken a room in the best hotel in town. It was only rated three stars and Graham was having some difficulty adjusting to the lack of five-star services. He was sitting up in bed when Jenny emerged from the shower.

'What are you doing?' she asked.

Graham quickly scooped up a bundle of papers and photographs and put them in an envelope. He passed her a small handful of press cuttings.

'Julia gave these to me. There's one here of the music festival where Alexander and Sally met – see, there's a photograph of her. It says underneath that she's a local girl, but no one I've spoken to remembers her. Isn't that odd?'

'Not really, it's a big town.' She slid beneath the bedclothes and put her arms around his lean waist. His skin smelt of lemons, whisky and cigars. It was uniquely his smell and she loved it. 'It's gone midnight,' she murmured.

'Uh-huh.' He lifted the brown envelope off the bed.

'What's that?'

'Surveillance photographs. They've just been delivered by my private detective. I asked him to follow Sally for a few days, and this arrived this evening, but there's nothing interesting yet.'

'You've inherited over fifteen million pounds. Why not let it go? You don't need the extra money.'

'I don't care about the money. It's far more than that. After listening to his friends today, I don't believe my father committed suicide. Somebody killed him, Jenny, and I think Sally could have had something to do with it. I certainly believe she tricked my father somehow, and I'm going to prove it.'

* * *

21

Alexander opened a bottle of Bulgarian Cabernet Sauvignon and passed a glass to Sally as she huddled in front of a tiny electric fire in their sitting room. It was threatening to snow again, but she still insisted on keeping the central heating thermostat to a level just sufficient to stop the pipes from freezing. He had only been married to her for two months after a whirlwind courtship, and there was so much about her that still baffled him.

'I thought the memorial service went well, didn't you, Sal?'

'It was fine. I'm just glad it's over at last. Some of them didn't leave until nearly seven o'clock. God knows what extras that hotel are going to charge us.'

'Not much. They need whatever business they can get right now. I just hired the room from them, plus the staff, and Mrs Willett did the rest, although she said she thought you'd been a bit tight with the budget you gave her.'

'Did she indeed! Well, you've got to remember that we're talking about *your* food and wine now, Alexander – and *she's* got to remember that she's *our* housekeeper! I'm not sure that Mrs Willett is going to work out.'

Alexander noticed the two pink spots of colour that glowed on Sally's cheeks and recognised them for the warning sign he had become accustomed to. She'd had a difficult time after the service, with first one relative, then another snubbing her deliberately, and he could see that she was spoiling for a fight. Best to change the subject.

'I saw you talking to George Ward after the service. I tried to join you but I seemed to be surrounded constantly by other guests. He's our chairman – what do you think of him?'

'Oh, all right, rather dull.'

'He didn't look dull; in fact, I thought he seemed really worked up about something. What did he say?'

'He was going on about your uncle's death, called it a tragedy, untimely, the usual. I thought he was a very nervous type, not chairmanship material at all.'

Sally picked up their empty dessert dishes and took them into their tiny freezing-cold kitchen. The treacle sponge had been too heavy for Alexander, but he'd known better than to leave it, as Sally wouldn't stand for that. Waste of any kind was an appalling extravagance to her. He would never be able to fault her on thriftiness. He had already forgotten how quaint he had thought her, and their household management was now one of simple, if meticulous, routine. He was struck suddenly by the magnitude of the change to their personal lives if they moved to Wainwright Hall. Worried that she wouldn't be able to cope, he caught her hand as she sat down at the table again.

'Sal, I don't want you worried by our move to the Hall. Do you need help with it?'

Sally looked at him strangely, and for a disturbing moment he thought she was going to laugh at him, but then she simply smiled and patted his hand where it rested still in hers.

'That's very sweet of you, darling, but I think I'll cope.'

CHAPTER FOUR

Detective Chief Inspector Fenwick settled back into a moderately comfortable chair and focused his full attention on the conference platform. It had been Assistant Chief Constable Harper-Brown's idea that he should attend this seminar. The division's training and development record was so appalling that any inexpensive opportunity to improve the statistics was latched on to immediately.

The room was almost full, a testament to the popularity of the subject even in these overworked, budget-constrained times. Two speakers stepped on to the platform and the lights dimmed. A slide flashed up on the screen. *Forensic Accountancy*, and underneath it, in smaller letters, *Cooperation Initiative*. The Institute of Chartered Accountants in England and Wales had joined together with representatives of the banking and insurance industries to fund a series of lectures for police forces across the country. Their goal, apart from playing the part of good corporate citizens and thus hoping to soften any further tightening of the already tough regulations, was to improve their ability to work with the police to reduce fraud and the laundering of criminal money through legitimate business enterprises.

In a dry but authoritative voice, the first speaker explained briefly what money-laundering was: how criminals would set up a series of complex businesses through which they could pass the proceeds of criminal activity. Simply put, the 'dirty money' went in at one end – say the exchange of currency at a bureau de change – and came out clean at the other as untraceable cash or balances in legitimate bank accounts. Most of the dirty money was from drugs or smuggling, but the system wasn't choosy and proceeds from any criminal activity could be processed.

Governments, legislators and law enforcement bodies across the world had recognised in the 1980s that preventing a criminal from benefiting from a crime would reduce crime itself, either by making the risks of using the money unattractive or by preventing the financing of bigger and more rewarding criminal activities. Wide-ranging laws and regulations had been introduced, some of which made it the responsibility of the banks and other financial institutions to ensure that the money they accepted was legitimate. Penalties for failing to do so were fierce, for the company and even for individual employees, who could be prosecuted for any personal mistakes or oversights. The speaker explained that bank clerks themselves could end up with a fine, a criminal record and even a prison sentence if they accepted suspicious money or helped to process it in any way. But the better the controls that were put in place, the more clever the criminals had become and the more difficult it was proving to expose their schemes. Fenwick took detailed notes and listened with interest to the unfamiliar technical, legal and accounting terms.

The second speaker described new European-wide legislation that he and others were trying to have introduced, but his explanation was so complex that several of his audience nodded off to sleep. During the fifteen-minute break before the next session, Fenwick poured himself an extra-large cup of black coffee and nibbled on a shortbread biscuit in a desperate attempt to raise his blood-sugar level and avoid the embarrassment of falling asleep when the lights dimmed again.

'Hello, Andrew! How are you?' a deep Welsh voice boomed out behind him.

'Davey! Good, thanks. Great to see you. Good Lord, it must be, what – three years now?'

'And the rest. We were at that damned refresher course out in the sticks for over a month. That was longer ago than I'd care to be reminded of.'

Davey Morgan was a powerful, rugby-playing man who had gone through the selection process to be made a chief inspector (in the days when the rank still existed) alongside Fenwick. They'd discovered to their mutual surprise a natural rapport and a shared dry sense of humour. Morgan was one of the few people with whom Fenwick felt he could relax. They'd always meant to keep in touch, but that was before Monique's illness and Davey's move away from the south.

'Where are you now?' Fenwick asked.

'Still Liverpool. It's a tough patch but the wife and kids live out on the Wirral and they love it. And you?'

'Harlden, West Sussex.' He couldn't bring himself to discuss his family, and Davey sensed his reticence.

'West Sussex. That rings a bell . . .' He took a thirsty gulp of coffee, the porcelain cup fragile in his giant hands. 'I know! Isn't that where Harper-Brown ended up, as ACC?'

'Yup. You know him?'

'Know him! By God, don't I just. Old Pencil-Pecker was my super for three bloody years. Boy oh boy, I don't envy you.'

Fenwick laughed. 'So it's not just me then? I thought the man had singled me out for his disapproval.'

'Lord, no. He's a nightmare, although I can see that you'd not be his type.' Davey joined in the laughter. 'I bet your paperwork's doubled.'

Fenwick shook his head grimly. 'Well, it *should* have done, but I can never seem to keep on top of it.'

That, he thought, was just one of the many problems he had in his relationship with Harper-Brown. It was as if they defined the fundamental requirements for being a police officer from different ends of the spectrum. Their only point of overlap was the importance of solving crime: Fenwick because of a driven search for justice in an unfair world, and the ACC for the statistical and measured satisfaction of a job well done, reflected in an improved ranking in performance league tables. This one common sense of purpose provided a tenuous link from which they both strove to create a credible working relationship at least sufficient to allow them to co-exist within the West Sussex Constabulary.

In the second half of the seminar, Fenwick was lectured on the legal protections that existed to prevent suspected fraudsters and money-launderers from incriminating themselves. He made very few notes and listened in growing disgust until the final talk about cross-force and international cooperation restored some of his faith in the system. The speaker, Commander Miles Cator, had been seconded from the Metropolitan Police to head a high-profile task force that coordinated Inland Revenue, Customs and Excise, intelligence services and police authorities in the UK, in cooperation with similar units in five other countries. He described how they had been working for three years to uncover a multimillion-dollar money-laundering operation that spanned three continents and ten countries, in an investigation that had employed over one hundred people. It had led to the arrest of fifteen people, spread across the US, UK and Monaco, who were still awaiting trial in custody.

Fenwick concentrated, barely blinking, on Cator's closing words:

'. . . So, if there is one message I would like to leave you with, one lesson from this case which is still at least a year away from trial, after which I'll be able to talk more freely about our methods, it is *never* underestimate the scale and complexity of the arrangements these gangs put in place. Crime, whether it's smuggling drugs or illegal immigrants, prostitution or plain old grand larceny, is *big* – and I mean *big* business. In fact, it is one of the most significant and universal sources of income there is in the world.

'Big businesses can buy the best legal advice, computer systems and accounting services they need in order to thrive. We have a world within a world today. The tentacles of organised crime, and the money-laundering arrangements needed to allow it to survive, spread everywhere in industry, our leading professions and even potentially into some governments.

'The people behind this are wealthy, organised, inventive and clever; ruthless and utterly without remorse. And it is only by combining the best of our talents that we will ever be able to compete with them and win. Ladies and gentlemen, thank you for your attention.'

Cator received the longest round of applause, and Fenwick was surprised by Davey's scepticism as they discussed the morning over a lunchtime pint.

'So you didn't rate what Cator said?'

Morgan shook his head. 'All conspiracy tosh if you ask me. Course crime is big business, everyone knows that, but most of it's ill planned and opportunistic. I've not met any of his "master criminals" in my life, have you?'

'Perhaps that's because they're the ones we never catch. You know as well as I do that if you add up the amount of money we know circulates from drugs alone, we only ever intercept a fraction of it. Where does the rest go?'

'Don't know, but what's your division's detection rate?'

Fenwick knew instantly: 'Twenty-two point three per cent last year.'

'Not bad! But my point is that the undetected money is accounted for by the seventy to eighty per cent of unsolved crimes. Where I come from, the great news is that the murder rate's up and it's mostly the daft buggers killing each other off! I bet more of them have been scared or injured out of the business than have ever been captured by any grand Inter-bloody-pol scheme.'

Fenwick couldn't help but laugh at Morgan's totally politically incorrect view on life – no wonder he and Harper-Brown had never seen eye to eye – but that didn't mean he agreed.

'That's only one side of the story, Davey. I think Cator's more right than wrong. There is another aspect to this business. It's just that those involved are so smart we rarely come across them.'

His remarks were greeted with another great belly laugh. 'That's because there's a little bit too much of the intellectual in you, boyo. You'd love to get your teeth into an arch-criminal – a real meaty challenge to whet your appetite. Me, I'm more of a realist. Come on, I'll buy you another.'

'No, can't, I'm afraid. I've got to get back.'

'You're going back into work again today? Forget what I said; it's just plain daft, it is, that you are.'

'No choice. H-B's called a meeting to review resourcing, case allocations, secondments, the lot, across the whole division. If I'm not there I'll find at least half my teams reassigned tomorrow morning.'

'Well, he's not changed. Go and fight the good fight then, and good luck to you.'

The meeting dragged on. They were expecting a difficult Easter, and the Assistant Chief Constable was looking for even more of his force to be deployed along the south coast to prevent any trouble. Organised protest groups were known to be planning riots and he didn't want a conflagration on *his* patch.

By seven o'clock Harlden had lost ten of its complement to secondments along the coast, manpower neither uniform nor CID could afford to lose, as they were already four under establishment as it was. Fenwick groaned inwardly as he thought of the extra work, standbys and long shifts that Easter would bring, just as the school holidays were starting.

Harper-Brown closed the meeting with a sharp reminder of the need to maintain efficiency. 'Some forces are achieving detection rates of close to thirty per cent, *regularly*, and rates of, say twenty-two point three are, frankly, looking anachronistic.'

Fenwick was keen to escape now that the meeting was over. The last thing he wanted was to hear Harper-Brown's infamous 'Ah, one more thing . . .' directed towards him that evening. He'd made it as far as the top of the stairs before he heard the call.

'Ah, Chief Inspector, just one more thing. Yes, you, yes, Fenwick. My office, if you please.'

'Yes, sir.' Fenwick hid his sigh of exasperation under a cough and turned reluctantly to follow the ACC. His boss from Harlden, Superintendent Quinlan, was standing close by.

'Problem?' Fenwick asked in a low voice as he passed him.

Quinlan shrugged and shook his head. 'None that I know of.'

When they reached the ACC's office, Harper-Brown left the door open, so it couldn't be an unforeseen disaster after all.

'How was the conference today?'

'Conference? Oh, this morning. It was good, really good. One speaker, Commander Miles Cator, was exceptionally strong.'

Harper-Brown's normal poker face turned dark at this unexpected praise before resetting into an expression of polite enquiry.

'Ah, Cator was there, was he? What d'you make of him?'

'Impressive, sir, from what I could tell. Young, of course, but bright, and seemed a good policeman.'

Harper-Brown busied himself with papers on his desk for a moment, avoiding Fenwick's eye.

'So you didn't find him, how shall I put it, a bit of a showman? You know, all smoke and mirrors?'

'Not at all, sir. What he could reveal of his methods seemed very sound and his results speak for themselves. Oh, I'm sure he's a bit of a diplomat, if that's what you mean, dealing with all those other authorities, and of course he's very young for his rank.'

The ACC was silent for a moment, and Fenwick gained a very clear impression that he'd upset him in some way.

'Very well,' said Harper-Brown eventually. 'I want you to produce a summary of all the sessions and circulate it within the constabulary. No point in a little learning not being shared, and money-laundering is a very hot topic. And Fenwick, make sure that it's a balanced paper – all the sessions, please.'

Fenwick had six open cases that he was working on, and he'd already lost a day to the seminar. Now he was going to have to spend further hours behind his desk producing this paper.

'Oh, and one other thing, Fenwick. I have a meeting with the Chief Constable and the Police Authority tomorrow afternoon and they've asked for a report on our complaints procedure. I believe that in Sergeant Warner's absence on secondment, you're the acting officer in charge of that at Harlden. I have all the other divisions' reports except yours and I'll need it for first thing tomorrow morning.'

Fenwick stared at him in disbelief.

'I don't think the Superintendent or I were aware that you needed a report, sir, otherwise I'm sure it would have been with you.' Even as he said it, Fenwick knew he shouldn't argue.

The ACC's thin mouth almost disappeared.

'You were sent a memo, Chief Inspector: here, see for yourself.' He thrust a piece of paper at Fenwick, who had no option but to look at it. The note was dated only the day before. At that moment it was probably sitting in his morning's post with a sticker on it from Anne, his secretary, marking it for his immediate attention.

'I see, sir. When in the morning do you need it?'

'First thing. The meeting's at two thirty and I'll need to have my report bound before I leave at one. Nine thirty at the latest.'

CHAPTER FIVE

The journey from HQ to Harlden normally took just under an hour, but there was an accident on the bypass and Fenwick waited an additional forty-five minutes in a tailback. He was so tired by the time he'd cleared the traffic jam that he drove on autopilot straight home.

It was only later, after he'd murmured a quick hello to the live-in nanny on his way to find a hot shower, that he remembered the complaints report for the ACC. With a smothered expletive he reached for the phone by the side of his bed and called the station. The duty sergeant was an old friend and ally.

'George, it's Fenwick. I've got a problem.' He explained his predicament and exactly where the complaints file could be found in his office. His secretary was frighteningly efficient when he allowed her to be, and it was one file he'd never had cause to open.

'Could you send someone over with it? I know you're short-handed, but . . . any chance?' If there was one person Sergeant George Wicklow would do anything for, it was DCI Fenwick.

Fenwick finished his shower and changed into jeans and a sweatshirt. It was a cold evening. He still had a tan from the half-term break he'd taken with the children, and the slight shading of grey in his black hair was stylish enough to look deliberate. All of which was an irrelevance to the man who gave the face that stared back at him from the bathroom mirror a cursory glance before turning to take the stairs two at a time in search of his dinner.

He'd almost reached the bottom step when there was a hushed call from the upper landing.

'Andrew! Hang on.'

A lithe twenty-year-old body leapt down the stairs, landing lightly at the bottom, right beside him.

'Hi. You didn't give me time to talk when you came in. There's been a bit of a problem.'

Fenwick's heart sank. He thought immediately of the difficulties they'd had with his son Chris the year before, and gritted his teeth in anticipation of terrible news.

'In here.'

The nanny led him into the kitchen. On the table were the half-assembled parts of a wooden box, with a pile of shiny pebbles beside it.

'Chris's been collecting those stones all week. Each of the children was given a box to fill and take in to class tomorrow. But he'd collected so many that when he tried to cram them all in, the box fell apart. And he'd spent ages finding, washing and polishing them.'

'I'm sure I've got a shoe box somewhere that'll do, Wendy.'

He realised from her expression that it was the wrong answer.

'He's absolutely sure he has to take the original box back tomorrow, and it needs glueing. I told him his daddy would be able to fix it. It was the only thing that stopped him crying!'

Fenwick looked at the rough pieces of wood, from which his six-year-old son, with absolute faith, expected him to create a suitable setting for his precious stones.

'This is going to take more than a bit of glue. Look, I'll have my dinner, then I'll take this lot out to the shed. Are you in for the rest of the evening?' It was already half past nine.

'Yup, Tony's coming over.' She blushed suddenly and Fenwick's heart sank. Wendy was such a great nanny, and he dreaded hearing the news that had so obviously thrilled her.

'Go on, what is it?'

'He's proposed,' she whispered shyly.

'And what have you said?'

'Yes!' she said with a small squeak of excitement.

Fenwick gave her a quick hug and kissed her cheek. 'Fantastic. Congratulations. I'm so pleased for you both. He's a great guy.'

He made himself a hasty supper of pasta with a basil and tomato sauce and a green salad, and resisted the idea of a glass of wine. He had too much to do and it was already ten o'clock. The complaints file still hadn't turned up by the time he'd finished his meal, so he decided to mend Christopher's box first. Before going out to the shed, he crept upstairs to check on the children. They still shared a room, despite the fact that they could have had one each. It was as if they clung together even more closely now that their mother had gone. It had been nearly two years, but every day without her still hurt him. He just hoped that they didn't miss her as much as he did. He banished the thought and pushed open the door.

It was always the same, always. That moment of listening intently for an indrawn breath; waiting for Bess's half-snore or the merest rustle from Christopher. Moonlight filtered around the edges of the curtained sash window, casting a blue glow over their twin beds.

A little grunt from Bess, an answering sigh from Chris, and his heart relaxed. They had become accustomed to seeing very little of him during the week, but for Fenwick it was a daily sacrifice and he felt its cost dearly. He bent and kissed Bess's smooth forehead, unable to stop himself from brushing her curls back and away from her face, despite the risk of waking her up.

She smiled faintly in her sleep and his heart turned over. At least she didn't look too much like her mother with her eyes closed. Chris was tucked into a ball, head burrowed deep in a fold of the duvet. Fenwick gently tugged the quilt away from his face and kissed his cheek. His son didn't stir. Fenwick straightened and walked carefully back to the door. A loud squeak disturbed the silence and he cursed inwardly as he bent and removed one of their latest toys from under his left foot.

WDC Nightingale was let into the surprisingly neat sitting room by Wendy. She tried not to stare as the slim dyed-blonde with a stud in her

29

nose removed the fireguard from the hearth.

'It was so cold I lit a fire earlier,' she said, in an unnecessary explanation that left Nightingale even more curious as to her precise place in the Fenwick household. 'I'll tell him you're here,' she added.

Nightingale looked around the room curiously, but the only hints of his family were in the framed photographs on the bookshelves. Nightingale wasn't wearing her glasses so she couldn't make out the faces without walking right up to them and peering. Acutely conscious of the open door behind her, she risked a quick look but was only able to make out a strikingly beautiful brunette holding a baby in her arms.

A clock on the mantelpiece chimed the half-hour and a block of ash fell soundlessly into the embers. After a moment's hesitation she bent down and threw a small log on to the fire. It crackled and blazed at once. Minutes ticked by. There was a CD player in the corner and she went to investigate. It was modern and expensive – she knew because she had one exactly like it. She bent and peered at the loaded CD, and the glass cover opened automatically in response to her movement: Schubert. She resisted the temptation to press Play. There was a faint creak and the door opened behind her. Nightingale snapped upright, her cheeks burning, and turned round.

A little girl of about seven years old stood in the doorway, staring up at her curiously, the toes of her tiny bare feet wriggling beneath the hem of a long cotton nightdress.

'Hello.' It was a confident little voice, almost that of a hostess welcoming an unexpected guest.

'Hello.'

'Who're you?' Deep brown, almost black eyes stared up at her from under a wayward mop of curly black hair.

'I'm Nightingale. Who are you?'

'I'm Bess.' A further appraising stare. 'Police?'

Nightingale suppressed a smile. 'Yes.'

'With my daddy?'

'Uh-huh, sometimes.'

'You're not in uniform so you're a detective, then.' It wasn't a question. Bess sat on the sofa to one side of the fire and pointed to another. 'Sit down.'

'Thank you.'

'He's late, I suppose.'

'No, I'm just delivering some papers but I was told not to leave them. I have to hand them to him personally.'

'Umm.' Legs swung inches from the floor. 'He'll be in the shed, I bet, mending Chris's project. Shall I get him?'

'No, he knows I'm here. Your . . . the lady went to tell him.'

'Wendy. Good.' Another restless glance around the room.

'That's Daddy's music,' she said, pointing towards the CD player. 'Would you like to hear it?'

Before Nightingale could answer, Bess was out of her chair and standing on tiptoe to reach the controls of the machine.

'Should you . . . I mean, is it all right?'

A haughty glance back over one shoulder.

30

'I'm allowed.'

The whisper of the opening notes of a Schubert piano sonata filled the corners of the room and crept up to Nightingale.

'This is one of my favourites, Bess. Good choice.'

'It was already in there. Daddy likes it too.'

Nightingale felt unaccountably uncomfortable. She stood up and started to pace the room.

'Do you know any stories?' asked Bess with more than a hint of appeal in her tone.

'Ah – no, not really.'

'You must know *some*!'

'Well, perhaps a few, but not very good ones.'

'Tell me some.'

'Pardon?' Nightingale's tone of voice, the raised eyebrow, the shocked stare were timeless. Bess reacted as if programmed.

'Tell me some, *please.*'

'That's better. Well, I'll need some time to think about this. What sort of stories do you like?'

'Adventures are best, they're my favourite.'

Bess patted the sofa and Nightingale obediently sat down beside her. At once, the little girl settled into her lap and stared up at her expectantly, one hand stroking and twisting a thick black curl of hair.

'Right, well then . . .' Nightingale took a deep breath and had made it as far as *Once upon a time* . . . when the sitting-room door opened wide and Fenwick came in. He stared at Nightingale and Bess in astonishment; words of apology for keeping her waiting died on his lips.

'Bess! What are you doing out of bed? It's nearly eleven o'clock and you've school tomorrow. Get back upstairs this instant.'

The tone was severe and Nightingale saw Bess's face cloud in surprised misery. It was obvious that her father didn't usually react so fiercely, and Nightingale realised with a flash of insight that it was because she had met one of his children that he was so annoyed. That was unfair on Bess and it was no big deal that she'd seen this side of him.

'It's my fault, sir,' she said, rising and placing Bess gently to stand on the floor. 'Bess was good enough to keep me company and I should have sent her to bed.'

'I didn't want her to wait on her own, Daddy.' Bess rushed over and hugged her father's thighs.

'But I've told you before about talking to strangers.'

'Even nice ones?'

'Yes, even nice ones. Now, go on, upstairs to bed.'

'Will you come with me?'

'Oh, all right, come on. Nightingale, you can go, there was no need for you to wait. Good night.'

Nightingale watched as the DCI bent automatically and lifted his daughter in a single, practised motion, so that she could cling on to his neck. She felt an unexpected lump in her throat and tried to swallow it discreetly. Bess heard her gulp and grinned over her father's shoulder.

'Night-night, Nightingale,' she whispered.

'Good night, Bess, sleep tight.' Nightingale let herself out into the chill night, closing the door firmly behind her.

Much later that same night, Fenwick sat stiffly in front of his personal computer and put the finishing touches to his report on the Harlden complaints procedure. He had meant to produce a cursory one-page summary, but something – his habitual pride in his work, or a determination not to let the ACC get the better of him, he didn't know which – had compelled him to do a thorough job. Harper-Brown wouldn't even read it, but Superintendent Quinlan would, and he'd be pleased. They needed to tighten up procedures to reach the new standards set by HQ and Sergeant Warner had never risen to the challenge.

It was nearly one o'clock in the morning but he was still wide awake. This house had been an extraordinary and unexpected inheritance from his great-uncle the previous year, but the income from the capital sum he had also received only just covered its upkeep and Wendy's wages. She was a good nanny, despite her dyed hair and nose-stud and her tendency always to be late. She hadn't demanded a huge pay rise to compensate for the inconvenience of living in the country, because it meant that she could be within a few miles of her boyfriend, Tony. If she decided to leave, Fenwick would never be able to afford an equally well-qualified replacement.

He tried to make an effort to compensate for being a single parent. Ever since the children had lost their mother after a suicide attempt had led to her irreversible coma, he had done everything he could to help them forget the terrible trauma. Everything except give up his job, because he couldn't afford to. He knew that if he ever had to decide between his children's welfare and his career, he would choose them, a thousand times over. He just hoped he would never be faced with that choice. He closed the file, switched off the computer and went to make himself a cup of tea before heading for bed.

CHAPTER SIX

On the day after he had delivered his report on Harlden's complaints procedure to Harper-Brown, Fenwick was surprised to receive a call from the Assistant Chief Constable concerning Alan Wainwright's death. There had been a lot of public interest in the investigation, enough to make the ACC uneasy and keen to see the whole case closed as quickly as possible. It had been handled by a colleague of Fenwick's at Harlden, DI Blite, a man he both disliked and distrusted. The investigation had been brief, and when the coroner's verdict was returned he had confirmed the cause of death as suicide. That the ACC should call him now, two months later, caused Fenwick to frown with unease. He doubted that this was going to be a welcome conversation, and he was right.

'Fenwick, I've had a call from Graham Wainwright, the deceased's son. It seems that he has his doubts about his father's death and the coroner's verdict.'

'Did he voice these at the inquest, and if not, why not, sir?'

'No he didn't. At first he says he trusted the verdict but now, it appears he's been hearing rumours. He wants us to have a quiet look, that's all. Wainwright's was in the news quite enough when his father died.'

'I see.' It didn't take a genius to work out why the ACC had called him now. Harper-Brown was too shrewd to show his intense dislike for Fenwick in obvious ways but he never hesitated to single him out for a potentially difficult and damaging case. He was handing him an impossible task: satisfy an influential and worried man who has just lost his father that his suicide is not suspicious, oh, but by the way, don't you dare stir up trouble now that we have successfully closed the case. It was suddenly obvious why the ACC hadn't called Blite, who would have been the logical choice. Handling this one without either upsetting the family or rekindling public interest would be a miracle.

'Graham Wainwright is an important man, his concerns have to be taken seriously but the last thing we need is the press forming any sense that we are unhappy with the verdict, *which we are not*. I told him you would call today and that you were renowned for your discretion.'

The ACC gave him Graham Wainwright's number and hung up. Fenwick studied the fingertips of his left hand briefly, deep in thought, then called his secretary.

'Anne, call Records and have them send up the file on the death of Alan Wainwright; it will be dated sometime in January this year. Then find Sergeant Cooper and ask him to join me.' Cooper could be relied upon to be

33

absolutely discreet, reliable and above all unexcitable. Just the man for the job.

The report arrived quickly. It was brief and Fenwick's heart sank as he read the few pages and waited for Cooper to arrive. Blite's team had interviewed family, friends and business colleagues of the dead man. At the time, no one could think of a reason for Wainwright to kill himself and only one acquaintance had raised concerns that his death might not have been suicide, concerns that were neither commented upon nor investigated, according to the papers in front of him. In the pathologist's report, attention had been drawn to unexplained abrasions on Wainwright's arms, knees and back and to further bruising down his left-hand side. It was all consistent with his having suffered several heavy falls shortly before his death.

There were traces of mud on his clothes and grit in his shoes that suggested he had walked in the wood before killing himself and one of his gloves, thick with mud, had been found in the clearing. There was no sign of the other. However, in the absence of any police suspicions, the coroner had had little difficulty in recording a verdict that Alan Wainwright had taken his own life whilst the balance of his mind was temporarily disturbed.

As he was about to close the file, Fenwick noticed a brown envelope tucked into the back. He opened it and read the two pages of closely typed notes it contained carefully. His secretary came in unbidden with fresh coffee as he refolded the papers and put them back in the envelope. 'Anne, please have DC Nightingale come up at once. If she's not in, find her.'

He remembered Nightingale vividly. She was a young policewoman still under training, and they had worked together on a case the previous year. She had impressed him then, but he hadn't seen much of her since. Sudden memories of that previous case crowded out his immediate concerns and he was frowning by the time there was a tentative knock on his door.

'Excuse me, sir.' As she tapped on Detective Chief Inspector Fenwick's half-closed door, Nightingale's heart beat faster.

'Yes?'

DCI Fenwick looked up, neither welcoming nor dismissive, his expression serious. Sight of his carefully neutral face did nothing to calm her nerves.

'You wanted to see me, sir?'

'Come in. It's about the Wainwright case. You were part of the team?'

'Yes, sir, I was first on the scene and then I did some of the interviews.' She had been given the less important ones: the housekeeper, gardener and maids on the Wainwright estate.

'And what was your conclusion?'

Nightingale blushed brick red and tried to think what to say. *Her* conclusion! It was a highly irregular question, particularly as she had disagreed so strongly with the officer in charge that she had gone so far as to put her own feelings on file. Still, she trusted Fenwick absolutely, so she said, without preamble:

'It wasn't suicide, that is to say I wasn't convinced that it was suicide.'

'Did you voice this opinion to the investigating officer in charge at the time?'

'Yes, sir, but . . .' How did she say politely that Blite and his team had all enjoyed the rare opportunity to laugh at her? Her professionalism and competence usually made her a disappointingly elusive target for ridicule – malicious or benign – so her continuous questioning and concerns about this case had exposed her to more teasing than she'd ever had to face before. Yet she had still persisted, which was typical of her if she thought that she was right.

'Well, quite honestly, he and the others thought I'd got worked up over nothing.'

Fenwick suppressed a grin. He had forgotten her absolute honesty.

'And yet you felt strongly enough about it to risk DI Blite's displeasure and to add your own note to the file?' Fenwick studied her closely as he waited for her answer, noting the tension in her shoulders and around her mouth. He remembered that off-putting intensity about her from the previous case. It was obvious that she was preparing herself to receive a reprimand from him, and he spoke quickly to reassure her. 'It's all right, you've done nothing wrong. Tell me why you had your doubts.'

'There were details that came up in the investigation that worried me, like the missing glove and the footprints all around the car. They looked as if they'd been made after the car was parked there.'

'That could be the result of the morbid curiosity of a passer-by without enough sense or civic duty to report the death. It happens.'

'But there was the bruising too – and the mud all down one side of his coat.'

'Remind me what the path. report made of the bruising?' He knew, having just read it, but he was curious to see how she supported her suspicions.

'That they were consistent with heavy falls just before his death. But if he'd driven to the clearing, what chance would he have had to fall down? It was a bitter night, so he wouldn't have been tempted to take a walk in the woods.'

'He might have stumbled as he went to attach the hose.'

'I thought about that, but he'd have used the car to steady himself.'

'Hmmm.' A few bruises and a missing glove proved nothing. 'It's weak, Nightingale. Was that all?'

'But there were the barbiturates, sir. His doctor was adamant that he didn't prescribe them and we've never been able to find the chemist who dispensed them, despite all our appeals. There was no label on the bottle in the car and I went through his rubbish three times looking for a receipt.'

Fenwick was forced to smile. Only Nightingale would be persistent enough to wade through a suicide's garbage so many times.

'And then there was the matter of his car keys. His housekeeper had been prepared to swear in court if need be that the keys I found in the ignition were the spare ones that he never used, whilst his main set had been on top of the chest of drawers in his bedroom, where he always left them overnight.'

Fenwick nodded, as if to acknowledge she had a point, then dismissed her with a curt 'thank you'.

'Might I ask why you were interested in my opinion, sir?' Nightingale knew that she should just go, but curiosity won out over discretion.

'No, you might not.' Fenwick watched the constable go with a determinedly expressionless face, but as soon as she had closed the door, his frown returned and he called Anne again.

35

'Have you found Cooper yet? I need him urgently.'

'He's on his way up to you right now, sir.'

Cooper arrived, breathless and pink-faced, moments later. He had just started an interview when he had received the Chief Inspector's message, and had hoped to wrap it up quickly rather than rearrange for another time, but it had dragged on and now he was late, something Fenwick hated.

Sure enough, the briefing he received was clipped and to the point. They had a difficult job to do and not a lot of time to do it in. Fenwick gave him the file and a list of people to interview that afternoon.

'The problem is, Cooper, that Graham Wainwright is convinced that his father did not commit suicide, whatever the evidence might say.'

'So why hasn't he come forward before?'

'Good question, and one that we will be asking him when we see him tomorrow morning – I've called him and he will be expecting us. Before then, I want you to talk to all the officers involved in the case, except DC Nightingale. I've already spoken to her.' He noted Cooper's surprise. 'You'll see why when you read her note in that file. She wasn't happy with the verdict at the time.

'This isn't going to be an easy one. We're going to have our work cut out to keep this out of the papers whilst we do enough to satisfy the son that his father's death wasn't suspicious. I hate these cases involving aggrieved and vindictive relatives at the best of times, but when they have influence as well . . .' He didn't need to finish the sentence, Cooper was already nodding and grimacing at the same time.

'I'll report back again tomorrow morning then, sir?' Cooper eased his tweed-clad bulk from one of Fenwick's notoriously hard visitor's chairs, trying to keep the look of despondency from his face as he did so.

CHAPTER SEVEN

Two poached eggs on toast, a slice of double back bacon with the rind trimmed off and grilled tomatoes, washed down with a mug and a half of strong sweet tea. Detective Sergeant Cooper was anticipating a difficult day, and that called for decent provisioning. His wife, sensing his mood of serious determination, said little as she made him a packed lunch. She knew that he was unlikely to find time for a proper meal if he was working with the Chief Inspector again.

'There you are, love.'

He gave her a quick kiss of thanks that left traces of toast crumbs in her wispy hair, and was on his way out just as his son was stumbling down the stairs en route to the second sitting.

'You're off early, Dad. Working with Fenwick again?'

'Aye, makes a change once in a while.'

Cooper lived within walking distance of Harlden Division, but today he would take the car. It took a couple of turns for it to start and he made a mental note to ask his son to have a look at it. He was a wonder with his hands, although being a mechanic at one of the local garages hadn't exactly been what his dad had had in mind for him at first.

The seven-thirty news bulletin was just finishing as Cooper parked. He was only a little surprised to see that Fenwick was there already. Hey up, he thought to himself, I knew it was going to be one of those days.

The Chief Inspector was in his office looking cool, refreshed and eager. His eyes were bright and he was whistling to himself through a half-smile. Cooper hid his astonishment in a cough that brought Fenwick's head up with a start.

'Sergeant! Excellent. I had a feeling this was going to be a good day.'

Cooper shook his head, forgetting to turn his unhelpfully expressive face away. The ACC had stitched them up with this case, cancelled all leave for Easter and was now sitting back waiting to see the Chief Inspector he disliked most fail. And here was Fenwick, happy as a sandboy, without an apparent care in the world.

'I know, Sergeant, I know. We're not in a great situation, but it's not hopeless either. I've had an idea and I'm going to join you today in this investigation!'

Cooper muffled a groan and unconsciously patted the lunch box under his arm.

'We'll interview Graham Wainwright, the other family members, the housekeeper and the management at the family firm, all very discreetly. I'm going to give us a day to see if we have grounds for further enquiry. Go and find DC Nightingale. She can help us out with the interviews.'

Cooper went to find Nightingale, fairly certain that she too would be in early. She was.

'What are you up to?'

'Packing, Sergeant. I've been sent off to the coast for three weeks over Easter.'

'When do you leave?'

'Tomorrow.'

'Busy today?'

Nightingale's heart quickened in anticipation.

'No, sir. One or two reports to finish before I go, but they're almost done and I can easily complete them tonight.'

'I keep forgetting just how keen you graduates are.'

Nightingale was on the accelerated promotion scheme, and now that Cooper had grown used to the idea, and to Nightingale, he no longer resented the new-fangled privileges it gave her. Besides, he had never seen anyone other than DCI Fenwick work so hard.

'Come on then, the Chief Inspector hasn't got all day!'

Nightingale tried hard not to grin like an idiot as she followed Cooper's broad back along the corridor.

Graham Wainwright had moved temporarily with Jenny to a country house hotel in one of the folds of the Sussex Downs five miles away. The three detectives became entangled in early commuter traffic and didn't arrive until nearly half past eight. There were new lambs in the fields that bordered the twisting drive up to the hotel, and Fenwick, Nightingale and Cooper each privately relished the first proof that spring had to be close at hand despite the lingering wintry weather. Graham and Jenny were still asleep when they arrived, so they drank coffee in a deserted cigar-smelling guest lounge as they waited.

'Nightingale, you talk to Jenny Reynolds separately, see what she thinks about Graham's worries and find out who else we should talk to as unobtrusively as you can. Cooper and I will work on Graham.'

They had to call the room a second time and in the end Nightingale was sent up to their suite to encourage Graham downstairs. He descended grumbling and unshaven as Jenny greeted the startled Nightingale wearing only a bath towel.

'I'm DC Nightingale from Harlden CID.' Jenny barely glanced at her warrant card. 'Do you have a few minutes? I wanted to talk to you about Mr Wainwright's concerns over his father's death. Has he shared these with you?'

'Oh, yes. Graham shares everything, can't keep a secret to save his life. Oops, now there's a slip. Forget I said that. Come in. I've ordered coffee and juice. Ignore me while I get dressed.'

Nightingale did her best, but Jenny had a model's disregard for nudity whilst Nightingale had been to a school where the girls still avoided communal showers. By the time refreshments arrived, Jenny had finally decided on old black jeans and an extraordinary fuchsia-pink cropped sweatshirt, having apparently tried on everything else from her wardrobe, cocktail dresses included. As she dressed she chatted to Nightingale as if they were old friends. Jenny was only a few years younger than the detective and supposedly in the third year of a four-year honours degree in psychology. Since she had met Graham, though, whilst out clubbing in London, she hadn't attended a single lecture. For the past three months she had abandoned her original plans for the future as she had fallen further and further in love with him. She explained that he had a certain schoolboy charm under the playboy façade that she found captivating, and a warm heart and generous nature that he was usually at pains to conceal.

She explained to Nightingale that Graham was genuinely worried but she had no idea why. In her opinion there had been nothing sinister about his father's death: no threats or unusual circumstances had preceded it. Other people, though, had been worrying at Graham and airing their concerns that his death had not been a suicide. It had come to a head during the recent Memorial Service for his father, after which he had felt that he had no option but to go to the police.

Jenny's theory was that Graham was experiencing genuine guilt and regret. Not that his father had ever shown him any affection, far from it. He had packed him off to boarding school with glee at the first opportunity and they had never formed a close relationship. As a result, Graham had virtually ignored his father whilst he was alive and Jenny's theory was that, now that it was too late to make amends, he felt guilty.

It all sounded plausible to Nightingale, who listened, made notes and gathered the names of other family members. As Jenny talked, she became curious about her relationship with Alan Wainwright's son.

'How long have you known Graham?'

'Since January, nearly three months. I think it's a record for him!'

'He's in demand, then?'

'Oh, always. He's one of Britain's more eligible bachelors, but I don't mean to make him sound awful. Once you get past the fact that he's just an overgrown, spoilt schoolboy, he's lovely. A very kind man.' She hesitated for the first time and Nightingale sensed that she was holding something back.

'There is something that's worrying you, though. What is it?'

Jenny sat down on the edge of the crumpled bed and ran her fingers through long blonde hair.

'He's become obsessive about Alex's wife, Sally. He has a private investigator following her around and they meet nearly every day. He won't tell me what they discuss.'

'I thought you said that he was open with you, couldn't keep secrets.'

'He is on everything else. It's just this thing with Sally. He can't stop thinking about her and he believes she's somehow involved in his father's death.'

'Forgive me for asking, but is Sally very pretty?'

Jenny flushed and glared at Nightingale, but her voice remained controlled.

'Yes, she's a perfect English rose – gorgeous complexion, natural ash-blonde hair, very pretty and great legs – but I don't think he fancies her. In fact, quite the opposite. I think he hates her. To be fair, her past is pretty vague, and in the few times I've met her I have seen her wrap men around her little finger, but that's hardly grounds to suspect her of murdering his father!'

'Is that what he thinks?'

'He's never said so directly, but he can't get over the fact that his father died so conveniently after changing his will and only a few months after meeting Sally.'

'I see. This is all conjecture, isn't it?'

'Of course it is! But you don't understand Graham. He doesn't work, he jumps from hobby to hobby, desperately trying to find something meaningful, and he's eaten up with guilt over his father. He's not a playboy, he's just a caring, deeply sensitive, unfulfilled man.'

'You're fond of him, aren't you?'

'Yes, very.'

Nightingale left to rejoin Fenwick and Cooper where they sat enduring Graham's chain-smoking. Although he was unshaven and scruffily dressed, he exuded a certain charm that was about more than money. After he left Fenwick turned to her with quizzically raised eyebrows.

'Anything?'

'Not really, sir. Jenny thinks it's guilt, and she seems to know Graham quite well. She's very worried about him, though. Since his father's death he's become obsessed, and he blames his cousin's wife Sally in some way. He's even hired a private detective.'

'I know, he told us, but so far all the man's found out is that Sally Wainwright-Smith changed her maiden name years ago and that there are rumours she somehow manipulated Alan Wainwright into dividing his estate into two so that she and her new husband would inherit.'

'Fifteen million pounds is a powerful motive.' Cooper was studying his notebook carefully. 'We've known murders for much less.'

'True, but the problem here is that all we have is conjecture. No one can understand why Alan killed himself; they're unhappy with the will so they look for a suspect. Sally's new, and an unexpected beneficiary, so suspicion falls on her. It would be different if the coroner hadn't already recorded a verdict, and Inspector Blite should have probed more, but he was under enormous pressure to close the case at the time.

'Now, though, in order to reopen the case, we will need much more than this, and even Graham admits that his private investigator has found nothing. I'll talk to the deceased's sister, Julia; Cooper, you call Alexander Wainwright-Smith, see what he has to say, then speak to Alan's friends at his clubs; and Nightingale, here's the number of the investigator Graham's hired. Call him and do a PCN check for any mention of anybody associated with this case. You'd best leave Councillor Ward to me. He's a tricky bastard and not a great fan of the police.

'Nightingale, this will be a lesson in discretion for you. You must stick to the script. We are tidying up loose ends, that's all; no ad-libbing or becoming carried away. I'll see you both back at the station at three, and make sure that you have enough information by then for me to call the ACC.'

They arrived in his office at the end of the afternoon foot-sore and despondent. Cooper was still clutching his now empty sandwich box under his arm.

Fenwick looked as bright and fresh as he had done seven hours before.

'Any progress?' he asked.

'Nothing, sir.' Cooper shook his head wearily. He'd endured five hours of spite and rumour without finding a trace of any real substance. 'As soon as the people we interviewed realised that the police were taking their suspicions seriously they clammed up, didn't want to be pointing any fingers. And you?'

'No hint of anything out of the ordinary, although there is a lot of resentment about the will. I spoke to about a dozen people and only one other, Julia Wainwright-McAdam, the old man's sister, was suspicious. She hates Sally Wainwright-Smith and alleges she had an affair with her brother, but there's no evidence, and even she admitted it was all hearsay. Councillor Ward was particularly circumspect in what he said. He's suddenly very reluctant to see the inquiry reopened. Nightingale, did you find the private investigator?'

'Yes, sir, he hasn't found out anything unusual other than the change of name. He's still trying to discover her original maiden name, but he says that he comes across name changes all the time in his line of work, and he refused to speculate on why she might have changed hers. The PCN check came up blank.'

'So, my report to the ACC will say . . .?'

'Suspicions investigated thoroughly but no new grounds for further enquiry.'

'I'm afraid so. Don't look despondent, Nightingale. Sometimes we just have to take the evidence at face value and live with it.'

The phone rang and Cooper and Nightingale left Fenwick to talk to the ACC. If they had remained in his office, his words to Harper-Brown would have confused them both.

'Yes, sir, we have concluded, and officially there is insufficient basis for reopening the file; there simply isn't any hard evidence to justify taking it further. But, sir, Graham Wainwright is not a fanciful man, nor do I believe he has made this up. We can't prove anything, but if ever there is even a hint that all is not well at Wainwright Enterprises, we're going to have to take it seriously. I realise that that is not entirely what you wanted to hear, but it's what will be going in my report . . . And a good afternoon to you too, sir.'

CHAPTER EIGHT

Alexander and Sally's move to Wainwright Hall went smoothly. Its architecture was late-Victorian gothic, ornate chimneypots, an improbable tower, gargoyles, flying buttresses. The internal decoration was heavy-handed Victorian, virtually unchanged since Alexander's great-great-grandfather – the original Alexander Wainwright, after whom he had been named – had furnished it. There was a portrait of him above the main staircase, painted when he was in his late forties, on the occasion of his third marriage, to the woman who later became Alexander's great-great-grandmother.

There was a portrait of her too, tucked away in one of the guest bedrooms, holding his grandfather as a baby. She reminded him so much of his mother that Alexander insisted that the painting be moved into the sitting room, his favourite of all the reception rooms. The rest he left to Sally, who was in her element.

Mrs Willett, the housekeeper, was resolutely positioned 'below stairs' to spring-clean the kitchen, pantries and other utility rooms. Mr Willett kept out of the house and contented himself with his late spring gardening, as he had done for the past thirty years. His wife came home to their tied cottage each evening with dire warnings that 'Her Majesty' had plans for the garden too, so there was no point him being so cocky, his time would come. Willett merely whistled between his teeth and went back to his pricking out.

Alexander stayed out of the way and concentrated on holding the business together in the aftermath of Alan Wainwright's death. It had shocked the whole company, but so far he had pulled everyone through with an unexpected toughness. As he strode through the corridors, startling management and staff with his sudden presence, people began to recognise an almost eerie resemblance to his uncle.

Within days of their moving into the Hall, Alexander surprised Sally by saying he'd invited his Cousin Graham to dinner. It was time, he said, to try and close the rift created by his uncle's will. Jenny was still around and she would be coming too. He suggested that they eat out at a restaurant to avoid the potential embarrassment of welcoming Graham into the house that he must surely have assumed he would inherit. To his relief, Sally agreed.

The dinner started tolerably well, except that Graham insisted on asking Sally probing questions about her background and refused to be put off by her evasions. Alexander was in need of relaxation after weeks of intense activity at work, and as soon as they had finished their main course he took advantage of Jenny's obvious boredom and need for a cigarette to suggest that the two of them take a brief walk outside in the cool evening. She accepted gratefully, and they strolled for a while around the village green in companionable silence. Jenny suddenly broke it.

'I'm not a gold-digger, you know.'

'What makes you say that? I'm sure nobody thinks so.'

'Oh no? Your wife does, for one.'

'Sally? Oh, you're quite wrong there.'

Jenny gave him a strange look, opened her mouth to argue but then changed her mind and shrugged.

'Whatever. Anyway, as long as you don't think so.'

'Of course I don't. I can tell you're very fond of Graham, and he needs someone decent to keep him on the straight and narrow.'

Jenny laughed and squeezed his arm. 'I know what you mean. He's been spoilt so badly that I don't think any woman in his life had said no to him before I came along.'

'That's probably why your relationship has lasted as long as it has. You're good for him, it's obvious.'

'I love him,' she said simply, and slipped her hand from the crook of his arm.

'I hope it works out and that you'll be as happy as Sally and me.'

Jenny gave him a long sideways look which he missed entirely and then shook her head. They lapsed into silence until they had completed their turn of the green. When they returned to the restaurant, the atmosphere between Sally and Graham had deteriorated and they were obviously not speaking to each other. As soon as Alexander walked in, Sally stood up and placed a hand to her forehead.

'I have a terrible headache, Alex. I need to go home.'

Alexander glanced from his wife to Graham and back. His cousin looked furious.

'Of course. I'll just go and settle the bill and bring the car round.'

As he stood by the reception desk, waiting for them to ring his credit card through, Graham strode up to him.

'Your wife . . . How well do you know her?'

'What are you implying, Graham?' Alexander's tone hardened, and he frowned down on his much shorter cousin, who reacted with surprising diplomacy.

'Alexander, please, we're family. Don't get me wrong. I just need to find out if—'

'What's happening here, Alex? Where's the car?' Sally's imperious voice cut across Graham's conversation and he stopped talking at once. The maître d' filled the awkward silence.

'Your bill, sir: if you could sign here?'

Alexander bent to sign, acutely conscious of the simmering presence of Sally by his side and of Graham hovering by the door. Jenny arrived and took Graham's arm gently, her face full of concern, but Graham smiled to reassure her that there wouldn't be a scene.

'I've got to go, Alexander, but call me, please? We do need to talk.' Ignoring Sally, Graham turned and left with Jenny.

Alexander waited until they were in the car to talk in the hope that Sally would have calmed down.

'What was all that about?'

'Your cousin is an insufferable bastard, Alex.'

'Sally!'

'Well, he is, and he's dangerous too. He's going to start spreading rumours around that we can do without, and if we try and deny them he'll just make more noise. It will ruin the company.'

'I don't think Graham would deliberately harm the business. He still owns five per cent of the shares, remember. And what is there, other than the will, for him to start rumours about?'

'You don't know him, Alex! He's just the sort of vicious nuisance we can do without. We need to think very carefully about how to manage him.'

Alexander said nothing – there was no point trying to argue with his wife once she had made up her mind – but privately he thought she was overreacting and it worried him. She was showing signs of strain even though they had now moved into the Hall, and she refused to talk to him about it, insisting that everything was fine. He had noticed that the level in the gin bottle was reducing with alarming rapidity, and he had never known her to drink spirits before.

'I've been thinking, Sally, whilst the decorators are in the Hall, why don't you take a short holiday in the sun somewhere?'

'Don't be stupid, Alex. Who is going to oversee them and make sure they don't cock things up? Certainly not you, you're always busy at work.'

'It was just an idea.'

They drove the rest of the way back to the Hall in silence.

CHAPTER NINE

The report and accounts for Wainwright Enterprises were brief to say the least, just the minimum required to be lodged with Companies House. Nevertheless, Alexander read them with great interest on his return from the office each day, working back over the records for the past ten years. In the few weeks since he had been appointed managing director he had taken his new responsibility very seriously, as had his wife. He impressed on her the importance of understanding the accounts in detail and they developed a shared obsession with the financial aspects of the business. Now that they were personally wealthy Sally transferred her fixation with money from their still meagre housekeeping to the millions of pounds passing through the business.

They quickly devoured the published accounts and soon mastered their content, but what they found intrigued them and inflamed their desire for yet further information.

'So what do you make of these latest accounts, Alex?' Sally asked one evening. He had just reread the most recent set.

'They don't say much. In fact, I would say that they are deliberately succinct – just the bare minimum required. The company's extremely profitable and keeps on paying a healthy dividend to the shareholders.'

'Exactly! It's far too profitable. There's simply too much cash in there.'

'I agree. I've compared our results with those of other companies in a similar line of business, and in every single year Wainwright's has made ten times their profits.'

'Well, you've always said that it's a very well-run company, Alex.'

'Not to this extent. I think there's something strange about it, and what's more, I can't get a straight answer from either Neil Yarrell or Arthur Fish. Neil insists that he leaves all the detailed running of the finances to Arthur whilst he focuses on shareholder relations and acquisitions; and Arthur never gives me a simple answer to a straight question. If I don't receive the information tomorrow that I asked him for over a week ago, I'm going to lose my temper with him!'

'Is he incompetent or crooked, do you think?'

'Perhaps he's both. Come on, we've done all we can for tonight. Let's go to bed.'

The accounts department at Wainwright's was silent and dark except for a solitary yellow glow from under the closed door of the office of the financial controller, Arthur Fish. It was very late. Normally he would have gone home over three hours earlier, but he had called a neighbour and asked her to sit with his wife so that he could stay behind in the office and sort things out. Now, as he stared at the mound of paper in front of him, he felt sick. His hands shook as he tried to put the bundled files in order, and he knocked over a box of paper clips as he tried to save a huge cascade of computer printouts from falling to the floor. The whole lot went crashing down and he had to sit there with his head in his hands, struggling to control his breathing.

It was awful . . . everything was out of control. He had been told to have the information ready for the new managing director by the next day or start looking for another job. Arthur knew that he was facing exposure and ruin. Old Mr Wainwright had never been like this. He and Neil Yarrell had made it very clear how they liked the accounts department to be run, and he had followed their instructions to the letter. The problem was that the new MD and his wife were playing by different rules, and Neil Yarrell had created so much distance between himself and the mess he *knew* they would find that Arthur felt very much alone.

He stared balefully at the orange rent-a-crate in the middle of the floor and cursed the Wainwright-Smiths' dangerous curiosity. There had never been any trouble before. He, together with their external accountants, had always dealt with the year-end audit very nicely; no awkward questions and just enough testing to make sure that the files looked correct in case they were examined by someone other than their compliant auditors, which they never were. Now Mr Wainwright-Smith was demanding full access to the files, and Arthur knew what he would find – or rather, what he wouldn't, if he was any good. He would not find the records and ledgers that would make the whole thing balance, simply because the books didn't balance. Mr Alan Wainwright had known that and had never asked awkward questions. There was no way in which Arthur would be able to sort things out by morning. Neil Yarrell wasn't worried because he thought that Alexander could be persuaded to be less inquisitive – for his own good. But Arthur didn't agree. He detected a stubborn streak in young Mr Alexander and a toughness that he thought Neil was underestimating. And as for his wife! Well, he hadn't met her yet, but by all accounts she was even worse than her husband.

He glanced nervously at the clock on his desk: in less than twelve hours either Mr or Mrs Wainwright-bloody-Smith would arrive and expect to see that crate full to the brim with orderly management accounts. Arthur picked up the printouts that littered the floor and composed them into piles, sorted roughly by year. At eleven o'clock his phone rang and an irate neighbour summoned him home. He locked his door on the mounds of paper and tried not to think about the morning.

'Sally, my dear, what a pleasant surprise. How lovely to see you again. You'll recall we met at the Hall, just before your wedding?'

'Yes, of course, you're Neil Yarrell, the finance director. I've been looking forward to meeting you again. Alex is busy so he asked me to collect the accounts and take them home so that he can study them tonight.'

'This is my financial controller, Arthur Fish.' Sally and Arthur clasped hands and locked eyes. An alert observer would have noticed Arthur's widen momentarily in shocked recognition, but Sally missed it as her gaze moved on restlessly to the crate full of paper behind him.

'Are those the accounts?'

'Yes, all of them. You didn't need to come in personally, you know, we could have had them sent to the Hall for you like before.'

'No, I wanted to come in, if only to meet you all. Anyway, within a month I shall start work here as Alex's PA. I'm looking forward to it, but in the meantime he has asked me to help him pull the numbers apart.'

She smiled brightly, a predator's grin. Yarrell and Fish glanced at each other with barely concealed concern.

'Wainwright's is a very complicated company. You might not—'

'Yes, yes, I know all about that. Don't worry, Alexander and I haven't yet found a problem involving money that has defeated us.'

With that she motioned to the doorman hovering behind her, who picked up the crate and followed her out.

Arthur scurried back to his office and closed the door once again on his bemused secretary. In the privacy of its confines he rubbed his hands with glee. He had her now, the mysterious Mrs Wainwright-Smith. She could pretend all she liked but he had recognised her instantly, and he had only to remember her real name to secure the hold over her that would mean that he would never again have anything to fear from little Miss Sally.

That night Arthur returned from work at Wainwright Enterprises and eased his key into the lock of his wide front door. He put his shoulder gently behind the swing of its weight as it opened noiselessly on well-oiled hinges. At first he could hear muffled conversation and his spirits rose, then he realised that it was the radio and his mood deflated in an instant.

Nurse Brown had heard his quiet entry and walked into the hall. He raised his eyebrows in a silent question but she shook her head and his spirits sank even lower. In the kitchen he set a white-and-green M&S carrier bag on the island unit. To his left, past the built-in oven, fridge and larder unit, was the door to the utility room; straight ahead a double-width back door led via a ramp into the carefully tended garden. To his right there was a passage, and beyond, a purpose-built extension where his wife now spent the remainder of her days.

Behind him, in the hall, Nurse Brown was putting on a lightweight coat.

'I'll see you tomorrow morning, then, Mr Fish, just before eight. I've left a note of things we need on the worktop – and there's a new prescription to pick up from the doctor if you have a moment at lunchtime.'

He thanked her and wished her a good evening. When she had left, the silence of the house surrounded him, broken only by small mechanical noises in the kitchen. The fridge motor clicked on and hummed, the tap dripped erratically, and away to his right, faint in the distance, the radio chattered.

He walked through the passage and into the pretty sitting room cum bedroom beyond. His wife was half lying, half sitting on her bed, the radio beside her. As soon as she saw him her eyes rolled slightly and the left eyelid flickered. She was welcoming him home.

'Hello, love. How's today been?'

With great effort she closed and opened her left eye twice. One was good, and three bad.

'Oh.' Arthur wasn't quite sure what to say; he never was. He put all the troubles of his day at work behind him and focused on the next hour he would spend with his wife.

'I've got us a bit of a treat for tea tonight. A Marks and Spencer steak and kidney pie – your favourite – and a summer pudding with cream to follow.' Even as he spoke he knew it was for his own comfort; she ate like a bird these days, pecking at the mashed food he served her for a few minutes at a time, before dozing off. How could anyone be so ill and yet continue to live? It baffled him, and yet she remained the only sane, controlled part of his awful life.

He walked back to the kitchen and set the oven to warm whilst he went to change out of his suit. His bedroom was neat and tidy, the double bed carefully made up with envelope corners that would have pleased the sternest nursing sister. In a freshly laundered casual shirt, cardigan, check trousers, socks and slippers, he made his way back down to the kitchen and popped the pie in the oven. He'd bought ready-prepared runner beans and it took him only a moment to peel the potatoes. At seven o'clock precisely, his early-evening chores complete, Arthur went to join his wife in time for *The Archers*. He told himself she still looked forward to the series, but there was no way of really knowing any more. Still, she always blinked once when he asked her whether she had enjoyed it.

Arthur looked at her now, her eyes closed. Was she asleep or conscious? What went on behind that paralysed, twisted face? He tried hard to remember her as she had been: a smiling, quiet, contented wife with not a bad word to say about anybody. She'd had no great gifts save her ability to be a wonderful, calm wife and mother. Their three grown-up children were a testament to her abilities; Arthur took no credit for their upbringing. And now look. All that goodness trapped inside a sick, bloated body that needed twenty-four-hour care. It made him very angry. No wonder he had gone so badly wrong.

The buzzer went off on the cooker, reminding him that he still had the beans to cook. He raised himself to his feet and returned to the kitchen, steeling himself to prepare his wife's mush and talk to her for the next half-hour until the night nurse arrived and he could escape to hours of mindless television before bed and the guilty pretence of sleep. As he picked up the fork, his mind switched to the memory of his meeting with Sally Wainwright-Smith, and he set about mashing the food with a passion that smashed the innocent potato into fragments that shot across the edge of the plate and on to the floor.

He was surprised at the violence of his feelings towards Sally. Look at her now, so smart and smug, probing into the company accounts and consequently into his past as if she owned both. Her butter-wouldn't-melt-in-the-mouth looks filled him with contempt. Who did she think she was, parading around like the lady of the manor? He knew better, oh yes. Arthur had recognised her at once; there was no forgetting that face, particularly those eyes. He had seen them gleam in malicious delight, narrow in anger and close in ecstasy, but she had no idea what he knew.

The sense of power this knowledge brought him was disorientating, and he had to rest his hand for a moment on the worktop to steady himself before lifting the pie from the oven. He had rarely felt this strongly, and adrenaline pumped into his system as he realised that he might be able to reclaim some control of his life. Let her probe and bully all she liked; there was a point beyond which she would not be able to push him, and when the time came he would tell her so. The thought made him lick his lips with pleasure, and he actually smiled as he placed his wife's small bowl of food on the tray next to his own plate.

'Supper's up, love!' he called as he walked down the short passage whistling the familiar theme tune.

CHAPTER TEN

Throughout the following Friday night and the whole of the weekend Alexander and Sally worked their way diligently through boxfuls of Wainwright accounts. Sally was baffled within the first hour; Alexander admitted his confusion not much later, but between them they gradually worked out a solution. They would concentrate on just one year and on one part of the business in order to try and understand it completely. At first they would work independently and then compare notes.

By eleven o'clock on the Saturday morning they were ready to discuss their conclusions for the first time. Sally started.

'This part of the business received forty-five million pounds in income, had costs of only eleven million and transferred twenty to another subsidiary company.'

'I agree. Let's look at the subsidiary that received the twenty million next.'

They worked on until one, when they ate a hurried salad, and completed their analysis by three in the afternoon. This time Alex spoke first.

'Total income for this subsidiary of the company was eighty-three million, including nineteen and a half million it received as an intercompany transfer. In other words, half a million pounds went missing in the year. It also transferred forty million to two other parts of the business.'

'That's what I have too. Now you look at one of the divisions that received some of the forty million and I'll look at the other.'

Throughout the rest of the afternoon and into the night they followed a daisy chain of transfers among Wainwright Enterprises subsidiaries. They stopped for a few hours' sleep and resumed again before dawn. By the end of Sunday afternoon they had trawled through just three-quarters of one year's detailed accounts and had calculated that five and a half million pounds had so far 'disappeared' in the web of intercompany transactions.

Sally defrosted some leftover goulash for supper and laid places for them at the kitchen table. She poured two glasses of a supermarket wine and served large bowlfuls of the stew with potatoes and chunks of Saturday's bread refreshed in the oven.

'Five and a half million! Where's it gone, Alex?'

'No idea. We need to finish going through the papers for the rest of the year, and if we don't find it there we have to assume it's been siphoned off.'

'By whom – your uncle, Neil Yarrell, Arthur Fish?'

'Or all three, perhaps. There's no point speculating, though. Let's finish supper and get back to work.' They ate quickly and in virtual silence, their minds preoccupied with the mysterious disappearance of so much money from Wainwright's.

It was midnight before they closed the final file and refolded the last computer printout. The amount of missing money had risen to seven million pounds out of a total of one hundred and eleven million that had been passed from subsidiary to subsidiary for no apparent reason.

The following morning they confronted Neil Yarrell together. At first they just asked about the transfers of money and he gave them a detailed and plausible explanation involving income tax and VAT. He seemed relaxed and confident until Alex sprang the matter of the missing seven million on him. The finance director looked as if he had been slapped in the face, but said nothing.

'You sign off the accounts, Neil. A discrepancy that large must have been spotted by you or the auditors.'

'There was no discrepancy, I can assure you. It must be a miscalculation on your part.'

'We don't think so.' Sally's voice was hard and uncompromising. 'It looks like fraud, and if you know nothing about it, I suggest you ask Arthur Fish. He must have been stealing from the company consistently.'

'Now look here . . .' Their voices were so loud that none of them had heard the tentative tap on the half-open office door, and Neil Yarrell stopped in mid-sentence as his financial controller walked in. It was obvious from Arthur Fish's face that he had overheard them, and he looked about to faint.

There was a silence, which was eventually broken by Sally.

'It was as well you heard that, Fish. If you and Neil want to avoid a scandal, you've got twenty-four hours to come up with a credible explanation.'

Arthur looked to Alexander, but the managing director merely shook his head, his expression unreadable, then took his wife by the arm and walked out, leaving his senior accountants to confer.

As soon as they had gone, Neil Yarrell told Fish to leave and called James FitzGerald. He explained their problem succinctly.

'Bloody hell!' exclaimed FitzGerald. 'That didn't take them long. And the tax explanation didn't work?'

'It doesn't explain the missing seven million. Given time, I'm sure I could work up a missing set of accounts with Arthur, but they're like bloodhounds on the trail! Now that they've got the scent of missing money beneath their noses, I bet they'll work through every year.'

'I'm going to have to pay them a call, then. It's sooner than I would have liked but it can't be helped. You just do what you need to on the figures and leave the rest to me.'

'Alexander's going to be in the office all day but I've no idea where Sally went when she left – to the Hall probably.'

'I'm going to sort them out today, Neil, separately. They're an unhelpful partnership and, if we can drive a wedge between them, it will make controlling them easier. It's about time we created some distance between those two love-birds.'

'You think that this is a love-match?' Yarrell sounded surprised. 'Haven't you heard what everybody's saying about her?'

'Oh, I've more than heard, mate, don't you worry. I think I know exactly where Sally's coming from. You just stay shtoom, OK? And tell your pal Fish to put a sock in his whining, it's getting on my nerves.'

James FitzGerald arrived at Wainwright's in the middle of the afternoon and blew a kiss at the receptionist as he made his way unchallenged to the lift. As it climbed slowly, he glanced at his watch. It was nearly three o'clock, plenty of time for him to sort Wainwright-Smith out before going on to visit his wife at the Hall. On the top floor, he knocked lightly on Wainwright-Smith's door and walked straight in, closing the door behind him.

'Yes? What do you want?'

FitzGerald ignored the anger in the new managing director's voice and flopped down in one of the armchairs. He leant over easily and poured himself a small whisky, then waved the crystal decanter towards Alexander, his whole manner proprietorial.

'Just who the devil do you think you are?'

'Alexander, you probably don't remember me but I'm James FitzGerald, an old friend of your uncle's.' He smiled and the flash of canine enamel was wolfish. 'I need to talk to you, now.' The man's hard-edged accent grated on Alexander's nerves and he let his annoyance at the interruption show in his face.

'I'm very busy, Mr FitzGerald. Make an appointment with my assistant. If it's urgent then I think I have some time left tomorrow morning. Now if you'll excuse me . . .'

'I'm afraid that won't do, Alexander. You seem to forget that I'm a rather substantial shareholder in Wainwright Enterprises, and I take a great and personal interest in this company. Whilst I have every confidence that Alan knew what he was doing in recommending you as MD, I'm not sure you yet realise the *full* extent of your responsibilities.'

There was something about the man's tone that stopped Alexander giving a blunt response and he paused to let FitzGerald continue.

'That's better. We need to have a private chat, just you and me, not a word to anybody else, you understand, particularly that pretty and determined young wife of yours.'

'What's this all about?' Wainwright-Smith stood up from his desk and walked over to the group of chairs in which FitzGerald was sitting.

'It's about money, Alexander, death, money and family obligations – your obligations now, to me and others.'

Wainwright-Smith sat down, his expression studiedly neutral.

'Go on, Mr FitzGerald, I'm all ears.'

'I understand from Neil that you've been asking questions about the company's finances that would be better, quite frankly, left unasked or answered. He's tried to persuade you but you've ignored his advice. I'm not here to argue with you, I'm here to tell you. Let it go.'

FitzGerald could see the expression of indignation and anger that crossed Alexander's face, to be replaced with a stubbornness that reminded him so much of his dead uncle it made his heart sink. Alan Wainwright had been a proud man as well, and it was only his dire money troubles in the nineteen-seventies that had allowed FitzGerald and some of his friends to gain the

52

influence they had needed over Wainwright's. There had been no persuading him until necessity had driven him to accept their offer, and FitzGerald could see that there would be no persuading the nephew either. He had no option, then, but to tell him and hope that greed or fear – perhaps both – would do the rest.

'I'm going to tell you a secret, Alexander, known to a very few people, and if you ever reveal it to anyone, including your wife, I promise you that I will personally cut your tongue out and choke you with it.'

The threat was delivered so coldly that Alexander could feel the hairs on his arms and at the back of his neck rise with a chill of fear. He had no doubt that the man sitting before him was capable of doing exactly what he had just described.

'OK,' he said and marvelled that anger had kept his voice steady. 'Get on with it.'

'I mean it. There is a skeleton in your family's cupboard that I've helped keep hidden for over thirty years. Just view it as part of your legacy now and we'll all be fine.' He smiled again, with a white flash of enamel, and bent forward confidentially to tell Alexander his secret.

The phone was ringing when Sally returned to the Hall from a brief shopping trip, just before five o'clock. Before she could reach it, Mrs Willett had answered.

'Yes? She's here.' The receiver was banged down on the mahogany side table with a disregard for property that made Sally's blood boil. 'For you, madam.' The housekeeper retreated into the passageway that connected the entry and main halls.

'Sally Wainwright-Smith.'

'James FitzGerald here, Sally. We don't really know each other, but we met briefly at Alan's funeral.' His voice crackled as the signal from his mobile phone weakened.

'Oh yes.' She vaguely remembered meeting him, a common little man with bad manners and worse breath.

'I need to see you, it's quite urgent.'

'Not today, I'm very busy. Shall we say—'

'I'm already on my way, Mrs Smith, and believe me, you will want to see me.'

She had only just hung up her jacket when she heard the crunch of tyres on the gravel outside. A silver-grey Mercedes pulled up in front of the main doors and a thin man in a lightweight suit climbed out of it with athletic ease. He was carrying a large brown envelope. For a moment she considered denying him entry but then curiosity overcame anger and she opened the door.

'Sally!' His tone was intimate and patronising.

'What do you want?'

He pretended to look hurt at her bluntness, and then smiled. It was an unpleasant, knowing expression and Sally suddenly realised what was coming. Her eyes strayed to the brown envelope.

'Yes, exactly. Shall we . . .' He gestured with an easy familiarity towards the study to one side of the entrance hall.

'You seem to know your way around.'

'Oh, I was a regular visitor here in Alan's time. Please, after you.'

Behind them, in the shadow of the passage, Mrs Willett put her duster and polish on the floor noiselessly and waited for the study door to close before moving towards it.

The room was dark and smelled of a lemon-scented polish. FitzGerald handed the brown envelope to Sally and waited while she flicked through the glossy black-and-white pictures. A few made her smile.

'You could have published some of these, they're really very good.'

FitzGerald regarded her with admiration; this was hardly the reaction he had expected.

Another photograph caught her eye and she burst out laughing, a sound full of innocent enjoyment.

'Oh, poor Alan! Look at his face.' They both laughed together then Sally's expression suddenly hardened.

'So is this what you do to get your money, then, Mr FitzGerald? Are you a grubby blackmailer, making money by taking blurred photographs at other people's windows? Are you no more than a peeping Tom?'

For a slender man, James FitzGerald's grip was surprisingly strong. He squeezed her arm tighter, but the pain only made Sally smile. The sight of it made him close his fingers until their tips locked and she gasped out loud, but it still sounded like a sigh of pleasure.

'They were my insurance policy, that's all, in case Alan ever misbehaved. I never expected them to come in handy after his death. Tell me, do you believe in the power of three, Mrs Wainwright-Smith?'

'Oh yes! Grant me three wishes is a particular favourite of mine, although I've rarely known a man to manage more than two.'

Her assurance incensed him and he twisted his hand, burning the bare skin of her arm, but her eyes never lost contact with his, nor did they blink to shed the tears of pain that gathered there.

'Did *you* go to church as a child, James? I did, and I can still remember my favourite hymn. Forget Father, Son and Holy Ghost; forget father, mother, child. It is the three in *one* that matters. Yes, I believe in the power of three, but I believe in the power of one even more.'

Her face glowed an ethereal white in the gloom, her eyes were brilliant with the power of mastery over pain, and her voice recited the words with an inexorable rhythm that drew him closer. But James FitzGerald was not another Alan Wainwright.

'You see, Sally, there were always three of us to keep things steady for the company. When Alan died, it left me a little short-handed, which means I haven't got the resources I need and I'm having to become more personally involved than I would like to keep things under control. Wainwright's is a special company in which I take a very close and personal interest.

'Drop your investigations, don't ask any more questions and stop encouraging your husband to be more curious than he needs to be. You wouldn't want these photographs made public, would you?'

Sally appeared to consider this for a moment.

'So I *am* right about the company: there *is* something going on there. What is it?'

'Never you mind.' He stroked her cheek gently with one finger of his free hand without once releasing his grip of her wrist. The contrast made her shudder and pleasure showed in her eyes.

'You remind me of someone, Sally, and I can't think who. Where have you come from? Is your past as interesting as your present?'

Under the pretence of finally giving in to the pain, she moved her free hand to his and, with a muttered 'please', lifted his fingers away. Her mind was working rapidly. If James FitzGerald really was somehow linked to what was happening at Wainwright's – the huge cash flows, the secrecy, the tolerance of substantial fraud – it meant that he had to have criminal connections, and that made him a dangerous man to cross.

'We'll drop the investigation, James, just as you ask, but you have some tidying-up to do as well. Arthur Fish is a nervous man,' she saw his face darken and hurried on, 'and he's inept. You need to get rid of him, quickly.'

FitzGerald said nothing as he picked up the photographs and replaced them in the envelope. He saw himself out.

Alexander arrived home earlier than usual, keen to stop his wife from working on the accounts. He removed his tie as he walked through from the entrance hall to the sitting room on the left. Sally was reclining on the window seat, staring out into the garden. She didn't look well and was wrapped in a thick long-sleeved jumper.

'Are you OK? You look whacked.'

'I am a little tired, to be honest; it's this never-ending winter.'

'Come on, I'll talk to Millie about supper. You put your feet up. Would you like a drink?'

'Got one.' She shook a tall tumbler at him and then took a long swallow, the ice clinking against her teeth as she drained the glass.

'Another? What was it, Perrier?'

'Gin and tonic, and yes please, I'll have another.'

Alexander took the glass from her and went to the drinks table in the corner. Her voice followed him, disembodied.

'I've been thinking about what Neil Yarrell said today. You know, I think I believe him – so long as he's got a good explanation for the missing seven million, I think we can relax, although I still think Fish is inept.'

'I'm amazed, Sally, you were so certain something was wrong. But I agree with you. I think we've become worked up over nothing. I'm sure there's a logical explanation for the gaps in the accounts.'

They stared at each other in amazement, both trying not to let shock show on their face. Neither had expected such an easy capitulation from the other. The suddenness of Alexander's about-turn confused Sally, already vulnerable from her confrontation with FitzGerald, and she burst into tears. Alexander was by her side at once and enveloped her in a huge hug.

'There, there, it's all right, hush now, it's OK. You're tired. You've been working far too hard. Why don't you lie down for a while? You can have a nice rest while I talk to Millie about a meal. Come on.'

He coaxed his wife towards the stairs, noting with concern that she picked up her fresh glass of gin and tonic on the way. Millie Willett was hovering in the hall.

'Mr Wainwright-Smith, if I could have a word?'

'Not now, Millie, can't you see my wife's a little unwell? We'll talk later. I'll be down in a minute.'

'Very well, sir, I'll wait for you in the kitchen.'

Sally looked at her housekeeper with sudden curiosity. She stopped crying abruptly and straightened her shoulders.

'It's all right, Alex. I'm fine now, really, much better. You go and have a shower. Millie, if you need to say something, you can talk to me in the kitchen. Off you go, Alex. Go!'

The next morning Alex was eating a rushed breakfast before leaving for his weekly eight-fifteen meeting with the director of production when Sally casually mentioned that Mrs Willett was working her notice.

'What!' He spilt his coffee over the pine table they used for breakfast in the morning room. 'She and Joe have been here with Uncle for years. You can't just get rid of them.'

'They're an unnecessary extravagance, and besides, we really don't need a full-time housekeeper and gardener.'

'But the Hall is huge – there's more than fifteen bedrooms – and the grounds need a heck of a lot of work. And anyway, you've just told Sue to retire so that you can become my PA. You'll never do it all!'

'Sue was very slow, dear. I'll be much quicker. Joe hasn't done a decent week's work in years, and as far as Millie Willett goes, I can arrange local cleaning help for a fraction of her cost. I've already found two girls who'll do very well.'

He was in a rush to leave for work so he didn't have time to argue. He meant to have it out with Sally that evening, but somehow the conversation never happened. He was tired, she was beautiful, and after his bath and dinner he couldn't bring himself to raise a topic that was bound to result in another argument. And so the Willetts went, paid in lieu of notice, and all trace of them disappeared from the Hall.

When Sally casually mentioned a few days later that temporary tenants were moving into Bluebell Cottage, he realised that she had evicted the Willetts from their tied accommodation as well. There was a row then, terrible for its fury if not any more for its rarity, but it was too late, they'd already gone. Alexander was appalled. What would people think of him? The Willetts had been a bit of a nuisance, and he had to agree with Sally that they were one of his uncle's least valuable legacies, but to evict them so callously would reflect badly on both him and Sally. It was a small world, and word would soon go round that the new master and mistress of the Hall were complete bastards. He was jealous of his reputation and intensely angry with her for damaging it so soon.

After a few weeks his relationship with Sally recovered, but he took to sleeping in his uncle's old room if he came in late from a business dinner, which he did now several times a week. When he did arrive home on time they would always talk over the business of the day, and she would sometimes have an opinion or an idea that brought a new insight to his management problems, but the warmth in their relationship had cooled beyond recovery.

CHAPTER ELEVEN

The pebbly beach was almost deserted as the biting wind whipped the sea to a froth of white horses and blew fragments of rubbish to lie trapped against the breakwaters, flapping helplessly. This was a strange time of year on the south coast, full of both potential and threat. If the Easter weekend was bright and sunny, spontaneous crowds would arrive, bringing prosperity and short-term relief to the thousands of small businesses that relied on the trippers for their livelihoods. Every night the owners of these enterprises listened to the long-range weather forecast, tapped their barometers or gazed ominously at strips of seaweed in an attempt to read their fortunes for this year. So far the signs were not good. Despite Easter being one of the latest on record, the weather was hanging on obstinately to its trappings of winter. With less than a week to go, there was frost on the ground at night and even a flurry or two of snow on the North Downs.

The woman who walked along the stony beach above the line of seaweed discarded by the retreating waves was huddled into a thick winter coat worn above jeans and trainers. She had a woollen hat pulled down over her ears, and the hands she stuffed into her pockets were wrapped in mittens. It was impossible to tell her age – she could have been anywhere between sixteen and sixty – but that her mood was solemn and distracted was obvious even from a distance.

Arthur Fish watched her walk the long miles of deserted shore, keeping his distance on the promenade above the beach. He had followed her from Harlden that afternoon as part of his obsessive interest in everything she and her husband said or did. He had been alarmed at first when she bought a ticket to Brighton, but then the realisation that she was being drawn back to her past, the past he knew too well, had warmed him. The Wainwright-Smiths had dropped their ridiculous investigation into the company finances, but Neil Yarrell had told him that Sally still didn't trust him and wanted him fired. That was the last thing he needed. The thought of being trapped in his tidy house with his dying wife filled him with horror. So he had started following his nemesis in his spare hours whilst trying to decide what to do. This afternoon, seeing her here on old turf, looking so vulnerable and worried, had made him decide that he needed to take direct action.

She had reached a particularly tall breakwater and was walking up the incline of the beach towards stone steps that led in turn to the promenade. He quickened his stride and went to meet her, arriving a few moments before she did.

'Hello, Sally.'

She looked up at him in shocked surprise, her face for once vulnerable, mouth open like a child's – so like a child's, in fact, that it reconfirmed he had been right, he did know her from another age.

'You don't remember me, do you?'

'Of course I do, Fish, now get out of my way.'

'No you don't, dear, not really. Look closely, because I remember you . . .' He paused, and his tone made her catch her breath. 'From a *long time ago*.'

'No.' The word was barely a whisper, but he could see the acknowledgement grow in her eyes.

'Oh, yes. I think we should talk, don't you? Would you like a cup of tea, or would you prefer a beefburger and chips – I think that was your particular favourite, wasn't it?'

Sally was clinging on to the railings to hold herself up, and the sight thrilled him. He loved to see this upstart pulled down from her recently inherited heights. He took her elbow and steered her across the road towards one of the few sea-front cafés that had opened for the weekend. Inside, the windows were fogged with the patrons' breath and the heat from iron radiators. He sat her down at a corner table next to the window and brought over two brimming cups of steaming tea.

He talked to her softly, in a low voice that wouldn't carry to the other customers, who stared at them with a natural curiosity. It wasn't often that you saw such a beautiful woman, particularly in the company of a tubby little man like that, old enough to be her father.

Sally ignored her tea and stared down at her hands as Arthur's voice droned on, telling her a story that she knew was true. Here was an unexpected tendril from her past, snaking out to catch her by the ankles and trip her up. It was all so unfair, when she was so close at last to achieving her dream of complete financial independence and control of her life. How had this happened? She thought back, to the time when Arthur insisted they had met. She couldn't deny any of what he was saying, despite having no recollection of him at all. She spoke for the first time.

'How did you recognise me? I look so different now.'

Arthur grinned at her and patted her hand in a way that made her feel sick.

'It's your eyes; I'll never forget your eyes looking at me the way they did back then, full of contempt and anger, just like you looked at me the other day in my office. How times change, eh? What does little Master Alexander know of the woman he's married, then?'

In one swift motion, Sally removed her hand from under his and upended her tea over his bare fingers. He yelped as the near-boiling liquid scalded his skin, and had to rush to the counter for a cold dishcloth with which he dabbed at his fast-blistering flesh. Two fingers were already pink and swollen and the woman behind the counter clucked over him as she placed his hand in a glass of cold water.

Sally watched him as he walked back to their table, a cruel smile on her face. As soon as he was seated, she spoke in a soft whisper that people nearby probably mistook for concern.

'You've made a mistake, Arthur. Don't ever threaten me, do you hear? You may think you have a hold over Alex and me, but you haven't. Who will believe you, a fat little bastard who gets his kicks in ways that would turn most decent people's stomachs? You'll be a laughing stock.'

'It's not just me! There are others who'll remember.'

'I doubt it. Mine was not a profession that encouraged long memories.'

'Maybe, but I'm not the only one you left behind. I can think of at least one other person who would love the opportunity to get back at you for what you did to her. She won't have forgotten little Sally Price, the bitch whose evidence put her away, and I'll be seeing her again very soon. You're not impregnable, Sally – whatever you like to think.'

Sally studied him with a detached interest and then picked up her hat and mittens. She stood up and bent to whisper in his ear.

'Just remember, Arthur, dead men don't tell tales.' Then, with a playful nip on his ear from her sharp little incisors, she was gone, leaving Arthur to gaze at his throbbing fingers with a look of horror on his face.

PART TWO

Death pays all debts.

Seventeenth-century proverb

CHAPTER TWELVE

It was the third Thursday in the month, which held a special significance in Arthur Fish's routine. Normally he would already have had the day mapped out precisely to the minute, but things were different today. He had been unable to concentrate since the previous Saturday and his encounter with Sally Wainwright-Smith. His hand was getting better but the occasional pain from the one remaining blister only served to remind him of her parting words, and then the fear he had been trying to cope with all week would return with a vengeance.

At first he had been determined to confront Alexander with his revelation at once, but the idea of his own secret past becoming common knowledge deterred him. He was also scared of the new MD. Alexander Wainwright-Smith had changed. All trace of the boy Arthur had known had disappeared, and there were times when he was reminded of Alan Wainwright, complete with all the older man's arrogance. So he had spent most of his time pretending that nothing had happened. His ability to retreat into a fantasy world where there were no problems and he was a decent, law-abiding citizen was one of his greatest strengths. It was also a fatal weakness.

He waited quietly in his kitchen, ready to start another arduous day, finding simple enjoyment in his second cup of tea as he watched the cooker clock creep towards seven forty-five and the arrival of the day nurse. As soon as her key was in the lock he would reach for his overcoat, a short, smart camel weave that his wife had bought him eight years before as an anniversary present. It was the last present she had ever bought him, as it turned out, but they weren't to know that at the time. It had been cleaned frequently since. Each time it came back he would strip away the plastic and check the collar and cuffs for wear, hoping to find that it was still all right for another year. In moments of melancholy he would consider the likelihood of the coat outlasting his wife, although the tenacity of her spirit frightened him with its determination to see through another day.

The minute counter moved on and the nurse arrived. The cooker clock said 07.48. She was three minutes late. He drank the rest of his tea and rinsed the cup swiftly. He considered going back into the annex to say goodbye to his wife again, then thought better of it. He hated to be late for the eight-fifteen meeting.

Nurse Brown was in the hall, adjusting her coat so that it hung neatly on the peg.

'Morning, Mr Fish.'

'Nurse Brown.' He picked up his coat, finding his cap in the pocket where he had tucked it the night before.

'Six o'clock, then, this evening?'

'Yes . . . er, no. I'm late tonight. A faculty day.' Arthur felt himself blush as he pulled on the green cap.

'Oh, it's a faculty evening, of course.' Nurse Brown grinned at him. Did she know? How could she? Of course not, it was just his guilty conscience.

'Edith Wilmslow will be here at five thirty as usual. She'll stay till I'm back as it's the night nurses' evening off.'

Edith Wilmslow was eighty if she was a day, but she was a good neighbour, blessed with the health and vigour his poor wife so sadly lacked. Nurse Brown nodded her acknowledgement. She was an unstintingly cheerful individual and he didn't know how his wife coped with her all day long. Thinking of the invalid once more, he felt guilty as he closed the front door with a satisfying snick. He really should have said a second goodbye.

The day at Wainwright's passed quickly, but Arthur still found that he was looking at his watch every fifteen minutes. As he sat in yet another meeting, his mind drifted to the evening and he pressed his thighs together in anticipation like a little boy. At five fifteen, a quarter of an hour earlier than usual, he picked up his coat and tweed cap and closed and locked his office door for the night. His secretary had left already, sent home early by her impatient boss.

At the station he bought a cheap day return to the south coast, controlling the tremor that had already started in his hands now that the evening was so close. He sat down in the corner of an empty second-class carriage and opened his *Daily Mail* in an attempt to look normal, but he couldn't focus. In his imagination he was already with Amanda, her stern eyes reprimanding him if he even dared to look at her directly, her black gown gaping open to reveal the cut-away leather bra and suspenders underneath. His trousers felt hot and tight as he gripped the paper and tried to control the flush that suffused his whole body.

His reverie was shattered as the carriage door slammed open. Three teenage girls and a nondescript youth clambered in, followed by a neat-looking woman with a little white dog on a lead. The girls were shrieking with laughter at some unheard remark. Their accents were vulgar; their language, when he finally deciphered their guttural half-sentences, was vile. He couldn't believe young girls could be so coarse and he hoped desperately that they would sit well away. As if sensing his discomfort, the leader of the pack saw him, grinned maliciously and shouted, 'Over 'ere!' to the others before plumping down on the seat opposite. Arthur automatically removed his cap, remembered his flushed state and dropped it in his lap. All thoughts of the evening ahead vanished. Defiantly he shook the paper free of creases and started reading it properly for the first time.

The other two female louts came and crammed their scantily clad, pale-limbed bodies next to their friend. The dark-haired youth who had followed them into the carriage, after a cursory glance at Arthur, chose a seat at the opposite end of the compartment. Arthur briefly considered the idea of joining him, then thought, Blow it, why should I move? and tried to concentrate on the morning's news.

Everything he did – each cough, twitch, change of crossed leg – caused the venomous trio opposite him to descend into fits of expletive-ridden cackles as they speculated openly about his sex life, whether he picked his nose and ate it, and whether it was he who had just farted. They kept on repeating the same suggestions and dirty innuendo – their imaginations limited by poor schooling, weak vocabulary and lazy intellects. His only defence lay in silence and studious concentration; they had to grow bored some time. But no, stop after stop, as the slow train crawled towards its destination, they mocked Arthur and his respectable middle age as only vicious teenagers could, with a lack of alternative occupation that allowed ample room for their spite. If they had been boys, he told himself, he'd have given them a piece of his mind, but their femininity confused him. Brought up never to hit girls, to be a good boy, to raise his cap promptly to ladies in the street and offer his seat on the bus – and smart-like, otherwise he'd feel the sting of his grandmother's hand on the back of his bare thighs and worse to come at home – he couldn't cope with naked female aggression, at least not this sort.

Their pale, bare limbs did nothing for him; the exposed white midriffs, pierced navels and unfettered skinny breasts left him unmoved. Nowadays he liked his women fully formed, mature, with creamy rich flesh that offered a proper handhold – always assuming Amanda would let him touch her tonight. At the sudden thought of her, he had to recross his legs and adjust his cap. This brought shrieks from the bitches opposite, while their leader belched loudly and repeatedly. Cheese and onion crisps! Disgusting. Ha! he thought. Laugh away, you stupid . . . Even in his mind he couldn't say the word. If you only knew what the evening held for me, you wouldn't laugh. You'd show me respect then.

Something of his bravado must have shown in his face. The girls grew quiet suddenly, and as the train plunged into the long, twisting tunnel that was a prelude to the final descent to the south coast, the carriage became eerily silent. The electric lights flickered once and went out, leaving them all in a rolling pitch blackness. Emergency lighting flared on, casting a supernatural blue glow across the empty seats. Arthur blinked and looked around. The youth in the far corner was staring at him, his intense blue eyes reflecting back the emergency light in an unreal, inhuman glow. He seemed to be looking directly at Arthur, his concentrated gaze disconcerting in the half-light. Then the carriage flickered yellow as full power returned, and Arthur gave him no more thought.

As soon as the train slowed in the terminus, the girls roused themselves from their bored stupor and fell shrieking on to the platform, tripping and stumbling towards the exit. Arthur contemplated the evening they had in store and pitied, briefly, their next victims. At least if they were of another generation they would have fewer scruples in dealing with that coven, who deserved whatever was coming to them – that night, that life. Arthur shrugged them off.

It was a cool, clear night. He stuffed his *Daily Mail* into the nearest litter bin and breathed deeply. He felt cheated. Normally by now he would have replayed in his mind the memories of previous visits and blended them carefully with anticipation until he had relished the best of both reminiscence and expectation. Instead, he'd arrived at his destination flat and in incipient bad humour, with his underlying fear since his confrontation of Sally barely in check. He glanced at his watch: six thirty. The train had arrived on the dot and he would have no difficulty reaching Amanda's in time for seven o'clock. After they'd finished – except he didn't like to think that far ahead – he had something to give her for safe-keeping. They'd known each other long enough, and it would ease his mind to think of it being hidden somewhere. He had decided not to mention Sally tonight. It would spoil the whole evening, and despite what he had said in the café, he wasn't sure that Amanda would want to become involved all these years later. He decided to walk to clear his mind for the evening ahead. Behind him, a slight figure slipped unnoticed into the shadow of a car park wall and followed at a discreet distance.

CHAPTER THIRTEEN

Detective Constable Nightingale walked out on to the rusted balcony and took a deep breath of tangy salt air. A second breath, redolent of rotting seaweed and ozone, and her head started to clear. Behind her a police officer walked on soft feet across the faded chintz carpet and sat down to touch a pallid, plump arm. They had been on the scene within fifteen minutes of uniformed's call. She was coming to the end of her short placement on the coast and had lost count of the number of assaults she'd attended, but this was her first murder.

She stretched her cramped shoulder muscles and realised that she was far too tense to be able to blame her work. The real problem lay deeper. In February she had finally agreed with her fiancé that it was very unlikely they would be getting married that year – or any year for that matter. Now that the relationship was a fading memory she was shocked to find that she had under-estimated the loneliness.

She looked out into the orange neon glow of the street below, the streetlamp shaded on the near side to protect residents in the flats. Well, here was one resident who wouldn't need the council's consideration any more. Nightingale twisted and looked back into the room. The woman was slumped on the worn sofa, almost naked, eyes closed, with one hand arranged defensively across the tops of her sagging breasts. One eye was blackened and closed, her nose had been bleeding and her lip was split. Other bruises showed beneath her loose dressing gown, some new, others a dirty yellow. There was blood in her hair and some had trickled from her ears. Nightingale could see the paramedic still trying to resuscitate her, but it looked hopeless.

She couldn't guess the victim's age – fifty, perhaps even older. It was difficult to tell, as the heavy make-up showed every facial line and flaw. And yet there were apparently enough customers who had fallen for her temptations after reading one of the cards that advertised her services in the telephone boxes by the pier to have allowed her to pay the rent on this squalid flat.

It had been easy enough to work out her profession without the willing help of the neighbours, who'd been only too delighted to share their observations and suspicions with the police. Still, Nightingale couldn't fathom the attraction. She turned back to the street below in disgust.

It was twilight, cool but fine. The days were starting to lengthen quickly now and the air almost hinted at spring, which made the sight of the funny little man scurrying north along Chalk Avenue all the more odd. He had his tweed cap pulled down tightly over his ears and the collar of his camel-hair coat was raised. He looked guilty, and for a moment Nightingale wondered whether he had an appointment in the flat in which she stood. If so, he was late and his meal had gone cold. But no: after casting a furtive look towards the rotating blue light on the patrol car, he turned east and away towards a housing development optimistically christened Sea View.

Nightingale watched him go with no doubt as to his purpose, and she despised him. She remembered suddenly an uncle, her father's brother. A grotty little man who turned up on Boxing Day and at Easter and had to be found a place at the table next to his young niece.

She had stumbled across him once, tucked in the lee of a wall, the sun hot on his face, with a tail of shirt where his trouser zip should have been and one of her teenage magazines cramped in a sweaty palm. God, what a sight! She'd tried to creep backwards but somehow had made a noise, a twig or a stone, enough to give her away and make him look up. And that grin – surprised, welcoming, aroused. She'd wanted the ground to open up; her cheeks had flamed, the bile had risen in her throat, but she'd been trapped there by that grubby little pervert. The hairs rose along her forearms at the memory and she turned back to the distraction inside.

The paramedics had finally given up and DI Chambers was asking about the cause of death. Nightingale listened, pity warring with contempt within her, before she was dispatched to interview more of the neighbours.

Arthur Fish scuttled inland towards Sea View, feeling the easterly wind on his cheek. Although he was early as always, he was still anxious to make good time. Night was falling prematurely as clouds from the horizon closed out the setting sun. As he neared the top of a small hill, he noticed the blue strobe light ahead. He immediately thought of ambulances, and from there his thoughts slipped effortlessly towards his wife. Was she all right?

At the top of the hill he realised that it was a police car and guilt flooded him. Were they raiding Amanda's? Had she already divulged the names of her clients? Was his secret about to break? But no, the car was parked to the left, opposite the turning to Sea View. He pulled his collar up about his ears and walked briskly past the pulsing light.

All thoughts of passions past or to come fled as he turned east into the wind. He felt frightened, old and a fool. For a brief moment he looked ahead into the next hour and saw it stripped of all the lust and emotion that usually clouded his perspective. He was a middle-aged man about to fulfil his appointment with a whore past her prime. Worse, what he allowed, no begged her to do to him could never be described as the result of a normal sex drive. He shivered inside his coat and shrank within his skin.

Amanda had seen the lights in front of the flats opposite and for a moment prepared herself for the dread of rapping knuckles against her solid front door. She had worked incredibly hard to achieve the respectability of her own permanent address. The fact that it was in a neighbourhood clinging to the edges of respectability made it even more of an achievement. A mere one hundred and fifty yards separated her from the blue light and the sort of run-down flats that her current charitable work and church attendance now helped to push into a distant memory.

Amanda was forty-five – still young enough to have made the break from street life quite well – and she owed it all to three things: an iron will, hard work and an intuitive insight into human beings. Were it not for the nature of her profession, her grandmother would have been proud of her achievements.

She watched the reflection of the blue lights on distant trees and realised that it would be a difficult evening. Arthur Fish was her next appointment. He was the last of her old customers. All the others had been quietly discouraged over the past few years, as she had carefully managed her transition from street life, via prison, to owner-occupation. It was five years, seven months and two weeks since she had been released from prison, an experience that had finally convinced her to do anything she could to slide her fingers on to the bottom rung of the ladder that was her only way out of the swamp in which she struggled to stay alive. She'd made it, and only Arthur and her occasional nightmares reminded her of the real source of her sizeable deposit on the house. It was her new regulars who now paid for her mortgage, private health insurance and pension.

Why was Arthur still a client? All the other originals had gone, taking the hint or the threats as necessary, but he clung on. In the past she'd had to admit, but only to herself, that she was almost fond of him, and he'd had such a tough life. His needs were so simple as to be almost laughable. He had never hurt her, and he was the only one who had turned up at the hospital that time she'd been beaten up. Despite his age – he was only fifty – he was as close to a father figure as she had ever known, her own being a changeable figment of her mother's raddled imagination.

Thinking of Arthur, she glanced at the clock and decided to get the room ready. They always used the downstairs back room; it was the only one with a fireplace, and he so loved a real fire. He'd give that little shiver that made her hide a smile, and go to warm the back of his trousers against it. There was a big sofa on the opposite wall on which she had spread a soft pale blue candlewick bedspread. A large old-fashioned galvanised bath stood in front of the fire, and next to it talc, flannels and baby lotion. The birch was kept hidden in the cupboard until later.

Amanda thought the bath was pushing matters too far, particularly as he'd admitted to her once that it had never actually been part of those memories he dredged up to become aroused. But these days he was so preoccupied that she needed all the props available to have him finished promptly in an hour. And that was all he paid for. She adjusted her outfit. The apron had been starched so fiercely that it cut into her neck. He was likely to be early. He was.

A bare hour later, she had run herself a proper bath, poured in some lavender oil and settled back for a long soak. She had at least two hours before her final appointment. This spare time was one of the precious luxuries she could now relish. As she eased back into the scented hot water, a frown creased her forehead. He'd been so screwed up she had almost run out of baby lotion, and then, at the end, just before he left, he had given her a sealed envelope. She was so used to little gifts that she had automatically started to open it.

'No!' he had shouted. 'Don't do that. Just keep it for me. And if anything should happen to me, take it straight to the police.'

Very odd. He wasn't normally a melodramatic man, but his fear had been real and Amanda had accepted it. Only now, as she lay back and thought about it properly for the first time, did her worries start. What was in that envelope? Why had he given it to her – and this talk of death, what did that mean? Unable to relax, she clambered out of the hot bath. Wrapped in a fluffy pink towelling robe, she padded downstairs and opened the envelope by delicately picking at the glue with her long varnished thumbnail.

Inside was a small cassette tape, about two inches by one. There was no letter, no label or writing of any sort on it apart from a tiny figure 10 in pencil. She looked at the envelope. Nothing, simply plain manila, and yet Arthur had been scared as he'd passed the packet to her. Tapping the cassette thoughtfully against her cheek, she tried to decide where to hide it. There was a large china cabinet in the front sitting room full of porcelain dolls in period costume. Some were tiny, others over two feet high. All were in immaculate condition, their costume colours fresh, faces clean and bright. Amanda took a small key from a jar on the mantelpiece and unlocked one of the ornate glass doors. She lifted out Priscilla, one of her favourites. Priscilla was dressed in a green velvet winter coat with rabbit-fur trim. She was twenty inches tall and carried a cosy little muff to keep her delicate china hands warm.

Amanda tucked the tape inside the coat and put the doll back, carefully arranging others in front of it again. She felt slightly foolish but relieved as she switched off the light. A shadow passed across the curtained front window. Someone had just walked between the streetlight and her house, and they would have to be close for their shadow to reach here. She shivered and glanced at the clock. There was still plenty of time to finish her bath and relax before her next client.

She was halfway up the stairs again when there was a knock at the front door. Amanda had no intention of letting whoever it was in, and she stood stock still on the stairs, waiting for the unexpected caller to go away. It was probably an old customer hoping to renew his acquaintance, but he should have known he would never be let in without an appointment.

The knocking came again, an insistent rap that would annoy her neighbours. Amanda swivelled on the stairs and went back down to a door that could have graced a maximum-security prison. There were two deadlocks, bolts top and bottom and an industrial-strength safety chain. A peephole had been inserted exactly at her eye height, which allowed a fish-eye view of the whole front garden, designed specifically to eliminate blind spots. There was an entryphone with camera attached tucked in the shelter of the eaves' overhang.

The view from the fish-eye was of a lean silhouette, back half turned; a baseball cap worn with the peak forward threw the face into shadow, but a margin of pale hair shone in the light. As she watched, the caller knocked again, long and hard. A light went on in next door's front room, and Amanda swore under her breath. No stranger was ever allowed into her home. Even potential new clients were vetted first on neutral territory. But now she had no option but to depress the entryphone switch.

'Who is it? What do you want?' her voice rasped electronically from the speaker in the porch. The figure turned round and smiled at the security

70

camera. Amanda took a step back in shock – to see that face again after all this time.

'It's me, Amanda. Let me in. I'm freezing out here.'

She felt a surge of nervous excitement that made her fingers shake as she undid each lock and bolt, one after the other. The safety chain rattled as it fell, and she finally turned the latch.

'It's you,' she said simply, as her unexpected visitor stepped into her hallway and she pushed the heavy door closed behind them.

Next door, the neighbour's front light went off.

CHAPTER FOURTEEN

Arthur shivered inside his coat as he waited on the platform for his return train. As always, on nights when he had seen Amanda, he felt guilty, but tonight in addition, he felt desperately scared. He glanced around him. The platform was empty except for a courting couple. The signal light turned green and the slow stopping train drew into the station with a weary sigh of brakes. Seconds before it pulled away again, a slim youth in designer trainers and tracksuit rushed down the stairs and grabbed at the door handle. Ignoring the guard's angry shout to 'Stand away!' he clambered in, almost falling across the feet of a middle-aged woman. She glared at him, and he grinned back before making his way steadily through the carriage towards the front of the train.

Up ahead, Arthur huddled in misery in the corner seat of an empty compartment. He always felt low as he returned to his invalid wife, but tonight he was so depressed he couldn't think straight. He kept dropping his head into his hands and rubbing his eyes. His life was a mess: work, home and sex – wherever he looked, he had messed it up. And he had tried so hard to do his best.

At first things had been fantastic. Despite his lack of accounting qualifications, he had slowly worked his way up from a humble accounts clerk at Wainwright's in the 1970s. He had been a self-taught amateur, so when he'd started noticing discrepancies he had been reluctant to draw anyone's attention to them. Eventually, though, the problems became too big to ignore. A cheque was issued for double the amount of the invoice received, then the invoice mysteriously disappeared; a dubious claim for a refund on damaged stock was waved through with no query; a payment was made to one of their major suppliers, and though the amount was right it was paid into a different bank account. And then there was all the cash. Most bills were settled in bundles of twenty-pound, then later fifty-pound notes. He'd thought it old-fashioned, but his suggestions for improvements were always ignored and the cash continued to flow. He had plucked up courage on more than one occasion to go to his supervisor, only to be shouted at and promptly thrown out of the office. Word went round that Arthur Fish was stupid, not an accountant, and with little idea of what he was talking about. There were rumours that he would be dismissed. As a young newly married man with a huge mortgage and a wife who was expecting a baby, Arthur had stared ruin in the face. Then came the afternoon he was notified that he would have to attend a review meeting with the chief accountant the next day. Even now, when things were really stressful at work, he still dreamt of that awful night of waiting, accompanied by fears of failure and destitution. If they sacked him he'd have no references, no credentials, nothing but debts.

The following morning, sick to his stomach, exhausted from lack of sleep, he had arrived expecting to be fired, but he hadn't been, not that day, nor the next. Instead he was praised for his diligence but firmly told that it was misapplied. Wainwright's was a unique and highly profitable company. It worked in its own way, and if he was smart and fitted in it would be to his advantage. At the end of that month there had been an additional fifty pounds in his pay packet without any explanation, a fortune in those days. He had banked it. When he noticed further discrepancies, which gradually became larger and more frequent, he just closed his mind to them and continued authorising the cash and cheques that paid the company's bills.

Arthur huddled in his corner, rocking with the motion of the carriage, and realised that those early months of turning a blind eye and hoping that he wouldn't be fired had marked the beginning of what he now knew with certainty had been a criminal career. When had he first started to think of himself as a criminal? Certainly not back then. Even when he was mysteriously promoted, after his supervisor had a fatal heart attack, he had been too naïve to realise what was going on.

Now he was the financial controller and Wainwright Enterprises comprised a vast array of businesses employing thousands of people. The original company was a tiny relic in the spreading empire. They had weathered recessions and benefited from recoveries more strongly than any of their competitors. Arthur had been proud of the company and its management. Whilst their competitors floundered and collapsed, Wainwright's prospered, never wanting for orders, never experiencing cash-flow problems and all within a private company, owned by a few long-term shareholders and the family. The accounts team had been kept small and a local firm of auditors never found fault.

Arthur hugged himself for comfort. His long-dead supervisor had called him an idiot, and that was what he was. As he'd started to suspect what might really be going on, so the number of surprise cash bonuses grew, until he and Jill, his wife, could afford to move to a really nice house that she loved. Her respect for him increased and with it their love for each other. The idea of risking it all was unthinkable, so he'd carried on turning a blind eye until the arrival of Alexander and Sally Wainwright-Smith.

He should have left when Alan Wainwright, the previous managing director died. He had saved enough, but by then his wife's health had deteriorated even further and he had chickened out. Throughout her illness Wainwright's, of course, had been fantastic. They paid for the best possible care, flew in specialist doctors, funded experimental medicine, even helped him re-equip the downstairs extension when it became obvious she would never be able to do anything for herself again. Now it was too late. He was trapped in a web of deceit and lies that he had, however unwittingly, helped to construct. There was no way out. He knew he should retire and be with Jill in her last few months, but he didn't dare leave. He realised with sudden and awful certainty that he would never enjoy a long retirement.

The connecting door between compartments opened and closed quickly, bringing a chill draught of night air. Arthur looked up and saw a lean, black-

73

clad youth weaving his way unsteadily between the empty seats. There were just the two of them in the carriage now, and he quickly looked away, avoiding eye contact.

The young man flopped down diagonally opposite and swung his muddy trainer-clad feet on to the seat next to Arthur's knees. Arthur huffed loudly and risked a quick look up. Two ice-blue eyes stared back at him, full of contempt. The youth grinned and Arthur turned his head away hurriedly.

No one joined them at the next stop, and Arthur began to feel very much alone in the carriage with this strange man. He calculated the number of minutes left before the train arrived at Harlden, and started to count the seconds patiently. The young man was still staring at him insolently and had started to fiddle with something in his pocket. The silence that lay between them became threatening. Arthur, already on edge from the evening's close encounter with the police and his own guilty memories, came to a sudden decision that he would change carriages. He picked up his cap and started to stand.

'Uh-uh.' The youth shook his head and leant forward to block Arthur's path. He was still smiling, but now his expression had a crazy edge to it. He was enjoying Arthur's sudden and obvious fear and wanted him to know it.

'Excuse me!' Arthur put on his most authoritative tone, but the other man just laughed at him and pushed him back in his seat with a rough hand.

'How dare you! I need to leave.'

'Indeed you do. You should've left a long time ago, from what I hear.'

The man's threatening tone sent a jolt of adrenaline through Arthur. His heart contracted painfully and his stomach churned. He leapt to his feet again, determined to push by and make his escape, but the youth blocked his way. He felt two sharp punches to his ribs and had to sit down quickly as his knees buckled in shock. He put his hand to his side to rub the dull pain away and felt a sticky wetness. He looked down at his fingers to see them covered with blood. He started to shiver, petrified now by the awfulness of the reality of what was happening to him. The youth was still standing there above him, rocking easily with the motion of the carriage, a blood-stained flick knife in his hand. He was watching Arthur intently, obviously relishing his growing terror.

'Why?' Arthur was stunned. There was no pain now, just a freezing cold around his ankles and sickness at the back of his throat.

'You've been a naughty boy, Arthur, and naughty boys get punished.' The youth spat out the words, laughing at the older man's pain. Blood trickled down Arthur's shirt to join a spreading damp stain on the front of his trousers.

'And now you've pissed yourself too. You prat!'

The train lurched over an uneven set of points and entered a cutting. Arthur recognised the familiar motion and sound and realised that they were nearing the next stop. Someone might get on. He could hammer on the window and someone might see him. He might yet escape!

It was as if his attacker could read his mind. Reluctantly he stopped tormenting his victim and looked around.

'Time to go. Say goodbye, Arthur.'

Then he lunged forward, knife in fist. Arthur raised a hand to ward him off but his fingers were swatted away easily and the blade went home. This time it didn't miss. The sharpened point slid between ribs and cleanly into the main cardiac muscle. Arthur's heart took one more stuttering beat and then simply stopped.

The youth flipped the blade shut, pulled out a wallet from Arthur's inner pocket and calmly buttoned his victim's jacket over the bloody wounds. He placed the cap on his lap, where it covered most of the stain. Then he smashed the light immediately over the slumped body. With luck, no one would recognise it for what it was until the end of the line.

As the train slowed in anticipation of the next stop, he flicked through the wallet, looking for cash. He took the solitary twenty-pound note, then threw the wallet to the floor. He got off the train at the next station, which was busier than he would have liked. The buzz of the drugs he had taken in Brighton was starting to fade. He had needed them to steel his nerve, as he had never before gone so far as to kill someone in cold blood. His head felt too big for his body and his hands started to shake. He stuffed them firmly into his pockets so that no blood would show. The Gents' was stinking but empty and he rinsed off the worst of the mess under a begrudging trickle of cold water. Amazingly, there were paper towels, and he wiped off most of the rest of the blood on three or four of them.

There was one remaining taxi in the station car park. Cash wasn't a problem tonight, it wouldn't be for a while, so he decided to take the easy way home. In the back of the cab he popped his last tiny grey pill into his mouth and swallowed. It wasn't until he was excavating the dirt and blood from under his thumbnails with the tip of his knife, feeling the shock recede and the high return, that he remembered that he had been supposed to take the man's wallet with him to make it look like a mugging. That was going to piss off his employer, and he was suddenly worried that he might not be paid the second half of his money. Still, hopefully they'd never know and he would get away with it. He usually did. He told the driver to stop in the middle of town and walked the remaining short distance to the club, where he knew he would be able to buy what he would need to see him through until morning without nightmares.

CHAPTER FIFTEEN

It had been a long day – correction, it had been a long, long month – but there were only a few more days to go and she'd be back at Harlden. The three-week secondment had been good experience but Nightingale was glad that the Easter weekend had finally arrived and that it would soon be over. She missed her old division more than she had ever expected. It wasn't in her nature to form sentimental attachments to places or colleagues, but she had done so there, and when she actually thought about the idea, it worried her. It was uncomfortable to think about what – or really whom – she might be missing so badly.

It was nearly ten o'clock and she had been working for over fourteen hours. She was alone in the duty room. The others on her shift had gone home and the new team was in the canteen buying coffee and bacon sandwiches. All she wanted to do now was run a deep bath sprinkled with aromatherapy oil, put on some Schubert, pour a glass of chilled Chardonnay and slide into the warm scented water to lie there until it cooled. The idea was so compelling that she could almost smell the lavender as she grabbed her jacket and headed for the door.

The phone rang and she kept on walking. There were others on duty, much fresher than she was; they could answer it when they returned from the canteen. It kept on ringing, again and again. The urge to answer it was almost impossible to resist – she was as conditioned as one of Pavlov's dogs – and as she opened the door, the automatic response finally overcame the phantom scent of lavender. With an angry backward kick, she slammed it shut and grabbed the nearest receiver, hoping even as she did so that the caller would have hung up.

'Yes?'

'About bloody time too. Who's that?' She recognised the voice of the duty sergeant.

'DC Nightingale, Sarge.'

'Who? Oh yes. What took you so long?'

'I was just leaving, Sarge.' Behind her, Nightingale heard the chatter of returning colleagues, suddenly louder as the door opened.

'Well, you can forget that. Find DI Linden or DS Pink and get over to Sea View, Cheyne Terrace. Two of my team here responded to a report of a domestic disturbance and found a body; death looks suspicious. SOCO are already on their way.'

Nightingale groaned. There was no point in arguing. DS Pink was drinking a cup of coffee noisily as he gossiped behind her. He was bound to tell her to go with him, as he never missed an opportunity to flirt with her. So far she had been able to maintain a façade of icy disdain whilst she'd seethed inside but tonight she was already so tired. Could she keep her cool?

Sure enough, Pink told her to join him in his car. He spent the twenty-minute journey chatting her up. The problem with Pink was that he thought he was such a smooth, good-looking hunk that she was supposed to fall for him immediately, despite the fact that everyone knew that he was married. He treated her disinterest as a clever 'come-on', but his patience was obviously wearing thin after weeks of concerted attention had failed to make any impact on her. As they reached their destination, he delivered his *pièce de résistance*.

'You like classical music, don't you?'

'Yes.'

'Thought so. Well,' he leant unnecessarily close as he bent to undo his seat belt, 'I've got two tickets for a concert at the Royal Pavilion on Saturday night.'

'Really? Lucky you.'

'So, would you like to join me?'

'I don't think so, thanks all the same.' She reached for the door handle to get out. His hand went to her arm with enough force to pull her back.

'Come on, Nightingale. Stop being so hard to get. You know you want to, you can stop the play-acting now.'

His fingers squeezed her arm then opened enough to brush just below her breast. Without warning she felt long-suppressed anger well up inside her.

'I said no and I meant it. Will you just stop pestering me!'

'Pestering you, you stuck up little bitch! Who do you think you are? Jesus, anyone can see you're desperate for it. The boys are right, you're just another frigid dyke, with an arse so tight you only shit on Sundays.'

He slammed out of the car, causing an oncoming motorist to swerve wildly. Nightingale stayed where she was, fighting back tears of hurt and anger. He was a stupid bastard and she cared nothing for his opinion, but his reference to the rest of the boys and their supposed contempt hurt her badly. She had worked hard, helped out and backed them up when they fell behind with the paperwork. All for what? Nothing. They'd been laughing at her all the time behind her back. After a moment the tears disappeared unshed, but the anger didn't. She swallowed hard, buried it deep and followed Pink into the neat semi-detached house.

SOCO were already on the scene, and flashes from a camera flickered irregularly from a room to the right of the hall. Pink was talking to one of the uniformed constables who had been first to arrive.

'The neighbours, Mr and Mrs Wells, reported sounds of a disturbance at about nine o'clock.'

'What sounds?' asked Pink.

'Raised voices followed by screams.'

'Who was she?'

'Amanda Bennett.'

The constable consulted his notebook: 'Married? Live-in partner?'

'Mrs Wells says not. Lived alone. Moved in less than a year ago.'

Nightingale craned her neck and peered over Pink's shoulder. The police surgeon arrived and made his way delicately into the front room as the SOCO team moved to one side, and she saw the body for the first time. A white woman, perhaps in her late thirties or a little older; slender – her body had been in good condition; a bit too much make-up but otherwise she'd probably been quite attractive. That was before her murderer had finished work on her.

There was no obvious pattern to the cuts to the woman's face and neck so far as Nightingale could see. Some were slight, no more than nicks; others were deep, biting right into the flesh. She watched without revulsion as the police surgeon went about his business.

'Been dead less than two hours.'

'Cause of death?' Pink was always impatient.

'The pathologist will tell you that.'

Work continued impersonally around the corpse. There was no banter, not out of respect but just because everyone was so tired. Pink and Nightingale searched the house, not speaking to each other. When the surgeon left, Nightingale finally entered the murder room. It was neat and tidy, furnished on a modest budget. The only obviously expensive item was a delicate china cabinet containing a collection of ornamental dolls.

'We've found out what she did for a living,' Pink called out to Nightingale and she followed him up the stairs. He nodded towards one of the rooms with a knowing smile on his face.

One bedroom contained a large double bed, with a mirror above it and another where the headboard should have been. There were two built-in cupboards discreetly set behind ornate wooden screens. Inside, rows of bizarre costumes had been arranged in order from innocence to deeply disturbed. Among the more innocent were a schoolmistress's outfit with short pleated skirt, gown and gym knickers and a nanny's apron with a bottle of baby lotion tucked into the pocket.

In the other cupboard, in shades of red, purple and black, were skin-tight costumes in every conceivable material, with strategically cut holes. Rubber, lurex, leather, PVC, silk, they were all there. Stacked tidily in shelving to one side was a wide range of studded collars, boots, sex aids, canes and whips. Despite herself, Nightingale was intrigued, though she hoped it didn't show.

'A client turned nasty, then.' Pink sounded certain.

'Could be, but why risk all that noise? And she didn't look dressed for a client.'

'No, dear, you've got it all wrong, she *undressed* for clients.'

Nightingale ignored him. 'There was another murder earlier this evening just over the road – Tracie Grey. She was a prostitute too.'

'Why didn't you say so at once, you idiot? They could be connected.'

'The cause of death looks completely different, sir. But I'm sorry, you're right. I should have mentioned it straight away.' *And I would have done*, she thought, *if you hadn't been so intent on seducing me.* She walked away from him. Following her nose, she pushed open the bathroom door. A full bath of clean water on to which dried rose petals and lavender flowers had been sprinkled reflected dying candlelight. To one side an open book and a solitary glass of something that could have been vodka stood waiting. To a connoisseur such as Nightingale, this was all the evidence she needed that the woman downstairs had been preparing to indulge in a long private bath before she had been so brutally interrupted. Unfortunately, Pink had already made up his mind as to motive.

'Nightingale, get down here and go and interview the neighbours. Come on, get your finger out, this is a murder inquiry, not a guided tour.'

Ignoring Pink's aggression, she left quietly and went to visit Mr and Mrs Wells. A uniformed constable had already broken the news that their neighbour was dead, and the elderly couple sat in shocked, horrified silence.

A cup of tea was offered and accepted, but sitting down in one of Mrs Wells' comfy armchairs was a big mistake. Fatigue swamped Nightingale and she had to struggle to keep her eyes open. Mrs Wells, however, made a good witness, observant and to the point, and Nightingale woke up in interest.

'Amanda moved in nine months ago. Haven't seen much of her since, kept herself to herself. Friendly, but not one to mix.'

'Was there ever any sign of a husband or lover, anybody close to her?'

Mrs Wells paused, looking embarrassed.

'No one regular, but she did have visitors.'

'Male friends?'

The elderly woman nodded, not meeting Nightingale's eyes.

Nightingale didn't push her. They already knew the victim's profession; what she needed to find out now was the identity of her killer.

'Can you describe any of her callers for me?'

'No. That's what's odd. Until tonight you'd hardly know they were there. Ever so discreet: a light tap on the door, then they'd be let straight in. Not like earlier on. That's what made me look out. All that banging. There'd never been anything like that before.'

'So you saw tonight's caller. Can you describe them for me?'

'Well, he was slightly built, fair, a bit skinny, I think. I couldn't see much more but she knew him, I could tell.'

'How?'

'Well, Geoff had just opened the door a crack – we keep the chain on – and we were deciding whether to ask him to be quiet when she opens her door and says, "Oh, it's you." And lets him in.'

'You said "him"; are you sure it was a man?'

The old couple looked at each other, shocked.

'Well, I couldn't be certain. They weren't overly big, so it could have been a woman. What do you think, Geoff?'

'Couldn't say. I assumed it was a man but . . . well, I never saw the face and there was no making out their figure.'

'What happened after they were let inside?'

Mrs Wells went on to describe the sounds of an argument, then a woman's screams so awful that they called the police. They hadn't heard the front door open or close again, and nothing else had happened until the police arrived.

There was nothing more for Nightingale to learn from Mr and Mrs Wells, and she returned reluctantly to DS Pink.

CHAPTER SIXTEEN

At exactly the same time, twenty-four miles to the north, DCI Fenwick crouched down between worn train seats to stare up into the surprised, glazed eyes of a man whose driving licence identified him as Arthur Fish. Fenwick picked up his wallet from his feet, handling it carefully in case there were any fingerprints on it. Fish had been found a short while before by a cleaner too used to late-night drunks to have been much surprised by the solitary hunched figure, but who was now struggling with the shock of finding a dead body. Fenwick had been at home, relaxing with a good book, when he received the phone call summoning him back to work. His house was less than fifteen minutes' walk from the railway station, so he had jogged down easily, arriving well before the rest of the team. The uniformed constables from the car patrol were outside, keeping the few potential witnesses together in a waiting room.

It was a strangely peaceful moment. He was on his own in the carriage, and only the small pool of blood that stained the seat cover gave any hint of the violence surrounding this sudden death. He touched nothing more, contenting himself with searching the scene with his eyes. The man's coat had been buttoned up askew, the middle button fastened through the lower hole. It was old-fashioned camel hair, three-quarter-length, expensive but hardly stylish. The victim's cap lay on the floor between his suede lace-ups. He looked to have been in his fifties; balding, rather overweight.

Fenwick straightened up and climbed back out of the train to wait for the others. He was growing impatient: he could never stand to wait. Then he heard a siren in the distance, growing louder, and the flashing blue of the light lit up trees by the tracks. A few minutes later the SOCO team arrived, donned their white suits, caps, gloves and overshoes, and started their work. The first thing they did was to screen the windows from the outside, spoiling the view of the few would-be travellers who'd had the nerve to ignore their own train and stay to watch. Serves them right, thought Fenwick, pleased that they would now have a long, boring wait for the next service.

There were sounds of heavy feet on the concrete stairs to the platform, and Detective Sergeant Cooper arrived, pink-faced and puffing.

'You took your time!'

'Sorry, sir, there was another accident on the bypass. Whole road was blocked so we had to back up and come in across town. What've we got?'

'We appear to have landed a Mr Arthur Fish, very recently deceased. Found by the cleaner,' he glanced at his watch and raised his eyebrows at Cooper, 'nearly an hour ago. PC Dane was first on the scene and called it in.'

'Suspicious?'

'Could be. There's blood on the seat and his coat. No sign of a weapon, so unless he's haemorrhaged, it looks unnatural. Let's find out what Pendlebury has to say, he's just arrived.'

The two men entered the train and found the morose pathologist in almost exactly the same position that Fenwick himself had adopted earlier. He'd opened Fish's coat, jacket and shirt, and was studying the flabby pale skin beneath.

'Evening, Doctor, have we got work to do?'

There was no answer for a moment whilst Pendlebury finished his short-sighted scrutiny of the wounds. Then he simply said: 'Yes, you have,' and carried on.

Fenwick waited, a tactic which usually worked with this most taciturn of men. Tonight, though, it failed, and he was finally forced to ask: 'How did he die?' adding quickly, in the hope that it would pass as one question, 'And when?'

'There are three stab wounds to the chest with enough bleeding to suggest that at least two of them were not immediately fatal, but as to whether they were the cause of death, I can't say until after the PM.' Fenwick's second question he completely ignored.

Fenwick caught Cooper's eye and grimaced. Pendlebury was a great pathologist but he could be laborious to work with, and recently he had been getting worse.

Pendlebury checked that the photographer had finished and then called out abruptly for someone to help him move the body so that he could take a temperature. The detectives left him in the stuffy carriage with its smells of dying evacuations and went back to the platform. Cooper called Operations for more resources and then asked Fenwick the question that had been bothering him since he'd arrived.

'Why'd they call you in for this one, sir? There's at least two other DIs on duty who could've handled it.'

Fenwick opened the dead man's wallet with his gloved fingers and showed Cooper a plastic identity card with a photograph of the dead man on it. Beneath it were the man's name, his business title and the name of his employer – Wainwright Enterprises.

'Constable Dane looked to see who he was and George Wicklow was bright enough to realise the significance of the case when it was called in.'

'Well, he was right. There's going to be a lot of interest in this one.'

Fenwick nodded but added nothing. His suspicions about Wainwright's had been raised the previous month, but he hadn't expected to be encountering them again so soon. Part of him, with all due respect to the dead man, was glad that he was.

Within an hour the body had been removed, they'd interviewed the cleaner, station staff and potential witnesses, and arranged for the whole carriage to be subjected to forensic tests. The train had left the coast at 21.12, arriving at Harlden just over an hour later. There were eleven stops in between. By midnight, the operations centre at Division had arranged for posters requesting information to be put up on platforms and in car parks along the route. Litterbins were being collected from all stations in case the murder weapon had been thrown away – though that was unlikely – and a search along the tracks, starting at the Harlden end, had been arranged for first light. In the morning, police officers would be interviewing staff at other stations and then questioning passengers in the hope that someone might remember Fish. A team would join and work the 21.12 train for several days in the hope of tracing regular travellers.

At about the time that the incident room manager was finishing the duty schedule, Fenwick, Cooper and a WPC were knocking on the late Mr Fish's front door. A very old and tired-looking woman answered. She seemed ready for an argument.

'Mrs Fish?'

'No. Who're you?' She peered through a six-inch sturdily safety-chained gap. Fenwick showed her his warrant card and announced them all. She studied it closely, inclined to take it off him had he not held on to it, then begrudgingly opened the door to allow them in. They were taken straight into an orderly kitchen, where a single cup of tea had just been made.

'Well?' She bristled with hostility. Fenwick would not have wished her welcome on anyone, and felt a moment's sympathy for Arthur Fish.

'Excuse me, you are . . . ?'

'Mrs Wilmslow, from number sixty-three. I sit in until the night-nurse arrives on the Thursdays Mr Fish goes to his faculty meeting, but she's late and so is he!'

'Sit in for whom?'

'For Mr Fish, of course.'

Fenwick merely stared her out, unmoved by the show of brusque obtuseness.

'Oh, I see what you mean. Well, for Mrs Fish really.' A pause, then the first volunteered comment. 'She's very ill. I don't know what with, but I think it's MS. Can't do anything for herself now, poor dear. It's a miracle she's lasted this long.'

Her brief attempt at taciturn control broken, Mrs Wilmslow then couldn't stop talking. She told them all about Mrs Fish's illness; Mr Fish's important job; his monthly faculty meetings; how normally he was back by now – very regular and punctual in his habits, was Mr Fish. Would they like to wait for him?

'Is Mrs Fish awake? How well would she understand us?'

'Oh, there's nothing wrong with her mentally, that's the tragedy. It's her body that's let her down. There are some days better than others, of course, but she can't speak now – that went about two months ago – and the blindness is becoming more frequent. I can't recall the last time I saw her out of bed. It's tragic. Here I am, eighty-three and as fit as I was twenty years ago whilst she, poor dear . . .' Mrs Wilmslow seemed to be enjoying her tragic story a little too well.

Fenwick suppressed a shudder and then relaxed as he heard the matter-of-fact voice of the night-nurse calling from the hall behind them.

'Sorry I'm late. The traffic was terrible.'

She walked into the kitchen and stopped dead when she saw the serious-faced strangers standing there.

'Oh no, she's gone,' she said in a whisper.

'No, that's not why we're here, Miss . . .?' Fenwick showed her his warrant card.

'Hay, Alice Hay. What's happened?'

'We believe her husband, Mr Fish, is dead.' Fenwick watched Edith Wilmslow's and Alice Hay's faces closely as he broke the news. There was no mistaking the shock he saw there as they both instinctively covered their mouths in horror.

'How did he die?' The nurse recovered her wits first.

'I can't tell you at this stage, but we will need someone to identify the body if his wife is so ill. Does he have children?'

'Yes, but not nearby. I'll do it.' Alice sounded calm and professional now that she was over the shock so Fenwick accepted her offer gladly.

'Is Mrs Fish well enough to be told the news?'

'She's poorly but it's a chronic condition and she's been stable for some months now.' The nurse paused, deep in thought. 'She will start to worry soon anyway as he's not back. On balance, I think you should tell her, but let me call her doctor first. I have his emergency number.'

They all waited whilst Alice Hay completed her hushed call to the doctor, using the phone in the hall, despite there being one in the kitchen as well. It appeared that Fenwick wasn't the only one to mistrust Edith Wilmslow's obvious nose for gossip. The nurse returned within minutes.

'He agrees. Waiting until morning would only add to her anxiety and increase the risks of a severe reaction when she is told, and she'll have to be eventually. Come with me, I'll show you the way.'

Fenwick followed Alice and made it clear to Cooper that he should stay with Mrs Wilmslow and keep her out of the way.

'It's one blink for good or yes, and three for no or bad,' the old woman called after them, determined to have her say in the drama.

The invalid suite was in a lavish extension at the back of the house. A large, airy room faced south with a conservatory-style wall overlooking a landscaped garden. Concealed spotlights picked out specimen plants, a fountain and a gentle stone statue of a deer and fawn. It was a serene setting in which to die.

Most of the paraphernalia of nursing and care was kept out of sight in a small room fitted with cupboards and a sink. Opposite it, on the other side of a short entrance corridor, was a specially equipped bathroom with wheelchair access, hoists and other lifting equipment. Whatever money could achieve had been achieved, with no concern for cost.

A low nightlight candle flickered gently on the bedside table, quaint and reminiscent of nursery scenes long past. It was impossible to tell whether the patient was awake, and Fenwick let the nurse go first.

'Mrs Fish? Are you awake? Do you mind if we put the light on?' Alice gently coaxed her patient awake. 'It's me, Alice. I'm sorry, my love, but something has happened and you need to be told.' She held on to her patient's hand, unobtrusively finding the pulse.

Fenwick sat down in the bedside chair and explained who he was.

Mrs Fish's surprisingly attractive brown eyes were open and fearful. A practised deliverer of unwelcome news, Fenwick went straight to the point.

'Mrs Fish, I'm terribly sorry, but you must prepare yourself for some very bad news.'

The look of fear deepened and the nurse squeezed her limp hand in a gesture of comfort. Fenwick went on, knowing that no delay could change what he was about to say.

'There is no easy way to say this. We believe that your husband died this evening, on the train back to Harlden. I am so very sorry.'

As Fenwick explained why they were almost positive that the man found on the train was Arthur, a huge tear formed slowly and rolled down her cheek, to be followed by another and then more. Soon her whole face was wet with tears she was unable even to brush away. It went on for a long time as the nurse gently wiped her face with clean tissues.

'Are you up to a little conversation, Mrs Fish?'

A single, fierce blink.

'You want to know what happened?'

Blink.

'It looks as if your husband's death wasn't natural. We don't think it was suicide either. We suspect he might have been attacked and killed.'

She continued to stare at them intently. There was no sign of shock or surprise, just an incredible anger in her expressive eyes.

'Did your husband have any enemies?'

Three blinks.

'Anyone who might have had a grudge?'

Another three blinks.

'Was your husband worried or frightened at all?'

Hesitation, then three blinks.

'You don't seem very sure. Please, if he was acting differently from normal, it could be significant.'

There was no reply, and the tears welled up again.

'Do you have a friend we can arrange to sit with you? Mrs Wilmslow, perhaps?'

Three definite rapid blinks.

'I'll be here until Mrs Brown arrives in the morning, Chief Inspector.' The nurse's soft voice was comforting, and immediately tears started again. 'I think that's enough for now. Could you see Mrs Wilmslow out when you leave while I stay here?'

As he left the house with Cooper, Fenwick sighed deeply.

'She knows something, I'm sure of it, but she's decided not to tell us. Poor woman – I bet she never expected to outlive her husband.'

The next morning Fenwick and Cooper attended the post-mortem. The sergeant hung up his tweed jacket outside, convinced that the smell of the autopsy would stay with him for days if he wore it. The trousers would go straight in the wash that night, along with every other stitch of clothing he was wearing, but the jacket still had plenty more wear in it before it would be sent to the cleaner's. He hated this aspect of the job. The boss always seemed impervious but Cooper found autopsies hard and resented the need to be there. He'd even turned down a cooked breakfast that morning and was hoping the single slice of toast and marmalade he had managed would stay put.

Pendlebury was waiting for them, gowned and ready, beside the body of Arthur Fish, which was lying face up on a steel table. He nodded at them

84

both as they walked in but said nothing. Really, thought Cooper, his moods are worse than ever.

Pendlebury started dictating his external examination of the body, then undressed it and place the clothes into sterile plastic bags for forensic examination.

'Apart from recent scalds to his left hand there are no other signs of violence on the body except for these stab wounds' – he read out precise measurements of the wounds. 'Three wounds, same blade. The first two weren't fatal, he bled from both for a short while. The third looks to be at the right angle and with sufficient force – see here, the faint bruise of the butt of the knife – to have reached his heart. It was a narrow, sharp blade; from the shape of the wound it could have been a flick knife or something similar. I'll be able to tell you more about the weapon after I've looked inside.'

Cooper swallowed hard.

'There's a substance under his fingernails and around his groin – I've sent samples to the lab. It smells like some sort of powder – here.' Pendlebury lifted one of the dead man's hands up for them to sniff. Cooper caught a trace of Johnson's baby lotion that took him right back to bathing his baby daughter all those years ago, and was angry that such a wonderful memory should now be tainted forever.

'It's baby lotion, Doctor. I recognise the smell.'

'He'd had sex shortly before his death and had used a prophylactic. He hadn't washed afterwards, and we've got plenty of trace evidence.'

'But why baby lotion?' Cooper was struggling to find the relevance. Fenwick and Pendlebury exchanged a look, and the pathologist carried on.

'Let's turn him over – Ken, thank you.' His assistant rolled the body on to its flabby stomach with practised ease and then straightened the limbs.

'Now, take a look at this.' Long red welts stretched across Fish's buttocks and lower back. 'A cane, I think, certainly not a belt or whip. Probably done a matter of hours before his death.'

'Sado-masochism?'

'You tell me, but I couldn't disagree with the conclusion.'

He inspected the rest of the back and limbs, lifting flecks of towelling and lint from the skin and hair, then asked for the body to be turned over again.

Without further preamble he started with a strong Y-shaped incision, his dry commentary recorded by the overhead microphone. The suddenness with which the taut grey skin sprang back from beneath the scalpel made Cooper choke. The micro-thin layer popped open, allowing subcutaneous fat to expand. Fish had been unfit and had carried at least an extra twenty pounds, and that layer of fat suddenly became the most prominent part of him.

Cooper glanced down at his own comfortable paunch and felt the acid remains of his toast and marmalade scald the back of his throat. He coughed loudly and blew his nose. Fenwick appeared unmoved, although it was always hard to tell. Unlike Cooper, he was able to keep any trace of what he was really thinking from showing on his face. He watched now as Pendlebury carefully removed and weighed each internal organ. All appeared relatively healthy given the man's age, with no trace of heart disease despite the obvious lack of exercise and excess weight. Pendlebury pointed out the death wound to the heart and gave them the blade length and width.

Fenwick and Cooper waited patiently as the pathologist removed and weighed the brain, but there was nothing more for them to learn, and they left as the body was being sewn up. Outside, in the car park, Fenwick paused to lean across the roof of their car.

'I want the relevant divisions on the coast informed of this death. I know it's jumping the gun, but Brighton or somewhere close is the most likely source of whatever sex it was that poor bloke was buying. I'll lay money on the fact that it's where he visited last night. It would be far enough away and busy enough for him to feel anonymous.'

'Do you think there's a connection between the sex and the murder?'

Fenwick paused, then shook his head slowly. 'It's a possibility, but why wait until he's on the train?'

'Just a mugging gone wrong, then?'

Fenwick looked at the sergeant in exasperation.

'So why do we have his wallet, complete with credit cards? No, that doesn't make sense either. It doesn't feel like a random crime, and yet it's too callous and casual to be premeditated. I'm not jumping to any conclusions; we'll have to wait and see what today brings.'

CHAPTER SEVENTEEN

Fenwick was studying the contents of Arthur Fish's wallet when Cooper tapped on his office door and walked in.

'Ready, sir?'

'In just a sec. Sit down. What do you make of this?'

Cooper eyed the angular visitor's chair in Fenwick's office with something approaching hatred but moved to obey. The DCI held out a small silver key for his inspection.

'For a padlock or a suitcase? Where'd it come from?'

'It was in the lining of Fish's wallet, tucked away. There's a reference number on it. Get it checked out, would you, and we'll keep it quiet for the time being. Any news from the railway yet?'

Cooper shook his head. 'Nothing. This evening will be more likely, but so far there's no clue at all as to whom did this or why.'

Fenwick's poker face carefully blocked out his reaction to his sergeant's appalling grammar as he stood up and threw Cooper his set of car keys.

'You drive. I need to think.'

It would be a silent journey.

Wainwright Enterprises had five offices in the UK, but none so grand as their head office, on the outskirts of Harlden. It was the landmark building in a development four miles from the town centre. Five storeys of dark blue tinted glass set in brilliant steel frames towered above a landscaped park like a contemporary ziggurat. The development occupied a natural rise, and Wainwright Enterprises had built on the summit, assuming an automatic authority much as it had done over the county's commercial life. Stepped fountains and sculpted shrubs covered the slope of the hill, cleverly concealing a functional car park to the rear of the building. Cooper chose one of the few visitors' spaces and parked neatly but with considerable puffing and effort. His bulk made three-point turns an effort, even with power steering, and his habitual tweed jacket restricted his manoeuvrability as he twisted and turned in the driver's seat. When he had finally finished and switched off the engine, Fenwick broke the silence.

'Wainwright's again. It seems strange that two senior executives – the managing director and now the financial controller – should have died within a few months of each other.'

'Accidents usually happen in threes, sir. Who do you think will be next?'

Fenwick didn't like that thought at all, and continued with his original theme.

'You have to admit that this is a bizarre coincidence.' He slammed the door shut. 'And I have a deep distrust of coincidences.'

They were escorted from the reception area to a small meeting room dominated by a circular cherrywood table, where they were served fresh coffee.

The finance director, Neil Yarrell, arrived a few minutes later. A slim man of average height, he looked much younger than they had expected, no more than thirty-five. He offered them a perfectly manicured hand to shake and Fenwick recognised discreet Italian tailoring in his suit and tie.

'Chief Inspector Fenwick, good morning. I'm sorry I kept you waiting but I was just on the phone to the Assistant Chief Constable. You're here about Arthur Fish. Terrible business.'

Fenwick introduced Cooper, who promptly took out his notebook.

'Extraordinary! In this day and age you still use paper.'

Cooper raised his eyebrows in surprise. Was the man deliberately trying to be rude?

'It works, sir.'

'I'm sure it does, but it's still fascinating. Right, what can I tell you?'

'Everything you can about Mr Fish, starting with his employment here.'

'Well, I hope you've got plenty of time – and paper, Sergeant. He'd been here nearly thirty years.'

'Sight of his personnel file will be sufficient for the background, sir. If you could perhaps describe his role and responsibilities?'

'He was the company's financial controller, which means he dealt with management accounts, internal controls and so on.'

'And how does that vary from your role as finance director?'

'I tend to focus on strategic developments, capital funding, shareholder relations – more up and out than inwards and down, if you understand my meaning.'

Yarrell went on to describe Fish's job at monotonous length. Cooper found it hard to take notes, as there was no way of knowing which aspects were relevant and which just so much detail. At the end of ten minutes Fenwick moved the conversation along.

'What was his mood recently?'

'Fine. Same as usual.'

'He didn't seem troubled or preoccupied?'

'No. He was naturally a bit of a worrier, but I like that in a financial controller.'

'How about his personal life?'

'His wife, you mean? Well, that was very sad. We were all terribly upset when she became ill. It would've been a blessing to poor Arthur if she'd gone, quite honestly.'

It was all said by rote, with a callous disregard that betrayed a complete lack of true sympathy for his late colleague. Fenwick could feel his dislike growing for Neil Yarrell. At the end of half an hour he called the interview to a close. They had learnt nothing of relevance. Yarrell promised to send the personnel file to them and agreed to arrange for the finance staff to come down one at a time for questioning.

There were seven staff in all, including Fish's secretary. By the time they'd finished seeing the third, Fenwick was utterly exasperated.

'Nothing!' he exploded. 'Not a damned thing. Each one of them is prepared to swear that Fish was a nice, quiet bloke, decent to work for, never got angry or upset. They've no gossip about him or the rest of the place, and not a bad word to say about anybody. And nobody knows a thing about faculty meetings.'

'Well, perhaps it's just a decent place to work. It does have an excellent reputation.'

'No, Cooper, they all seem word-perfect to me. It's as if they've been primed before they saw us. When we leave here, find out if he was a chartered or certified accountant, and whether either of those august bodies holds faculty meetings he attended. If not, I think we can conclude that they were his cover story for his visits to prostitutes.'

Cooper nodded and left to usher in the fourth member of staff to be interviewed. The questioning went quickly and predictably, as it did with the fifth and sixth members of the finance department. The last person to arrive was Fish's secretary, Joan Dwight. In her fifties, already tearful and upset, she looked a little more promising than the others. She'd just sat down when Yarrell tapped on the door and beckoned Fenwick outside.

'Is it really necessary to see Mrs Dwight?' he whispered. 'She's really terribly upset.'

'It's relevant to see everyone who knew Mr Fish.'

'Yes, but she won't be able to tell you anything – she's not that bright. I can't think that she'll help you in any way.'

'Nevertheless, if you'll excuse me . . .' Fenwick turned his back on the man and closed the conference room door behind him.

Mrs Dwight was indeed tearful and distraught, and it required considerable patience to coax her story from her. It was basically the same as all the others, but this time at least they gained an insight into Arthur Fish's working life.

'He was very regular in all his habits. He arrived at a little before eight fifteen every day and liked the first half-hour to himself. I'd always be in just before nine, make the coffee and open the post. Then he did his dictation.'

'Did you take shorthand?'

'Sometimes, for short pieces, but a few years ago he started to use one of those dictaphone things and I just had to get used to it. Here,' she leant forward and wagged a soggy tissue at Fenwick in emphasis, 'this'll show you just what a kind man he was. I used to get in a terrible muddle with his tapes, could never remember which ones I'd typed. I used to erase new ones and retype the old ones – I was all over the place. Then Mr Fish worked out a system just for me. We always have ten of those little cassettes on the go, each one numbered, and he'd keep a list of them for me, showing which one I should be working on at any time. We had no more problems after that.'

Fenwick marvelled at the patience of a man who could cope with this sweet but muddle-headed dinosaur, but she had obviously been devoted to him and was desperately loyal.

'So did he seem upset at all recently?'

She looked down at her lap and twisted the soggy tissue.

'No,' she said hesitantly, 'same as usual. Although he'd been working very long hours over the past few weeks, and I know, although he never told me as much, of course, that things had got worse at home.'

'How did you know?'

'Oh, little ways. He always used to keep the door between his office and mine open, unless he had a meeting, of course, but he'd taken to closing it recently.'

'And this had been going on for how long?'

'A few weeks or so. And just last night, before he went off to his faculty meeting, he closed his door so that he could do a whole load of dictation.' Her face suddenly showed shock. 'Oh, I must do that, of course I must. He did a full tape's worth, I know, because I've only got numbers one to nine in my rack upstairs.'

'And he showed no signs of being upset or different in any way?'

'Well, no.' Joan shook her tightly permed head emphatically. 'I'd have known.' She pursed her lips.

Cooper asked his first question, gently, in his soft local Sussex voice.

'Have you ever known him out of sorts, Mrs Dwight?'

Tears flooded her eyes again and her face was washed in a pink wave of colour. She nodded almost imperceptibly.

'A little bit just recently,' she whispered. 'I think his wife's illness had finally worn him down. Normally he'd never even so much as raise his voice to me but he shouted at me last week, really shouted!'

'And you think it was because of the situation at home?'

'Well, what else could it have been? I know that he and the new managing director never really saw eye to eye, but why should that upset him?'

Mrs Dwight suddenly realised what she had said and was obviously regretting her words. Fenwick could tell she was about to close up on them.

'Sergeant, might I have a brief word outside?'

Mrs Dwight butted in. 'I really should be getting back now, I'll be missed. And there's that tape to see to.'

'Please give us a few more moments. We won't be long.'

Fenwick and Cooper stepped outside and Fenwick leant close to the sergeant's ear.

'Why don't you take it from here? I'm a little too much the figure of authority to get any more, and she's done her respectful bit now. Mentally she's decided she's given us more than her due. Ask her to show you the way to the canteen and then invite her for a cuppa.'

As Cooper slipped back into the meeting room, Fenwick decided to go and find the new managing director of Wainwright Enterprises. Behind him he heard the sergeant complimenting Mrs Dwight on her cardigan, and they were into a conversation about his wife's knitting before the lift door closed behind him.

Fenwick walked the long corridor from their conference room, curious to find out more about Wainwright's. He quickly completed his inspection of the ground floor. It contained only meeting rooms, the post room, access to the delivery yard and a small staff rest room. As he walked towards the lifts, the ever-vigilant receptionist called out to him.

'Can I help you?'

'No thanks.'

'Where are you going?'

'To have a look around.'

'We really prefer our visitors to stay on this floor. The office layout is very confusing.'

'I'll be fine, don't worry.'

A bell announced the imminent arrival of the lift, and the receptionist grew agitated.

'Really, sir, visitors are to stay on this floor.'

'I'm not a visitor,' he said, and stepped into the lift. Technically he shouldn't be doing this. He had no warrant, no powers of search, but he didn't want to give senior management any warning that he was on his way. It was already nearly midday and he wanted to catch them before they left for lunch.

There was no guide in the lift as to what happened on each floor, so Fenwick pressed all the buttons with the intention of holding the lift as he quickly stepped out to check. The first and second floors contained a quiet rows of small offices, none large enough to belong to the managing director. On the third and fourth floors, groups of people in suits worked or talked in low voices in a spacious open-plan office.

The top floor was noticeably smaller than the rest, and Fenwick emerged from the lift on to thick carpet in a panelled lobby. Heavy mahogany doors stood open to his right, through which he could make out a large empty desk with a PC to one side. He turned towards it.

The surface of the desk was immaculate. A half-used shorthand pad lay open beside the computer, with about a dozen letters ready for signing arranged over the mahogany top. Apart from a leatherbound diary, that was all that the desk contained. Fenwick thought about the state of his own secretary's desk and marvelled at the contrast. This person was either the height of efficiency or vastly underworked.

There were two more desks opposite, both cluttered but unmanned, and two offices, doors closed, completed the scene. Fenwick glanced down at the letters and started to read one without meaning to.

'Can I help you?'

The voice was cultured but sharp and he found himself blushing like a naughty schoolboy. He turned around to face his accuser, to be confronted by a beautiful blonde of no more than twenty-seven or eight. She was taking off an overcoat under which she was wearing a tailored black suit and pale pink blouse that showed off her figure. Her hair was pulled back from an oval face with a perfect English rose complexion. The eyes had a slight Asian tilt and the full mouth had been painted in a way that invited kisses. She had set down a full jug of fresh coffee on the desk.

'Yes, I'm with Harlden police, Detective Chief Inspector Fenwick.' He showed her his warrant card. 'As a matter of interest, who answers the phone on this floor?'

'Voicemail, with a divert to the operator for urgent messages. It's cheaper than having secretarial cover. Come this way.'

'And you are . . .?'

'Mr Wainwright-Smith's assistant. What do you want? I'm sure you don't have an appointment today, so why are you here, please?'

'Surely you must have heard about Arthur Fish?'

She continued to stare at him blankly, but the delicate rose tint left her cheeks.

'As you can see,' she gestured towards her coat, 'we have only just arrived. What's happened to Arthur Fish?'

'He was murdered yesterday. I'm the officer in charge of the investigation.'
She said nothing but stretched out a hand to steady herself.

'You'd better come in and see Alex . . . Mr Wainwright-Smith. He doesn't know.'

She tapped on one of the large, anonymous mahogany doors and walked straight in without waiting for an answer, leaving Fenwick behind her. She spoke before he could stop her, and whilst her body and the door still shielded his view of the room.

'Alex, this is Chief Inspector Fenwick from Harlden police. He's here because Arthur was murdered yesterday.'

It was neatly done, and now he would never know how the managing director of Wainwright Enterprises had reacted.

Wainwright-Smith's assistant showed Fenwick to a chair with a graceful open-palmed gesture, and he looked around at an office the size of a large conference room. Considering its size, the furnishings were modest, even understated. A desk was positioned before the landscape windows, surrounded by comfortable chairs. Wooden filing cabinets occupied all of one wall. At the opposite end of the room from the desk, two sofas and three easy chairs were loosely grouped about a huge coffee table. Between the desk and the sofas an oriental rug occupied a sort of no-man's-land of dead space.

Cooper had interviewed Wainwright-Smith about his uncle's death, so Fenwick had never met him. He was much younger than Fenwick had expected. He had reddish-blond hair, astonishing blue eyes and a smattering of freckles on a disconcertingly open face. At first Fenwick appraised him as lacking in character, but then he shook hands and looked him in the eye, and the strength and intelligence he found there warned him not to underestimate this man.

'This is terrible. When did it happen?' He sounded appalled but in control.
'Yesterday evening.'

'But I only saw him at five o'clock, just before he left for the faculty meeting.'

'It seems everyone knows about the faculty meetings. What were they?'

'I'm not sure exactly, something to do with one of the accounting bodies, I think but, yes, we all knew about them because Arthur was fanatical about them. He went monthly and never missed one; they should have given him an attendance medal!'

Fenwick thought briefly about the body and the signs of recent sexual activity with sado-masochistic overtones, and wondered what impact this knowledge would have on the memory of Arthur Fish. Would he go up or down in people's estimation?

He went through his standard questions about Fish's last days, but as managing director, Wainwright-Smith knew little of his financial controller's routine.

'Neil Yarrell, the finance director, could tell you more. He keeps very tight control of the department.' Wainwright-Smith hesitated. 'You said it was murder, definitely? It couldn't have been suicide?' He looked anxiously at his assistant as he spoke. She had remained in the room throughout the interview, sitting neatly on the sofa with her perfect long legs modestly inclined at an angle, knees and ankles together.

'We're fairly certain it was murder – no weapon was found at the scene and the way he died would have been an unusual, not to say impossible method of suicide.'

'How *did* he die?'

'We're not releasing details yet. Why did you ask about suicide?'

'Oh, nothing.' Again the look to the woman, as if for guidance. 'It's just that . . .' Wainwright-Smith hesitated and his assistant walked over to him.

'Murder is such a shocking and extraordinary event,' she finished for him.

Fenwick stared at the pair. There was something more here than a boss – secretary relationship. What had Wainwright-Smith been about to say before he had been cut off?

'I assume he was mugged, then.' She seemed so calm and in control, almost disconnected, as if violent death had to be expected from time to time.

'Why do you think it was a mugging?'

His question clearly shocked her.

'Why not? Surely most random murders are.'

'And why do you assume it was random, Mrs . . .'

'Wainwright-Smith, Sally. I'm Alex's wife. I naturally thought that it would have to be random. Why would anyone wish to kill Arthur Fish, of all people? He was so harmless.'

'Did you know him well then?'

'No, I hardly knew him. Did you, Alex?'

Her husband still looked shocked, a deep frown on his face.

'Of course I did. I've worked for Wainwright's since I left school, and he had been in the finance department for years even then.'

Fenwick decided it was essential to separate this pair. They were forcing him to ping-pong his questions from one to the other and it was distracting him.

'Mrs Wainwright-Smith, could I trouble you for some coffee, no milk, one sugar.'

She would have to make it fresh, as the jug on the desk outside would be cold by now. With obvious reluctance she left the office. Fenwick closed the door firmly behind her.

'Why did you really wonder if it might be suicide, Mr Wainwright-Smith?'

The man sitting opposite him nodded, as if admitting that it was inevitable Fenwick would ask the question.

'Arthur had been having difficulty with his workload, even though we are computerised now. I was concerned that we had worried him so much that he had killed himself. He was a very nervous man.'

'Why should he be nervous?' Fenwick's question sounded mild, a matter of routine, but it masked how much Wainwright-Smith's comments intrigued him. They were in such contrast to the tutored answers he had been given by the finance staff.

'Did I say nervous? I meant nervy. He was a man who fretted over details and as the business has grown, so he appeared to become somewhat over-worked.'

'Despite the computerisation?'

For some reason, the question unsettled Wainwright-Smith.

'Perhaps because of it. He didn't like change of any kind.'

'Is there anything more you can tell me, sir?'

Wainwright-Smith looked away, unable to meet Fenwick's eyes.

'No, except that I shall miss him.' He paused. 'Sally's a long time. I'll just go and give her a hand.'

The last thing Fenwick wanted was for them to compare notes. He shot up out of his chair and made it to the door before the other man could reach it.

'Don't trouble yourself. I'll go and find her. I need to ask her a few further questions and I've already detained you long enough.'

They shook hands and Fenwick retreated to the small executive kitchen, where he found Sally reheating in the microwave the coffee she had made earlier. She saw the look of disbelief on his face and smiled.

'Waste not, want not, Chief Inspector.'

'Of course.'

As he sipped his stale but hot coffee, he asked her directly about her automatic assumption that Fish's death had been a mugging. She avoided his questions with deftness born of practice, which left him suspicious and frustrated. As soon as he had finished his coffee, he left.

Sally. He began to understand why the Wainwright clan disliked and distrusted her so much, and she was certainly beautiful enough for people to believe her capable of any entrapment. Fenwick continued to puzzle over her as the lift descended uninterrupted. It was an odd relationship up there on the top floor, and not altogether helpful for their enquiries.

The receptionist visibly relaxed as he reappeared from his unauthorised tour. Cooper was waiting for him in reception with a grin on his face. He really was impossible.

'Wait until we're in the car, Sergeant.'

Fenwick drove this time, impatient to be doing something.

'Well, go on.'

'She was *very* chatty over a cup of tea and a fruit slice. Apparently, Mr Fish had been worked up ever since Alexander Wainwright-Smith took over, and even before that you could hardly have described him as relaxed.'

Fenwick told Cooper what Alexander had revealed about Fish's growing workload and difficulty coping with the computer.

'Well, that explains it then.'

'Does it? I disagree. The Wainwright-Smiths were too quick to volunteer an opinion about his death – a suicide brought on by anxiety, or a mugging. In my experience, very few innocent people, or at least very few of those with nothing to hide, make such suggestions to the police without even hearing the facts first.'

Cooper frowned, in obvious disagreement, then voiced the thought that was troubling him.

'You don't think that your previous concerns about Wainwright Enterprises are making you a bit overly suspicious, do you, sir?' It was said with deference, but answered firmly.

'No, Cooper, I do not. We need to find out much more about Fish. Talk to his bank manager, friends and lawyer. How much of an estate has he left? Wainwright-Smith was holding something back and his wife was a completely closed book. I don't trust her at all.'

'So you met the famous Sally? Can you understand why Graham Wainwright distrusts her now? Mrs Dwight told me all about her and I can't wait to meet her myself. It's a pity we neither of us interviewed her last month. I wonder what Nightingale thought of her. She did the re-interview, didn't she?'

'I don't think she did. Sally was ill, or something, and by the time she was better, we'd already concluded our work.' Fenwick signalled left, off the by-pass.

'Mrs Dwight says she's into everything. She's only been working here a week or so and she's already disliked. Even Neil Yarrell watches himself around her.'

'Why on earth is she working as her husband's secretary?'

'Cost efficiency, according to Mrs Dwight. Hey, watch that cyclist. Bloody idiot!' Cooper turned and shouted at the startled teenager who'd just rushed out directly into their path from a side road.

Fenwick had braked, swerved economically and continued without a backward glance. He didn't even look shaken, let alone angry. Cooper wondered, as he frequently did, whether the Chief Inspector had any real feelings left at all, apart from his obvious love for his children.

'Apparently Mrs Wainwright-Smith is fanatically mean with money despite the fact that she and Alexander inherited half his uncle's estate,' Cooper continued. 'Sally used to work somewhere else, but she packed it all in, moved them into their new family estate, sorted it out in double-quick time, got bored and then turned her attention to the business. Now she's into everything, cutting back and proposing efficiencies everywhere.'

'So she's not really his secretary then – that's just a convenient label.'

'Oh no, she is. She may not be popular but she works like a trouper, Mrs Dwight says. And the economies included the top floor. She cut out a PA and an assistant, put in voicemail and now runs things with a rod of iron. She's got a junior secretary working for her, and Yarrell has his own PA, who sits in his office.'

'It might be cheap but it's not effective. When I went up there, she was the only one in the office – and she'd only just arrived. We'll need to speak to Graham Wainwright and the rest of the family again. This is the opportunity we need to reopen the Alan Wainwright inquiry. I'll speak to the ACC this afternoon to clear it.'

Fenwick pulled up beside a bakery.

'Sandwich? We're not going to have time for lunch.' Cooper nodded reluctantly and comforted himself with the thought that at least his waistline would benefit if he skipped his usual meat and three veg in the police canteen. And of course the fruit slice he'd had with Mrs Dwight earlier, just to be companionable, had filled a few corners.

CHAPTER EIGHTEEN

The railway station was less than half a mile from Police Division in Harlden, so Fenwick had ordered an incident room to be set up conveniently one flight up from his office. By the time he and Cooper returned from Wainwright's, the room was fully equipped with desks, phones, computers, printers, a direct fax, secure filing and the inevitable whiteboards. He had called a briefing for two o'clock. The Superintendent and the ACC wanted this one solved as soon as possible. Everyone there knew that this was a high-profile case and the pressure for an early result had already started.

A team of over fifty officers from divisions along the railway line had been at work since first light, and Fenwick had been given a detective inspector to run the work in Harlden whilst he co-ordinated the whole inquiry. Unfortunately, the only inspector available was DI Blite, who had a tendency to cut corners.

The incident room was well organised. Photographs of the murder scene had been pinned up next to two of Fish, alive and smiling at an office party. The train timetable from Brighton to Harlden had been copied and enlarged, together with all the connecting routes. On one of the boards someone had set up a neat chart with all the stations on the line down the left-hand column, with a checklist across the top detailing the actions required at every one: collect and check the contents for all rubbish bins; interview staff and regular passengers; post notices to the public describing the incident and asking for help; check taxis; collect any security-camera footage, and so on. Fenwick was pleased to see that the board was already more than half completed.

His secretary, Anne, arrived just before the meeting was due to start.

'The ACC wants to talk to you straight after the briefing, sir.'

Fenwick nodded, resigned to the inevitable. He called the meeting to order briskly. Extensive work had been done, all well organised, but so far with few results. Ten minutes into the meeting the door was flung open with unnecessary force and a young detective constable walked in hurriedly. Fenwick vaguely recognised him as a year-two graduate on the accelerated promotion scheme. There were unanimously raised eyebrows and shakings of heads as the young man lurched forward, trying without success to catch the door before it crashed against the wall. Fenwick deliberately let silence descend as, with blazing cheeks, the graduate hovered at the back of the room.

'Sorry, sir. A lead came in and I was just checking it out. I'm very sorry I'm late, sir.'

Cooper glared at the lad and motioned him to sit down at the front of the room. He liked to think he ran a tight team and he was old-fashioned on matters of discipline. He saved Fenwick the bother of deciding how to react by ordering the latecomer to report.

'Yes, sir, we have had a report of a blood-stained ticket and paper towels being found at Burgess Hill station. The ticket's a return from Harlden to Brighton, bought the same day as Fish was killed. I've passed the ticket number on to the station here so that they can tell us when it was bought, and the local team at Burgess Hill are stepping up their interviewing.'

'It could be anybody's blood. Bloke cut himself on a beer can for all you know.' Inspector Blite was dismissive of such naivety. The detective constable coloured but kept his head up and looked to Fenwick, who nodded once.

'It will take a while to get the results of the blood test from forensics and you did the right thing in the meantime. The case is less than twenty-four hours old and if we're going to get a break it will most likely be today or tomorrow. Just remember, all of you, to remain objective and keep up the work at other stations, particularly Brighton. What's the feedback from there?'

'Not a lot, sir. We have one sighting of Fish which confirms he got off the train at the main station but none of the regular taxi drivers recognises him and so far no bus driver recalls him either.' DS Gould had been put in charge of the checks along the railway line. He had experience of working with the other divisions involved and with the railway police.

'He had sex shortly before he died, and from the marks on his body, it could be sadomasochistic. How far have enquiries reached with known prostitutes in Brighton and the nearby towns?'

'Not very.' DI Blite shook his head dismissively. 'They had two prostitutes murdered last night at the end of a terrible Easter Weekend. The whole division is working flat out, and they're trying to help but . . .' His voice died.

'Two prostitutes murdered last night? Any link with our Mr Fish, do you think?'

'I doubt it. The Brighton police are looking for connections between the two local deaths – they were discovered less than a mile apart – and they aren't that keen on adding Fish as an unnecessary complication. I'll chase it anyway.'

Fenwick read out the highlights of the pathologist's and forensic reports. The forensic report confirmed the pathologist's suspicions; traces lifted from Fish's nails and body included baby lotion and talc. The microscopic fragments from the weals on his lower back were wood, and they were working to find out the species, not that it was likely to help particularly. Fenwick ignored the explosions of laughter that mention of the baby lotion brought to the room.

'All right, all right. That's enough. One last thing: we have a full set of fingerprints lifted from the victim's coat, with more on his wallet. It is unlikely that they were the murderer's, unless he was particularly inept, but we're running full checks against the national index.'

The briefing concluded, and once the others had left, Cooper brought up the subject of the key.

'It's to a small fireproof lock-box but our locksmith can't give us any idea

97

of the make. He's taken an impression and sent it to the Met. Apparently they have experts there who might be able to help but it'll take a while – a week or more, maybe.'

'Keep an eye out for anything it might belong to – it's curious that he would keep it hidden in his wallet.'

After the briefing, Fenwick descended the stairs, determinedly ignoring the twinge from his right knee that had started inexplicably to ache again. His old injury invariably chose moments of stress or intense activity to reawaken. In his office he removed his jacket and hung it carefully over the back of a visitor's chair. Then he sat back in his own chair, head resting on the hands laced behind it, and simply stared at the contents of the pin-board opposite his desk. From the earliest days of his career, he had found that creating his own visual imprint of the case from the evidence as it was assembled, helped him to focus. As soon as he had been given an office, he had put up a cork board – the same one that graced it now, tattered as it was – on which to pin copies of the key exhibits that the incident team were assembling. It was almost half full already with material from the Fish case, and Anne had tacked the report from Alan Wainwright's suicide in one corner.

When his phone rang he ignored it; an urgent fax was delivered and it wasn't even given a second look; fresh coffee arrived, and his secretary, recognising the signs, set it down without a word and left, closing the door behind her.

There was no science or process to describe what was happening in his mind. He was waiting for inspiration, for the moment when the right random half-thoughts found their way into his active mind. After a time, he picked up his pen and pulled a clean sheet of paper on to the immaculate white blotter that covered the centre of his desk.

He wrote swiftly, in sketchy, economic letters, dashing one word off after another:

Why Fish? – Why the train?
Is MOTIVE personal- or business-related?
Why the closed office door?   ➡ guilt?
                                  ➡ phone calls?
                                  ➡ fraud?
                                  ➡ *FEAR?*
                                  ➡ Final tape – what's on it?

Sally ⟷ Arthur Fish ⟷ Prostitute

Murders

Alexander ⟷ Wainwright's?

The scribbling stopped and he looked down at the jottings that covered the page. They made little sense, but even so, he pinned it on his cork board beside a photograph of Arthur Fish, smiling into the camera at some office party.

His phone rang again and he snatched it up, annoyed at the interruption. 'Yes?'

'Fenwick. Didn't you receive my message? That damned secretary of yours . . .' The ACC sounded furious.

'I'm sorry, sir. I did get it but there was a late development and I was diverted. I apologise.'

'Yes, I've already heard about it, this blood-stained ticket. Let's hope it is the break you need. Now look here, I've had Alexander Wainwright-Smith on the phone most upset. I told you to handle Wainwright Enterprises delicately, and instead you go in there and charge around the place as if you own it!'

Fenwick didn't bother to ask how the ACC already knew about the discovery of the ticket at Burgess Hill station. Blite had probably called him personally as soon as the briefing had finished. But the complaint from Alexander surprised him, particularly as he thought he'd discerned a certain subtlety in the managing director. He guessed that Harper-Brown was overreacting to a mild comment and judged the tone of his response accordingly.

'I certainly didn't charge anywhere, I can assure you, sir. In fact I was very conscious of your guidance and behaved accordingly. Was he very upset? Would you like me to call him?'

'That won't be necessary. Just be more careful in future. And I'm still waiting for today's report on the case. I don't expect to have to remind you again.'

'I'm working on it now, sir, and I shall let you and Superintendent Quinlan have a copy in the next hour.' Superintendent Quinlan was, after all, Fenwick's direct boss, in charge of Harlden Division. He tolerated the ACC's direct involvement in sensitive cases with a patience Fenwick could only admire.

The phone call left Fenwick in a bad mood, and word soon reached the team that it would be better to leave him alone that afternoon. An hour later there was a hesitant knock at the door and Cooper's head appeared round it. Seeing Fenwick standing by the board, he visibly relaxed and came into the room.

'Any new ideas, sir?'

'Not really. I've spent most of the afternoon on the phone to the other divisions. There's no further breaks so far. We must find out whether either of the prostitute murders in Brighton is connected in any way to our case; and obviously analyse the blood and fingerprints as quickly as possible. Has Gould strengthened the team at Burgess Hill station?'

'Yes, sir. He's tracing all staff and taxi-drivers who were on duty last night in case it is the station where the killer left the train, and we have a listing of all care in the community cases with any record of violence. It's a long list.'

'Have you traced Fish's family?'

'One son lives in Canada and is on his way back home. The daughter works for a voluntary association in Africa; we haven't reached her yet. No trace of the third son. Apparently he's on a back-packing tour somewhere.'

'Call Joan Dwight. I want to know what was on the tape that Fish dictated before he left work on Thursday, no matter how trivial.'

Cooper glanced at the clock surreptitiously: six fifteen. The Chief Inspector saw his glance and swore out loud.

'The children! Excuse me, Cooper, I've a phone call to make.'

He was dialling as the sergeant left. The phone was answered, as it nearly always was, by Bess.

'Harlden two-six-five-nine-two, who is speaking, please?'

'It's Daddy.'

'Daddy!' A high-pitched, excited yelp shrieked into his ear and made him laugh. It was always the same: whenever he called, she was so warm, loyal and openly loving. It almost broke his heart sometimes, and the absolute trust filled him with the fear that he would some day not prove worthy of it. She knew at once that he would be home late, and with a generosity and understanding way beyond her seven years, she saved him the difficulty of having to explain.

'I'll tell Wendy to have your supper ready for when you get back tonight, shall I? She's half expecting it.'

'She shouldn't make me supper but if she already has, yes, please tell her I'm going to be late. Now, what sort of day have you had?'

She chatted on happily about school and her recorder class.

'We're learning "Three Blind Mice", a real song, and I can almost play it without the music! Shall I go and get my recorder – hang on.'

She was gone before he could say a word. In the distance he could hear her calling out to Christopher, 'Daddy's on the phone,' then the sound of pounding, uncoordinated feet, the rattle of the receiver on the wooden table and his son's voice.

'Hello. Are you going to be late again?'

'Afraid so, Chris. How are you? Have you had a good day?'

Through a series of almost monosyllabic answers he learnt that his son had not had a good day but had enjoyed his tea. He was so unready for life that Fenwick worried about him constantly. How was he going to cope in a world that was cruel and twisted? Chris couldn't even handle playground sniping without brooding over it for days. Bess helped him of course but she was only a year older and would not always be there. He was so like his mother it made Fenwick shudder.

Chris passed the receiver back to his sister and the sounds of an uneven triplet reached him, the descending notes faltering as Bess nervously either blew too hard and squeaked or too softly to make a noise. The tune never progressed beyond the first few lines but three simple notes make a tune and he could hear the wonder of it when Bess burst back on to the line.

'Did you hear, Daddy? Did you hear? Real music!'

'Brilliant, sweetheart; really good. You go and practise some more now.'

Moments later he replaced the receiver and stared at the wall again. Another two and a half hours and it would be twenty-four hours from the time the body had been found. On impulse he decided to go and join DS Gould in Burgess Hill.

CHAPTER NINETEEN

Nightingale eased herself into scented hot water and rested her head back against a folded towel. The lights were off. Candles flickered as air currents caught them and sent hundreds of points of light to scatter across bright tiles and the bubbles that tickled her chin.

She waited to feel clean, imagining the heat of the water opening her pores to let in the cleansing oils so that she could then sluice away the film of dirt and poverty that coated her whole body. Setting her near-empty wine glass down carefully, she closed her eyes, held her nose and sank beneath the surface. She stayed down for as long as possible, but it was no good: the feeling of grime wouldn't leave her.

Restlessly she drained the bath, finished her wine and then stood rigid under the shower as she swung the dial from freezing to scalding and back to ice cold again. After five long minutes she had no choice but to stop; the discomfort had become too intense for her to continue. The sense of dirt was all in her mind, she knew that, but she could still taste the smell of the streets at the back of her throat, and the sense of greasy grit on her skin wouldn't go away.

It had been, quite simply, an awful day. At twilight she and her partner for the evening had taken a bus down to the terminus where they agreed to split up and meet on the hour, every hour unless something developed in the meantime. Nightingale walked until she stood among mean streets whose only decorations were the girls draped against lampposts, in doorways and on street corners. She had tried desperately not to look smart, but even her oldest jeans were tailored, and the T-shirt she wore was fresh and clean. She stood out like a beacon in the night, in cruel contrast to those around her. Even the youngest – and she must only have been thirteen – looked used and faded when Nightingale walked by.

There would be no easy way into the conversations she needed to have. A group of four women with skin colours ranging from ebony to pasty white were standing on a corner, talking in a disjointed chatter as they kept their eyes on the passing traffic. Nightingale walked up to them and they kept on talking.

'Excuse me, might I have a word with you?'

A plump Eurasian girl replied without once taking her eyes off the passing cars.

'You reporter or what?'

'No, I'm with the police.'

They all burst out laughing: not cruel, just amused at the thought that she could imagine they would want to waste any time in conversation with her.

'We're investigating the deaths of Tracie Grey and Amanda Bennett last night. They were pr—' Nightingale stalled on the word, suddenly aware that she had no idea whether it would be taken as offensive or not. The group sensed her discomfort and turned their slow eyes on her. Unbelievably, Nightingale felt her cheeks glow hot; she swallowed hard.

'They were prostitutes. Amanda lived in Sea View and we're trying to find anyone who knew her. Tracie lived in Black Rock Heights, number three.'

'How old're you?' The thin, pale one chewed gum, moving it incessantly from cheek to cheek. Lipliner had been used imaginatively to draw a Cupid's bow on her face, even though her lips were pencil thin and pursed into a disapproving line. Thick carmine lipstick filled in the improbable shape. Nightingale dragged her eyes away from the distraction.

'That's irrelevant.'

'No, I'm curious to know the experience of the officers they put on such an important case.'

'There are over ten of us working on this.' Nightingale realised that the interview had slipped from her control; the more she had to explain herself, the less she would achieve. 'Did any of you know Amanda Bennett or Tracie Grey?'

A silent shaking of heads from two; loaded lack of interest from the others. She gave up and moved on. Looking back on the night, that first interview had perhaps been the least unpleasant. She'd been spat at, propositioned and 'accidentally' knocked into a concrete pillar. At the end of six long hours, she had found no one who admitted to knowing the murdered women and neither had her colleague.

She learnt something, though, just by watching at the railway terminus. There were the regulars: men who got off the train, walked straight through a side exit and signalled to one of the women there. The woman would return within thirty minutes. God knows where they'd gone, but it was obvious what they'd done. Then there were the ones new to the game: furtive, curious, excited, who hovered around inside for a while and ducked out of sight as soon as a police uniform appeared.

The children were the worst to watch. Knowing at thirteen or fourteen, the sharp ones recognised who might be a punter and homed in quickly, cutting out would-be competitors. Sometimes there was a courting ritual over a burger and fries. Very occasionally the buyer – whilst Nightingale was watching, it was always a man – made it clear he was interested in two and the kids would pair up – boy/boy, boy/girl, girl/girl. When they disappeared it was usually for several hours. Some didn't return at all.

The most pathetic were the older teenagers with lank hair, acne, skeletal arms and bruises. Addicts, used and abused, they hung around, desperate for a trick, too afraid to go back to their pimp without having scored. They all had one thing in common, though: none of them knew anything about Amanda Bennett or Tracie Grey.

She could see the acknowledgement of danger in their eyes – they lived with it every hour – but she wasn't part of their hope or solution. As one of the most articulate, tired and depressed had said to her, shortly before she gave up for the night: 'And how're you lot going to save me?'

'We can find murderers and put them away.'

'And what about the next one, and the one after him? Where'll you be when I'm out here?'

Nightingale had nothing left to say.

'Exactly. You can't do nothing for us, and there's nothing we will do for you.'

Despite her bath, it took a determined effort to relax her mind and try to sleep, but she managed it and woke, almost refreshed, when her alarm went off at eight. It was a bright, crisp morning and she decided on a jog in the small park opposite her apartment. A circuit took her five and a half minutes on a good run, and today she did five simply to make the blood flow and wake up her sluggish circulation. She was at the station, showered, fresh-faced and alert before half past nine.

There was no sign of Pink or the rest of the late-night team, so she decided to start her paperwork. Pink was determined to find the connection between the two murders, but no matter how hard she tried, Nightingale couldn't see any, and her six hours on the streets the previous night had been a complete waste of time.

She was finishing her depressingly brief notes as Pink walked in, closely followed by two other detective constables. They each carried an oily greaseproof bag, and the smell of smoked bacon filled the room. It was just one of the many rituals that Nightingale had learnt to avoid during her short secondment; a perfect opportunity to make her feel different, either as a target for unwanted advances or by excluding her.

The smell of fried bacon made her mouth water. She had been so sickened the previous night that her supper had been two large glasses of wine and some bread sticks. Now she was famished and a bacon sandwich was exactly what she wanted. It was a quarter to ten; just enough time to go to the canteen before the briefing.

'Morning,' she called out as the others walked past. Her eyes left the keyboard but her fingers kept on typing. Pink looked at her suspiciously and she returned an open, neutral smile, then stood up, swinging her bag over her shoulder. It was another clear day and she had decided to wear a mint-green linen suit and ivory blouse. The outfit was cool and crisp and fitted perfectly.

'Where're you off to?'

'Canteen. Breakfast.'

'Briefing in fifteen minutes. Don't be late.'

She ignored Pink and found her way to the basement. The queue at this time of day snaked out into the corridor. She joined it and started watching the clock. Ten minutes later she had her sandwich – toasted granary bread, brown sauce and three rashers of bacon. The heat of the bundle penetrated the paper bag and napkin, and greasy pressure points formed where her fingertips grasped it away from her suit.

The lift always took an age to arrive, so she chose the stairs, running up them two at a time to arrive precisely one minute before the briefing was due to start. She opened the door as the others were starting to leave.

'Incident Room Two, now.' Pink seemed in an even worse mood than usual.

Nightingale turned on her heel and was about to follow him.

'No food in briefings, you know that. Leave it.'

It was true, that was the rule, but no one ever followed it unless the Superintendent was going to be there. The others had finished their sandwiches; hers was juicy and hot. She swallowed hard, her mouth awash with saliva.

'Right.' She walked over to her desk and left the warm bag on a pad of paper. A couple of officers grinned at her, without sympathy; others avoided her eye entirely. One, confident and good enough at his job not to care, grimaced and soft-punched her shoulder. 'Ignore him,' he mouthed.

Incident Room 2 was half full with a mix of uniformed police and detectives. Pink was already deep in discussion when Nightingale arrived, wire-rimmed glasses perched on the end of her nose in anticipation of notes on the whiteboard. She chatted easily with a couple of other DCs; nothing significant, but the normal conversation was a quiet relief from Pink's usual charged remarks.

He called the meeting to order and within minutes had confirmed what she'd thought privately earlier. Despite his determination they had found no obvious links between the two cases. However, he was keeping the investigation teams combined and emphasised that they were still to look for connections in all avenues of enquiry. Nightingale's brief update was as unexceptional as all the others, and Pink enjoyed every moment.

They had their duties reconfirmed and Pink told Nightingale to go off duty until she resumed her questioning of prostitutes that night. It meant that she had several hours unexpectedly free. On the off chance she called Nick, another graduate on the APS scheme in Harlden, to see if he was free and could travel down to Brighton for lunch. Amazingly, he was.

They carried their drinks into the pub garden and he listened as she described her current case. She explained how her interviews in every pick-up area had been fruitless and emotionally draining. She had sensed the women's resentment, and her presence upset the punters who either crawled the kerb or studied the lurid cards in the phone booths. It was Nightingale's first brush with failure and she didn't like it. She couldn't empathise with these people, and they either distrusted her or treated her with a contempt that made her angry. She was only trying to do her job and prevent another murder, but they just didn't want to know. For once she gave in to her frustration and had a good moan.

'Don't they realise I'm here to help them? I'm just doing my job!'

Nick looked at the scrupulously neat and elegant woman sitting opposite him. Perfect skin, clear eyes, manicured nails and at least a fifty-pound hair cut that had shaped her rich auburn hair into a contemporary bob. She wore virtually no make-up and didn't need any, yet she looked as if she was ready for a fashion shoot. One slender foot, encased in a fawn suede pump, swung over the side of the bench they were sitting on.

She looked what she was, the product of a privileged, upper-class home and an exclusive education system. How could he tell her that for most of the people she would ever have to deal with in her chosen career she was utterly alien and would be vulnerable to any view they chose to hold of her? Yet as a policewoman she was one of the best.

'It's hard for them to trust you. You're different, not just because you're the law but also because, well, you're from a different class.'

'Oh, please! You can't work in the new millennium and still be talking about class.'

'Yes I can. That's the reality you've got to deal with. You have had a privileged upbringing and it shows. For a lot of people that means you don't understand their problems, so why should they trust you?'

'But I do understand, and I want to help. They must see that.'

'People see what they want to see. Don't get me wrong: once people get to know you it's different, and I'm not saying you're difficult to work with or anything because you're not – you're great. But you have to understand that to the average prostitute hanging out by the pier, you represent everything they don't have. It's a wonder you weren't assaulted!'

Nightingale shrugged disconsolately and Nick decided to change the subject.

'Come on, I'll get you another drink. Same again?'

'No, just a lime and soda, thanks. I'm driving.'

After another fruitless night, Nightingale returned to her flat at just after one in the morning. The answerphone light was blinking. Her mother had rung twice to remind her it was her brother's birthday on Saturday. There would be a family lunch and she was expected. She erased the tape, checked her doors and windows carefully, showered and went straight to bed.

The next morning she woke gritty-eyed and stared vacantly at the ceiling. She had showered, dressed, eaten some fruit and was driving once again towards the station when an idea occurred to her. If she moved quickly she would have time to follow it up before the noon briefing.

At Division she made enquiries and found her way to the office of the local vice team, where she hung around the coffee machine. Being young and good-looking had some advantages, and she was soon in discussion with a scruffy detective constable. He had no objection to explaining the basics of vice in Brighton and suggested they have a decent cup of coffee in a nearby café. Over an excellent cappuccino he started to talk.

'Essentially you've got three types of prostitutes around here: first there's the casuals – they're the housewives who handle a little business from home. They are low-key, modest-cost and not affiliated to any of the gangs. We hardly ever hear about them unless some neighbour complains or they get beaten up for intruding on more organised territory.

'The second group is drugs-related; usually that includes the new arrivals in town. A bloke they think is their white knight picks them up and gets them hooked on drugs, then they start scoring tricks to please him and feed their habit. It's organised and territorial, and it involves boys as well as girls. The more successful pimps go on to back clubs or local bands but they'll be earning their serious money from prostitution and drugs.'

'What happens to the girls?'

'Essentially they die young. By the time they are in their early thirties they look fifty and have lost their appeal. Their pimps dump them and they spend the rest of their days sliding further down the social ladder until they are homeless and destitute. Like I told DS Pink this morning, your Tracie Grey was in this group. The flat she was found in was one of half a dozen

105

owned by her pimp, and judging from her age, she wouldn't have had it for much longer.'

Nightingale stared at him in astonishment. Why couldn't Pink have found out the name of Tracie Grey's pimp at once, rather than have Nightingale and others still out walking the streets, facing daily humiliation and failure? She swallowed her anger at his inept handling of the case so far and tried to concentrate on the rest of the conversation.

'At the very top end you have the escort agencies and specialised services. These are usually run by syndicates, highly organised and very lucrative. They aim their services at wealthy men – businessmen, public servants – who can later find themselves compromised into doing favours for people they would rather not know.'

'So it's part of organised crime and there's blackmail involved?'

'It's always organised, yes, but the blackmail is selective. These days, prostitution probably only accounts for about a quarter of earnings. The rest is smuggling, car rackets, grand larceny.'

'And Amanda Bennett?'

'Until she was murdered I would have put money on her being a survivor. We knew her quite well; I even arrested her myself once. She had a record but somehow managed to work her way out of the low end of the business. She did time for living off immoral earning a few years ago: she ran a house of young girls – none underage, she made sure of that, but still young enough to be the daughters of most of her clients. And she catered for very particular tastes.'

'So which syndicate did she belong to?'

'Very good question. We never did find out, and that's one of the reasons she did so much time. She insisted she was in it alone, and we couldn't prove otherwise.'

'Could I see the file?'

'Don't see why not. Ask DS Pink – he has it.'

Nightingale finished her coffee with difficulty and thanked the DC for his help, neatly side-stepping his suggestion that they meet for a drink later. She only had two more days to go until she could return to Harlden, and the thought helped to ease the intense indignation she felt.

Later, at the station, Pink heard what she had done, who she had seen and what she had learnt on her own initiative. As he stared at her neat head, bowed over her keyboard as she typed up her report, his face showed a rapid series of expressions from fury through embarrassment to a grudging respect, but he said nothing. He did, however, allow Nightingale to spend her last two days tidying loose ends before returning at last to Harlden.

CHAPTER TWENTY

'We've been invited to dinner again by Alex and Sally on the twenty-eighth.'

'We only saw them last month, Graham.'

'I know, but Sally called and pressed me hard, and I said yes.'

'That's next Friday. I thought you didn't like their company.'

'Alex is all right in small doses, and there are some matters of business I need to discuss down south anyway. I'll go a couple of days early to sort things out, and you can join me there.'

Graham sounded casual but Jenny could see the tension in his shoulders and it worried her. He had been so withdrawn in the last few days.

'I'll come with you.'

'No!' His tone was sharp and Jenny was taken aback.

'What is it, Graham? What's worrying you? Why don't you let me come with you; some company would do you good.'

'I don't want you involved, darling. There's some plain talking to be done and I'll be better off doing it on my own. Come on, don't look like that. After the dinner we can go to London and I'll buy you a present.'

'I don't need presents, Graham. I just want to be with you.'

'Ah, but this will be a very special present, one I have never bought for anyone before. I'll only be gone for a couple of days and then we'll be together again.'

He tried to hug her but Jenny resisted his embrace in a rare show of pique that caught them both off guard.

'This isn't like you.'

'I know, Graham,' her voice was tearful, 'but you're so preoccupied these days. We came up here to Scotland in such a hurry it made me think you were running away from something, and you've hired beaters you don't need who stand around doing nothing and look more like security guards. Every time you think I'm not looking, you seem worried half to death.'

He put his wiry arms around her and this time she didn't resist.

'I'm sorry. There's no way I wanted to worry you, darling. You're right, I am uptight. Something's not right and I've got proof now from the private detective.'

'I thought he was following Sally?'

'He was.' Graham looked grim and Jenny felt scared all over again. 'I've got all I need now on Sally; that's not the problem. Finding out about her has just led me into a bigger mess.'

'Tell me about it, I'd like to help.'

He squeezed her tight.

'No, Jenny, you're too special. I couldn't bear it if anything happened to you. I love you.'

The suddenness of his declaration shocked her into silence. He had never said it before and when they had started living together he had made a point of explaining that love wasn't part of the bargain. Something had changed in the past few weeks, and the realisation made her feel happy yet also incredibly vulnerable.

'I love you too, Graham, so much.'

She kissed him fiercely and started to lead him towards the bedroom. The sound of the telephone on the landing stopped them in their tracks. Graham picked up the receiver. A minute later he replaced it, having barely spoken a word. He looked grey.

'That was George Ward. Arthur Fish is dead. George has just returned from a golfing holiday and found out that he was murdered on Thursday night. I shouldn't have run away. Perhaps if I'd sorted this out sooner, he'd still be alive.'

'Surely you don't think it's connected to your father or the business?'

Graham shook his head, sat down heavily on the top stair and rested his head in his hands. Jenny wrapped her arms around his shoulders, unable to think of anything to say. She was worried sick that Graham – idealistic and without an ounce of business acumen – was becoming embroiled in something dangerous, and that was now being played for stakes high enough to perhaps even cost a man his life.

'I'll set off on Wednesday.' Graham stood up abruptly and helped her to her feet. He saw the expression on her face. 'I'm going alone, Jenny. I'll meet you at the Hall on the twenty-eighth.'

'Be careful, Graham, please. I couldn't bear to lose you, not now. Not when it's all starting to work out between us. I don't know what it is that's worrying you, but please watch yourself. Two people who worked for your family's firm have died and it's obvious you don't think it is a coincidence. I know that I didn't share your concerns about your father's death, but perhaps I was wrong. If you know something, or even suspect it, please go to the police.' The raw pleading in her voice made him hold her tight and stroke her hair. He whispered into her ear.

'I will, sweetheart, after the dinner, but I have to be sure first. I won't take any unnecessary risks, I promise.'

Graham squeezed her hand and led her slowly along the landing towards the bedroom.

CHAPTER TWENTY-ONE

On the Saturday night two days after Fish's murder, Fenwick arrived home from the station just in time to read his children a story before bedtime. Cooper called him an hour later. Even though the forensic laboratory had been able to lift a whole handprint from the shoulder of Arthur Fish's jacket, it had taken them a painstaking four hours to match the fingerprints conclusively to those on the bloody ticket found at Burgess Hill, and a full day before these were run successfully against the national criminal fingerprint index.

'We've got a match, sir. The prints lifted from the scene all belong to one Francis Fielding, who is well known to Brighton Division. He has a string of convictions, starting with delinquency as a minor and then three drugs-related, one of procurement and two for GBH. He did nine months for the last one and was released four months ago.'

'So it could be a mugging after all. Have you let Brighton know yet?'

'No, I called you first. Do you want me to?'

'Yes, but ask DS Gould to do it. He knows them well and we need to be absolutely sure they don't cock it up. Come and collect me now and we'll make our way there. They don't need to wait for us unless they have doubts about proceeding. Get the officer in charge to call me on my mobile to confirm where we'll meet.'

As he replaced the receiver, Fenwick could feel his pulse thumping in his throat. This was the break they needed. Within hours he could close the case, with one of the strongest chains of evidence he had ever had. It would be an incredible result for him personally, and for Harlden. He was in the car with Cooper, less than a mile from the suspect's address, when the call came through from Brighton that shattered his hopes. Cooper answered his phone.

'Brighton, sir. They've found Fielding. He's dead.'

The scene of death was brightly lit by the bare hundred-watt bulb that swung from the ceiling in the unheated one-room flat. The body lay face down on the bed and the pathologist estimated that he had been dead over twenty-four hours. Rigor had left the upper body and was present now only in the legs. A scene-of-crime technician had already found a used hypodermic and a bag of what seemed to be heroin. Fenwick waited for the local officer in charge to make the introductions and ask the questions.

The pathologist was clipped and professional in her replies.

'Looks like he died as a result of a massive heroin overdose. There's classic pinpoint contraction of the pupils, but I'll need to wait for toxicology to confirm. Time of death is within the last thirty-six hours and at least twenty-four hours ago. So far as I can tell at this stage, he died here on his bed and hasn't been moved.'

DS Winters nodded, his body language territorial.

'As soon as he's been identified, give me a call and I'll join you. It looks fairly conclusive, though. Judging by the amount of heroin we've recovered, he must have come into a lot of cash suddenly, got overexcited and fried his brains.'

Fenwick looked around the grubby kitchen. Plates still showing scraps of food were stacked in the sink. Two clean coffee mugs had been placed in the remaining space on the draining board, next to a jar of instant coffee powder and a stale carton of milk.

'Looks like he was expecting a visitor.'

DS Winters shrugged but otherwise ignored the comment.

'We're interviewing neighbours and known acquaintances, so I'll keep you in the picture, Chief Inspector.' Winters was polite but clearly didn't feel that Fenwick would add a lot to his inquiry.

'That's fine. If you find any further connections that might link him to the murder of Arthur Fish, or your two prostitutes here, let us know. We're interested to know how he got his hands on so much money. And if you find a knife, could you send it to our lab as soon as possible? It could be the murder weapon we're looking for.'

With the death of Fielding, Fenwick immediately came under immense pressure to close the case. DS Winters found a flick knife that was proven to be the murder weapon and the ACC argued that it was the final evidence they needed. Fenwick didn't agree, but not even all his powers of persuasion could convince the ACC and Superintendent Quinlan to give him Sergeant Gould and his officers for one more week. Then the Brighton team discovered two thousand pounds in cash in a brown paper bag hidden beneath Fielding's floorboards, and Fenwick argued that this could be evidence of a contract killing. Despite his addiction to drugs, Fielding hadn't been anything other than a minor pusher on the local scene and there was no explanation as to how he had come by so much cash immediately before his death. Grudgingly Harper-Brown gave in and Fenwick was granted his precious week.

He briefed DS Gould immediately. He was to try and trace the money found in Fielding's flat; probe whether there was any link between Arthur Fish and Amanda Bennett or Tracie Grey; and generally be alert for any hint of a motive that linked the killing back to Wainwright's. It was a tough assignment but Gould was a diligent officer. Fenwick had every confidence that if he was right and this wasn't a simple mugging, then this sergeant would find the connections they needed.

PART THREE

Murder, like talent, seems occasionally to run in families.

G. H. Lewes

CHAPTER TWENTY-TWO

Fires had been lit throughout the Hall, in the hall, sitting room, drawing room and main dining room. The refurbished rooms glowed in the light of the flames. Everything was perfect. Alexander and Sally were determined to welcome the family to their new home with a style they had always thought had been lacking under its previous owner.

The fire in the main drawing room was devouring dry pine logs with hungry tongues of flame, spitting embers against the fireguard. Pockets of cold air huddled stubbornly in corners and against windows. The drawing room was bigger than the whole of the downstairs of their previous house, and Alexander had never known it to be warm enough. Sally had turned the central heating down almost as soon as they had moved in and he knew it wouldn't go up again until November – it was one of her rules.

They were expecting seven guests: Jeremy Kemp and his wife; Graham and Jenny; Julia and Colin and their daughter Lucy. Sally had prepared for the event with an awesome precision, and Alexander's only responsibility now was to keep the fires blazing obediently. Outside an early dusk had fallen and a dull grey mist surrounded the house.

The telephone rang.

'Alexander? Hi, it's Jenny. Could I speak to Graham, please?'

Her voice carried over the unmistakable static of a mobile phone.

'He's not here yet, Jenny.'

'But he was due with you on Wednesday. He said he had an early meeting or something. It's not like him to go off and not tell me where he is. I'm worried about him, Alexander. He was in such a state when he left. Has he called you at all?'

'No, but I can check with Sally if you like.'

Alexander rang off and went in search of his wife. The kitchen was the most obvious place to start looking, but she wasn't there. In the dining room, all the candles had been lit. Two thick waxy altar candles graced flower arrangements in the centre of the mahogany table, and Victorian ruby wine glasses caught and held the light so that the table appeared to be bathed in an ethereal fairy glow. His uncle's solid silver cutlery had been polished to an intense lustre that caught and held the candlelight. There was still no sign of Sally, then Alexander remembered the flower room. As he walked down the back corridor her voice reached him.

'Now, Irene, that's for Julia and Colin's room, you know, the Oriental Room. Take it carefully! Don't spill it and make sure you set it down on a mat. I don't want to find water marks on any of the furniture. And hurry back, this last one's for Graham's room. Our guests could be here any minute.'

Irene, one of their daily helps pressed into service for the evening, squeezed past him, both hands clutching a tall, gangly arrangement that looked vaguely Japanese.

Sally was concentrating so hard on the final touches to the last arrangement that she didn't hear him arrive. A large plastic apron, tied loosely at the back, protected the evening clothes she was already wearing. She'd chosen a pink silk trouser-suit with a long-sleeved tunic top tied with an ivory sash about her tiny waist. The trousers clung to her, flattering her slender figure and making her alluring yet somehow fragile. The pink and ivory set off her complexion perfectly. She had put her hair up for the evening, and the smooth chignon looked almost too heavy for her long, slender neck. The diamond and pearl drops in her ears had been his aunt's but they had never looked so perfect and appropriate as they did on Sally, like fresh dew on an immaculate rose, setting off its velvety perfection.

'Hi.'

He said it softly but it still made her jump.

'Oh! It's you. You startled me. Are the fires all right?'

She went back to her arrangement. The bronze and oyster of the chrysanthemums clashed horribly with her dress, and the bowl of flowers she was so delicately adjusting reminded him of a funeral wreath.

'I'm glad you're here,' she went on. 'I couldn't fasten the safety chain on my watch. Could you do it for me?'

'This is beautiful. When did you get it?' Alexander stared in awe at the elegant gold and diamond-set dial and the pink crocodile-skin strap.

'It was a present from your uncle last Christmas. It's a Patek Philippe; very sweet of him.'

She held out a too-thin wrist from which the loose gold safety chain dangled. He closed the clasp up tight and tried to fix the chain. A sharp slither of gold, part of a sheared link, slid into the tender nail bed of his thumb.

'Ow! Damn thing pricked me.'

'Mind the blood! Don't get it on my sleeve. Here, wash it off under the tap.'

Alexander rinsed off the blood and gently pulled the spike of gold from under his nail.

'The chain's broken.'

'Never mind, it'll be OK. Did you want something?'

'Jenny's just rung, asking for Graham. She thought he'd already be here, but he didn't say he was coming early, did he?'

Sally took a pair of fine long-bladed scissors and snipped off a recalcitrant bud that was refusing to do her bidding.

'No. Not as far as I know.'

'That's what I told her. She sounded worried.'

'Oh, you know Graham, he's a law unto himself. He's probably found another Jenny somewhere and sneaked a day with her.'

Irene bustled back into the room and squeezed her generous figure past Alexander. Sally thrust the flowers at her roughly.

'Here, take these! Don't spill the water, you stupid girl! Now look what you've done!'

114

A slow puddle of water spread across the tiled floor. Alexander grabbed a cloth and bent to mop it up as Irene inched past him on tiptoe, her hands full.

'She'll have to go,' hissed Sally.

'Come on, Sal, it was an accident, no big deal.'

'Not because of that, idiot! She's pregnant again, any fool can see. And she's only nineteen.'

Alexander squeezed the cloth out in the sink as his wife carefully removed her apron. One of the girls would tidy the flower room the next day; they could forget it for now. Their guests were due at seven o'clock. Sally hurried off to the kitchen, and Alexander went in search of his uncle's grand piano and one last moment of calm.

The music room was cold. He turned on the lights and at once the evening outside the windows grew dark. The mist was thicker now, an indiscriminate fog that blanketed the green of the lawns and the delicacy of the borders in a grey monotone.

He lifted the solid cover of the Steinway and started to play. Chopin's E-flat minor nocturne flowed automatically to his fingertips and he closed his eyes, willing the steady Andante to surge through him. It was a brief piece but it blotted out his thoughts about Sally. Something about his wife made people scared, and it was starting to worry him.

'Alex? There you are! Come on, our guests are here. The butler's taking their coats. Do hurry up.'

Downstairs in the drawing room the fire had inexplicably decided to sulk. It had been blazing only minutes before but now the logs smouldered, sending out thick woody smoke. Sally glared at Alex. It was unforgivable that he should spoil the grand entrance. Everything else was perfect.

The butler took the bellows to the fire, and after a few puffs it started to flicker and glow. Sally was showing her guests the changes she had introduced in the room, unaware of – or perhaps simply ignoring – the jealousy and suppressed anger in her audience. After a moment Lucy detached herself from her parents and joined Alexander by the fire, accepting a glass of champagne on her way.

'Alexander, I have a favour to ask. Today's my boyfriend's birthday and we had planned to celebrate together, only I've had to come here. Not that I mind, I always like seeing you, but . . .'

'Why didn't you call? We could easily have accommodated another.'

'Mummy said it was out of the question, but I did tell Ryan I'd ask you, and he could be here in twenty minutes.'

Alexander laughed. 'Go on then, call him. There's a phone in the hall.'

'It's all right, I have my mobile. Thanks, Alexander!' She planted a kiss on his cheek.

They had all drunk at least two glasses of champagne before Jenny arrived by taxi from the station. She was dressed as if to go clubbing; her black lacy mini-dress was transparent enough to reveal a matching bra. As soon as she walked into the room she looked around expectantly for Graham.

'He's still not here?'

'No, dear, but don't worry, he's bound to turn up soon. I bet he's hanging around somewhere, oblivious of the time.' Sally air-kissed Jenny casually as she made the empty attempt to reassure her.

'But it's not like him. He hasn't called in two days, and he's never done that before.'

A knowing look was exchanged behind Jenny's back as Sally and Julia shared an unspoken thought 'so he's tired of her at last – about time.'

Jenny's concern was eclipsed by the arrival of the Kemps, followed closely by Ryan, much to Lucy's delight and her mother's annoyance.

'Will he be staying the night?' Sally asked Lucy coolly, pointedly ignoring her husband.

Ryan answered her directly, saving Lucy the embarrassment.

'No thanks. I don't drink, so I can drive back later.'

The smoked salmon canapés circulated, and still Graham hadn't arrived. More champagne was served, the clock struck eight and an uncomfortable break developed in the conversation

The butler saved them by announcing in a grand voice: 'Dinner is served.'

His pomposity made Lucy giggle, which upset her mother further. Sally suggested they start without Graham or the dinner would spoil. Muriel Kemp had to coax Jenny from her chair by the window, and Ryan asked Alexander loudly whether he'd inherited the butler with the house. So it was with a fragile, insubstantial attempt at conversation that they made their way through the great hall to the dining room.

Alexander had chosen the wines wisely from his uncle's cellar and even Colin was impressed, going into rhapsodies about the Gevrey-Chambertin when it was served. At the other end of the table Sally glowed and sparkled with pleasure as her guests started to relax. Each compliment was taken with self-effacing grace, but Alexander could see how much they meant to her. Jeremy Kemp sat to her right, in Graham's intended place, and she charmed and cajoled him to such an extent that it was obvious he was besotted with her.

Alexander laughed inside as he watched his wife gently resist the solicitor's overaffectionate pats and hugs. To his right, Jenny sat in virtual silence, pecking at her food. Alexander and Ryan worked diligently throughout the long meal to try and lift her spirits, but it was to no avail. Her concern was almost palpable now, and they all felt its contagion.

After coffee, in an attempt to take Jenny's mind off Graham, Alexander suggested they move to the music room, which was at the front of the house, over the hall.

He was still in the mood for Chopin and played the E-flat minor first, before moving on to one of his favourite études. He was part-way through another nocturne when he noticed Lucy waving to him. 'We're going for a walk,' she mouthed, and pointed towards the door.

When the music concluded, the whole group, minus Lucy and Ryan, returned to the drawing room to sip coffee and armagnac. Apart from Ryan, they were all staying overnight, and no one was in a hurry to go to bed. The music's magic had worked on them all except Jenny, who remained frantic and tearful with worry. Around midnight some of them started a game of cards.

'What was that?' Julia looked up sharply.

'What?'

'That noise, like a cry.'

'Probably a fox, that's all.' Sally was dismissive but they waited silently in case it came again.

'There! Did you hear it?'

They all nodded. The shrieking cry could be heard clearly now, although the mist formed an impenetrable veil around the house.

'Where's Lucy?' Julia's voice was sharp with concern.

'She went for a walk with Ryan almost an hour ago.'

Alexander wasn't too worried. True, the Hall was miles from anywhere, but the two lovers would be together.

'Colin, go and find your daughter. She shouldn't be out there on her own.' Julia looked accusingly at her husband.

Colin obligingly lumbered to his feet, his face pink and sweating, and weaved from side to side as he tried to find the door.

'I'll go too.' Alexander was on his feet and into the front hall before anyone could disagree. Apart from Jenny, he was the only one who seemed completely sober.

Outside the air was chill and damp and he regretted not stopping to put on a jacket. Where to start? He could hardly see more than five feet ahead. The cry came again and the hair rose on his arms and neck. It sounded so human – a terrified, panicky bleat. Instinctively he moved towards it, calling out Lucy's name.

'Lucy? Ryan? Where are you?' He could hear sobbing now. That was no animal. He started running but then made himself slow down, fearful of missing whoever it was in the night.

'Lucy! I'm over here. Lucy!'

A shambling form came at him from the mist, two-headed, arms waving. It was Lucy and Ryan, clinging on to each other, faces ghostly white, mouths hanging open. They both looked petrified.

'It's all right. I'm here, come on.' He threw his arms wide around them both. Lucy was sobbing uncontrollably now, shaking in his arms. Ryan rested his head on Alexander's shoulder, breathing heavily. Alexander could smell the sharp, sour taint of fear on his breath each time he exhaled.

'It's OK, you're safe now. Come on back to the house.'

He imagined them lost and confused in the mist, baffled by the night and the trees to the extent that they had become disorientated and frightened. They were only young, and it was a night fit to create demons of the shadows in even the most prosaic mind.

'You don't understand.' Ryan's voice was husky still with fear.

'What don't I understand?'

'It's . . . we . . . he . . .' Whatever it was, Ryan couldn't bring himself to speak of it.

Lucy took two deep, ragged breaths.

'It's Graham, Alexander. We found Graham. I think he's dead.'

CHAPTER TWENTY-THREE

'Oh God!' Alexander's first thought was of Jenny. How could he tell her? Then he thought guiltily of his cousin; he should have been worrying about him, after all.

'Are you sure, Lucy? Ryan?'

Lucy nodded. Ryan said: 'The man we found was certainly dead – I'm sure.'

'It was horrible, Alexander.'

'Tell me where he was and I'll go and look. Meanwhile, stay here.' He didn't want them blundering into the house until he was there to support Jenny.

Their directions were vague. They couldn't remember where the body was – 'Under a tree' was the best they could do – nor how long they'd been running before Alexander had found them. He soon realised that there was no chance of finding Graham on his own. He needed help.

Julia was standing on the front terrace, her coat around her shoulders as she peered out into the mist. As soon as Lucy saw her, she broke away from Alexander and Ryan and ran to fling herself into her mother's arms.

'Lucy, darling. Ssh, ssh, it's all right. You're safe now. Come on in and get warm. You're frozen.'

Safety, love and a sympathetic voice immediately had their traditional effect and Lucy was reduced to an uncontrollable sobbing heap.

'There, there, it's all right.' Julia threw her coat around her daughter's shaking shoulders.

'What is it, Alexander? What's happened?' Sally stood erect and bright-eyed next to Jenny, who stared at him in horror. Somehow she already knew; some instinct had warned her to fear the worst.

'Lucy, Ryan – go and sit by the fire in the drawing room, you're freezing. Off you go.'

The two left quickly, relief and exhaustion outweighing any desire to be the centre of attention. Julia and Muriel Kemp went with them.

Alexander went to Jenny and put his arms tightly around her. He tried to find words that would ease the pain he was about to cause, but it was impossible.

'Jenny,' he said softly, ignoring the others, 'Lucy and Ryan think they've found Graham. They say he's dead.'

He braced himself for hysterics and more tears but Jenny stood perfectly still.

'Dead, you say.' Her soft voice was calm, chilling in its flatness. 'We'd better go and find him, then.'

'We'll go – Colin, Jeremy and I. You stay here with Sally.'

'No! I must be there. He'd want me there. I'm coming.'

'Jenny...'

'Leave it, Alex, she's right. Anyway, I want to come too.' Sally signalled to the butler to get their coats and went to change her shoes. Her practicality disturbed Alexander more than anything else so far in that crazy evening.

Jenny stood rigid in the circle of his arms. He tried squeezing her to show comfort and support but she was oblivious to it. Jeremy Kemp and Colin, shocked into sobriety, waited mute by the open front door, peering with dread into the mist that was steadily thickening about the house. It was only a few minutes before the butler returned with coats and torches, closely followed by Sally.

'Would you like me to call the police, sir?' He exuded deference but it was clear that he felt his employers were going about this the wrong way. Sally pre-empted Alexander's answer.

'That's rather premature, don't you think, Jarvis? For all we know Graham might simply be dead drunk, not dead.'

For a split second they all looked at her, appalled. Alexander felt Jenny shudder at the callousness of his wife's words and he leapt in.

'Mrs Wainwright-Smith has been deeply shocked, Jarvis. She's not thinking straight. Of course you must phone the police. I should have thought of it myself. Good man.'

The butler merely nodded, unfooled but too professional to let his feelings show. Alexander could tell that his wife bitterly regretted her words but there was nothing she could do to take them back. At least say sorry, he willed her, but she didn't, and instead turned to lead the party outside.

All they had to help them was Lucy and Ryan's vague description of where they'd found the body. Alexander led the others back to the point at which he had encountered the pair and stopped to discuss tactics.

'They came from over there,' he explained, pointing into the now dense fog, 'and they said he was under a tree. Now there's a copse straight ahead and, I think, some stands of oak and beech to the left.'

'There's also that ancient beech to the right,' said Sally.

'Yes, of course. Well, there are five of us. I suggest we split into two groups and meet up again at the copse. If anybody finds anything, they're to shout out and we'll converge on the voice.'

'I'm happy to go on my own, old man – that would make three search parties and we'll be quicker. I know my way round these grounds.'

'OK, Colin. Then—'

'I want to go with you, Alexander.'

'Of course, Jenny. Then Jeremy, you and Sally take the—'

'We'll go to the old beech, dear.'

'Right, then we'll go to the farthest oaks and you the next stand along, Colin.'

The party split up, the yellow glow of their torches disappearing into the pearly-grey gloom of the night. Kemp followed Sally as she set off confidently. Her determined stride intimidated him, and they walked in silence until she stopped suddenly and sniffed the air.

'What is it?'

119

'The river, can't you smell it? We must be nearly there now, but we've come a little too far south. This way.' Sally set off again with barely a backward glance, her face flushed and her eyes bright.

Crazy shapes loomed in front of them as the torchlight threw black shadows of bushes and bullrushes on to the wall of fog. A paddock ran straight down to the river bank, and moments later they heard the rustle of wind over water and the fog cleared enough for them to see out across the whole stretch of the river.

'The beech is just beyond those trees. We'll see it soon.' Sure enough, the great upward-sweeping branches were soon visible. Sally lifted her torch to shine into the crown of the monstrous tree, where branches and new leaves swayed from side to side in the wind like huge seaweed fronds caught in a current.

'Shine it on the ground, Sally,' Kemp urged. 'We might miss him.'

But Sally appeared not to hear. Slowly she started to pace around the vast tree. Tendrils of fog fought to resist the fingers of wind and cling to its branches.

'What was that?' Kemp's voice was hoarse with fright. 'There, on the other side.'

Sally kept the torch on the branches of the great beech as she continued to circle its massive trunk steadily.

'For God's sake, woman!' Kemp ran on ahead of her, stumbling over roots and slipping on wet leaves.

'My God. Oh my God!'

Sally walked up calmly to his side and shone the torch on the white figure swaying and turning inches above the ground. There was no doubting that he was dead. His eyes bulged open, bloodshot from the force of slow strangulation; his tongue pushed out of his mouth, black and swollen. The rope that appeared to have killed him was embedded deeply in the bare skin of his neck, blood-stained where it had cut into him whilst he was still alive. He was naked, except for a tiny leather thong.

'We'd better call the others.'

'You can't bring Jenny here, Sally. She mustn't see this.'

'There'll be no stopping her. She'll want to see him.'

'But we have *got* to stop her. This isn't a sight for a woman!' His words shocked them both. It was apparent that Sally was by far the more composed of the pair. From time to time she turned to stare at the body with something approaching fascination, but she had shown no fear at all.

Kemp felt his own pulse drumming in his head, and his expression changed from shock to confusion. How could anyone be coping so well with the awful spectacle in front of them? He didn't know whether to be impressed or suspicious. Normally he was poker-faced, but where Sally was concerned there was no hiding his emotions. She could read his expression perfectly.

'You're right, Jeremy, as always,' she said. 'Take the torch and go and find Alex before they get here.'

'Will you be all right here on your own?'

Sally looked at the body and nodded. 'Go on.'

* * *

120

Alexander saw the light of another torch bobbing in the fog as someone ran towards them. His stomach clenched and he held on tight to Jenny's arm.

'It's OK,' he said to her softly. 'I'm here.'

Kemp came into view and they waited for him in silence. One look at his face was enough to tell them what he had found. They stood in a terrible circle, nobody wanting to ask the question that would confirm the drastic change in all their lives.

'Is he dead?' Jenny's whisper broke the stillness.

'Yes, Jenny, there's no doubt. He's dead.'

She nodded and leant heavily into Alexander, who hugged her instinctively.

'Have you left Sally with Colin?'

'No.' Kemp seemed surprised by the suggestion. 'She's with the b— She's with Graham.'

'On her own?' Alexander was outraged.

'It was her suggestion, honestly.'

'Oh, for God's sake, you know there are times when one just doesn't listen to her, for her own good!'

'Well, I . . . She was very insistent, very calm.'

Alexander glanced down at Jenny, who was hanging on to him compulsively.

'Never mind. Look, you take Jenny back to the house and wait for the police. I'll go to Sally.'

'No. I want to see him.'

'That's a bad idea, Jenny. Go on back with Jeremy, please.'

'No, Alexander. I have to see him. I'll always wonder afterwards how . . . why . . . whether he suffered.'

Kemp thought of the terrible straining face, the bulging eyes, the blood-stained rope.

'I don't think it's a good idea, Jenny, really. Better to see him later, when he's . . .' He was going to say 'tidied up', but stopped himself just in time. 'Well, later, inside.'

'Why? What's the matter with him? What's happened to him?' She was shouting now, nearly hysterical. 'Tell me!'

Kemp looked at them both, at a loss to know what to do.

Jenny struggled to break away from Alexander, desperate now to find Graham and to see for herself, no matter how awful the reality. There was no way they'd get her back to the house unless they both took her, and Alexander was anxious to go and find his wife.

'Tell her,' he urged Kemp. 'Not knowing is doing more harm than good.'

'It looks like he committed suicide. He hanged himself.'

'No! He wouldn't. Why should he? You've got it all wrong.'

'There's no doubt, really. He was hanging when we found him.'

An image of the grotesque scarecrow silhouette, twisting in a halo of fog, returned to Kemp, and he shuddered.

'It can't be.' An idea came to her and she smiled crazily. 'It's not Graham! That's it. It can't be Graham, he'd never kill himself. He loved life and he'd be too much of a coward. It's all a big mistake.'

Her relief was pathetic to see. Alexander looked at Kemp and the solicitor

121

shook his head. There was no doubt on his face. Unlikely as it seemed to all of them, Alexander's cousin was dead.

Another torch appeared in the dark up by the house, then a second. Minutes later two uniformed policemen materialised behind the points of light. Colin, approaching the group from the direction of the river, spotted their uniforms and waited in silence for someone to speak.

'Mr Wainwright-Smith?'

'Yes, that's me.'

'We've had a report of a body being found.'

'Yes. My cousin, Graham Wainwright.'

'No, it's not! I keep telling you. It can't be him. He wouldn't kill himself like that!'

The policeman looked at the group. Their distress was obvious.

'Call this in as confirmed, would you, Bill, and make sure a female officer comes out with the police surgeon.' He turned to Alexander. 'If you could take us to the body, sir . . .'

Alexander hesitated, glanced at Jenny, then nodded. Kemp led the way along the narrow footpath by the river. Virtually all the fog had disappeared along its banks, torn away by the rising wind. The coppice, with its one huge beech, appeared before them.

'He's under that beech. I'll show you.'

'Did you find the body, then, sir?'

'Yes. I was with Mrs Wainwright-Smith. I'm Jeremy Kemp, by the way, the family solicitor.'

They circled around the tree, Kemp dreading the sight of the hanging man.

'It's gone!' he croaked in disbelief. 'The body's gone. It was there, hanging from that branch.'

'Round here.' Colin's voice called to them from behind the huge trunk.

He was crouching next to Sally with his arm around her shoulders. She was sobbing quietly. The body lay on the ground a few feet away, the rope still tight around its neck. His sudden proximity to a dead body and a crying woman seemed to make him nervous, and he spluttered as he attempted to explain his response.

'I heard her crying as soon as we arrived. Bloody stupid, Kemp, to leave her on her own.'

The astonished solicitor stared at the ground and wondered how on earth Sally had been able to lower Graham's body. He said nothing, too aware of her apparent distress. He could hardly protest that it had been she who had assumed command, dry-eyed and perfectly calm, ordering him to leave her and find the others. Given the state of her now, it just wasn't credible.

Alex moved towards his wife, and in that instant Jenny broke loose from his grip and ran over to Graham's body. She threw herself to her knees in the leaf mould. One look at his distorted face confirmed instantly that it was indeed Graham, and that he was incontrovertibly dead. She let out a terrible wail and started to rock over him.

Constable Parks tried to regain control of the situation.

'Right, everybody, over here, please, away from the body.' His colleague tried to coax Jenny away, but she fought him like a tiger, kicking and punching as they grappled beside the body. He eventually managed to lift her

122

and carry her away. Jeremy Kemp and Colin held on to her and after a few moments her cries subsided into a constant low weeping.

Alexander encouraged Sally to move, and the five of them were finally corralled together far enough distant to allow the policemen, belatedly, to secure the scene.

Parks returned to the group, notebook in hand.

'A few questions, just to establish the basics.' He thought of the body taken down from the tree, the footprints all over the site, and the marks of the scuffle between Jenny and his colleague. He would be in serious trouble.

'Who actually found the body?'

'My daughter, Lucy,' Colin explained. 'She's up at the house with my wife.'

'Was she on her own?'

'No, Ryan was with her, he's her boyfriend. They came back to the house and we organised ourselves into a search party.'

'Rather than wait for the police?' Parks couldn't stop thinking of the mess they'd made of the scene – why couldn't they have just waited for the professionals to arrive?

'We thought he might still have been alive.'

'So Lucy and Ryan were unsure, were they?'

'No,' said Alexander. 'They were clear, but we – well, Sally in particular – thought he might just've been drunk or something.'

'I see. And Sally is?'

'My wife, Constable Parks, Mrs Wainwright-Smith, but you can't talk to her now. As you can see, she's terribly upset. I need to get her back to the house, and Jenny too. They're both in shock and it's cold out here.'

'Very well, sir. If I could just have all your names, and I'd ask that none of your party leaves the house. We'll need statements.'

'Statements? But why? This is a suicide. You don't need to trouble this family any more, surely?' Kemp sounded every bit the family solicitor.

'All we have at the moment, sir, is a sudden death that is obviously not by natural causes. The detective in charge is bound to want statements.'

CHAPTER TWENTY-FOUR

It was a silent party that huddled around the low remains of the fire in the drawing room, awaiting the arrival of the detectives who would soon assume control of their lives. Alexander had calmed the cooks and butler and bribed them into waiting, even though they protested that they had seen nothing and would be of no help to the police. Lucy was fast asleep upstairs. Ryan had phoned his mother to explain that he would be late, and was engaged in a silent challenge on his Game Boy.

There was the sound of tyres on gravel, car doors opening and closing and then a low murmur of voices from the entrance hall. The butler showed a tall, dark man and a woman in uniform into the room. Alexander recognised the man at once.

'Chief Inspector Fenwick. How good of you to come. We didn't expect you for such a . . .' he struggled to find the right words, 'domestic matter.'

'Mr Wainwright-Smith. My sergeant was on call and he decided I should know. I chose to come. This is WPC Shah. I know it's late,' the grandfather clock in the hall obediently chimed two as he spoke, 'but I shall need statements from you all individually. Is there a room we could use?'

'Of course, the sitting room next to this, or there's the library on the other side of the great hall, although it might be rather cold.'

Julia stood up.

'My daughter Lucy's fast asleep. She's only seventeen; do you have to take a statement from her tonight?'

'It was Lucy who discovered the body, wasn't it?' Julia nodded. 'In which case I'm afraid I would prefer to speak to her as soon as possible, unless she's been given a sedative.'

Julia nodded reluctantly and went to wake her daughter. There was a sudden explosion of weeping from the sofa closest to the fire.

'Oh, it's all too terrible! I can't bear it. Oh God!' Sally dropped her head into her hands and rocked back and forth, tears streaming between her fingers and spattering her evening trousers. Jeremy and Colin rushed over to her, then stood back somewhat reluctantly to let her husband reach her side. He tried to comfort her but she was almost hysterical.

'This is no good, Chief Inspector. I'll have to take her up to bed.'

'You should get a doctor to see her.' Colin glanced at Alexander accusingly.

'I've got some valium in my bag. Would that help?' Muriel Kemp stole a nervous glance at her husband as she rummaged in a large paisley handbag.

'She needs a proper prescription, Muriel, not your comfort drops. I agree with Colin, we need her doctor here.'

Alexander helped Sally to her feet.

'It's OK. She has her own prescription. Thank you, Muriel, it was a kind thought, but she had best take her own tablets. She does need to rest now, though.' He turned to Fenwick. 'Chief Inspector, would you mind? She's in no state to help you as she is.'

Fenwick paused and studied Mrs Wainwright-Smith. Odd, this violent grief in one otherwise so controlled. Had they been that close, then, she and Graham Wainwright; more than cousins-in-law? Her crying irritated him. It was theatrical and off-putting. He decided that questioning her could wait until morning and said so to her husband. As the pair of them disappeared up the grand wooden staircase, Lucy and her mother came down it. Lucy stared at Sally, obviously upset by her loud distress. Fenwick could see her mother tutting and shaking her head at such a display from a grown woman who wasn't even a relative. Interesting: all the men wanted to protect Sally, but the women saw something entirely different. He wondered what it was.

'Lucy.' He smiled his best father-figure smile at the blonde beauty who stared at him with tear-magnified eyes from above the upturned collar of a candlewick nightgown two sizes too big for her. 'I'm Andrew Fenwick. I'm a policeman and I'm here because your Cousin Graham has died. Do you understand?'

'Of course. It's all right, I mean, I'm OK, not like her.' She turned to look back up the stairs.

Ryan put his Game Boy to one side and came to take her hand.

'You OK, Luce?'

'Yeah, fine. You?'

'Uh-huh, sort of.'

They stood shyly in front of the others, too old to behave naturally and just hug each other; not old enough to have the confidence to do it anyway.

'This way, please, Lucy. Would you like one of your parents to be with you?' Lucy shook her head, and Fenwick and WPC Shah escorted her across the grand hall and into the library. The air was chilly but they none of them appeared to mind. Lucy cuddled the candlewick to her, then pulled her feet out of overlarge flip-flops and tucked them up into the folds of warm material beneath her thighs. Fenwick started without preamble.

'You found the body, with Ryan.' It was a statement.

'Uh-huh. We sort of went for a walk and it – he – was there, under the tree.' She swallowed hard but seemed to be reasonably in control. He decided to continue in the same matter-of-fact way.

'I want you to tell us everything you remember. Everything.'

'Well, it was very dark and misty. We'd got lost but I could hear the river and I knew that once we'd found it I could get us home. The tree just appeared in front of us, you know?'

Fenwick nodded.

She hugged her knees up tight to her chest, eyes glazed as she concentrated on some distant memory, then she refocused on the policeman and grimaced.

'Sorry. The tree. When we found it, my first thought was one of relief. We weren't lost any more. The mist was really thick by then and we were soaked. The next bit's the horrible bit,' she said, in a small voice that reminded Fenwick of his own seven-year-old daughter.

125

Without thinking, he got up and went to sit beside her, lifting one stiff hand away from her knee and into his own comforting grasp. He saw WPC Shah raise her eyebrows and he gave a slight shake of his head. It might not be politically correct, but he knew that it was the right thing to do.

'Go on. We're not in a hurry, take your time.'

'It's all right, it's just that . . .' She squeezed his fingers and he saw the policewoman relax. 'Oh, I don't know. No matter how I try to think about it, it's so horrible.'

'Finding a body *is* horrible, but you need to help us by telling us exactly what you saw.'

'OK.' She took a deep breath and looked away again. 'Somehow we circled around the tree, and then I could see this figure moving in the mist. I realised that there was something odd about its shape. Instead of coming any closer it just stayed there, swinging from side to side, almost like it was dancing. It was spooky.

'Ryan thought it was a peeping Tom and got really angry. He went striding up to it and said, "Oi, what do you think you're looking at." But of course there was no answer, so I went too and as soon as I got there and I could see the face I knew it was Graham. The hair, how he wears it, nobody else has it like that these days. And I thought, how unlike him to be prowling. But he had no clothes on, only this leather thong-type thing, with his, with his . . .' again a pause and then a whisper, 'you know, his thing poking out over the top. Then I looked at his eyes.' She stopped speaking and swallowed hard.

'Go on.'

'They were wide open and staring. All red in the light of Ryan's torch. I knew he was dead. He had to be. Graham was weird but there's no way he was a pervert. I screamed. Ryan yelled and grabbed my hand, and we both started running. The fog was all around us and we seemed to run for ever. Then Alexander was there, and he was so calm and he brought us home and I went up to bed and, well, that's it. That's all.'

'Well done,' he said, and patted her hand. 'That's incredibly helpful. I just need to check a few things. When you and Ryan were on your walk, did you hear anything?'

'No, nothing. An old dog fox howling and an owl that made Ryan jump, but nothing else.'

'You didn't get the sense that there could have been anybody else out there?'

She shuddered, but shook her head.

'No. Not until we saw the body. It was absolutely quiet and the mist seemed to make any noises louder.'

'Let's go back to the body. You said it was swinging from side to side?'

'Yes, he was hanging, didn't you know?' Lucy looked surprised. 'He had a thick rope around his neck. I know we should've tried to get him down, but I never even thought about it at the time, and he *was* dead, there was no mistaking that.'

'You did the right thing to leave him where he was. With a sudden death the police always have to be involved, and it's best to leave the scene undisturbed.'

'Oh good. I'd been feeling guilty about that.' She looked relieved and yawned suddenly.

'Anything else about the scene that you can remember – the colour of the rope, how it was tied? Where his clothes were, for example?'

She thought hard. 'No, nothing. Except that, well, there was litter on the ground around the tree. I noticed it before I saw the body.'

There was nothing more Lucy could tell him about finding the body, and Fenwick moved on to her return to the house. Her memory of this wasn't as good. She'd obviously slipped further into shock by the time she had run into Alexander. She described her cousin's concern clearly enough, their return to the house and the disbelief they found there that Graham could be dead. Her only detailed recollection, though, was of Sally saying sharply, 'dead drunk, not dead,' and how bitchy it had sounded. But Jenny had believed them. She'd been so worried about Graham all evening, and she was sure something had happened to him.

He thanked Lucy and asked WPC Shah to take her back to her parents and bring in Ryan, without letting them talk to each other.

Ryan was also seventeen, and Fenwick again offered to wait until his parents could be with them in the interview, but the lad just laughed briefly and told him to get on with it. He confirmed Lucy's story and added a few points of detail of his own. He'd noticed more about the rope around Graham's neck. It looked like a hangman's noose, properly knotted, and the long length of it had gone down under a thick exposed root to the right-hand side. The 'litter' on the ground had been a few pornographic magazines, but he couldn't tell him what type they were. Fenwick thanked him and arranged for a police car to take him home, annoyed on the lad's behalf that neither of his parents had bothered to come and be with him.

Who next? he thought. What was the best order going to be? He decided it would be ladies first. Jenny he had to see quickly, and he was curious to find out what people thought of Alexander and Sally before he interviewed them.

Jenny came in, leaning heavily on Shah's arm, and the WPC sat next to her on the settee. Jenny slumped back into the cushions and closed her eyes. In the hall, the clock chimed quarter past three. Before they could start the interview, there was a gentle tap on the door and Muriel Kemp came in carrying a tray of tea and biscuits.

'I thought you could do with these.' She smiled hesitantly and placed them carefully on a low table in front of the empty grate. Fenwick thanked her and poured them all a large mug of hot tea, putting sugar into Jenny's, despite her mild protest.

She was obviously deeply shocked, and it had spun over her a web of exhaustion and disbelief that was so thick it restricted her movements to those of a sleep-walker. She had sunk deep into lethargy. Fenwick couldn't recall her saying anything since he'd arrived, and now he needed her statement, perhaps above all others, to help determine whether this sudden death might be accident, suicide or murder.

He studied her closely as she sipped her tea mechanically, grimacing occasionally at its sweetness. She was a pretty woman: lots of blonde hair; a winter tan on smooth arms and long skinny legs; and big blue eyes that he knew were the type that could captivate a man's heart, although not his. But the bone structure beneath the youthful bloom was not exceptional, and he thought her looks would fade gently over time in a way that would surprise the wrong type of husband who'd thought of her as a trophy wife.

The tea seemed to revive her. She suddenly shook herself and looked at Fenwick for the first time.

'You're being awfully patient, but I suspect you're keen to get on and question me. I'm OK now. Go ahead.'

Her whole attitude was in such contrast to Sally Wainwright-Smith's that it made Fenwick wonder again whether there had been anything between Sally and her cousin-in-law. He questioned Jenny gently but steadily, working through from the time she had last seen Graham, over two days before.

'He left Scotland early on Wednesday, driving his Jag. We were going to meet here tonight.'

By Thursday morning I was worried. Graham always calls me in the evenings, and he hadn't rung the night before. I didn't know which hotel he'd booked so I couldn't check that he had arrived safely.'

'Why were you worried?'

'He had been so preoccupied lately, but secretive too, which was right out of character. He refused to talk to me about what might be worrying him. He said it was better that I didn't know.'

'Do you have any idea what it was that so concerned him?'

'I think it must have been something to do with either Sally or the business; those seemed to be his biggest hangups. He'd had this private detective digging into Sally's past for weeks.'

'And he told you nothing about what he had discovered about Sally?'

'No.'

'What about the business?'

'I don't know what was bugging him, but it definitely concerned Wainwright's. Graham,' her voice caught again on his name, as if saying it had brought back a reality she'd forgotten during their conversation, 'Graham had no interest in the business before his father died. But then George Ward started pestering him at the Memorial Service about how his father's death couldn't have been a suicide. And others kept commenting on how unbelievable it was that Sally and Alexander had inherited half the estate. So he called the Assistant Chief Constable, and you came round. That's when he hired the private detective too.

'He told the detective that he thought Sally had somehow persuaded his father to change his will, so the man concentrated all his attention on her and her private life. But then, something happened – I don't know what – but it made Graham's attention turn to the company itself. He was worried by something he or the private detective had found out, and I think he was going to come here to confront somebody about it. In fact, I'm sure of it now – why else would he have come alone, without me? When he heard that Arthur Fish had died he was really worried, and so was I. I told him to come to you, the police.'

'Why didn't he?'

'He said he was going to, after tonight but then . . .'

Her eyes filled with tears and Fenwick decided to close the interview quickly. He asked a few more questions: an estimated time for Graham's departure from Scotland; a description of his red XJS which was still missing; his mobile phone number; and confirmation that he had taken a whole bundle of papers with him on his final journey.

Finally, after absent-mindedly finishing her cold, sweet tea, she looked up at him, meeting his eyes warily.

'I wasn't with Graham for his money, you know. I didn't expect to be around for long enough to help him spend it. He usually changed his girls with the season.' Her eyes suddenly started to drop their tears.

'But you seem very upset at his death?'

'Oh, I loved him. I would have done anything for him.'

He asked her gently: 'Why do you think he killed himself, Jenny?'

She looked at him blankly.

'Killed himself? You think it's suicide?' She shook her head violently at the thought. 'Graham would never have killed himself. No, this is murder.'

The clock chimed another half-hour and Fenwick took pity on Jenny. He asked her for details of her movements over the past few days and then let her go to bed. Once she'd left the room, he turned to WPC Shah.

'Did you believe her?'

'Yes, completely. Everything she said had the ring of truth.'

'I'm inclined to agree. There was no guilt there, and the right level of shock and sadness.'

'Excuse me for saying so, sir, but you didn't ask about Graham Wainwright's will – or who'll inherit now.'

'No, I didn't. I'm saving that for Jeremy Kemp. We'll see him next, but I want to check how Cooper's been getting on first. You wait here and make sure no one goes off to bed.'

It was nearly four o'clock in the morning when Fenwick found Cooper. He had interviewed the kitchen staff quickly and had then gone straight to the scene. The body had finally been removed and the pathologist would undertake the post-mortem at 'nine a.m. sharp'. Cooper walked his boss over to the tree where the body had been found, dreading his reaction. A familiar white tent had been erected under the vast spreading branches of the beech, spilling bright light out on to the leaf mould and twisted roots that surrounded the massive tree on all sides. Inside, Fenwick found two SOCOs still hard at work, so he waited carefully at the entrance.

'I need to get back and continue the interviews, so just the key facts, Sergeant.'

'The scene was a mess when we got here: body taken down from the tree; attempts to remove the noose from the neck had failed; footprints everywhere, coming and going.'

'We need to find out who did all that. It wasn't Lucy or Ryan. They left the body exactly as they'd found it. Any view yet on murder, suicide or accident?'

'According to the police surgeon, all the signs are, and I quote, "that it was accidental strangulation during auto-erotic stimulation". He had a leather posing pounch on, and there were several of *these* around.' Cooper handed Fenwick two bagged pornographic magazines full of explicit but straight sex.

'Any buts?'

'One or two. The noose was very professional, and the way it was looped around that branch there and back down to the ground . . .' Cooper walked delicately over to a large exposed root and pointed from over a metre away, 'here . . . doesn't make sense. I don't know how he could've gradually increased the pressure from where he was. Looks like a job for two people to make it work.'

'Make sure somebody stays here when SOCO have gone, and then come up to the house.'

Colin and Jeremy Kemp were lying in wait for him in the entrance hall, tired and angry. They demanded that the interviews be speeded up but Fenwick was determined to do them all himself and told them so firmly and politely. He saw Kemp next and learnt that it was he and Sally who had discovered the body for the second time.

'And Sally was calm when you left her?'

'Completely, Inspector—'

'Chief Inspector.'

'Completely. She's an extraordinary woman, y'know. I wouldn't have left her had she not been all right, but she was in remarkable shape, virtually insisted I went.'

'Really?' Fenwick raised his eyebrows. He could see Kemp immediately regret the remark, but the solicitor was wise enough to hold his tongue and not make it any worse.

'So her breakdown this evening – the hysterics – that was out of character, was it?'

'Course not. She's been through hell tonight, coping and being strong for Jenny's sake. It's completely understandable that she should collapse at some point. Seeing a man hanging from a tree is enough to frighten anybody half to death. She really is very sensitive. She has so much to manage in her life – you've no idea what she does, how much Alexander relies on her, not that he's even aware of it half the time! The man doesn't know the luck he was born with.' The last was said with such bitterness and jealousy that if anything ever happened to Alexander, Fenwick would be inclined to put Jeremy Kemp near the top of the suspect list.

'What about Graham Wainwright's will, Mr Kemp? Did he change it, given his inheritance?'

'Probably, but I can't say. He was no longer a client of mine. I passed his affairs over to a Mr Sacks, in Reigate. We'll give you the address first thing.'

'Why did he change solicitors?'

'He was upset over his father's will; blamed our firm in general and me in particular. Said we should have done something to prevent his father changing it. Relationships improved later, but by then he'd already appointed another firm.'

'Tell me about Alan Wainwright's will.' He could tell that Kemp wanted to plead client privilege but had thought better of it.

'Originally the whole estate, apart from token bequests, was left to his son, Graham. Alan disliked his sister and brother-in-law intensely and hated the idea of them having any influence over the business, so they were never going to inherit much, despite their expectations.'

'And the will was changed so that Alexander and Sally Wainwright-Smith inherited a substantial share of his uncle's estate?'

'Yes, effectively half. Shortly afterwards Alan brought me a copy of a letter, approved by the board of Wainwright Enterprises, nominating Alexander as MD should Alan die.'

'Were you surprised?'

Kemp hesitated a moment, then said shortly, 'Very.'

It was the only opinion he was prepared to express on the subject. Nor was he very forthcoming about Sally. Fenwick was given again the familiar description of a remarkable woman who had worked ceaselessly to unravel the complications of her husband's inheritance, on top of being Alexander's personal assistant and reorganising the managing director's office.

Cooper joined the interview quietly and sat in a hard chair by the empty fireplace.

Fenwick returned to the recovery of the body, but Kemp seemed reluctant to talk further. His sentences became clipped, his tone studiedly neutral. Not once did he volunteer further fact or opinion.

'So by the time you returned with the others, the body was lying on the ground. How did Mrs Wainwright-Smith do that?'

'The devil knows—' Kemp broke off and stared at Fenwick open-mouthed. It was almost possible to see the cogs in his tired brain click into place. It was quite clear that he'd said something he felt he shouldn't have, and he looked to Fenwick like a guilty schoolboy, caught out for not remembering his lesson. There was a silence, in which Kemp's eyes darted shiftily around the room. He was trying to replay everything that had been said, to calculate a way out of the mess he had placed himself in. But he was too tired to remember all the moves in the deceptively simple conversation, and in the end he simply clamped his fleshy lips even tighter and said nothing.

Probably the most sensible thing he's done tonight, thought Fenwick.

After Kemp had promised him full details of his movements over the past three days and the names of the rest of the bridge four with whom he and his wife had spent Thursday evening, Fenwick wished him good night.

Mrs Muriel Kemp came in swiftly afterwards. She was a short, thin woman of bird-like movements, given to fluttering her hands when nervous and to speaking in half-sentences, as if she didn't quite trust herself to conclude an opinion. Her eyes were small, hard, brown, tired now in the early hours of the morning, but still alert.

After five minutes Fenwick concluded that there was little she was going to contribute to the sum of his knowledge about the night's events, but he was curious to find out her view of Sally Wainwright-Smith.

'What's Sally like?'

Mrs Kemp's hands fidgeted in the air, inches above her lap.

'All right.'

That was it; no 'extraordinary woman' stories here.

'How well do you know her?'

'Not well at all. We rarely socialise with the Wainwright-Smiths.'

'But she had a lot of work to do unravelling Alan Wainwright's estate, so she must have spent quite a bit of time with your husband.'

'I don't know what you are implying, Chief Inspector, really I don't.'

'Nothing at all, only that he must have got to know her quite well, and perhaps expressed an opinion about her.'

'We rarely talked of her. Now, may I go? I'm rather tired.' She picked up a fringed cushion from the sofa and started to fiddle with the tassels.

'Mrs Wainwright-Smith's reactions tonight: did they strike you as odd in any way?'

She snorted in reply and concentrated on the plait she was making in the fringe. 'She's an odd woman. Nothing she does surprises me.'

'In what way is she odd?'

'She just is, Chief Inspector; a woman of contrasts, let's say. She's not a woman's woman, you know. She really gets on much better with men . . . It's hard for me to judge.'

Muriel Kemp would say no more and Fenwick let her go.

The interview with Colin Wainwright-McAdam, Graham's uncle by marriage, followed a strangely similar pattern to that with Jeremy Kemp, but revealed nothing new, other than the fact that Colin was an objectionable, snobbish man. He too was full of praise for Sally, explaining to Fenwick how delicate she was beneath the deceptively robust exterior.

'A wife like Sally would be an asset to any man, Chief Inspector, no matter how competent he was in his own right.'

Finally, as the clock chimed the hour yet again, Alexander Wainwright-Smith was woken from a deep slumber on a couch in front of the dying embers of his sitting-room fire. Cooper guided the dozy man through the great hall to join Fenwick and Shah, then positioned himself quietly out of everybody's line of sight. He didn't think that this death was suicide – it smelt wrong – and until he'd discovered Wainwright-Smith fast asleep in his drawing room he had been his prime suspect. The sight of the sleeping man, mouth sagging open, one arm thrown wide, the other holding a floral cushion tight to his chest, had changed his mind. It wasn't just that he looked innocent, he *slept* innocently. He'd never known a guilty man, unless he was a true psychopath, sleep so well on the night of his crime, whilst waiting for his first police interview.

Alexander yawned noisily, then covered his mouth in a hasty apology. WPC Shah contorted her jaw as she tried to stifle a sympathetic response.

'Sorry, I'm just so groggy.' He rubbed his face briskly, then shook his head. 'There, better. You must be exhausted.'

Fenwick shrugged, then started his questions for the last time that night. Alexander answered him thoughtfully. Despite his best attempts, he was still befuddled from his sleep and the drug of the pre-dawn hour. Perfect, as far as Fenwick was concerned; the man didn't appear to have the wit or energy to be anything other than honest. He repeated the detail of his meeting with Lucy and Ryan, the subsequent search parties, the discovery of the body and the return to the house. When Fenwick quizzed him gently about his guests' reactions, including those of his wife, he answered simply, with clear recall of the various conversations. Even when Fenwick challenged him on Sally's hysterics, his composure didn't falter. Yes, he'd been surprised, but then it had been an extraordinary day, and who was he to criticise such a human reaction?

'How is Mrs Wainwright-Smith?'

'Asleep. She took a couple of tablets and went straight out.'

'Is this a regular prescription?'

'Sadly, yes. She's being treated for mild depression by our doctor. He said it's nothing to worry about, although he'd like her to see a specialist and get more rest. Fat chance now.'

'What's caused her condition?'

'I'm not really sure. We've been through a hell of a lot since my uncle died in January and at first Sally seemed to cope really well. We moved into the Hall last month and she redecorated, helped me analyse the business, worked through the mess of our inheritance, tried to heal the rift with my family and then came and organised my office. But in the last few weeks it has all seemed to get on top of her.'

'Any idea why?'

'None at all, except that I'm working long hours now, so perhaps she gets lonely. We've only been married a few months, so I suspect this sudden change is a shock.'

Fenwick sensed that Wainwright-Smith was holding something back, but he was wide awake now and fully in control. He decided to change the subject for now.

'So you didn't know her long before you married?'

Alexander laughed. 'No. We had what is called a whirlwind romance. I met her before Christmas and married her in January.'

'Big wedding?' Fenwick wanted to probe into Sally's background without alerting her husband to his interest.

'No, just a few of my family. Sally didn't invite anyone.'

'That's unusual.'

'She's a very private person, Chief Inspector, and she said she wanted a new life and a break from the past.'

'Why was that?'

'You're asking a lot of strange questions, in the circumstances.'

'You're right. My mind's drifting. Forgive the idle curiosity, we're all tired. I'll leave the rest of my questions until tomorrow morning, when we'll be back to interview your wife. Good night, Mr Wainwright-Smith.'

'Good night, Chief Inspector.'

CHAPTER TWENTY-FIVE

'How was he dressed when you found him?'

'Surely you've seen the photographs – just the leather posing pouch, nothing else. Why do you ask?'

'Look here.'

Fenwick peered at Graham's neck, where the rope had contused the skin as he had strangled slowly. There were scratch marks, presumably from his fingernails as the noose was tightened.

'What am I looking for?'

Pendlebury gave a deep sigh, as if a promising pupil had just failed an elementary test.

'Look at the pattern of bruising and rope burns. See anything odd?'

Fenwick peered harder, not wanting to disappoint Pendlebury.

'Well, the patterning is very irregular. Towards the back – I assume where the knot pressed in under his left ear – there's a fully developed rounded bruise. On the right side the heavy contusions are all in a narrow line with spots of subcutaneous haemorrhaging beneath – and there seems to be a thin darker bruise, a sort of indentation, running round about half his neck.'

'Not bad. What does it suggest to you?'

'Uneven pressure, changes in the angle of the body? I've no idea, you tell me.'

Pendlebury bent down beside him, winced with pain and then used a little finger the size of a chipolata to point delicately at the various wounds.

'I think that he was clothed when the noose went round his neck. This is the clear indentation of a shirt collar – no, don't peer; I've taken some magnified images. It would also explain why the bruising on the right varies above and below a clear line.'

'So he was undressed after he died?'

'Very possibly, and here – wait, I'll give you the magnifying glass – look at the pattern of this bruise.'

Fenwick peered closer.

'I think that's the imprint of a chain. It's cut into his neck in most places, but just there I think we'll be able to record a clear pattern of the links.'

'I'll find out from his girlfriend if he wore a neck chain.'

'And check what sort of ring he wore too, whilst you're at it.'

There was a clear imprint of a ring on his right little finger, with a callus on the rise of his palm where it would have worn against the metal with each daily activity – holding a pen, drinking, eating.

'I hadn't considered robbery as a motive!'

134

'Could have been taken as souvenirs, or he was stripped by someone else – an opportunist thief who wasn't squeamish, perhaps, though I don't think so. The leather pants he was wearing were brand new; they still had the plastic staple from the purchase tag in the label. It would have scratched and been uncomfortable, but there's no mark on him. Either he had only just put them on before he died, or someone put them on him afterwards.'

'We'll try and find out who makes them, and with luck we may even be able to trace the purchase. Are these fresh?' Fenwick pointed to two long bruises running under the dead man's armpits.

'They're faint, hardly developed, but yes, they are fairly new. I'd say that they had been caused shortly before his death.'

'Was he tied up?'

'No, they're too short. I've never seen anything like these before.'

He backed away to allow his assistant to photograph them in close-up, then continued with his minute examination of the outside of the body but found nothing further of significance. Next he opened Graham's skinny torso and started on his internal examination and removal of the vital organs. Fenwick listened to the unusually brief commentary Pendlebury dictated into an overhead microphone, worried by the man's apparent preoccupation. From time to time he had to stop and straighten his back, and when he did so Fenwick noticed the sweat of pain on his face.

'He'd had breakfast before he died, but the stomach contents aren't fully digested. I'd say he was dead within an hour of his last meal. If you find his hotel and when he had breakfast I'll be able to give you a clearer time of death. Right now, all I can tell you is that it was between twelve and eighteen hours before his body was found. I just need to take samples for toxicology, then I'm done.'

'Yesterday morning, up to noon. Well, that's a start. I'll leave you to get on.'

Pendlebury straightened his back and winced again.

'Lumbago?'

'Just sciatica. Rain coming.'

The pathologist was more morose than ever and dismissed Fenwick's attempted sympathy with a brusque shake of his capped head. He nodded to his assistant: 'You can finish him now,' then beckoned to Fenwick with a bloody gloved finger. 'My office in ten minutes?'

In the stuffy office, Fenwick squeezed into the one visitor's chair and waited patiently. To his surprise, the pathologist arrived early, his face grey with pain. As Pendlebury eased his bulk into the tiny space, the walls seemed to crowd in on them. The pathologist winced again as he lowered himself carefully into a leather chair and rearranged a faded cushion into the small of his back.

'Whisky?'

'Too early for me.' It was only eleven o'clock and Fenwick shrugged away a moment's concern for his old friend as none of his business.

'You're right, but I think I need the help.' Pendlebury poured a short measure and surreptitiously used it to wash down a small white pill. 'Well, this is a bugger.'

'Suicide, accident or murder?' Fenwick had to ask, although it was clear that the death wasn't nearly as straightforward as it had first looked.

'Exactly.' The pathologist spread his pristine podgy fingers on the desk top and studied them intently. 'It could be any one of them. You're including accident because of the auto-erotic strangulation possibility, I suppose? Hmm, yes, well it is a *possibility*,' he placed particular emphasis on the word, which indicated clearly that it wasn't his favoured hypothesis, 'but no, I don't think so. Of course, the scene was such a mess that anything's possible.' He looked accusingly over the top of his half-moon glasses, and Fenwick frowned.

'Don't tell me, I know, but the damage was done before we arrived. At least they didn't cut the rope.'

'Yes. Well, I don't favour accident. Apart from everything else, the noose was entirely of the wrong type. That knot would've been damn painful, enough to distract him no matter how much he tried to become aroused. And the pornography you found was very mild. You'd expect something more hard-core. As I say, we can't rule it out because of the scene, but it's highly unlikely in my opinion.'

There was a silence in which Fenwick let the older man compose his thoughts.

'This is a tough one, Fenwick. Whatever I think, it's going to be hard to prove because the chain of evidence is so badly disrupted. If it was a suicide it was an inefficient one. He was asphyxiated; his neck didn't break, so that rules out his having jumped from the branch above. He must have just kicked aside whatever he'd been standing on and swung there for quite a few minutes. Very painful way to choose to go but perhaps he didn't realise.'

Fenwick stood up, started to pace, but quickly reached the edge of the room. He leant his back against the glass-panelled door, suddenly frustrated and eager to be gone.

'And murder? Yes, that's another definite possibility. If there are fabric samples from his missing clothes on the rope, it'll help. Are there any?'

'It's been sent to forensic, but there was so much disturbance at the scene we'll never be able to prove a chain of evidence with absolute certainty. Anything else?'

Pendlebury shook his head. There were no other signs of injury to the body, no old wounds, nothing else of any help. He sensed Fenwick's impatience to be gone and concluded quickly. He would send the samples to toxicology as a matter of routine, and most results would be through within twenty-four hours.

Fenwick ran down the steps from the hospital wing that housed the mortuary and sprinted across the car park to his car.

'Bloody fool!' he shouted to himself as he ran. He wasn't talking about the doctor.

An hour later he was crouching inside the white tenting that spread from the branches of the huge beech. He'd missed the SOCO team, but a constable on duty outside gave him their message: a completed report would be with him by early afternoon. He stood now to one side of the death scene, staring up at the branches above. Twisted roots ran out from the knotted trunk to burrow into the leaf mould over twenty feet away. The ground under the tree was bare of grass and covered by years of leaves and debris in various stages of decomposition. With a caution he couldn't help but feel was redundant, given the trampling of the night before, Fenwick moved the thick leaves aside as he edged to where the body had been lying. He brushed the dirt away with his gloved hands, sweeping a path before him about a meter wide.

When he'd got to within a foot of the trunk, he tiptoed back to the perimeter and started the sweeping action again, widening the cleared space into a wedge. Again he reached the trunk and returned to the edge of the circle he was making around it. It was hot within the tenting, and he removed his jacket.

'Need any help, sir?' A constable was peering inside with a look of concern.

'Yes, Constable . . . Robin, isn't it?'

The man beamed, pleased to have been remembered and blissfully ignorant of Fenwick's knack with names. He wasn't to realise that his beaky red nose was the only clue the DCI needed.

'Come in. Be careful. Clear the leaf mould to your right away from the path I've made. Tread lightly.'

'What am I looking for, sir? They were pretty thorough, you know.'

Fenwick raised an eyebrow and the man shut up at once. It wasn't his place to offer opinions.

'Indentations. They'd have been concentrating on finding trace evidence, and with the poor light this morning they could have missed the marks I'm looking for.'

The two men worked silently for another ten minutes, sweating uncomfortably as weak sunshine burned through the shade of the tree to heat the confined air in the tenting below.

'Sir! Here, sir. What about these?'

Fenwick crouched down by the excited constable and examined the neat L-shaped pressure mark over an inch deep in the soil. Carefully they scraped the leaf mould away around it and discovered three more. Each measured about three-quarters of an inch by an inch, and they were spaced about eighteen inches apart.

'Good man. Give me your radio and stay here. No one comes near, do you understand?'

Fenwick called the station, and another scene-of-crime team was dispatched to the beech tree. He asked for all the leaf-mould to be removed and searched and casts made of the impressions. There'd be hell to pay on the budget, but the Superintendent would sort that out. And anyway, he now felt that he was dealing with a murder. That the body had been undressed after death was not conclusive proof, but Jenny's comments about Graham's concerns, and the fact that he was planning to talk to the police, had established a likely motive. Now, he had discovered that the box on which the man had been standing had been removed. On balance, it looked like murder.

The Wainwright household was sleeping in and the temporary butler of the night before had left. Fenwick knocked loudly for several minutes at the front door and then in exasperation found the tradesman's entrance. It was locked, but just as he was contemplating a break-in, a girl turned up on a bicycle.

'Can I help you?'

'Yes, I need to speak to Mr and Mrs Wainwright-Smith and I can't get a reply. My name's DCI Fenwick from Harlden police.' He showed her his warrant card. 'Who are you?'

'I'm Irene, I work here.'

'Were you working last night?'

'Yeah, till midnight, then I went home.'

'Which is where?'

'Other side of the park. Look, why are you here anyway?'

Fenwick explained briefly that he had an appointment with Mrs Wainwright-Smith, and the furtive look of the casual law-breaker crept into her eyes. Suddenly she seemed less inclined to let him in, and she blocked the door with her body as she unlocked it.

'I'll check with Mrs Wainwright-Smith to see if it's OK. You'd best wait where you are.'

'It's all right, I'm expected.'

She shrugged in defeat and he followed her into a long brown-and-cream-tiled passage with scuffed dark brown doors on either side. Mrs Wainwright-Smith's refurbishment of the house had not extended below stairs.

'Bloody 'ell.'

The butler and cooks obviously hadn't felt it was their job to tidy up at the end of the extended evening, and glasses, cups, mugs and leftover toast littered the surfaces.

'What's been goin' on 'ere? This was tidy when I left.' A note of anticipatory defence had crept into her voice and Fenwick wondered just what Mrs Wainwright-Smith was like to work for.

'It was a very late night.'

'What happened?' Sudden fear leapt into her eyes and she backed half a step away from him. 'Why're you here?'

'I'll explain it all in a moment. Now, tell me about yesterday evening while you put the kettle on.'

His jacket was flung over a chair; he loosened his tie and surreptitiously removed his cuff links before folding his sleeves up.

'You're filthy. Whatya been up to?'

He rubbed his face wearily and yawned noisily.

'Tell me about last night and I'll tell all.'

Sensing gossip, she made two mugs of strong tea, put a blue-and-white-striped sugar bowl in the middle of the table and settled her comfortable bottom on to an old leather-padded chair.

'Go on.'

'You first.'

'Fair 'nough. Not much to say, really. I was paid for the full day, plus extra after eleven, and I left at twelve.'

'How did you get here and back home?'

She raised her eyebrows at the dumb question. 'I cycle – remember.'

'Even at night?'

' 'Course. It's quite safe. I use the cycle track by the river, then the footpath through the woods, and there's only Badgers' Break to go through before I'm home.'

Fenwick made a mental note to get a large Ordnance Survey map. 'How long does that take?'

'Depends on the weather. When it's fine, between twenty and twenty-five minutes. When it's misty like last night, more like forty.'

'So what time did you get here yesterday?'

'Eight o'clock in the morning, sharp.'

'And you were here till midnight. That's a long day.'

A moment's hesitation, then a nod.

'Tell me about the day.'

'We were frantic. Guests due to arrive at seven and not one room made up – it was the decorators' fault. They were late finishing the last bedrooms. I told the missus not to use that firm but she did anyway 'cos they were cheap. And to be fair,' she nodded to herself in agreement, 'they did a better job than I thought they would. Mind you, there's no way you want to disappoint *her*, believe me.'

'So I understand.' Fenwick shook his head, as if in sympathy.

Irene looked at him appraisingly and took a long gulp of tea.

'Biscuit?'

'Please – I skipped breakfast.'

She disappeared into the pantry and came back with a fresh pack of digestive biscuits. His stomach rumbled loud enough to be heard, and she laughed as she picked up the bread knife and sliced into the shiny red plastic, a third of the way down the pack. She gestured to the spilled contents.

'Tuck in.'

'Thank you.'

'So you've 'eard about her. Boy, it's different now.'

'From when?'

'From when old Mr Wainwright was 'ere, of course.'

'You worked here then?'

'Yeah, off and on. Mr and Mrs Willett were the full-time staff. I came in casual. But she got rid of 'em, of course – economising, she calls it. Slave labour, I says. She's so bloody tough. You take yesterday. We gets here, Shirley and me, at eight on the dot. She's already up and charging about. There's a list of things a mile long to do which any sensible person'd know was a week's work. But oh no, not the missus.'

'What about Mr Wainwright-Smith: did he help?'

'Poor lamb. He was dead to the world. I went in his bedroom early on and there he was, snoring fit to burst the light bulbs.'

'And Mrs Wainwright-Smith, what time did she leave?' Fenwick decided to play a hunch. He didn't trust Sally, based on her behaviour the night before, and was preparing for the fact that she could lie to him when he interviewed her. If he could establish an independent corroboration of her whereabouts he would be a lot more comfortable.

A look of calculation passed across Irene's face, but he stared back at her, all innocence.

'You'll not tell 'er it's me saying this?'

'I can't promise, but I won't use names unless I have to.'

'Hmmm.' She thought about it for a while as she nibbled her biscuit. Fenwick kept quiet and finished his tea with a slight slurp.

'OK. You'll be interviewing Shirley too, won't you, so's it could be either of us. Well, she left 'bout half eight, pr'aps even earlier. Said she wanted to get

139

to market first thing to pick up fresh fruit and veg for dinner. And before you ask, I didn't see her again till lunch time, but she must've stopped by before 'cos all the veg were in the kitchen when we had our morning coffee.'

'At what time?'

'Don't know. Let's see. I did upstairs while Shirl was down 'ere. We 'ad a cup of tea at nine.' She looked guilty. 'For a few minutes is all. Then it was back to it till around eleven, I s'pose, and I think that's when we spotted the veg, right in the sun too. All that trouble to buy them fresh, then she just left 'em there. She must've been in a rush. In fact, she didn't come and check up on us once all morning; most unnatural, that.'

'And when did Mr Wainwright-Smith wake up?'

'What's this all about then? Why you asking all these questions?'

Fenwick told her simply and watched her face as the news sank in. Her look of horror was quickly replaced by curiosity and morbid interest.

'And when d'you reckon 'e died?'

'Sometime yesterday.'

'And he wasn't found until past twelve last night. I must've cycled right past him.' She shivered. 'And it was suicide?'

'Might have been, but we can't rule out other possibilities yet.'

'So it *might* be murder.' She relished the word, gave a nasty grin and said: 'Well, well. Another suspicious death. Wonder who the lucky one is *this* time?'

'Meaning who will inherit?'

'Yup. Be interestin' if it's her upstairs again, wouldn't it?'

'But it's really *Mr* Wainwright-Smith who would inherit, surely?'

'What's 'is is 'ers, believe me. 'E's a guest in his own 'ome half the time.'

'So what time did he get up yesterday?'

'I took him a cup of tea at twelve 'cos I was worried about 'im. I knew he should be at work and it just wasn't like him to oversleep. I had to shake 'im awake and draw the curtains back.'

'And then?'

'I left 'im to it. Made 'im some toast when 'e come down, and a fresh pot of coffee. Missus came back shortly afterwards, and once she'd had her shower and changed, they went off to work.'

'How did Mrs Wainwright-Smith seem when she came back?'

'In a rush, as usual. Surprised to see hubby in the kitchen with us, that's all.'

'We'll need to interview Shirley, and it would be helpful to have your address, just in case.'

'No problem.' She pulled a piece of scrap paper from a hook by the phone and printed the details out carefully for him.

There was a loud jangle, and she looked at the system of bells and pulleys on the wall.

'Front door. 'Scuse me.'

Fenwick looked around the kitchen. Thick green baize covered the door, and he could hear nothing beyond it. If Irene and Shirley had been busy elsewhere in the house, it would have been easy for somebody to slip in and leave the fruit and vegetables at any time after nine o'clock. Clumsy, though, to leave them in the sun and not in the shade on the other side of the room. Someone in a rush, maybe, or not wanting to risk being seen.

Graham Wainwright had died between six a.m. and midday. A six-hour period for which neither Alexander nor Sally Wainwright-Smith had an alibi.

The door swung wide, opening the way for a chatter of voices. Sergeant Cooper and the new team had arrived. Fenwick heard Irene and Cooper, laughing already at some unheard joke and he decided to leave the rest of the questioning in the kitchen to his Sergeant. WPC Shah was waiting silently in the front hall. As fresh tea was made, he walked past pantry, flower room and store rooms to the drawing room. It was dark, and smelt of stale brandy and cigars; he drew the curtains and forced open a window.

As he pulled the curtain cords, bright light flung shadows back to reveal heavy mahogany antique tables, footstools, sofas big enough for four, and gilt; gilt everywhere, in the candle sconces, candelabra and huge mirrors hung around the walls. As he walked the length of the room across faded Persian rugs and polished inlaid flooring, his image flitted from mirror to mirror on either side, a disturbing flicker from the corner of his eye.

There was a connecting sitting room, pretty and comfortable, opening on to the front hall, on the opposite side of which lay a small office with household accounts stacked neatly beside a personal computer. Then there was the library, in which Fenwick had conducted last night's interviews. Cracked brown leather chairs stood by walnut tables and a reading desk polished to a gentle luminescence. Huge bookcases lined every wall and bordered the windows. His breath misted in the chill, shadowed room.

A volume had been left out on one of the tables, and Fenwick opened it at a marked page: 'Roses – Ailments and Pests'. He heard a footfall behind him, and turned to find Alexander, unshaven, hair spiked in all directions, wrapped in a heavy towelling dressing gown.

'Chief Inspector, I didn't know you were here. Have you been offered coffee?'

'I've had tea and biscuits, thanks. Irene saw to that.'

'Good. I need some too. Would you mind coming down to the kitchen?'

'Actually it wasn't you that I came to see; it was your wife. Is Mrs Wainwright-Smith awake yet?'

A look of immediate concern crossed Alexander's face.

'I left her asleep in her room.'

So the Wainwright-Smiths slept apart, yet they had been married only a few months. Very curious.

'Do you really need to trouble her yet?'

'Yes, I do. Would you go and wake her, please, and ask her to join me here in, say, five minutes.'

It was an instruction, and Alexander left at once, frown lines of worry appearing on his face. Fenwick found Cooper and Shah and told them to join him, then completed his inspection of the rest of the ground floor.

On the opposite side of the great hall were the dining room and a marble-floored passage leading to an ornate Victorian conservatory. A second, steeply banked staircase rose from the back hall, disappearing into gloom above.

There were low voices from behind him, and he went to join the master and mistress of the house as they stood waiting for him beside the empty fireplace in the great hall.

In her five minutes, Sally Wainwright-Smith had dressed and combed her silvery fair hair back into a neat ponytail. She wore no make-up, but the fineness of her skin and the shape of her eyes were such that she needed none. Other than a pallor that made her natural delicacy seem almost waif-like, there was no trace of the hysteria of the night before.

Fenwick nodded a greeting, then walked towards the library. Cooper, Shah and Sally followed, but when Alexander moved to do so too, Fenwick turned and shook his head. Alexander watched anxiously as his wife disappeared into the room. Sally did not turn round, nor did she appear surprised to find herself alone with the police.

Fenwick moved swiftly through the preliminaries and asked directly for her account of her movements the previous day, from the time she woke up.

'Well, some of it's a little vague. I woke early, gave the girls their instructions for the day, and then went back to bed. I didn't tell them that because I wanted them to work hard; there was a lot to do and they don't concentrate if I'm not around.' She was looking him directly in the face, eyes wide open and frank.

'So you didn't go off to buy fruit and vegetables?'

She blinked, and hesitated for a fraction of a second.

'No, I simply said that to make them think I'd be back.'

'So you lied to them?'

'A white lie, Chief Inspector, of no consequence.'

'So who delivered the vegetables?'

'The man from the market, by prior agreement.' She said it smoothly but her cheeks flushed and Cooper made a note on his pad.

'Go on. What happened next?'

'Both Alex and I were exhausted. I woke just after eleven thirty, and went to have a long shower and to put my clothes out ready for the evening. When I went into Alex's room, he wasn't there. I found him in the kitchen, drinking coffee with one of the girls. We went straight to the office, did some work and came home. We were together for all that time. We were back here by about five thirty, something like that, and then worked like mad until our guests arrived.'

Fenwick then asked her to describe how she and Jeremy Kemp had discovered Graham's body. She hung her head and briefly covered her face with her hands. When she looked up again, her cheeks were wet. Cooper pushed forward a clean white handkerchief that she took from him with a grateful smile.

'Do you recall how the body looked when you found it?'

'No.' It was barely a whisper.

'When Jeremy Kemp left you, what did you do?'

She shook her head but didn't answer. There were more tears, and Fenwick waited them out.

'Sorry. I'm still finding it hard to talk about. And to be honest, it's all very vague. I can remember the sight of the body, then it's all a blank until Alex came and found me. And later – I don't know – it was just all too much.'

Fenwick pressed her about how the body had been removed from the tree, but she said that she thought Kemp had done it, and if he hadn't done, she had no idea. Under further intense questioning she avoided any comments by effectively claiming amnesia about the crucial time of her wait under the tree.

'Earlier in the evening, Mrs Wainwright-Smith, you'd dismissed the idea that anything could have happened to Graham.'

'Had I? Yes, you're right. It seemed so unlikely, he was so full of life, really carefree. And I never thought that he'd . . . that he could . . . Well, he seemed to enjoy life so much. But perhaps that was all a front. Jenny said that he'd been very worried recently – we should have listened to her.'

'You must have known him well to be so affected by his death.'

'No, I didn't know him at all.' Sally shook her head defiantly. 'We had only just started to become better acquainted in the few weeks since his father's death.'

Despite her tears, the hysteria of the night before and the obvious surprise that he'd known about her conversation with the girls, Sally was clearly in control and at ease. Fenwick debated with himself the merits of challenging her account of the day of Graham's death but decided to let it rest for now. She was likely to be more careless if relaxed. He'd already caught her out in one lie, so she was capable of making a mistake.

When Sally had gone, and he sat alone with Cooper and Shah, he turned to the WPC, deliberately ignoring Cooper, and asked: 'So, what do you make of her?'

Shah was as surprised as Cooper that she'd been consulted, but her reply came instantly.

'I don't trust her and I don't believe her.'

Fenwick didn't react, but looked to Cooper. The sergeant's face radiated disagreement.

'That's harsh, and premature. I don't see how you've decided that so quickly.'

'So what's your view, Cooper?'

'Seemed a sensible lass to me. Good to her husband. Very hard-working. A bit flaky on some of the details from yesterday, but she's obviously confused and upset.'

'Amazing, isn't it? Two completely different views – one from a man's perspective and the other from a woman's.'

'Sir! I gave my opinion as a professional officer, not as a woman.' WPC Shah had flushed in her indignation. 'I object to—'

'Calm down. It wasn't a sexist remark. It's a fact that if you look at all our interviews, none of the women have a good word to say for Sally Wainwright-Smith, while all the men, without exception, admire and want to protect her.'

'But her "poor brave little me" act is so obviously transparent.'

'To you, maybe, but not to her husband, Colin, Jeremy Kemp, or even Sergeant Cooper, for that matter.'

'Hang on, sir. I just gave you my immediate reaction – don't lump me with the others. I hardly know her.'

Fenwick brushed aside Cooper's discomfort with a small laugh. It was rare to see him uncertain and confused.

Cooper felt aggrieved; he didn't welcome being challenged by the DCI in front of Shah.

'So what did you make of her then, sir? I suppose you are immune to her charms.'

The laughter disappeared in an instant from Fenwick's face.

'Yes, I am. I don't have a firm opinion yet, but I think she could be a cunning and potentially manipulative woman who finds lying too easy for us to trust her.

'Now, Constable Shah, I want you to find the box the fruit and veg was delivered in yesterday, and see if you can trace where it came from. Ask Irene which markets were open yesterday that Sally would use. Cooper, you go and interview Julia Wainwright-McAdam. She and Colin were staying overnight. Check with Jenny whether Graham wore jewellery, and if he did, ask her for a description. Then I want photographs of all the house guests last night, and of Graham Wainwright and Neil Yarrell. Oh, and go and see if SOCO has arrived. I want casts taken of those imprints under the tree.'

'What're you going to do with the photos, sir?'

'I'm working on it, but they'll come in handy, I know it. I'm going to take a walk in the grounds until you've finished. I'll be at the car in half an hour.'

He needed time to think before the team briefing at ten. He had to make it clear that this was a murder inquiry without overstating the evidence, or DI Blite would be straight on to the ACC before he could say 'case closed'.

Sally stood at the double front door and watched the three police officers disappear down her long gravel drive. When she turned around, Alexander was standing behind her in the hall.

'There you are! Are you OK?'

Sally nodded and went to lean against him.

'You look terribly pale, Sally, and you've stopped eating properly again, haven't you? I saw you at dinner last night.' What he really wanted to say was that she had started drinking far too much, but he couldn't think how to.

'Don't fuss, Alex, I'm fine. I'll go and have some coffee to help me wake up.' She noticed suddenly that he was dressed for the office.

'You're going to work? But it's Saturday!'

'Well, yes, unless you particularly want me to stay.'

She shook her head, unable to summon the energy or the guile to compete with his constant obsession with work

'No, it's OK. You go. There was something I wanted to talk to you about, though. It's quite urgent.'

She led him outside on to the gravel and around to where his car was parked in the bright spring sunshine. He opened the driver's door and left it wide to allow cool air inside.

'Graham's death has made me think hard, darling, about things I normally try not to dwell on.'

Sally's voice was soft and tired; she sounded worn down, even sad. Alexander squeezed her shoulder reassuringly, then gathered her slight body against his chest, holding her tight. He kissed the top of her hair, relishing the feel of its softness against his cheek. She sighed and relaxed into him.

'I've been thinking about death, how fate can suddenly change all our plans without warning. We need to be more prepared, and I hate to say it, but we have never done anything about drawing up our wills.'

To her surprise, her husband laughed.

'Of course I have. As soon as we got married.'

'But Jeremy . . .' She stopped herself.

'Oh, trust Kemp to be worrying you unnecessarily. I didn't use him; I bought one of those do-it-yourself kits. There was no way I could afford his fees at the time.'

'But a lot's happened since then.' She waved her arm at the house and grounds. 'Shouldn't you update it?'

'I have done, several times, and it's lodged safely at the bank so it won't get lost. You have no need to worry, particularly now that Graham is dead. If I had died first, then our share would have reverted to him but, as it is we now inherit from him. It was a condition of the old man's will.' He tilted her head up so that he could kiss her lightly. 'I've made sure that you'll be all right if anything happens to me, and nothing is going to happen to you. Now, I have to go. I'll try to come home at lunch time to make sure you're OK. Bye!'

Sally watched him drive away, the expression on her face changing from tiredness to fury as soon as he was out of sight. As she stalked back inside, she ripped three long shoots of flowering honeysuckle from the wall, one after another, and shredded them as she walked, scattering flower buds and leaves on the path.

Irene was still on her own in the kitchen. She had started clearing the debris, stacking plates into piles and separating the china, glass and silver, with a depressingly small amount going into the dishwasher. She'd forgotten about the mugs and biscuits on the old pine table, something she'd normally never do.

'How dare you help yourself to my food!'

Irene straightened up from the dishwasher and turned to find Sally, white with anger, pointing a finger at the digestive packet.

'Half the packet has gone! It hadn't been started last night!' Her tone of betrayal would have served equally well had she been accusing Irene of an affair with her husband.

Irene blushed. She knew the rules; they'd been spelled out when Sally had arrived.

'It was for the policemen, miss. They hadn't had breakfast.'

Sally looked at the crumbs that still littered Irene's black leggings and cardigan, and raised her eyebrows in disbelief.

'Don't compound your problems by lying to me, Irene. Never lie to me.'

Irene felt a chill at the back of her neck as she stared into Sally's pale, slanted eyes. Part of her wanted to stick two fingers up and leave her right then to her house and the mess, but the woman scared her, and she was still owed her week's wages. She decided in that moment that after she'd finished this week and picked up her pay, she would give in her notice. Until then she'd best keep her opinions to herself.

'I am sorry, miss. You can take the cost out of my wages and I won't do it again.'

Sally nodded once, checked the price on the wrapper and then deliberately took five biscuits and crammed them into her mouth, one after another, as Irene stared at her in open disbelief.

* * *

In the car on the way back to Harlden, Cooper summarised his interview with Julia.

'Aunt Julia tolerates Alexander but detests his wife. She implied that old Alan Wainwright had an affair with Sally and that she seduced him into changing his will.'

'Any proof?'

'None. It's just like before, when Graham Wainwright came to us with worries about his father's death.'

'And now Graham is dead too. That's three influential and powerful men, all connected with that business, who have died in the last two months.' Fenwick paused, obviously deep in thought. 'Neither Sally nor Alexander's alibi for the morning of Graham's death is watertight. They both have motive, and Sally's reactions last night were bizarre, to put it mildly. I'm going to have tails put on both of them; until we have further evidence to the contrary, they're my prime suspects.'

Cooper regarded his boss with obvious concern.

'That's not going to be popular with the ACC, sir.'

'Tell me about it! But since when have *I* won any popularity contests?' He laughed with a confidence that Cooper could only envy. 'Changing the subject, how's DS Gould getting on with the loose ends on the Fish case?'

'Under pressure. Brighton Division keep telling him that the case closed when Francis Fielding died, so they aren't helping much at all. There's a right SOB down there called Pink who seems to take great pleasure in being as unhelpful as possible.'

'Well, the case isn't closed in my mind. There was a suspiciously large amount of cash in Fielding's flat with no obvious source, so we can't rule out that he was paid to murder Arthur Fish.'

'Conspiracy's always hell to prove, and the ACC won't like it.'

'If these deaths are linked in some way, and if Alan Wainwright's death was murder as well, then this is a very clever conspiracy.'

'Clever and bold, to risk killing Graham within a week of Fish's murder.'

'Bold or desperate. If there's a link, the person behind it has an appetite for risk that's almost suicidal, yet they're smart. Of all the people we have interviewed, does anyone fit that description?'

There was a silence, then Cooper spoke reluctantly.

'Alexander's brighter than he lets on.'

Shah chimed in, encouraged by Fenwick's previous interest in her opinion:

'So is Sally. I think she's the sharper of the two, and we know very little about her.'

'You're both right. Cooper, we must talk to that private investigator Graham hired. And have the local police in Scotland search his house in case there's any information there. We'll need interviews with the staff, too.'

They drove on in silence until they reached Harlden High Street and the inevitable Saturday lunch time traffic jam.

CHAPTER TWENTY-SIX

Harlden had once been a quaint market town. Now, traffic waged a constant battle in a one-way system that had proved to be a planner's delight and a motorist's nightmare. Fenwick dropped Cooper and Shah off on one side of a dual carriageway opposite the station so that he could use the time it took him to crawl towards the car park to think. Strangely, he didn't mind. Pieces of the case were beginning to come together into a vague picture. It wasn't in focus yet, but a shape was emerging and he needed to give it the space to solidify.

The ideas had started when he attempted to fit Sally's behaviour into a logical pattern. No matter how hard he tried, he could not make sense of her erratic mood swings. One minute she was hysterical, the next calm and in control. He decided to leave a message with a psychiatrist the force retained as an adviser, and was surprised when she returned his call immediately. He was negotiating an emergency set of traffic lights, a single lane caused by roadworks and a dysfunctional roundabout, yet remarkably he was still even-tempered when he responded to his mobile.

'Fenwick.'

'Andrew, it's Claire Keating. You rang.'

'Claire! Thanks for getting back to me. Have you got a few minutes? I have a case – well, a person involved in a case – that's perplexing me, and I need your help.'

'Go on, I'm intrigued.' Claire had a voice like honey on a warm day and at that moment it radiated pleasure. Fenwick, though, was in no mood to notice it.

He explained his dilemma about Sally's behaviour, expanding with examples and quotes from her statement. Claire listened without interruption, and when he had finished, there was a long pause before she spoke.

'What you are describing could be dysfunctional behaviour, or it could simply be the symptoms of acute stress or depression. Without meeting her, it's hard to tell.'

'But if it was dysfunctional behaviour, what would be causing it?'

'Mental illness, abuse, personality disorder, or all three. The symptoms are quite vague, but from what you've said, they do sound a little extreme. However, that is a long way from suggesting any form of abnormality or social imbalance.'

'Supposing for a moment that it is more than the result of stress, what might the root cause be?'

'Andrew, I won't base a diagnosis on a hypothesis, you know that.'

'Please?' He sounded so human and in need of help. There was an even longer pause, then:

'I really can't comment on this person Sally, but I can talk about previous experiences, just as long as you understand that this is off the record.'

'Of course.'

'Very well. In an extreme case, it's my experience that violent mood swings, erratic behaviour, obsessions, delusions of grandeur followed by panic and feelings of paranoia could all be symptoms of manic depression, which is treatable with medication.'

'She has pills the doctor has prescribed for depression.'

'Not the same thing at all.'

'Forget I said that. If it weren't manic depression, what else could create the symptoms I've described?'

Fenwick had inched his way around the traffic system until he could see the gates to the station car park in the distance.

'The degree of emotional insecurity that you've described has many causes, but a common one is some form of childhood trauma or abuse.'

Fenwick immediately thought of his own son and his terrible reaction to his mother's illness, and went cold. He had only been four years old when he had witnessed her attempted suicide and Fenwick's desperate efforts at resuscitation. Claire carried on talking, oblivious to the change in his frame of reference.

'A damaged individual can mature, even prosper. Sometimes they live and die without any visible sign of an earlier trauma affecting their lives. However, the latest thinking is that the likelihood of a normal adult life is increasingly rare. Modern-day life is extraordinarily intense. People are bombarded with information, opinions and arguments until reality becomes very subjective. Add to that an incomplete emotional development and a suppressed response to childhood trauma, and you can have a time-bomb in certain people who display an apparently well-adjusted personality that is barely sustainable. There are many people who live behind a carefully constructed façade, to all intents and purposes "normal", whatever that means, but who are actually precariously balanced on a knife edge of control, waiting for life to push them over. It happens all the time, and we call it a mental breakdown. Most recover, but sometimes the psychosis is malignant and they become chronically ill. Andrew, can you hear me? Are you still there?'

'Yes, bear with me, I'm just parking the car.' Fenwick's voice was faint, and he hoped that Claire would put it down to the physical distraction of manoeuvring the car. 'Go on. Could such a person be dangerous?'

'Normally no, only to themselves, but very occasionally the disturbance runs deeper and then matters are different. If there has been a serious trauma – for example the loss of a parent or sibling – left untreated and followed by, say, abuse of some sort, then you can end up with an explosive personality, capable of extreme reactions and unbound by any social conventions, but that's very rare.'

He could barely bring himself to answer her, and when he eventually did so, his voice was a whisper.

148

'Thanks, Claire, that's been very helpful. I'll call you again if anything more develops.'

'No problem. Are you sure you're OK? Look, call me again soon – you have my private number, so you can reach me any time; I'll look forward to it.'

It was several moments before Fenwick could stop his hands shaking. He kept telling himself that it was *Sally* they had just been talking about, not Chris. Chris was a six-year-old kid with a loving father who was determined that what had happened to his mother would never leave the indelible scars that Claire had just described. He swallowed hard and slowly made his way in to the briefing.

CHAPTER TWENTY-SEVEN

'Welcome back.'

'It's good to be back.' Nightingale slung her hold-all on to a scarred corner desk, next to the radiator that rarely worked, and felt that she had come home.

'Good time?'

'I've had better, but it was OK. How've things been here?'

DC Adams brought her up to date in lurid detail, spending more time describing the latest rumoured affair than he did their current case load. The murder of Arthur Fish the previous week interested Nightingale at once.

'Who's working that?'

'Fenwick and Cooper, plus more than a dozen others. DS Gould's on it, so you can ask him, if you dare.'

'What about you?'

'I'm on a sudden death: Graham Wainwright, a hanging that could be anything – murder, accident, suicide. The DCI reckons murder, but DI Blite thinks he's barking. My money's with Blite on accidental death; the guy was in a leather G-string, tackle hanging out all over, surrounded by porno mags when we found him. What would you think?'

'It would depend on the circumstances. Look, why's Fenwick on that one too?'

'Reckons they're linked. Fish worked for Wainwright's, and—'

'Wainwright Enterprises, here in Harlden?'

'Yeah, why?'

'Their MD died earlier this year; suicide, so the coroner said. I was first on the scene.'

Adams shrugged. If she wasn't going to join in a general criticism of the higher-ups, he wasn't interested. She left him to his report and went to find out if she could join the Wainwright case.

'Sir?'

Fenwick raised an impatient eyebrow and stared at Nightingale as she hovered in the doorway to his office. He did not invite her in.

'Yes, Constable, is it urgent? I'm very busy.' He was obviously deep in thought and seemed more than usually tense.

'Could I join the team, sir? On the Wainwright case?'

'Speak to the incident room manager, it's his call. He's organising the resources.' He lowered his head and returned to reading the papers in front of him. She was dismissed.

'Thank you, sir.'

She left his office realising that she'd been stupid to believe their previous working relationship meant anything to Fenwick. Yet her work for him the year before had resulted in a crucial breakthrough; she had even risked her life for him, and this was all the recognition she was granted. Subconsciously she rubbed her left arm, feeling the bump of scar tissue beneath her blouse. She had felt so alive during the months the case had lasted, and so close to Fenwick, that her life had assumed a different shape, one which she still craved.

Their joint search for a serial killer had consumed her completely, so much so that afterwards she had never recovered her relationship with her fiancé. With unwelcome insight, she suddenly realised that she had never wanted to. Shaking her head to dispel the unsettling thoughts, Nightingale went to find the duty officer, only to receive a bollocking for being late and a placement on general duties. An armed raid on a newsagents was reported within minutes and she was on her way.

Fenwick had organised a full briefing for ten and the hum of three dozen voices flowed out to greet him as he opened the door at the top of the stairs. He took his time walking down the corridor. It was one thing to prove to himself that he could still run up the stairs with ease, quite another to arrive pink-faced in front of the team.

Superintendent Quinlan had authorised more resources as soon as Fenwick had told him of his suspicion that they were dealing with a murder. This was the first time he would be briefing them all, and some of them had been drafted in from neighbouring divisions. He was curious to find out what he had been given.

As he entered the room the noise quietened at once. Cooper looked at his boss with grudging admiration. There was an aura of power about the man that simply commanded attention and it was real, not just an act; he doubted Fenwick was even aware of the impact he had on his teams.

As his deputy on this case, Cooper was responsible for coordinating with the office manager running the Wainwright incident room. Fenwick's insistence that the three sudden deaths associated with Wainwright's be considered as potentially linked would complicate the investigation into Graham's death no end, as the teams would have to cross-check all the records constantly and report any aspects that might match, no matter how coincidental.

Fenwick started without preamble, outlining the three deaths so far that year, all connected with Wainwright Enterprises, and his working assumption that they could, in some way, be connected. He described their concerns about Alan Wainwright's suicide, and the lack of proof that had prevented them from taking their investigation further. DS Gould was there, summoned by the DCI to explain the Fish case and the loose ends he was following up despite the death of his murderer, Francis Fielding.

'We still haven't managed to trace the missing tape, number ten. It's not in his office or at home.'

'Keep looking. It holds his last known words and I want to find it no matter what it contains. Any idea yet where Fish went in Brighton?'

'No, sir. None of the prostitutes we've interviewed recognises him.

Enquiries are continuing, but the Brighton team are still working flat out to try and solve their own murders on the same night.'

'It's still an odd coincidence, and I want to be absolutely sure there's no link. Have one of your team take the SOCO and forensic reports from Fish's death and check them against those for the Grey and Bennett murders.'

What he was asking was a huge task and would add another layer of complexity to their enquiries. Cooper saw Gould's shoulders sag slightly but he rallied quickly.

'Yes, sir. Is there any chance of additional resources?'

'Talk to the administrative officer and see what he can do.'

The new team had listened with polite interest as he had outlined the parallel cases, but the attention in the room focused immediately as soon as he started the briefing on Graham Wainwright's death, and the reasons he thought it was murder, despite the inconclusive results of the post mortem. The news caused a ripple of excitement and DI Blite raised his hand in a casual way.

'Yes, Inspector.'

'Will you be appointing an SIO specifically for the Wainwright death then, now that it's a murder? If so, I'd like to volunteer.' His comment could be taken as either constructive or insulting; Fenwick was after all the senior investigating officer on all the cases already. Fenwick chose to interpret it as constructive and replied with studiedly relaxed confidence.

'I'm discussing my proposed strategy with the Superintendent after this briefing and I will be recommending that we appoint an SIO for this latest murder. I'll bear your interest in mind. DS Cooper, carry on with your report of the investigation so far, and the interviews last night.'

Cooper started to speak but as soon as he described the scene of death, he was interrupted by DI Blite.

'How do you get a full-grown, healthy man to stand on a box with a noose around his neck in the first place?'

He was openly sceptical, which infuriated Cooper, given that he had just asked to be given full responsibility for the case. What would the team think now?

'We don't know – yet. Perhaps someone held a gun on him or persuaded him it was a game or a joke.'

'He was over forty years old, hardly the age to indulge in some sort of stupid prank.'

'You never know. He had a taste for young women. Jenny Reynolds is only twenty, and the one before that was apparently a seventeen-year-old model!'

Fenwick listened for a short while as they argued the probability of murder, then intervened.

'Whoever is given the SIO role will need to test rigorously the theory of murder by hanging. It is highly unusual, but given the other evidence so far, it would be dangerous to assume that he wasn't murdered, simply because of the method the killer chose – probably deliberately in an attempt to make us believe that this was an accident or suicide. Let's move on. Sergeant, where have you got to on the fruit and veg box?'

'A result.' Cooper smiled. 'We traced the box to a market stall. The trader remembers the order because it was a large one – took it on his mobile phone, the number's on his van. He definitely didn't deliver, as Sally Wainwright-Smith said he did. He says he was on the stall, and didn't even leave for a pee. The order must have been collected on Friday morning.'

'Can he remember by whom and when?'

Cooper grimaced. 'Not clearly, but he's positive it wasn't Sally Wainwright-Smith. I showed him her photograph and he said he'd have been sure to remember her. He thinks it was a bloke.'

'Have you shown him Graham Wainwright's photo?'

'*Graham*'s? No. I showed him Alexander's. Wasn't him.'

'Go back with Graham's. And did the box go to forensic?'

'Yes. It's smothered with prints, though. It'll take forever to identify and eliminate them.'

'Never mind. Do it anyway. And make sure you check it for the dead man's.'

DI Blite raised his eyebrows at the instruction, but fortunately he was in the front row, so only Fenwick and Cooper could see his expression of open disagreement with the authorisation of manpower to such lengthy task, for what he clearly saw as no good reason.

As soon as the briefing ended, Fenwick went to the Superintendent's office to wait for the call from the ACC. He had asked to be briefed urgently. It was now twenty-four hours since Graham had died, and he was anxious for an early result. The meeting started predictably enough with the ACC challenging the need to continue work on the murder of Arthur Fish. Fenwick defended his actions on the basis that they needed to eliminate any possible connection with the death of Graham Wainwright, and the Superintendent backed him up. The ACC gave in grudgingly but Fenwick knew he was on borrowed time. Harper-Brown had good reason for wanting the broader inquiry closed as it was consuming manpower and forensic resources that were in incredibly short supply.

He listened in attentive silence as Fenwick outlined the basis of their suspicions that Graham Wainwright had been murdered. He wasn't happy with the conclusion but accepted it grudgingly:

'So what's your strategy? Surely your prime suspect is Jenny Reynolds?'

'Well, it's certainly one theory, sir.' Fenwick's tone gave nothing away but he looked at the Superintendent over the top of the speakerphone and shook his head in despair. The ACC was speaking again.

'Look, I have to go to another meeting. Who are you going to appoint as SIO, Superintendent?'

Fenwick and Quinlan had discussed this before calling Harper-Brown. Fenwick knew that he needed a senior officer dedicated to investigating Graham's murder, but he wanted to remain in overall charge of all the Wainwright investigations. The Superintendent had agreed – he had absolute confidence in Fenwick and trusted his judgement – but he wanted to keep the team as local as possible, and the only senior officer available was DI Blite. Fenwick had reluctantly accepted that Blite would become SIO, but reporting to him.

'Our recommendation is that we appoint DI Blite . . .'

'Good.'

'. . . Reporting to Chief Inspector Fenwick, who will retain overall responsibility for all the cases associated with Wainwright's.'

There was a silence in which Fenwick imagined the ACC searching for arguments as to why this was inappropriate, but there were no easy ones, and after a pause he said, irritably, 'Very well, but I don't want this connections thing overplayed. Try and keep it simple and for God's sake don't give any hint of it to the press.'

Blite was delighted with his appointment, despite having to report to Fenwick instead of direct to the Superintendent. As they planned out their tactics for handling the case together, Blite returned to his point that hanging was a very unusual method for murder. Fenwick agreed. They would both study the post-mortem report carefully when it eventually arrived, and their researcher would check HOLMES for any similar cases.

'There's a lot to do, Inspector, and I'll help out.' Fenwick wanted to keep close to the case, particularly as Blite would be susceptible to any hints for quick closure that the ACC would inevitably throw his way. 'Any aspect you'd like me to focus on?'

Blite couldn't turn down the offer; he was to report to Fenwick and he wanted to make rapid progress.

'My team will focus on the interviews, forensic and SOC reports; testing the feasibility of the cause of death; tracing the investigator; liaison with Scotland; talking to Kemp about the uncle's will; and the press briefing. It would be helpful if you could interview Graham's new solicitor and obtain a search warrant for Wainwright Hall and grounds.'

Inevitably he had passed the sensitive and tedious parts of the case over, but Fenwick had expected nothing more. They agreed to reconvene at six.

Fenwick and Cooper teamed up to interview Mr Sacks, the dead man's solicitor. Unlike many law firms, Sacks' practice was open for business on Saturdays until noon. Fenwick was curious to discover why Graham had chosen a local firm, given that he seemed to have divided his time between London and Scotland since his father's death.

Mr Sacks was an elegant man who had obviously spent a fortune with his tailor in a not altogether successful attempt to disguise his weight problem. He showed Fenwick and Cooper into a modern, sparsely furnished office and promptly seated them around an expensive maplewood table. The immaculate, softly burnished top made Cooper reluctant to put even an elbow on it, let alone his notebook.

There was some preliminary skirmishing as Sacks sought to avoid revealing any details of Graham Wainwright's affairs. This stopped abruptly as soon as he realised that Fenwick was prepared to go to the courts if necessary. He buzzed for his assistant, who arrived moments later with the files – one bound in a soft calf-hide folder and two box files bursting with papers.

'Graham and I were at school together, so when he decided to replace Kemp and Kemp, he called me to suggest that he became a client of ours. We started acting for Mr Wainwright in March, shortly after his father died and he inherited a considerable part of his estate.'

'But not as much as he'd been hoping for.'

Sacks looked shocked at such a crude observation coming from the lips of a senior police officer.

'I really couldn't comment.'

'Did he ask you to consider pursuing the Wainwright-Smiths for the other half of the legacy?'

The solicitor opened the slender leather wallet with long dry fingers and flicked to some notes right at the back. A brief look of concern crossed his face but disappeared quickly.

'Initially, yes, but he changed his mind later.'

'Why?'

'I have no idea. He simply dropped the matter.'

'And what about the terms of Graham Wainwright's own will?'

'He didn't make one – he died intestate. I doubt he expected to die quite so soon, Chief Inspector.'

No will. It was another reason to doubt that his death was suicide. Surely, after inheriting so much, he would have put his affairs in order before killing himself.

Sacks continued speaking, oblivious to Fenwick's preoccupation.

'My dealings with Mr Wainwright were restricted to some investigation of title. As you will see, this is a very slender file.'

'And the others?' Fenwick pointed to the tatty box files.

'From Kemp and Kemp. We did nothing with them. In fact they arrived only a week before Mr Wainright's untimely death. My client had been extremely keen that we obtain them. It was most irregular. They were not, after all, Mr Wainwright's property but he was insistent and so we progressed the matter. Jeremy Kemp was very helpful, although it did take some time for them to arrive.'

'I see. Mr Sacks, I wonder if we might trouble you for some coffee?'

'Really? Are you going to be here that much longer?'

'Some time, yes.'

Cooper looked down to hide his surprise. He had thought that they were finished. The buzzer was employed again and Sacks' assistant diligently took an order for coffee. It arrived moments later: three cups already poured, and a tiny jug of cream which was placed delicately by the sugar. Fenwick added sugar and cream to his coffee until the cup was virtually overflowing. Then he made a show of pulling out papers from his leather folio, something Cooper had never seen him do before. He was clearly having difficulty finding a particular article, and Cooper watched in horror as notes, files, even a folded umbrella were dumped unceremoniously on the virgin maple. Every time something new was added to the growing pile Sacks winced. When a small stapler landed and fell over on to its side Cooper had to stop his own hand from darting out to catch it.

'Ah, there it is.' Fenwick appeared oblivious to the solicitor's growing horror. 'Now, do you know any of these people?'

He pushed a plastic folder of photographs aggressively across the table but somehow his aim was off. Instead of reaching Sacks, it slid rapidly towards Fenwick's brimming coffee cup. A corner of the folder caught under the edge of his saucer at full speed and knocked the cup over. Sacks watched in horror as dark brown liquid spilled out over the tabletop in a long trickle, heading towards the edge and the perfect beige rug below.

'Look what you've done!'

'I'm so sorry. Here, let me help.' Fenwick pulled out some paper tissues and thrust them at Sacks. He did it in such a rush that he caught the top of the milk jug and it tipped into the sugar bowl, which promptly upended. Now sticky demerara sugar joined the brown spill and started to dissolve.

'You idiot!' Sacks was furious. He stared for one further horrified second at the disaster that was already ruining his table and threatening his extravagant rug, and then darted for the door.

As soon as he was gone, all trace of the clumsy buffoon left Fenwick and he moved nimbly around to the leatherbound file and flicked through its pages.

'Sir!'

'Never mind. Go and keep an eye out in the corridor. Tell me when he's coming back.' He continued to check the pages rapidly, occasionally pausing for a few seconds to skim their contents.

'Coming!'

When Sacks and his assistant returned, they found Fenwick and his tissues desperately mopping at drips as they ran over the edge of the table. Cloths and a sponge were deployed rapidly, and it looked as though disaster had been averted by the narrowest of margins. The file of photographs, though, was ruined.

'I am sorry. Look, we'll come back some other time to go through the photos.'

Sacks could barely bring himself to bid a civil goodbye to Fenwick, and Cooper left quickly, purple with suppressed indignation and embarrassment. He said nothing until they were in Fenwick's car and the Chief Inspector was driving smoothly back to Harlden police station.

'We had no warrant.'

'Indeed not.'

'We had no powers of search.'

'Did I search? I don't recall searching.'

'But, sir!'

'But nothing. All I did was take a little look at papers he'd left open on the table. If they had been at all sensitive, a solicitor like Sacks would have taken them with him.'

Cooper subsided into censorious silence and Fenwick continued driving. They were almost at the station before Cooper's curiosity finally vanquished his principles.

'Anything interesting?'

Fenwick hid the smallest of smiles in the turn of his head as he pulled into the car park.

'Yes, very. Come on, we'll discuss it in my office.'

Fenwick waved a hand in the general direction of the duty sergeant, who buzzed them through the electronically locked door that separated the public and private areas of the station. He took the stairs two at a time, leaving Cooper way behind. When he was certain his sergeant was out of sight, he paused and rubbed his right knee, wincing as he touched the tender joint. Then he walked up the rest of the flight and had comfortably regained his breath by the time Cooper puffed into his office.

'Who would you say was the most reliable – and open – solicitor we know?'

Cooper was breathing heavily and glad of the pause for thought that the question gave him.

'Hmmm, tricky.' He scratched his head and eased himself into the bone-hard visitor's chair. 'Cook? He's a bit of a bugger, but he's all right.'

'Good idea. Pass me that phone directory, there, behind you.'

The call was answered within three rings, and Cooper could hear the distinctive Scots voice booming from the receiver.

'Andrew. Long time. What can I do for you?'

'I need some help, Richard, from someone with insight into our local legal firms.'

'Intriguing – go on.'

'What can you tell me about a certain Mr Sacks?'

'Relatively new, expensive and bloody arrogant. A piece of work. *Very* smart and very prickly. Not someone to get on the wrong side of.'

'Ah.' Fenwick's tone said it all.

'Too late, huh? Never mind. You'll survive. Was that it?'

'No, there is one other thing. Kemp and Kemp: what's the word about them?'

There was a long pause.

'That's a little more tricky,' Cook said at last. 'Are we on the record?'

'Certainly not.'

'And you're not on your mobile?'

'No, I'm in the office and there's no tape running. Go on, you've made me curious.'

'Why do you want to know?'

'The firm was acting for a couple of people who've died rather unexpectedly since the start of the year, and we have our suspicions over at least one of the deaths.'

'Ah, that would be the Wainwrights. Interesting.' Cook had no expectation of Fenwick either confirming or denying his supposition, so he simply carried on. 'Well, what can I tell you? And before I do, be sure that I'll never say any of this publicly. Let's see, there are one or two rumours about Kemp and Kemp – well, about their esteemed client Wainwright Enterprises, really. Nothing certain, just an odd smell.'

'What sort of smell?'

'The smell of funny money. Kemp's have been the legal advisers to Wainwright Enterprises for as long as anybody can remember, as well as the family's solicitors. Wainwright's is a strange firm, constantly prosperous; in good times and bad it just keeps on bringing in the profits.'

'Would you take on an ex-client of theirs – say, a member of the Wainwright family?'

'Probably not.' He paused. 'No, scrub that, definitely not.'

157

'That's very helpful, thanks, Richard.'

'No problem. Oh, there's one more thing. Again just a rumour, but the word at the golf club is that Kemp has been fishing off limits, dangling his tackle in waters outside the home pond. Seen in odd places and at odd times with someone not obviously resembling his wife.'

'I see. Any idea who?'

'None at all, not my scene, but James FitzGerald might be able to help you. He runs FitzGerald Financial Advisers in the High Street and sometimes hangs around with Kemp and the people from Wainwright's.'

As Fenwick replaced the receiver thoughtfully, Cooper looked at him with renewed respect.

'What put you on to Kemp?'

'Sacks' face when he flicked through that prissy neat file of his. He saw something in there that he'd rather not have brought into the room with him. There he was, displaying those papers, showing that he and his firm had nothing to hide, and then he suddenly realised they did have. It was written all over his face. I was curious to find out what it was.'

'So you meant to spill that coffee, then!'

'Cooper!' Fenwick feigned hurt surprise and then grinned conspiratorially. 'So what did you find out?'

'A memo from Sacks to the other partners advising them that Graham Wainwright had asked to become a client. There was an estimate of the likely fees – over fifteen thousand pounds – but then a line that went something like: "Given the family history of this client and the nature of the ceding firm, I suggest that we discuss this opportunity at the next partners' meeting, on the sixteenth." I suspect if he hadn't known Graham or that the firm hadn't been new and in need of a prestigious local name, they might have turned Graham away – and that's very interesting indeed.'

FitzGerald Financial Advisers was located in the middle of the High Street in elegant and expensive premises. There was a discreet counter towards the back where routine business was conducted, in front of which there were two businesslike desks and chairs spaced well apart.

An eagle-eyed receptionist behind the counter gave Fenwick a winning smile as he walked in.

'We'd like to see Mr FitzGerald. I'm DCI Fenwick and this is DS Cooper, Harlden CID.' He showed his warrant card and spoke quietly, not wishing to alarm any potential clients.

'Mr FitzGerald is on the phone to a client at the moment, but I'll let him know you're here. What may I say it's regarding?'

'It's a police matter.'

Fenwick watched as she stepped into an office in the corner behind the ashwood barrier. As he waited, he watched a smart young man's attempt to persuade two very sceptical people of the value of life assurance and a pension. He doubted he'd have much luck there.

'Chief Inspector Fenwick, Sergeant Cooper.' The receptionist's soft voice called him into the office.

James FitzGerald sat comfortably behind a battered oak desk that looked unpretentious and lived-in – rather like its owner. He had three telephones, one of which was housed in a unit nearly a foot long filled with preprogrammed numbers. It resembled a mini-switchboard, and as they walked in, FitzGerald was in the act of angling it so that his visitors couldn't read the names alongside the dialling buttons. He was tall and thin, with stooped shoulders, but his handshake was surprisingly firm.

Fenwick took a moment to judge the man and decided on a direct approach. He explained that they were investigating at least one murder and several suspicious deaths, and watched the man's expression change from shock to scarcely concealed concern. When he mentioned the connection with Wainwright Enterprises, though, the concern disappeared, to be replaced with caution.

'What's all that got to do with me?'

'Kemp and Kemp are the legal advisers to Wainwright Enterprises.'

It was a straightforward enough remark, but it had a significant effect on FitzGerald. He shifted in his seat and ran a finger around the inside of his shirt collar, as if his tie had suddenly become too tight. He drew his mouth into a thin, hard line.

'I still don't see why you need to talk to me.'

'I understand that you might be able to give us some background information on Kemp's.'

'I hardly know them; they're not our solicitors. You've come to the wrong man, Chief Inspector.'

'Word on the street says I've come to the right man.'

FitzGerald's lean face flushed from white to deep red and he opened his mouth to argue, exposing sharp white teeth. Then, in an instant, the anger evaporated and he burst out laughing. To Fenwick's practised ear it had the clear ring of artificiality.

'All right, all right. If I get on my high horse you'll only go all heavy on me. I'd love to know who fingered me for this, but I'm sure you won't tell. "Word on the street" – oh, please!' He laughed again and settled back comfortably in his chair, lifting a leg to rest a highly polished shoe against an open drawer.

'What is it you think I can tell you?'

'I'm trying to find out what sort of firm they are.'

'Well, that's straightforward enough. You could ask them that yourselves.'

'Anything unusual about them?'

'Nothing that I'm aware of.'

'No rumours of shady dealings or anything like that?'

'Nothing.'

'So why was I told that you'd be a good source of gossip?'

FitzGerald laughed again. 'Oh, that's old news. Kemp had an affair with my first wife, but that was years ago. As I said, you've come to the wrong man.'

There was an unmistakable ring of finality about the remark. Fenwick said a quick goodbye and left with Cooper.

As soon as he was sure the policemen had left his office, James FitzGerald picked up his phone and pressed a pre-set number.

'It's me. We need to meet. No, not here. The club . . . No, right away. We have a problem.'

'He was lying!'

Back at the station, Fenwick and Cooper were reviewing their day before going to the evening briefing. Cooper was astonished at how relaxed the Chief Inspector appeared to be about their meeting with FitzGerald.

'Of course he was. What's interesting is why. What makes a man like FitzGerald risk lying to the police? Did you see his phone? He had Kemp's number on automatic dial, and Wainwright's. And that story about his first wife!'

'I don't understand why you're so calm.'

'It's our first real break in this case. He's lying, which means there's something he thinks is worth lying about. I want you to run a full background check on him. Also, we need to interview Mrs Kemp again and find out more about her husband. Wainwright's is watertight so far; we need to find weak links outside. We need a tight team working these connections – you and one other officer.'

'Who'll I get to do all this? You've assigned everyone that came free on to the Graham Wainwright case. I've got no oppos left.'

'Talk to the admin manager.'

The briefing was a short one. Blite had traced Graham's private investigator but had found out very little more. The man's inquiries into Sally Wainwright-Smith's background had revealed nothing other than the fact that she had changed her name at some point, and before he could do more work on her, Graham had told him to focus on Wainwright Enterprises. He had done a little digging, found out the names behind the shareholding trusts and was then paid off. The post-mortem report on Graham had still not arrived, but Fenwick had obtained a search warrant for Wainwright Hall and grounds. Now that Fenwick's name was firmly on the warrant application, Blite had no hesitation in taking back the responsibility for the search.

'Have you made any progress with stress-testing hanging as a possible method of killing?'

Fenwick was keen to make sure that they would be able to defend such an unusual approach when the case came to court.

'Sure, it could be done.' Blite sounded dismissive, as if the answer should have been obvious after all, despite his previous scepticism. 'And there's a case on HOLMES looks very similar.'

'Good. That's a relief.'

Fenwick asked Blite to chase up the post-mortem – it was vital to the investigation and would slow it down if it were further delayed.

Later that afternoon, he was attempting to bring order to his desk when the phone rang. It was Superintendent Quinlan asking him to stop by his office.

'Ah, Chief Inspector. I was just talking about you.' Superintendent Quinlan peered at Fenwick over the top of his half-moon glasses. 'The ACC's becoming anxious again. Apparently some of your team have been turning up at local clubs and asking the wrong sort of questions regarding certain members. Messrs Kemp, FitzGerald and Wainwright-Smith to be precise.'

'Good. It's about time.'

'Not good. The ACC also happens to be a member of some of these clubs, and he's been receiving complaints. He has also had fresh doubts raised in his mind by somebody, and I don't know who, about the nature of your central theory that Wainwright's and the Wainwright family lie at the heart of it all. He is not a happy man.'

Fenwick brought Superintendent Quinlan up to date with the day's developments and confirmed that he still believed the cases to be connected. Quinlan listened thoughtfully and didn't contradict Fenwick, but he was clearly concerned.

'It's all very tenuous. It would be far simpler to close the Fish case now that the killer is dead. Forensics have proven that his flick knife is the murder weapon, and you have had witness after witness confirm that he was the man they saw on the train.'

'But why did he murder Fish after following him from Harlden to Brighton and back?'

'A man like that, dealing in drugs, mixing with violent associates, it's hardly a surprising crime.'

'Perhaps not, yet there are several reports of him flashing wads of cash around on the night before he died, which is completely consistent with my theory that he was paid to kill Fish.'

'I'll give you one more week with the full team, but after that, if you have nothing more, you'll have to leave Fielding's death to Brighton and simply focus on Graham Wainwright. Don't argue, Chief Inspector, just one more week.'

If the Superintendent was being this direct so early in the Graham Wainwright case, then he must be under intense pressure. Fenwick sighed and shrugged his understanding if not his agreement.

'We will focus, sir, but *please* allow me the freedom to continue to ask questions, even if it is in the wrong places.'

Quinlan looked worried. 'This is a sensitive time. The Police Authority meets on the ninth. I'll do what I can. In the meantime, you need to keep both me and Harper-Brown fully briefed.'

Fenwick had returned briefly to his desk to collect some papers he was going to take home to study when the phone rang. It was five o'clock, and he had already told the children that he would be home by half past.

'Yes?'

'Duty sergeant, sir. Sorry to trouble you, but I've got a Miss Wilson down here wanting to make a statement in connection with Fish's murder.'

'Have someone from the incident room take it, then.'

'There's no one there, sir. Sergeants Cooper and Gould are out, and DS Rike went home ill a short while ago.'

DS Rike was the office manager, responsible for the running of the incident room. Fenwick's rare temper exploded.

'What is the point of having an incident room if it's not manned, Sergeant? There's no excuse; it's here in the bloody station, for . . . heaven's sake. Call

Adams and have him send someone there right now. And put this woman in an interview room. I'll come down.'

He was the senior detective on the case, and to be required to take a statement like this betrayed an inefficiency in the team which worried him intensely. It could be symptomatic of a deeper problem. He thought immediately of Cooper, and had the operations centre patch him through to his sergeant's radio.

'Cooper! There is nobody here manning the incident room. What the hell is going on?'

'Rike should be there, sir.' Fenwick could hear his sergeant's discomfort and was glad.

'Well, he isn't, and since when do we have a single officer manning the phones in a multiple murder inquiry?'

Cooper could have pointed out that Fish's murder had virtually been solved with the death of Francis Fielding, and that Fenwick had started so many lines of inquiry that DS Rike was finding it impossible to cope. He *could* have said all that, but what Fenwick heard was:

'I'm sorry, sir. It won't happen again. I think we need to replace Sergeant Rike, sir. He's been under the weather and struggling to cope.'

'Do it then, Cooper. Talk to the duty sergeant and have that room properly staffed by the time I return from having to take a routine witness statement!'

Miss Wilson had been shown into one of the ground-floor interview rooms. Fenwick guessed her age to be mid forties. She was smartly dressed, well spoken and was accompanied by an obedient Highland terrier on a tartan lead.

'Miss Wilson, I'm sorry to have kept you. Detective Chief Inspector Fenwick. I'm in charge of the investigation into the death of Mr Arthur Fish.'

She extended a sensibly manicured hand for Fenwick to shake, and he caught a faint trace of a lemony eau-de-Cologne. Miss Wilson was exactly the sort of witness juries and judges loved, and he hoped, against the odds, that she had something significant to say.

'Firstly, Chief Inspector, I must apologise for not coming forward sooner. I have spent the last few days sailing with my sister and her husband and had no idea about the murder.' He waved aside her apology and she continued. 'I caught the six-seventeen train from Harlden on Thursday the twentieth of April and distinctly remember seeing Mr Fish. There were three young girls in the same carriage, very badly behaved, and they tormented the poor man all the way down to Brighton.

'Just before we left Harlden station, a young man clambered on board. I remember, because he pushed past me to board the train, and tripped over Hector here and swore at me.'

'Would you recognise him again?'

'I think so. He had very distinctive eyes.'

Fenwick pulled out bundles of photographs, including one of a sneering Francis Fielding and showed them to her. She pointed to the one of Fielding without hesitation.

'Yes, that's him, I'm positive.' Fenwick felt a surge of adrenaline. 'Is he the murderer, then?' Miss Wilson sounded surprised.

'We believe so. Why?'

'Well, it's odd really, because I saw him meet his girlfriend in Brighton and I assumed they had spent the evening together down there.'

This was entirely new. They had had no idea of what Fielding had done whilst waiting for the return train. He urged Miss Wilson to continue.

'I was first off the train at Brighton, as I was in a hurry to catch a bus to my sister's. Anyway, I missed it, and as I was walking back to queue for a taxi, I saw Mr Fish on the opposite side of the street. That man in your photograph was walking behind him, and I'm sure that he was with a woman.'

'Can you describe her?'

'Not really. I paid little attention, and there was traffic passing between us. Blonde and slim is all I recall.'

'And afterwards?'

'Nothing further, I'm afraid. I took a taxi to my sister's after a long wait, and we caught the morning tide.'

Fenwick thanked her and assured her that the information was useful, then asked a constable to take her statement. Within minutes of returning to his office, he was on the phone to DS Gould.

'We have a witness who saw Fielding leave Brighton station with a woman – blonde and slim is all we have on her. Have someone redo all the interviews at Brighton station and trace taxi-drivers working that evening. Also put up a poster by the cab rank, appealing for witnesses to come forward. There was a wait for taxis that evening and somebody may have seen Fielding and this woman meet or leave.'

He replaced the receiver, all trace of the gloom that had descended after his meeting with Superintendent Quinlan evaporated, leaving him determined and optimistic once more. There was more evidence out there; he just had to find it. The last of his files was packed quickly and he made his way home in the hope of seeing his children before they were asleep.

CHAPTER TWENTY-EIGHT

The next morning, Cooper saw the administration manager and asked for yet more officers for the case. Two had been found at short notice the night before, but he needed another. When Nightingale's name came up, he grunted in a noncommittal way and nodded, but the secret pleasure he felt at having the lass on one of his cases again went some way to compensate him for declining a cooked breakfast that morning.

Nightingale couldn't believe her good fortune. She was summoned unceremoniously and told to find Cooper in the incident room. He was there with DS Gould and DI Blite. They glanced up as she entered, registered her age and rank and then returned to their conversation. She sighed inwardly with relief. It was so good simply to be ignored.

The team began to gather for the first of the day's briefings. It was a Sunday but there were few long faces. Fenwick arrived just before nine o'clock.

'Good, you're all here. I want to review progress on each case, starting with Arthur Fish's murder. Have we made any headway on where he went when he left the station?'

DS Gould shook his head.

'How's the team getting on interviewing prostitutes? We know Fish was into kinky sex. That must make it easier.'

'Yes, but that's not so unusual. Believe me, most of the girls – and boys too, for that matter – are willing to indulge their clients in a little S and M – as long as it's not too rough.'

'But what about the baby lotion and talc – that can't be as common.'

The detective shrugged and Nightingale opened her mouth to speak, but then thought better of it. She had to learn not to be smart in every meeting. Fenwick, though, had spotted her.

'Something to say, Nightingale?'

She thought fast. She could recall the crime scene – the costumes in the closet, the galvanised bath, the nanny's apron with its bottle of baby lotion.

'Come on.'

'When did Fish die, sir?'

'April the twentieth.'

'There was a murder of a prostitute on that night. I attended it.'

'We know about that, but the detective in charge said there was no connection. If you disagree, we'll talk afterwards. Right, I think we need to re-interview Fish's wife.'

DS Gould was already struggling to cope with the new demands in Brighton.

'She's virtually comatose, sir.'

'Just the same . . . I'll do it if you're too busy.'

DI Blite had chosen to sit at the back of the room for the briefing, and during the whole of DS Gould's report he had been engaged in a whispered conversation with one of the sergeants on his team. It was an obvious signal that he felt the cases were completely unconnected. He perked up, though, when Fenwick called him up to the front to update the team. Inspector Blite finally had some good news to report and he was going to enjoy the moment, conveniently forgetting that the detective work that had led to this particular break-through had been at Fenwick's instigation, not his own.

The dead man's fingerprints had been found on the fruit and veg box, together with Sally Wainwright-Smith's, and the market stallholder identified him as the man who picked up the delivery.

'This could implicate Mrs Wainwright-Smith even more – and she has a very weak alibi, unlike Jenny Reynolds. We have a confirmed sighting of her on the train from Scotland on Friday morning.' Fenwick had shared his suspicions of Sally Wainwright-Smith only with Blite, as he had wanted the team to remain objective. Suddenly Blite was preparing to share them and he felt it was too early. He changed the subject.

'Anything new in the full post-mortem report?'

'We haven't had it yet, sir.' Blite's tone of defensive sarcasm revealed how embarrassed he was by his failure to cajole the report from the pathologist.

'That's completely unacceptable. I'll call Pendlebury myself and get it for you today.'

Blite nodded, relieved that Fenwick's actions would distance him from a potentially sensitive situation. He had called Dr Pendlebury's office less than half an hour before, and his finely tuned nose for political problems had caught a strong whiff of something far nastier even than the odours originating from the autopsy room.

After the meeting, Gould, Nightingale and Cooper stayed behind with Fenwick. Now that they were a smaller group, Nightingale relaxed and told it straight.

'On the twentieth of April, at around nine o'clock, Amanda Bennett's neighbours heard sounds of a struggle and breaking glass.'

'Fish wasn't the murderer, then; he was on his train back to Harlden by then.'

'No, sir but he might have visited her beforehand. You see, her house was full of costumes, whips, chains—'

DS Gould interrupted. 'Our boy was into gentle caning and having his bottom kissed better afterwards, Nightingale, not that sort of stuff.'

Nightingale blushed a deep red. 'I know, sir, but I think Bennett was really versatile, she didn't just do the hard stuff. In her cupboards we found a birch, baby lotion and talc. I know that it's not conclusive, but it could be a link.'

'I agree, we can't ignore it.' DS Gould was regretting his earlier sarcasm. 'I'll have forensic compare the traces of wood we recovered from the body with the birch at her house. If there's a match we'll do a full composition of trace evidence.'

Fenwick agreed. 'We've got a busy day ahead of us, but I sense we're reaching a turning point, at least in the Fish case. Cooper, you and Nightingale go and see Kemp's wife. Find out if there's any truth in the rumour that Kemp was having an affair. Then see the other girl up at Wainwright Hall, Shirley Kennedy, and get her account of Thursday. I need to talk to Fish's wife. And we must continue digging into Sally's background. But first I'm going to chase Pendlebury for that report. I don't know what's got into the man lately.'

The post-mortem report had been promised faithfully by Pendlebury for the previous day, but he had been taken ill and rushed to hospital, and no one else in his office would now sign it.

Fenwick called the pathologist's office number and was advised that Pendlebury had now returned home from his brief spell in hospital, and would the Chief Inspector like to visit him at his earliest convenience. Fenwick left at once.

He found the pathologist sitting in an upholstered chair in a conservatory full of exotic plants, his feet resting on a wicker stool. He winced with pain when he moved to shake hands, and the sight prompted Fenwick to be more direct than he usually was.

'What's wrong with you? Why did they admit you to hospital yesterday?'

'It was a bit embarrassing. I collapsed at work. Caused quite a stir.' He couldn't have been more off-hand, but it didn't deflect Fenwick.

'And . . .?'

'I've got a growth on the base of my spine. I've known for some time it was more than sciatica. It was bloody agony yesterday, and standing over the table just makes it worse. It's not cancer, thank God, but I will have to have an operation. Not without its risks.'

'Why aren't you in hospital now?'

'Discharged myself. The operation's not due until Wednesday and I can't stand lying around with a bunch of sick people, hearing their war stories. Soon as they know you're a doctor, you become a prisoner in your own bed. I'll go in Tuesday, that'll be time enough.'

'Why did you want to see me?'

'The Wainwright post-mortem examination.' He paused, obviously very uncomfortable with what he had to say next. 'I cocked it up, Andrew. I'm sorry, but I made a complete idiot of myself over it.'

'Tell me how.' Fenwick's voice adopted the neutrality that it always did when he was struggling to keep his emotions under control. A faulty post-mortem was very serious. It could jeopardise his investigation and potentially be a gift for the defence in court.

'I was feeling terrible. I'd had a couple of painkillers but they didn't have any effect. I'm fairly certain that my external examination of the body was sound.' He tapped a folder on a table next to his chair, and Fenwick realised it was the long-awaited report. 'I've reread my notes and had my deputy check the whole thing, and that part of the PM's all right. It's from the dissection onwards that I had a problem.

'Cause of death was obviously asphyxia, but it wasn't by hanging as I thought; it was ligature strangulation. He was strangled with that rope and then strung up to make it look like hanging. I'm sorry, Andrew. It'll never happen again. I shouldn't have been working yesterday.'

'How can you be so sure it was strangulation? You said that the post-mortem lividity supported hanging as a cause of death.'

'It does. The lividity was pronounced in his extremities: hands, fingers, legs and feet, with no pressure points. He must have been strung up immediately after he died, or perhaps even as he lost consciousness. And I am sure. In cases of homicidal strangulation, the murderer usually exerts too much force, which causes a fracture of the hyoid. In a suicide or accidental strangulation, it almost never happens.'

'And Graham Wainwright's hyoid was fractured.'

'Yes. And there's one other thing.'

'Go on.'

'There were traces of a barbiturate in Wainwright's body. The toxicology reports came through first thing. On the morning he died he had had a hundred and forty milligrams of Nembutal, washed down with a large whisky. Normally that wouldn't be enough to kill an adult male, even mixed with alcohol, but it would certainly sedate him.'

'Would it work quickly?'

'Fairly. If it's taken orally – and there are no signs of needle marks on the body; I've had my deputy check – it's absorbed through the small intestine. And if he'd been given, say, Rohypnol he'd be compliant and easily manipulated. Trouble is, there won't be a trace of that now.'

'So his killer could have administered the drug, waited for it to take effect and then strangled him whilst he was heavily sedated.'

'Exactly. I've asked Roy Maitland, my deputy, to redo the post-mortem. He's at your disposal any time today. You don't need to worry that the original PM will compromise the results, thank God. He says that the organs and all the samples are intact and uncontaminated. I didn't botch any of the mechanics, just my analysis of them.'

Pendlebury looked out from underneath his shaggy eyebrows. He knew that what he had to tell Fenwick next would confirm how inept he had been in his internal examination.

'I missed the signs in all the internal organs – I could barely focus my eyes by the time we had got that far – but they are there, in the lungs, brain and liver. It's a clear case of murder now, Chief Inspector.'

CHAPTER TWENTY-NINE

The Kemp residence was set back from a quiet wooded road on the outskirts of a village four miles from Harlden. Tall wrought-iron gates stood open at the bottom of a drive that curved away behind a glorious stand of beech and maple.

'Looks like he's done all right for himself.'

Nightingale nodded and said nothing, memories of her own home firmly pushed to a remote corner of her mind. There was little in them to be nostalgic about and enough legacy of unpleasantness for her to avoid them.

The drive curved through woodland, and as it thinned, a delightful Queen Anne house was revealed on a gentle rise of land.

'Smaller than I thought it'd be after those gates.' Cooper grinned.

'But original,' said Nightingale before she could stop herself.

'What?'

'It's the real thing. It may not be big, but believe me, it's worth a pretty penny.'

'How can you tell?'

What to do? How to avoid the remarks that would reveal too much and unfairly mark her as an affected upper-class snob? She decided to lie.

'We did a project at school. It's one of those things like, I don't know, recognising a real wood table from veneer. We were taught to look for that mellow richness in the bricks; the windows are just right, and the pitch of the roof – all the little details.'

'Hmph.' Cooper swung the car around in front of the house.

There was a bell pull to one side of the door, antique and delicate. Cooper yanked it and Nightingale winced. Murial Kemp recognised the sergeant at once and blanched.

'Mrs Kemp?'

'Yes.' Her hand fluttered to her face and hovered near her open mouth.

What's she so scared of? wondered Nightingale, and observed even more intently.

'I'm DS Cooper, Harlden CID. Could we come in, please?' He extended his warrant card for inspection, but she barely looked at it.

'Yes, I remember you, but what's it all about? Is Jeremy all right? I mean . . . Yes, of course, come in.'

She's petrified, thought Nightingale.

'Thank you. This is DC Nightingale, and, so far as I'm aware, Mr Kemp is fine. It's you we want to see.'

Rapid blinking, a tremor in her hand as the door was closed behind them, then she rallied.

'I'm not really sure I can help you, Sergeant. I suspect it's my husband you need to talk to.'

'No, it's you.'

Again the hands gave her away as she led them into the drawing room. It was cold in here, and Nightingale watched with nostalgic amusement as their breath misted faintly in the chill, still air.

'So, what do you want with me, Sergeant?'

'As you know, we are investigating the sudden death of Graham Wainwright . . .'

Cooper's voice droned on. He was giving the woman a neat précis of the case, but he wasn't getting anywhere. Nightingale could see her regaining her strength and with it the anger to protest. Once she did that, they would have the devil of a job breaking her guard. She recognised this type of woman from her mother's coffee mornings when she had been at home during those long, bleak school holidays.

Mrs Kemp was pleasant, kind, probably generous too, but something of a snob. She had ended up in a house and with a standard of living much better than she'd ever expected. Consequently she was bedevilled by doubts as to whether she deserved it, was living up to it and, above all, whether she had the right style. Even her voice was uncertain, her accent modulating between perfectly well-spoken middle English and an attempt at what she clearly thought was county. It was sad, but it was also a weakness Nightingale could exploit. All she had to do was use what she thought of as her school voice, which was terribly, frightfully correct.

'Mrs Kemp, I'm so sorry to interrupt, but I have the most terrible headache and I wondered whether we might trouble you for some tea. Would it be an awful bother?'

Both Sergeant Cooper and Mrs Kemp's jaws fell open at exactly the same time. Nightingale effected what she hoped was a brave little smile. Mrs Kemp reacted as if programmed to the request and left the room.

'Trust me, sir,' Nightingale said in her normal speaking voice. 'We'll get far more out of her my way.'

Cooper hesitated for a moment, trying to work out whether this young slip of a girl was cheeking him, but there was no trace of it. He nodded.

'Do it your way, then, but you'd better make this work.'

She smiled at him and winked.

Mrs Kemp was back within minutes with a tray replete with silver tea set and delicate porcelain cups. There was milk and lemon and delicate shortbread biscuits that looked as if they were going to melt in the mouth. Nightingale suppressed a smile as she saw that there was honey too, in a little china pot next to the sugar lumps. Oh my, she thought, just like the old days.

'How lovely,' she blurted out. 'And your tea pot is just like my dear mother's.'

Mrs Kemp flushed and managed the ensuing tea ceremony with gentle confidence and obvious pleasure. There was a nasty moment when it looked as though Cooper was going to spread honey on his biscuits, but the consternation on the solicitor's wife's face reached even him, and the danger passed.

Nightingale was chatting happily with Mrs Kemp. It had started easily enough with the delicacy of the tea set and had moved on smoothly to the importance of maintaining certain standards, clearly a favourite topic at 'The Maples'. Cooper's muttered excuses as he slipped from the room were barely noticed. As soon as he'd left, Nightingale changed tack.

'I'm so glad he's gone, Mrs Kemp. There's something I wanted to raise with you, and it's best done while we're on our own.'

Mrs Kemp looked suitably alarmed, and her tea cup rattled in its saucer.

'It's about Mr Kemp and some of his activities over the past months.'

Mrs Kemp's face was pale now, hard brown eyes staring fixedly at this charming young woman she'd considered briefly as a friend.

'There are rumours . . . well, no, I'm afraid more than that . . . real stories about your husband and his—'

'More tea, Constable Nightingale? Your cup's empty.'

'Thank you, no. As I was saying, we have been led to understand that your husband may be having an affair.'

Was that relief that showed for a moment then? How odd.

'Who's been saying such things?' It sounded forced, this defiance, as if she was trying to say what would have been expected.

'We've heard it from a number of sources, actually.'

There was a long pause, then Muriel Kemp placed her cup and saucer down emphatically.

'Well, there's no point denying it. Yes, Jeremy has had affairs, off and on throughout our marriage. Every now and then he makes an effort, but then he'll fall for somebody new. I'm supposed not to know, of course – that keeps things civil – but he knows that I do really.'

'And you don't mind?' Nightingale struggled to keep her tone one of polite inquiry.

'I didn't say that! It's a matter of coping, that's all. And he won't leave me.'

'Why are you so sure?'

'Because he becomes frightened as soon as they fall for him and comes running home. And as for his latest attempt, she won't have him, that's why! Keeps egging him on and then going all coy. He thinks I don't notice, but the whole golf club knows. Still, he's nearly served his purpose now, and soon it'll be over.' Her voice was trembling despite her attempt at nonchalance. It was clear to Nightingale that coping came at a very high price.

'You make this latest attempt sound so . . . mercenary, so calculated.'

'That's because that's exactly what it is – on her part, anyway, not his, of course. Poor fool.'

'Who is she?'

Mrs Kemp looked at her in astonishment. 'You mean you don't *know*? You're not serious!'

'I'm new to the case. Please, it'll save time.'

'Sally Wainwright-Smith, of course. I thought your lot knew that.'

Nightingale made a neat note in her book and carried on.

'You said your husband had nearly served his purpose. What did you mean?'

170

'Did I say that? I don't know.'

'Come on, Mrs Kemp, you know you said it, and you implied that the flirtation was completely calculated on her part. Why?'

'I'm an embittered, scorned woman, Constable. I'm entitled to my cynicism.'

'And I'm a police officer investigating several murders who's entitled to ask the question.'

Mrs Kemp looked shocked at the sudden sternness in Nightingale's voice. Still she defied her.

'I meant nothing.' She was obviously lying, and what was more, she didn't care that Nightingale knew she was. Even her conventionalism wouldn't incline her to more honesty. Nightingale decided on shock tactics and backed her instinct.

'Aren't you worried for your husband's safety; for your own?'

Mrs Kemp tried to keep her face blank, but the look of fear Nightingale had seen as she had answered the door was back in her eyes. She pushed her point.

'Three people connected with Wainwright's are dead so far this year – two murdered, one suspicious.'

'You're not suggesting that ... My God!' She covered her mouth in horror. 'My God!' she repeated, and looked at Nightingale with a renewed respect. She was silent for a long moment, twisting her napkin into a crumpled ball. Then she nodded to herself.

'All right. I'll tell you.' She took a sip of tea and almost dropped her saucer. 'The rumour is that Sally started having an affair with Alan Wainwright about three months before he died. Alan never liked her husband, Alexander, and made him the butt of Wainwright Enterprises' jokes. He gave him the worst jobs, and the more diligent he was, the more Alan ridiculed him.

'Alexander had met Sally shortly after his parents died earlier this year, and she immediately started to work to reduce Alan's hatred of Alexander. It brought her into contact with Jeremy, and she asked for his help in changing Alan's attitude.

'It was hard work, but Jeremy was so besotted with Sally that he devoted himself to her cause. Even when the rumours started that she and Alan were having an affair, he refused to believe it and went on helping her.'

'Did Sally really think that an affair would make Alan Wainwright change his will?'

'She was convinced of it, I'm sure. Jeremy used to tell me that they were increasingly confident that Alan was going to soften towards Alexander, although even he was shocked that he bequeathed them half his fortune.'

'Surely it would have been easier for Sally just to seduce and marry Alan and not bother with Alexander?'

Muriel Kemp gave Nightingale an appraising glance.

'Alan was infertile – he had a virus five years ago – and he was desperate for a Wainwright heir. Graham had told him years ago that he would never have children of his own. It was one of his more cruel taunts. He said he couldn't bear the thought of bringing children into this world.'

'And his father believed him?'

'Why not? Graham was well into his forties, and not one of his hundreds of lady friends ever came knocking at the Hall door claiming patrimony. Julia, Alan's sister, had only produced girls, and there was no way Alan would consider leaving his estate to a *step*son. He wanted family blood in the veins of his heir, male blood; that left only Alexander.'

'So Sally was a brood mare! Despite their affair, you're telling me that Alan would have been happy to see her bear Alexander's child!'

'More than happy, ecstatic. He told Jeremy so when he changed his will in favour of them both. He said that Sally had promised to bear him a great-nephew.'

'So the inheritance was a bribe for her to have Alex's baby?'

'I'm sure of it; so's Jeremy.'

'Why did your husband think he had any chance with Sally, then?'

'Another good question, Constable. It seems unbelievable to you and me, but we're *women*. For a man, particularly a hot-blooded man like Jeremy, it's completely different. Sally could make him believe anything!'

'I need to corroborate this, Mrs Kemp. Can you tell me how I might do that?'

Muriel Kemp grinned with such malice that Nightingale shivered.

'You should talk to Mrs Willett, Alan's old housekeeper. If you think I'm bitter, you wait until you speak to her.'

'Get anything?'

'Plenty.'

'Go on then.' Cooper slammed the driver's door shut and looked at Nightingale expectantly.

'I'll tell you on the way; we're being watched.' Sure enough, Mrs Kemp had pulled back the delicate lace that screened the front landing window and was staring out. Nightingale started talking as the car crunched across the gravel. She was still explaining what she'd learnt as they passed through the gates.

'I think we should go and visit Alan Wainwright's housekeeper.'

'Won't she be on Inspector Blite's interview list, sir? His team was handling everything to do with the Hall.'

'Yes, but he'll have his work cut out questioning Kemp about Sally's discovery of the body, and then he'll need to go straight to the Hall. He'll welcome some help. Trust me, he always does!' Cooper glanced at his watch: nearly eleven o'clock. 'OK. Let's give him a call – see if he minds.'

Blite was only too pleased with the offer. His team were working flat out to complete their search of the Hall's outbuildings and grounds, and were at least a day away from talking to Mr and Mrs Willett.

Cooper and Nightingale found the Willetts in a fifth-floor council flat in a neighbouring town. The lift was out of order and the concrete stairs were damp and smelly. On their floor some attempts had been made to smarten the place up a little, and the graffiti was almost decorative, perhaps in response. The door to the Willetts' flat was painted a cheerful blue; the brass heart-shaped door knocker glowed softly in the dimly lit corridor.

Both Joe and Millie Willett were at home. They welcomed the two police officers into their tiny sitting room without ceremony and turned off the television. Millie went to make some tea, leaving the other three to find small talk among the various conversation pieces that had been squeezed into every corner.

'This is an interesting bit of carving, Mr Willett.' Nightingale had instinctively chosen to comment on the most expensive item in the room.

'Mr Wainwright gave us that after we'd bin with 'im for thirty year. Nice, in't it?'

'Very. Thirty years is a long time. Did you live on the Wainwright Hall estate throughout?'

'Yup, in Bluebell Cottage. Pretty little place, good soil.'

The conversation died and they waited in uneasy silence until Mrs Willett returned. The tea was good and strong, but Nightingale had to argue determinedly against sugar – Mrs Willett being very concerned about her obvious need to put on weight.

'Then you'll have a piece of my fruit cake, won't you?'

Millie Willett was a small, tough woman with a short, simple haircut and stern eyes. The hands that passed the plate of fruit cake to Nightingale had traces of arthritis in thumb joints and knuckles.

Nightingale took the smallest available slice and nibbled a corner. It was delicious, and the rest of the portion disappeared far more quickly than she'd intended, much to Mrs Willett's delight. Courtesies dispensed with, Cooper set to business. His workmanlike, practical style suited the Willetts perfectly, and they were soon chatting away like old friends, whilst Nightingale took notes. The couple had clearly liked their employer and enjoyed their responsibilities on the estate. They didn't volunteer many comments, and Cooper was forced to broach the subject of the will. The mood changed at once.

'Why do you think Mr Wainwright changed his will?'

'Couldn't say.' Joe Willett clamped his lips shut and glared at his wife. His bulbous nose glowed pink as his eyes blinked in indignation behind his black-plastic-framed glasses. Mrs Willett opened her mouth to speak, but with a stern 'Millie!' from her husband, she took a sip of tea instead.

'I know you want to be loyal to your employer, and none of us wishes to speak ill of the dead, but we've already heard the rumours and we're trying to find out the truth.'

'You should know better'n to listen to gossip, a man in your position, Sergeant.'

'But if it's the truth – and the truth suggests that all was not well at Wainwright Hall before Mr Wainwright died – then we have no choice but to listen, Mr Willett.'

'Joe . . .' Millie had edged anxiously to the near corner of her seat. 'Joe, I—'

'No, Millie! That's enough.'

Cooper changed tack.

'I know Mr Wainwright was a good employer, good as anyone could look for, but you're not doing him or his memory any favours by staying silent, you know.'

'A good man's name is worth an ounce of discretion, Sergeant Cooper. And he *was* a good man, for all that's been said about him.'

'True, but . . .' Cooper leaned forward conspiratorially in his dralon armchair, and the others angled forward automatically in response. 'I think I should tell you – and this must remain strictly between us, mind.' Mr and Mrs Willett nodded vigorously. 'Well, there's a chance, that is to say we suspect, though we can't prove anything, that Mr Wainwright's death was . . . suspicious.'

'You mean . . .?'

'Yes. It may not have been suicide.'

'There! Told you, Joe, told you. Said it was too convenient by half, so soon after she'd—'

'Millie! That'll do.' Joe Willett turned to Cooper suspiciously. 'You just sayin' this, or 'ave you got *grounds*?'

'Oh, we've got grounds all right, we just haven't got any proof; only hearsay and gossip, and we need more.'

'So you came to us thinking we'd shop him?'

'No! Thinking you might be able to help us trap a killer, before they kill again. It's already too late for Graham Wainwright.'

That silenced him. It even silenced Millie, but Cooper waited patiently, sensing that the mood in the room had just shifted in his favour. They'd talk now.

Joe Willett stood up and took a battered leather tobacco pouch from a drawer, then reached down the side of his armchair and extracted a worn pipe.

'I think more tea's in order, Millie.'

Nightingale watched in open-mouthed amazement as Mrs Willett automatically stood up and started to gather their cups.

'Won't be a moment.' She stopped suddenly and glared at her husband. 'Don't you start without me, mind.'

There was no danger of that. The slow filling and tamping of the pipe proceeded with mind-numbing ritual as far as Nightingale was concerned, but Cooper watched with contentment.

'That's a lovely old briar, isn't it?'

'Aye. Lovely.'

The two men nodded in mutual understanding as Nightingale tried to find something to concentrate on that would dampen her impatience and irritation with the whole occasion. She spotted a photograph album in the wall unit.

'May I?' she asked. Joe Willett shrugged.

The photographs were old, mostly black and white, and taken with a camera with a fixed field of focus. Only the last few pages were in colour. She flicked through them as Joe Willett and Cooper started to talk about the merits of various pipes, reading the inscriptions printed painstakingly beneath the images: 'Joe and baby Joey at Yarmouth', 'Miss Selina Wainwright pushing Joey in his pram'. Then, several pages later, 'Selina's engagement (Joe in tails serving!)'. There were a lot of images of Selina, who was a clear-faced brunette with a determined jaw; then suddenly the photos of her stopped.

Others continued: harvest festivals, summer fêtes, several bonfire night celebrations, one complete with brass band. Nightingale realised that the Willetts' whole lives had revolved around the Wainwright estate, and Bluebell

Cottage looked idyllic. How must they feel now, having been cast out of it after nearly thirty-five years to live here in a concrete box stuck halfway up an inconvenient high-rise dwelling?

'Tea up!'

More tea, more cake. Mr Willett set his carefully filled pipe to one side. In all that time he hadn't put a match to the tobacco, yet he seemed content.

Nightingale put the album down. They all took a sip of tea. Without preamble, Millie started talking as her husband looked on.

'Well, where to start? At the beginning, I suppose. Mr Wainwright had one son, Graham, born forty-two years ago this September. I remember it because my mum was in service to Mrs Wainwright then, and she had a terrible time with the birth – Mrs Wainwright, I mean, not my mum, she'd had all of us by then, all seven, if you can believe that.'

Mr Willett raised a meaningful eyebrow which, mercifully, his wife saw. Suitably redirected, she carried on.

'Well, Mr Wainwright had wanted a big family, but that wasn't to be; there was no way the missus could have any more. Poor thing, but still, at least it was a boy.'

Nightingale seethed, but kept her feelings from showing.

'Master Graham was spoilt rotten; anything he wanted, he had. So, naturally, he didn't turn out quite as his parents had hoped. He went through that many schools. Anyway, he was the son and heir, that's how he was treated, and that's how he behaved.

'Poor Mrs Wainwright died a few years after, very premature, such a shame, and my mum was getting on then. So Mr Wainwright asked her, "Who could you recommend to be housekeeper?" and she says, "Why, my Millie," and just like that, there we were. Course, Joe had to come too, wouldn't've been proper otherwise, but the estate needed more help and it beat farming. We had a fantastic few years, didn't we, Joe? That was about the time that young Selina got engaged, but that didn't last long. Heavens, that was a scandal and a half. She was Mr Wainwright's youngest sister . . .'

Nightingale recalled the photos of the determined brunette.

'. . . and she was good to us. She lived with her brother, and he was so proud when she became engaged to Julian Sands – that was his best friend, see.'

'Millie, get on with it.'

'But this is relevant. No sooner is she engaged than she goes and elopes, and not with Sands either, but with that travelling salesman, Henry Smith.'

The clouds parted for Nightingale.

'Alexander's father?'

Mrs Willett nodded approvingly.

'Exactly. It was a love match an' no mistake. I can remember her in tears in the kitchen of Bluebell Cottage – we were almost of an age, y'see, and who else did she have to turn to? My, she was a headstrong miss. She had that stubborn Wainwright streak – ruthless, you'd call it in a man. But to be fair, it was the real thing with Smith, and if her brother had found out he would've killed them both rather than lose her. Anyway, "Millie," she says to me, "I have to follow my heart, even though I know it will break his." That was her brother she was talking about, not Sands – never did take to him.

And it did, of course – break Mr Wainwright's heart, I mean. He never forgave her. Worked for years to disinherit her, not just from any right to his estate, but also from her mother's trust fund. I've never seen such hatred as he had for Henry Smith. You never want to cross a Wainwright. Firm and fair they are if you're on their side, but if not . . . By 'eck, I've seen some fellas suffer for crossing them.'

'Get to the point, Millie.'

'Nearly there.' Mrs Willett was quite immune to her husband's impatience, and with a start, Nightingale realised that it was the wife who had the upper hand in this marriage, whatever the superficial tea tray evidence suggested to the contrary.

'Well, now then. The point is that Mr Wainwright spent a *fortune* on legal fees to make sure his sister had no claim to any of the family money, but, bless her, she didn't seem to care a bit. She was hopelessly in love and stayed that way, so far as I could tell, until the day she died.'

'So why did Mr Wainwright change his will to benefit her son – Alexander? It doesn't make sense.' Cooper sounded baffled.

'Exactly! It didn't. It doesn't. But I don't think he did it of his own free will.'

'Pardon?'

'What I mean is, I think he was *confused.*'

'Speak plain now, Millie, if you're going to speak at all. They haven't got all day.'

Millie shifted in her chair and poured more tea. Now it had come to it, she appeared reluctant.

'Well, first of all, Miss Selina wrote to her brother begging him not to cast off his nephew. She didn't care about herself, and knew there was no hope for her husband, but young Alexander was a different matter. She was desperate for him to know his family, and so the poor lad was sent to Wainwright Hall during the school holidays. He had a miserable time. Graham was ten years his senior and as cruel as teenage boys can be. His uncle barely tolerated him; poor lad's blessed with his mother's eyes, so he was a constant reminder to Mr Wainwright of the sister he'd lost.

'And his other cousins, the daughters of his Aunt Julia, were part of a smarter set. They didn't wear trousers with three-inch hems bought so they'd last two winters, and home-knitted jumpers. Poor kid. All it did was show him that he didn't belong, but he knew how much the visits meant to his mum, so he pretended he loved it, for her sake. In truth, I thought it was going to ruin him at one stage, but then he seemed to grow a tough skin and survived.'

'Did Alan Wainwright never acknowledge him?' Nightingale felt a touch of sympathy for Alexander Wainwright-Smith.

'Acknowledge is a tricky word. I think he got used to him. He was a decent enough lad, obliging – ask Joe, he was always helping us in the kitchen or garden. But he was shy, and so out of place it irritated his uncle, a real burr in his side. Mr Wainwright was wont to blame the lad's father for all Alexander's weaknesses, and that got in the way.'

'And yet he left him half his estate!' Cooper was growing impatient.

'Hmm, well, left *him*, you say . . .'

'Millie, I said now—'

'Oh, hush, Joe, it'll out. But it's from folk who'll tell it straight.' She fixed Cooper and Nightingale with a bird-like eye and took a deep breath, fully into her stride. Joe pulled at his pipe and retamped the bowl.

'Well. Where to start? Don't worry, Sergeant, I'll be brief. Alexander left school with three A levels and was all set on university when his uncle suddenly ups and offers him a job at the works.'

'The works?'

'The old brickworks. Shoulda been sold years ago, but Mr Wainwright wouldn't part with it. Anyway, as I was saying, it was a take-it-or-leave-it affair, and he took it.'

'What was the job?'

'Oh, I don't know, but it was at the bottom, right at the bottom, in the dust and the dirt. Still, his mum was pleased, and of course Alexander never let on what he was actually doing. And by gosh, he worked hard. He was soon out of the yard and in the works proper, then into an office job. When the brick business closed up, he was moved on to Wainwright Enterprises. I don't know what he was doing, but he was in a suit by then.

'Young Alexander was a real worker, but I think that irked his uncle even more, what with Graham so unlike his cousin. Anyway, within a couple more years he had his own office and his career looked solid. But then he upset Mr Wainwright all over again. He started evening classes – some sort of Open University degree, I think it was. I remember him trying to explain it to Joe once – and he joined the music society; that's where he met little Miss Butter-wouldn't-melt-in-her-mouth Price.'

'At which? The society or his evening classes?'

'Mm, not sure.'

'Why did that upset his uncle?'

'It was a show of independence. Mr Alan was a decent man, but he was a tyrant with his family, he ruled all of them with a rod of iron. That's why Alexander's mum ran away. He'd of never let 'er marry for love. Alexander's going to night school was right out of order, but he went ahead and did it anyway. That's the Wainwright stubbornness – he's got his fair share all right. As a consequence, he stayed in the same job for all the time he took the course, nigh on three or four year, I reckon.

'Then 'e goes and marries Sally-my-lass, and within months he's on the up again. And he and the new wife are favourite guests of his uncle.'

'So that's why he was given an inheritance?'

Mrs Willett looked sly.

'P'raps, p'raps not.'

'Millie! I will not have unfounded gossip in this house, 'specially if it's slanderin' the dead.'

'It's not gossip, Joe Willett, as well you know. There's no smoke without fire, and there was *plenty* of smoke, believe me.'

Joe Willett eased himself up out of his chair and grabbed at his pipe and jacket.

'Where're you off to?'

'Pub.'

Millie shrugged and grinned at his receding back.

177

'Lift's out!' she called after him as he slammed the door.

Cooper and Nightingale stared at her warily, but she seemed completely unconcerned.

'It's not the gossip 'e minds, it's the,' her voice dropped to a whisper, 'talk about sex. It's embarrassing for him. Isn't that nice?'

Neither of the police officers could think of an appropriate reply, so they nodded and waited for the final chapter in Millie's never-ending story.

'Well, it's true that Mr Wainwright was pleased with his nephew's work, but Alexander was too much of his own man for his uncle's liking. The old man would summon 'im into the study at the Hall sometimes, and you should've heard the shouting – the old man's, that is. Alexander would answer mild, but his eyes – ooh, you could see rebellion in them.

'Which is where Miss Sally came in. Always the pacifier, meek and mild as you could wish. As soon as Alexander left the study she'd be in like a ferret after rabbits. And she'd stay in there too, for ages.'

'How long, for example?' Cooper had at last opened his own notebook and was making a few jottings of his own.

'Half an hour – nearly an hour once. And when she came out it was like the cat with the cream, her face. Saucy and self-righteous.'

'That all seems innocent enough, Mrs Willett. She sounds like a natural peacemaker to me.'

'Met 'er then, have you, Sergeant? She has that effect on most men, saving poor old Joe. Well, it wasn't as innocent as all that. I saw things. Speak to Irene's mum – she walked in on them at it once. I started to suspect something wasn't quite right when I found her earring under his desk. How'd it get there? Then there was that time I went to clear his supper tray without realising she was still in there. I just walked in, natural-like, and there 'e was, bright red in the face, sitting behind that big desk of his, gasping.'

'And Sally?'

'Oh, no sign of her, miss, *none at all.*'

'So where was she then?' Cooper looked confused.

'Behind the desk on her knees, if you want my opinion. There wan't anywhere else she could be – you check it out yourself, it's not that big a room.'

'But that's pure speculation!' Cooper's cheeks had taken on a ruby hue and he couldn't bring himself to look at Nightingale, who calmly asked Millie Willett the obvious question.

'So you believe that Alan Wainwright and Sally were having an affair?'

'Bingo. Less than three months afterwards, he changes his will and then goes and kills hisself, and guess who becomes mistress of Wainwright Hall! Even if he'd been minded to leave *something* for Alexander, there's no other explanation, to my mind, for his disinheriting his own son from the family home.'

She had nothing more to say. Cooper and Nightingale said their goodbyes and left Millie Willett to her cold tea and the sweet taste of revenge.

178

CHAPTER THIRTY

As he parked in the drive of the late Arthur Fish's much-extended house, it occurred to Fenwick that Mrs Fish might not even be living at home any more. He was in luck, however. She was there, in the charge of a full-time nurse, who explained that arrangements for her patient's care had been set out explicitly in the late Mr Fish's will. There were funds to ensure that his wife could die without ever leaving her home. The nurse whispered to him whilst they were still in the privacy of the hall.

'She is a very poorly lady, Chief Inspector. And she only communicates through blinking. Would you like me to stay and interpret?'

Fenwick declined, but asked for a reminder on how to read the invalid's feeble eye movements: one blink for good or yes, and three for no or bad.

She was lying just as she had been when Fenwick had first seen her, head propped up and turned as if expectantly towards the door; eyes open but unfocused. He sat down next to her and, on an impulse, took her hand. The watery blue eyes became more intent and moved fractionally in his direction.

'Mrs Fish, it's DCI Fenwick, Harlden CID. Do you remember, we met a few days ago.' There was no response.

'I came to tell you that we are making every effort to close the investigation into your husband's murder, but progress has been hampered by some important loose ends.'

The flicker of her blonde eyelashes was so faint Fenwick almost missed it. He decided to take it as a sign and carry on.

'Part of the problem is that we can get nowhere with Wainwright Enterprises, and I believe there could be a connection between his work and his death.'

A definite blink this time; that meant 'yes'. Was she agreeing with him?

'You think I'm right?'

Blink.

'The problem is that his employers are giving nothing away.'

Her expression didn't change – how could it; her muscles had long been paralysed – but Fenwick felt again the intense anger on top of her grief at her husband's death. Then the intensity passed, and he was beginning to think she had dozed off when her eyes opened suddenly again and stared at him.

'Do you know something, Mrs Fish? Something that could help us?'

Blink.

She had finally agreed to help him. Fenwick spent the next five painful minutes asking questions in an attempt to unlock Mrs Fish's knowledge. He could feel her frustration grow with his own, and her desperate fight against exhaustion was terrible to watch. Even blinking her eyes became too much

179

of an effort eventually, and she closed them in despair.

Fenwick looked at the ravaged face and wondered what kept the spark of life alight within her. With bitter irony he thought of his own wife, and of how her youthful, healthy body was a carrier for a mind her doctors were now calling vegetative; while here in front of him was a woman with an active mind, a warm character and intelligence, but virtually no means of expression because her body had failed her.

He moved to stand and started to let go of her hand. The fingers twitched and her eyes opened in alarm, their expression close to panic.

'I have to go. I'm due back at the station.'

She was definitely pleading with him not to leave. If only he could think of the right questions!

'You're saying that there's more for me to learn here, but my men have searched this house thoroughly.'

Three definite blinks – she was disagreeing with him.

Fenwick thought hard. They'd looked everywhere. Why was she so certain there was a clue here to her husband's death? Then it struck him.

'Did they search this room, Mrs Fish?'

Three blinks, then one. No. Yes. It didn't make sense. He tried one last question.

'Should they search in here again?'

Blink.

At last! Her eyes closed gratefully and he left her in peace.

Progress on the Fish case was good enough – especially as it allowed him to keep the investigation alive – but it wasn't Fenwick's main concern. He was dissatisfied with the pace of the inquiry into Graham Wainwright's death. Blite was struggling in his search at the Hall. He suspected it was because Sally's presence, and Blite's desire to avoid doing anything that would upset her, just in case her husband called the ACC, were hampering him. He had called the inspector as soon as he left Pendlebury's house because they could now put any doubts about cause of death out of their minds, and he had been unimpressed with the man's response.

It was Sunday and Fenwick was keen to see his children, yet he couldn't bring himself to turn the car towards home. Instead, he drove out into the country and towards Wainwright Hall. He wanted to shake things up, and push Blite to close as many of the loose ends as possible before Monday when he would have to provide yet another report to the ACC. He phoned Cooper at home and told him to join him at the Hall, and wasn't in the least surprised to find that his sergeant had brought Nightingale with him.

Blite was not a happy man when he and his team assembled in the library to brief Fenwick on their progress. He resented the Chief Inspector's presence, suspecting, rightly, that it signalled discontent with his lack of progress. His team of over fifteen had found nothing, and one of them, PC Shah, had managed to lose her warrant card in the process. When Fenwick told them they had conclusive proof that it was murder, he felt the ripple of excitement that passed through them echoed in his own adrenaline rush. They were hunting now.

'What about the medicine cabinet?'

There were a few raised eyebrows at Fenwick's question and some puzzled looks but Blite understood. The Chief Inspector had asked him to find out, without Sally realising, the nature of the prescription that she was taking under doctor's orders.

'Well, it was difficult to search because she's always there watching us like a hawk. In the end I pleaded a call of nature, so she had no option but to leave me alone!'

There was a smattering of laughter at his comment. Blite wasn't a popular officer and the story of him poking around in the lady of the manor's boudoir under the pretence of relieving himself would be around the station within minutes once the briefing was over.

Blite ignored them. He was enjoying his moment in the limelight. 'I found some regular sleeping pills and, get this, some barbiturates! Very unusual these days.'

'Sir!'

'Yes, Nightingale.'

'The drug which Alan Wainwright took when he killed himself was a barbiturate. If we could match the samples taken from his body with Mrs Wainwright-Smith's prescription *and* with the samples taken from Graham Wainwright . . .'

'. . . It could be an interesting coincidence. Well done, Constable. Inspector, see to it, would you, and make absolutely sure that our rights of search and seizure are watertight. Is there anything else of interest?' Blite shook his head.

Fenwick took in the mood of the team. It was only day two after the murder, and they should be fresh and ready for the hunt, yet they looked resigned, not hungry. He had never rated Blite as a leader, and there was no point having a large team if they were unmotivated.

'It may be that there is nothing here to be found, but being sure of that is key,' he told them. 'We are dealing with a clever and manipulative murderer, someone who almost tricked us into thinking that this death was an accident or suicide. Well, it's not. It was cold-blooded, pre-meditated murder, and it may not have been the first. Remember Arthur Fish? On the way here, I heard from DS Gould that forensic tests have confirmed that Fish visited Amanda Bennett before he died. They've matched wood fibres from his body to a birch in her cupboard and some very distinctive carpet fibres on his shoes, coat and trousers to a rug in her house.

'We now know where Arthur went on the night he was killed. The fact that the woman he visited was murdered immediately after his visit, adds weight to our belief that he was not killed by a random mugger. So why was he killed? And why was Graham killed less than a week later? Both murdered in a way to throw us off the scent. We don't know if this is the last killing, and until we discover the motive, we cannot be sure that other lives are not at risk. Motive is vital. Keep your wits about you. A clue may not be obvious. Look for anything out of the ordinary – even coincidences could count. I'm banking on you, and so is the Superintendent. Now you'd best get back to it. You've had enough of a break!'

The team left the room with straighter backs and Fenwick watched them go with relief. This wasn't going to be easy, but he was convinced there was evidence out there, perhaps under their noses, if they only had the brains to spot it.

'Cooper, Nightingale, come on, we might as well have a bite of lunch. There's a pub just down the road which does good food.'

Cooper spooned a large helping of horseradish on to his plate and picked up his knife and fork with an anticipatory sigh. It was a while since he'd had Yorkshire Pudding with his roast beef and his mouth was watering. They had found a table in a corner meant for two, but large enough for the three of them as Nightingale was only eating a sandwich. A boisterous family group next to them was making so much noise that Fenwick was comfortable they could talk freely without being over-heard.

'Did you mean what you said about other lives being at risk, sir?' Cooper's expressive face radiated concern.

'Yes. If there is a link, then somebody is being ruthless to make sure we don't find it. Graham told Jenny he was going to see us after some sort of meeting but he was murdered before he could. What did he know and why was it enough to cause him to be killed?'

'And we still don't know where the missing tape is, sir, number ten that Fish supposedly dictated on the day he was killed,' Nightingale put in. 'He might have left it at Amanda's.'

'Good point. Why don't you go to Brighton with Sergeant Gould tomorrow since you attended the original scene? See what you can find. Cooper can come with me to the Fish house, there might be something there. What else don't we know?'

'You had your suspicions about Sally, sir, early on – do they still exist?'

'Very definitely. We need to find out much more about her. She just suddenly turned up here in Harlden and the private investigator Graham hired could find out nothing of her past.'

Cooper made a note in his book. That was something Nightingale could get on with once she had finished in Brighton.

'Who benefits financially from Graham's death? That could be a motive.' Cooper talked as he mashed the last of his roast potatoes into the puddle of gravy on his plate, causing Nightingale to turn her eyes away.

'Alexander Wainwright-Smith. Blite tracked down Kemp at the golf club first thing this morning and he confirmed it. The residual estate reverted to the survivor should either Graham or his cousin die within twelve months of Alan Wainwright. On this half of the estate, though, Sally Wainwright-Smith doesn't get a look in. It all goes to Alexander.'

'I wonder who would benefit if *he* died?'

'Good question. When Blite asked Kemp he professed ignorance – said he'd never drafted a will for him. It's another thing worth checking on. And who is finding out more about James FitzGerald? I know it's not a priority but he was definitely disconcerted by our visit, so we mustn't lose sight of it.'

Cooper made another note.

The family at the next table departed in a noisy rush, leaving an empty silence behind them.

'That's our signal to go, I think. I'll see you tomorrow at 8.30, Sergeant, at Mrs Fish's house.'

CHAPTER THIRTY-ONE

Half a dozen searchers crowded the invalid's room, and Fenwick went to stand by her protectively. He looked down into her infinitely weary blue eyes and asked his first question almost as a statement.

'We've missed something. In here.'

Blink.

An abstract version of Hunt the Thimble followed, which left Fenwick and his officers staring in confusion at a blank wall to the right of Mrs Fish's bed. He tapped it firmly with his knuckle – solid. Someone started at the other end, about ten feet away. When they were less than four feet apart, the tone of their knocking changed.

'It's hollow behind here, sir.'

They searched fruitlessly for a concealed way into whatever lay behind the innocent magnolia wall, then Fenwick called for the saw. Mrs Fish was wheeled up to the farthest corner, away from the noise and dust, and then the circular saw bit into plaster. Five minutes later, the officer wielding the machine completed his final incision and rammed his shoulder into the oblong of wall he'd carved out. There was a creak, and one of the corners fell inwards. Two more attempts later they were staring into a dusty black hole, big enough for a man to step into.

Fenwick took a heavy-duty torch and shone it into the swirling dust. The beam flitted off metal shelving and fireproof boxes. He called for a photographer to record the scene before anyone else was allowed to move forward. Then he and Cooper stepped into the void. Ten metal boxes were stacked neatly on shelving in a room about the size of a large broom cupboard. On the third side was a safe that would have graced a small bank.

Fenwick shone the light up to the ceiling and found an entrance: a loft ladder attached to a hatch directly above his head. With a delicate gloved finger he hooked it down, then climbed up, trying not to obliterate any prints. The hatch opened easily at first, then caught on a rug that had been concealing it. He thrust it to one side and climbed up into Fish's bedroom closet.

The officers numbered every exhibit in the secret room, photographed them, then sealed the boxes with police evidence tape and wrapped them in plastic.

'Those are going to be opened in the presence of the Superintendent, and not before,' Fenwick told Cooper, who looked bemused. 'I'm guessing, but I think we'll find financial records from Wainwright's in those boxes, and I don't want *anything* to happen to break the chain of evidence that links them to this house rather than Wainwright's. That organisation has too much influence in this county for us to give them any excuse to interfere with this investigation and what we find.'

Before he left, Fenwick had the nurse witness Mrs Fish's acceptance that she had authorised his search. The safe, suitably sealed, was being lifted out as Fenwick said his last goodbye to her. A little plaster dust had settled into her hair, and her face was grey-white, with the look of a death mask. Her eyes barely moved as he thanked her, and her hand in his was as light as a feather. He knew that he would never see her again.

Fenwick's hunch about the boxes proved to be correct. When they were opened back at the station he discovered photocopied financial ledgers from Wainwright's, starting from 1983. In 1992, the ledgers became Excel spreadsheets, and then, only that January, changed again into a new computer-printed format. The thousands of columns of figures meant nothing to Fenwick, and he stared at them with a sinking heart.

'We're going to need a specialist, sir,' he said to the Superintendent, who had stayed to witness the whole thing.

'A forensic accountant, you mean? I'll talk to the ACC. He'll be able to recommend somebody.'

'I'm sure he could sir, but the best man to contact is someone who spoke at that conference I went to earlier this year, the one chaired by Commander Cator. Could you find some way of getting the ACC to recommend him?'

The Superintendent looked incredulous. 'You ask a lot, Chief Inspector, but leave it with me. I'll see what I can do.'

Ten minutes later, Fenwick was called back to the evidence room. A locksmith had managed to open the safe. When he arrived, it seemed that half the station was crammed into the evidence room, staring over the shoulder of a little man in overalls who was pulling open the door of the safe even as Fenwick entered the room.

'Thank you. Leave that inside, sir, if you please; you can go now. And you lot,' Cooper glared at the loiterers, furious that Fenwick should find them here, 'back to work.'

He pulled on thin latex gloves and bent his bulky frame to lift out the contents of the safe.

'Wait.' Fenwick disappeared then came back with a photographer. Cooper raised his eyebrows but said nothing.

The contents of the safe were photographed and then spread out on a long trestle table: a strong box without a key; two thick manila envelopes; and a small leather-covered book filled with page after page of numbers arranged in neat columns. Fenwick recognised Fish's handwriting and felt a surge of intuitive adrenaline as he flicked through the pages. He removed the small silver key he'd found in Fish's wallet from its evidence bag and slipped it into the lock of the strong box. There was a gentle 'click' and the lid sprang open. Inside there was a diamond engagement ring and a lock of brown hair tied with green ribbon. No sign of tape number 10.

In one manila envelope he found copies of Fish's will and other personal documents; nothing unusual or suspicious. The second envelope contained a passport in the name of William Herring but with Arthur Fish's photograph in it; a driving licence in the same name; an open first-class air ticket to Sydney; and £1,000,000 in bearer bonds.

'His escape kit.'

He picked up the air ticket. It had been issued on twenty-first February that year. Immediately after Alan Wainwright's body had been found.

Fenwick stared at Fish's photograph in the false passport and tapped it gently with his finger.

'What scared you so much that you forced yourself through the danger of buying false documents, and contemplated leaving the wife you loved so much? Sydney's a long, long way away. Did you think you'd be safe there?'

Cooper was down on his knees again, reaching into the safe.

'Here, there's something at the back. Gotcha!'

He leant back heavily, his face red from the effort, and handed Fenwick a black velvet-wrapped bundle.

'I can guess what this is,' Fenwick said as he unwrapped it carefully. A 9mm pistol glinted softly in the electric light. A box of ammunition fell to the table. Fenwick shook his head at the passport photograph.

'So you'd even bought a gun. Fat lot of good that did you. There's no point having it locked up. Here, Cooper, it's not loaded. We need to log this and get it fully checked.'

The phone rang in the evidence room.

'It's for you, sir. The ACC's going to be with Superintendent Quinlan here in Harlden at about six o'clock. When he arrives, they want you to join them.'

A new, more concentrated, regime had settled within the finance department at Wainwright Enterprises since Arthur Fish's demise. Neil Yarrell had moved swiftly to fill the vacuum, installing an ambitious young man with new-born twins and a massive mortgage as deputy financial controller. Superficially, at least, things had returned to normal.

When the phone rang in Neil Yarrell's office, he looked up irritably, annoyed at the interruption.

'Yes?'

'Mr Yarrell, it's Detective Chief Inspector Fenwick here, Harlden CID.'

'What can I do for you, Chief Inspector?'

'I was wondering whether you could tell me how your late financial controller came to have one million pounds in bearer bonds in a secret safe at his home?'

Yarrell stared at the handset in disbelief. He couldn't believe what he had just heard. A dreadful sinking feeling dragged at his stomach, and his throat was suddenly dry.

'Mr Yarrell, do you have a comment?'

The finance director swallowed in an attempt to find his voice.

'I have . . .' The words came out as a high-pitched squeak. He coughed and swallowed again. 'I have no idea. Please don't waste my time, Chief Inspector. How should I know what Fish got up to in his spare time. He had enough of it.'

'Really, and there was I led to believe by your managing director that he was over-worked. Never mind. I'm sure the ledgers and accounts we found hidden with the bonds will help to explain how he came to be a millionaire. They are on their way to our experts right now.'

As soon as he had replaced the handset, Yarrell rushed to the marbled executive bathroom and was violently sick. As he bent over the bowl, he felt the blood drumming in his ears. Only one thing troubled him more than the news he had just received from Fenwick, and that was the imminent prospect of the call he was going to have to make to James FitzGerald. He doubled over and was ill again.

News of the find at Fish's house spread through Harlden Division as Fenwick waited for the summons. By supper time it was the subject of open speculation in the canteen.

'It'll be a nightmare, mark my words.' DI Blite was, as always, an instant expert. 'These financial cases – terrible to bring to trial, expensive, lengthy and rarely successful.' He chuckled maliciously. 'Old Fenwick's done it this time. He still has a high-profile unsolved murder on his hands and he goes and rakes all this up. He will *not* be popular.'

Blite was right. At that moment Fenwick was standing to attention in front of the ACC in Superintendent Quinlan's office. He was in black-tie and it was obvious he was on his way to a function somewhere, which would explain his rare visit to the Division.

'What the devil d'you think you're playing at, Fenwick? You're asked to deal with the fatal mugging of a respectable businessman; instead, you go and half demolish his house and come back with some cock-and-bull request for a forensic accountant to investigate supposed financial irregularities at Wainwright's! Are you mad?'

The question was not entirely rhetorical. Had Harper-Brown ever considered what his worst nightmare might be, it would not have been too different from the situation he now faced. Wainwright Enterprises was the financial lung of half the county, directly or indirectly bringing employment to thousands and donating small fortunes to local charities. The Wainwright family – now just Colin, Julia, Sally and Alexander – were still closely associated with the power of the family firm and held positions in the key local charities, on the council and, Harper-Brown remembered with a sudden chill, within his own Lodge. His anger intensified. Why was it always this bloody man who created problems where none should realistically exist?

'A forensic accountant is out of the question. You've no grounds for suspicion.' He raised a pre-emptory hand as Fenwick drew breath to interrupt. 'Arthur Fish was the victim of a mugging that went wrong, that's—'

'His wallet wasn't taken, sir; he'd been terrified for weeks before he was killed; he was followed on the night he died; and the prostitute we think he met was murdered within hours of his visit.'

'Let me *finish*. His state of mind is only speculation, and the secretary who told you about it was incompetent and has since been dismissed!'

Fenwick swallowed hard. The ACC was uncannily well informed and it hadn't been by him.

'But the Brighton police found two thousand pounds in used twenty-pound notes hidden in Francis Fielding's flat. There is a strong possibility that he was hired to kill Fish.'

'That's hardly compelling.'

'Arthur Fish had a million pounds in bearer bonds in his safe, sir, along with false identity papers and a gun. Hardly the possessions of an innocent man!'

Harper-Brown was for once shocked into silence by the news of the contents of Arthur Fish's safe. Fenwick couldn't tell whether it was the news of the falsified documents, or of a million pounds in bearer bonds just sitting there that had shocked him more. When he eventually spoke his words had their usual effect on Fenwick who tightened his jaw to avoid feelings of disappointment from showing on his face.

'I don't need to tell you, Chief Inspector, that these are very delicate matters. I have already had Neil Yarrell on the phone from Wainwright's and you should anticipate an attempt by him to have all materials relating to the company returned.'

'I think, technically, those papers were the property of Arthur Fish, sir. He was the financial controller.'

'That is a moot point, as you well know. Stolen company property – which is what those documents probably are – should be returned to the owner on recovery.'

'Unless required as evidence in a reportable crime, sir.'

'Don't tell me the law, Chief Inspector!'

'No, sir. There are rumours, though, sir, and not just about Wainwright's either. Kemp and Doggett are not well regarded in Harlden.'

This made the ACC look up.

'Really? Why?'

'Hints of something not quite right – you know, just talk at the golf club, but it's persistent.'

The ACC hummed tunelessly under his breath and tapped the side of his chin with a finely sharpened pencil. Fenwick could almost see the cogs in his mind clicking into place. If there *were* rumours and he did nothing then there would be talk about police bias. That wouldn't do at all.

'Very well. You can have one week . . . I know it's not long enough for a full investigation, but it should be sufficient to see whether a more detailed and specialist inquiry is needed. And I want the report to come to me directly, Fenwick. Understand?'

When Fenwick called to ask for the name of the accountant who'd spoken during his seminar, Commander Cator just laughed at him. A week was no good to anybody, he explained impatiently.

'I realise that, sir, but at least give me an hour of your time to talk through this case.'

It was the best that Fenwick could negotiate, and a meeting was arranged for the following morning in London. As he made his way back to Harlden, his fury at the ACC's distorted sense of political survival almost blinded him, and he was hooted at by three motorists before he had the sense to pull over and calm down.

* * *

Fenwick returned to his office and asked Cooper to join him at once. His secretary, Anne, brought in two fresh mugs of coffee, remembering that Cooper liked milk and extra sugar, and Fenwick diverted his calls.

'How are you doing on the investigation into Sally's background?'

'DC Nightingale is going to do it, sir, once she gets back from Brighton.'

'Alexander's will?'

'No joy. We're going to have to ask him for it – do you want me to?'

'Not just yet. I don't want it to seem important to him. An opportunity should come up to meet him again in the next few days; we can do it then.'

'Where do you put Alexander in all of this, sir: lucky dupe or accomplice?'

'Could be either; he's a hard man to read. He could even be the next victim.'

Cooper couldn't work out whether the DCI was joking or not.

'Maybe she genuinely loves him.'

Fenwick merely raised his eyebrows, but the look he gave Cooper silenced any further conversation. It was clear that he thought Sally incapable of any affection and Cooper wasn't about to argue with him. Talking to the DCI on matters of the heart was dicey enough at the best of times but right now, with him in this sort of mood, it just wasn't worth it.

'I want Nightingale to dig into Sally's background as a high priority.'

'I'll put her on to it as soon as she's back.'

Cooper levered himself up out of the chair, bearing his empty coffee mug with him. Fenwick watched him go with a frown on his face. The next day he was due to see Miles Cator in London. He knew it was the right thing to do, but he begrudged the time away from Harlden. Cooper and Gould were excellent officers and he trusted them completely. Blite was a different matter, but at least he wanted a result as badly as Fenwick. Yet none of them had the fierce intensity and passion for results that he believed to be so essential.

He was driven by a burning desire, which he told himself was for justice, though deep down he knew that it was also for success. He was compelled to win at all costs, and he just couldn't see that same hunger when he looked into the eyes of his three senior officers. With a small start of surprise, he realised that the only person in whom he had seen an answering spark of determination was DC Nightingale. The thought filled him with new hope as he returned his attention to his crowded desk and overflowing in-tray.

Anne interrupted Fenwick just as he had finally rediscovered the wood of his desk.

'You have a visitor, Chief Inspector. She doesn't have an appointment and they've asked her to wait in Interview Room Two. It's Mrs Wainwright-Smith.'

'How long has she been waiting?'

'Only five minutes. I told her I didn't know when you'd be free, but she said she didn't mind waiting.'

Fenwick took the stairs back down the two flights to the ground floor, distracted and deep in thought. Since Graham's death, Sally had made a point of joining him whenever he had visited Wainwright Hall to meet DI

Blite. She was like an unwelcome shadow he couldn't shake off, and her obvious curiosity was disconcerting and suspicious. Now she had decided to visit him on his own territory, away from the Wainwright seat of power, and for no reason that he could fathom.

'Chief Inspector! Oh, thank you. I am sorry to trouble you, but I needed to see you.'

'No problem, Mrs Wainwright-Smith. Please sit down, there's no need to stand up for me.'

She disturbed him, increasingly so. She was slight and willowy, tall but not so tall as to detract from the impression of fragility she created. Despite himself and a deliberate defensiveness that he found he maintained in her presence, he could understand the pull of her attraction. She had a porcelain-perfect face and a demeanour that seemed to cry out for protection, and yet she was sexy too. There was something in the sway of her hips and in her gestures that seemed to caress the air. It appealed to the masculine within him. She reminded him by her very presence that he lived without female companionship, and at the same time she radiated a need of her own.

'Mrs Wainwright-Smith,' he ignored her obvious attempt to flirt, 'why do you need to see me?'

'I can tell that you're busy, so I'll come straight to the point. It's Jenny, Chief Inspector. She worries me.'

'In what way?'

'I don't precisely know. It's as if she doesn't care about Graham. I'm going to have to ask her to leave the Hall and go to a hotel whilst we wait for the inquest to adjourn, because she's hovering around as if she owns it. And she keeps returning to that tree as if she's fascinated by it. But she doesn't appear in the least upset by his death – just look at her clothes! She says she doesn't believe in wearing mourning black, but really!'

Fenwick took a moment to study the blue-grey cashmere twinset Sally was wearing, the single strand of heavy pearls, the black trousers and delicate and obviously expensive black suede shoes. For once he let his true feelings show on his face, and she responded at once.

'I can see that you think I'm overreacting, but she really is behaving very strangely indeed.'

Rather as you are, he thought, but said nothing.

'Well?' Sally had clearly expected him to take her concerns seriously. Perhaps she thought that Jenny had no alibi for the time of Graham's death, but Fenwick knew otherwise. She had stayed the night with friends in Scotland before travelling down to Harlden for the dinner party, and they had confirmed the time of her train. He was suddenly irritated by Sally wasting his time and stood up, making it clear the conversation was over.

'She's young and unconventional, but that doesn't make her a suspect. Naturally I will make a note of this conversation and bear it in mind.' That was completely true; all Sally had done by coming to see him was to increase his suspicions of her further.

'Of course I know that, but I thought you ought to hear my concerns.'

'Well, I appreciate you sharing them with me, Mrs Wainwright-Smith, but if that's all, the constable will show you out.'

Sally drove fast on her return to the Hall, cutting corners, jumping lights, swerving around cyclists at the last minute without braking. There was a growing sense of frustration inside her; she felt as if she was only just hanging on to control, and she hated that feeling. Ever since childhood she had been the mistress of her environment. She had decided who was allowed to enter her domain and why, but now, with these clumsy police oafs plodding around *her* house, *her* gardens, *her life*, she could feel that precious control slipping away, and that made her angry.

Sally's anger was a strange creature; it had no visible symptoms and often disappeared with the suddenness of a light being switched off. But now each time it came back it was stronger, less predictable, and more dangerous. She could feel it there inside her in the way her foot reached for the accelerator rather than the brake, and in her absolute disregard for the curses and raised fists that accompanied her passage home. She didn't care; other people had ceased to be of any consequence. What mattered now was managing a return to control as quickly as possible.

She swung the car into the drive in front of the Hall with a screech that destroyed the gravel finish her part-time gardener had slaved over. Irene was just leaving.

'What are you doing using the front entrance? How many times do I have to tell you?'

Irene had just about had enough of Miss Hoity-Toity's airs and graces, and she was about to tell her so when she saw the expression in Sally's eyes. The sight made her shiver and, as she said to her husband when she got home, 'There was murder there, Stan, I tell you, pure murder.' She phoned in her notice that evening.

Sally waited patiently for Alex to finish pouring the tea.

'Biscuit?'

'No thanks, Sal. Not hungry.'

'Alex, we need to talk.'

He looked at her with something approaching dread, but said calmly enough: 'Go on.'

'I'm worried about Jenny. I don't begrudge her the house room, but it's not right for her to mope around like this. She'll never get over Graham this way. I want her to go to a hotel.'

'Sally! He's not even buried yet, and the poor girl has no relatives to talk to. Her mum and stepfather are in South Africa and she's an only child.'

'She has friends. She should be mixing with them, not sitting like a ghost at the feast each night.'

'She doesn't. Most evenings she has her meal in her room.'

Sally smiled at him sweetly, but her eyes were hard.

'You're too soft, Alex. I want you to talk to her, find out what her plans are. Take her out for a drink this evening; it would do her good.'

'I'll see.' He drank his tea in silence, but Sally was relaxed. She'd made her point and he hadn't really argued, which meant that he was likely to follow her suggestion. Perhaps he would be as pleased to see the back of Jenny as she would be.

A ring at the front door made them both look up, startled. They weren't expecting visitors.

'I'll go.' Sally was on her feet before Alexander could stop her.

It was James FitzGerald; standing huddled out of a brief rain shower in the stone porch, framed by two massive gargoyles.

'Come in. The sitting room's warm.' Then, in a softer voice, 'Alex is here.'

Alexander joined his wife and their unexpected visitor in front of the small fire that he'd lit to cheer the house, despite Sally's reservations about the waste.

The two men shook hands cautiously. They hadn't met since FitzGerald had told Wainwright-Smith the little family secret, before Graham's death. James was obviously weighing Alexander up and the younger man didn't appreciate the scrutiny.

'You're an unexpected visitor.' At one time he would have been polite, but his months as managing director had already changed him. Apart from his wife nobody was able to impose on him any more. He could feel FitzGerald's surprise at the resistance he found in his returned stare, just as he had felt first Jeremy Kemp's and then Neil Yarrell's.

'Unexpected! Hardly, after what's happened this last week. Another Wainwright's bitten the dust and the police are crawling all over the company. It's not what I'd call ideal management, Alexander. Your uncle ran the business for nearly thirty years without a whiff of trouble. You're in charge for a couple of months and "bang" – the whole bloody lot starts to fall apart!'

Alexander and Sally merely raised their eyebrows in synchronised surprise. It was obvious that they didn't know about Fish's papers yet and FitzGerald wasn't about to tell them.

'Naturally, we are all very upset by my cousin's death.' Alexander's voice was flat and unyielding. 'But so far, the police have found nothing to connect it to the family or the business, nor will they. There is no connection; it was an unfortunate accident.'

FitzGerald looked at him with open disbelief.

'I don't give a fuck what it was, it was clumsy and very bad timing. Your uncle may not have told you this, but I've been the shareholder's unofficial representative for a number of years. Behind those Trusts, is a group of very powerful and private men. They have a lot of money invested in the company, and they will not appreciate all this police interest, I can assure you. If things go on as they are, they'll look to me to, ah, sort things out.'

'Thank you for letting us know, James. I'll remember that – should the need arise.' Alexander started to walk to the door, keen to show his unwanted guest out before his displeasure took hold.

'You haven't quite got it yet, have you? The need *has* arisen. They've asked me to stop by, to see what has to be done. Whatever I say will happen, I can assure you.'

'I see. Well you can tell them that things are under control. There will be no more deaths and the police are running around all over the place, in a complete mess. Give it a month or so and things will calm down.'

FitzGerald looked appraisingly round the comfortable sitting room, at the new décor and original antiques. He stared hard at the portrait of Alexander's great-great-grandmother over the fireplace and waved his hand towards it.

'A hundred years ago the Wainwrights owned this house, the company and the souls of every single person for miles. They were virtually the only employer of any size around here, and their word was law. Your grandfather continued the tradition but he was unlucky between the wars and never did make the fortune that some of his contemporaries did. And then your uncle, dear old Alan, well . . .' he smiled, deliberately unpleasant. 'What an absolute wanker.'

Sally drew breath sharply; Alexander opened his mouth to protest, but FitzGerald waved him down with a bored gesture.

'I know, I know, shouldn't speak like that in front of ladies, but she,' he gestured towards the painting, 'can't hear us, and I don't see any other lady present.'

'Now look here . . .' Alexander was tall and well built, details that people tended to forget when they were dealing with him. Sally went to stand by him and laid a restraining hand on his arm. Her eyes were cold, her expression just as calculating as FitzGerald's as she spoke to her husband.

'Don't. He's trying to provoke you and he doesn't deserve a response. I'm not offended. I have to respect someone before I care about their remarks.'

FitzGerald chuckled. 'You are a cool one. Kemp said you were, and he was right.' He saw the expression of surprise on Sally's face and went on: 'Yes, I *know* you trusted him to keep his mouth shut, but you should have known better. Anyway, I've said what I came to say. Remember, any more trouble and you can be sure that I'll be around.'

He left without another word. Sally and Alexander stared at each other, briefly united by concern.

'That was a threat.' Sally's voice was pensive.

'I know. Is he involved, d'you think, with all the . . .?'

'Deaths? Who knows.' She was dismissive. She needed Alex out of the house so that she could think straight. Her feigned disregard for James FitzGerald had taken more out of her than she cared to admit, and she was having to fight a suffocating sense of being overwhelmed by events cascading out of control. She needed space and time to think and plan. In a voice virtually devoid of emotion, she carried on talking to her husband as if nothing else mattered.

'Go and find Jenny; she'll be skulking in her room. Take her out for that drink.'

Jenny received his invitation for a drink with more pleasure than he'd expected, and they left within minutes.

The pub was dimly lit and smoky. Alexander had found a quiet corner table far enough away to provide a degree of privacy. Even so, he'd nearly finished his drink before she uttered a word.

'Why? I just don't understand why. I've been over and over it and yet . . .' Tears choked her voice and she had to stop.

'Would you like another?'

She nodded, and downed the rest of her drink in one gulp.

The pub had grown busy during their silent first drink, so there was a long wait at the bar, and when he returned to their table she was staring out of the rain-spattered window at the poorly lit car park.

'There's a man out there watching us, I'm sure of it.'

He looked at her, startled.

'I know you think I've got paranoid delusions, but I'm convinced we're being watched. When we left the Hall a car pulled out behind us, a Saab, and I'm sure it's parked there in the shadows, look.'

Alexander wanted to dismiss her fears as nonsense, but they echoed too much of his own concern. He suddenly found himself talking as if he couldn't stop: of Sally's original suspicions about the company finances; of his pain at Graham's death; and finally of his long-standing worry that his uncle's death might have been suspicious too.

Jenny listened with acute interest, interrupting only to clarify an occasional point. At the end of his long monologue she stood up and went to the bar. Either the queue was shorter or she received preferential service, because she was back within moments. She put a whisky in front of Alexander and took a long, considered swallow of her own gin and tonic.

'So do you believe Graham was murdered?' Alexander asked. He was regretting his own monologue and didn't want any questions about it.

'Yes . . . no . . . I don't know any more, Alex. I've no idea what to think. But suicide? It doesn't fit, no matter how scared he was. He'd hired a private investigator, you know.'

'I agree. Do you think he found out something from this investigator?'

'Yes, I'm sure of it.'

'What was it he'd asked him to look into?'

Jenny gazed at him with an open pity so stark that even he noticed.

'What? Why're you looking at me like that?'

Jenny shook her head sadly, and squeezed his arm compassionately.

'He didn't trust Sally.'

'Why not? Go on, tell me.'

But Jenny clammed up and refused to answer, retreating instead into her watching from the window. After a long moment in which neither of them touched their drinks she spoke again.

'I think Graham was killed, and so was his father. The question is, by whom. You're the obvious suspect, you've benefited from both deaths, but somehow I don't think it's you.' She laughed, an awful sound without hope or care. 'Which could be the biggest error of judgement I'm likely to make.'

'I didn't kill them, Jenny.'

'I believe you.' The words were a whisper, but the ones that followed were quieter still. 'But what about Sally? Can you be as sure about your wife?'

Alexander's mouth dropped open in shock.

'That's a terrible thing to say, Jenny. Such an accusation . . .'

'You've just told me that she stopped you going to the police about your uncle and the finances of the firm, for heaven's sake.' Her voice was rising, and a couple of people nearby turned around.

He realised that they had both had enough to drink.

'Come on, let's go home.'

He had to steady her as they crossed the uneven tarmac of the parking lot in the pouring rain. They were both soaked by the time they reached his car, and the windows misted up immediately. Their journey was completed in silence along twisting country roads, the only sound the thump of the windscreen wipers as they beat out double time, and the swish of the occasional car passing in the opposite direction. From time to time a pair of headlights appeared brightly in his rear-view mirror, only to disappear as the road dipped or twisted away.

'It's the Saab,' said Jenny as they neared the gloomy outline of the Hall. 'They know where we're going so they don't need to keep close.'

Sally was already in bed when Alexander and Jenny returned, even though it wasn't yet eleven o'clock. Alexander put the guard in front of the fire and went to make some tea. Jenny joined him in the kitchen.

'I'm sorry.'

'Don't be. You were upset. Tea?'

'Yeah.' Her voice was husky with unshed tears.

'Hey, come on. It's OK.'

She started crying then, long, terrible sobs that went on and on. He gathered her in his arms, felt her skinny little body shake and quiver and the tears soak his shirt, then his skin. He rested his head on top of hers and rocked her slowly to and fro. She cried herself hoarse and then kept on crying, making herself sick with the effort. As he steadied her over the sink, holding her whilst she retched, a dry terrible sound, he realised for the first time the awful depth of her grief.

'You really, really loved him, didn't you?'

'Oh God, Alex, he was my life. He was all I wanted. I didn't care about the money, just him.'

She was shivering now, and he sat her down next to the Aga and found an old blanket in the airing cupboard. He remade their tea, feeling a terrible sadness that he refused to analyse. Once she'd drunk it, with much coaxing, he wrapped the blanket around her shoulders and guided her upstairs and to her room.

In his own room the double bed was crisply made and his side was turned down – not that there was a his or hers side any more, as Sally never came to him now. A note had been propped against the lamp; it was from his wife.

I've gone to bed early. I'm very tired so don't disturb me. If I don't see you at breakfast, make sure you use up the old loaf for toast.

That was it. No good night, not even an 'x'. He slipped between the finely laundered cotton sheets, in the largest bedroom in his mansion. With a deep, resigned sigh he set his alarm for six o'clock and switched off the light. It was a long time before he fell asleep.

CHAPTER THIRTY-TWO

Miles Cator's attachment to the National Task Force into money-laundering had many advantages, not least a large modern office, the use of two dedicated research assistants and full computer support. Cator saw Fenwick's envious glance and cut into his thoughts.

'You'd hate the politics, believe me.'

Fenwick was sure he would, and returned his concentration to briefing the Commander on the Wainwright case. He desperately needed the man's cooperation. At the end of half an hour he'd shared everything he knew. Copies of Wainwright's ownership structure, report and accounts lay scattered on the coffee table, mixed incongruously with colour photographs of the various murder and death scenes and the personal account book that he had found in Fish's safe. Cator said nothing, but sat with his eyes screwed tight shut, fingertips drumming both temples. Then, without a word, he reached for a phone and summoned an assistant.

'Get me Weatherspoon in Jersey.' He glanced at his watch then turned to Fenwick. 'Leave this with me. Can you come back in two hours? I'll have an idea by then whether this is worth our involvement.'

With only six days left to prove to the ACC that Wainwright's had a case to answer, Fenwick had no choice. It was a glorious day in London, and he found his way to some gardens on the Embankment overlooking the Thames, where he drank a superb takeaway coffee and phoned every senior investigating officer on his team, one after the other.

He broke the last connection and sat back in shirt sleeves to watch the world pass by around him. He let his mind drift, empty of all conscious thought. The threads that he had confidently been following had become twisted. Dreams of tangled ivy haunted his sleep, waking him every morning at three. He knew there were connections but he was tormented by the idea that he kept making the wrong ones, whilst more glaring clues went unrecognised.

Fenwick thought long and hard, staring into the middle distance of the gardens with enough intensity to worry passers-by and cause an old lady opposite him to change benches. He forced himself to set his theory out logically. First, he believed that all three deaths could be connected. In both Alan and Graham Wainwright's case, the main beneficiaries were Alexander and Sally. Of the two, he still considered Sally the more likely killer – it was gut feeling unsupported by any logic, but her behaviour since Graham's death was erratic and suspicious. If she was the killer, and if the killings were all linked, she had to have a motive for killing Arthur Fish. That was a real stumbling block in his argument. There was nothing to connect Sally with Fish, whereas Alexander had worked with the accountant for years.

He scratched his head absent-mindedly and frowned. Was it worth asking DS Gould to try and find a connection between Sally and Fish? Perhaps, but he decided to wait until Nightingale had finished her investigation into Sally's past, in case she found a link there. Then there was the fact that Fish had known Amanda Bennett. If her murder was linked to his, then the web of deaths extended even further. He told himself it would be logical to drop his insistence on a connection, but even as his mind was convincing him, his instincts were screaming at him to give it one last shot. He would have to decide soon, as he was already under pressure to allocate DS Gould and his team to the Wainwright case. He decided to let the parallel inquiries run for another forty-eight hours, and turned his thoughts to the means of death.

The killings had been designed to look unconnected, and two had been set up as suicides, which meant that they were premeditated and well planned. Only eight days separated Arthur and Graham's murders, which suggested panic or an urgency that he could not understand. Graham's 'suicide' had been clumsy, and had they not had a poor post-mortem it would have been treated as murder at once. It felt rushed – why? If only he could find a way to link Sally to Arthur and a reason for the speed of Graham's killing, he would be able to sustain the combined investigation.

'She's as guilty as hell on all three, I can sense it,' he said to himself, unaware that he was speaking aloud. 'There's just one link that I'm missing. She had nothing to gain financially from Fish's death, so in what way did he threaten her? Find that and I find motive.'

A determination filled him, so fierce that it made him clench his fists and hardened his face into an expression that startled a courting couple as they passed by and finally caused the little old lady on the far bench to leave the gardens altogether. Somewhere a clock chimed, reminding him that he was due back to meet with Cator.

The Commander agreed to help, but he cautioned Fenwick to be patient.

'Six days isn't really long enough to do anything, Chief Inspector. In Jersey, where the owners of Wainwright's have their interests registered, the authorities are always very helpful. Their islands are legitimate financial centres and they want them to be seen as such, so they will do all they can to cooperate, but the trusts involved all appear above board; they are long-standing and the trustees are very well connected. As for the Wainwright development in the Caribbean,' he paused to sip his cooling tea, 'it's backed by a bank that is old school and has never caused any problems.

'It's Wainwright's here in the UK that we'll need to concentrate on. I've had somebody look at the accounts you retrieved from Fish's safe, and he described them as "bizarre". They certainly intrigued him, and he's the best forensic accountant I know. The personal ledger you found particularly excites him. He thinks it's some sort of record of all the anomalous payments that have passed through Wainwright's. He's going to do his best by the end of Monday – that's when your time's up, isn't it?' Fenwick nodded. 'At most, all we will be able to do is confirm the need for a thorough investigation, which should be enough to persuade your ACC to maintain a tough attitude towards

Neil Yarrell. Don't rely on us for any early convictions though. This could take years.'

Fenwick had always known that it would, and he was delighted that Cator had agreed to become involved. 'If you can find out anything that helps me to persuade the ACC to keep Wainwright's at bay, I'd appreciate it.'

Cator smiled, and Fenwick realised with surprise that there was no love lost between the two men.

'This will pass out of his jurisdiction soon enough if what you suspect is true. You'll have to cope with the fall-out when he realises that you've handed these papers over to me, but now that I have them, he'll find it hard to get them back without going way over my head, and I doubt he'll want to do that. You don't realise it yet, but you've put yourself in a very difficult position with your boss.'

Fenwick remembered his promise to the ACC not to part with the Fish papers. He would be accused of insubordination and would have no defence at all.

Outside, the weather had changed and blustery south-westerly gusts brought a hint of rain into the late afternoon. A storm was forecast for the end of the week, and already the windspeeds had risen as if in anticipation.

Fenwick hailed a taxi to take him back to Victoria station and checked his answering service. There was a message from Harper-Brown, asking him to meet him at his golf club that evening at seven. Fenwick completed a quick calculation and realised that he would barely make it, even if he did catch the 17.03 from Victoria. He leant forward and rapped on the glass partition that separated him from the cabby.

'Could you step on it, please, it's essential that I catch a train at five o'clock.'

The taxi driver gave him a look that clearly said, *If I had a fiver for every time I've been asked that, I'd be a millionaire by now*!

Fenwick intercepted the expression, interpreted it correctly and immediately turned it to his advantage.

'There's a tenner in it for you if we make it.'

Amazingly, they did.

The Harlden Golf Club, to which the ACC belonged, was the best in the county. An air of rarefied calm wrapped itself around Fenwick as he walked into the flagstoned entrance hall.

'Can I help you, sir?' The man in front of Fenwick had a proprietorial air.

'I'm meeting a member, Mr Harper-Brown.'

'Ah, yes, the Assistant Chief Constable. He's in the visitors' side of the bar, to your right.'

Fenwick spotted the ACC straight away, standing next to a bay window with two other men. As soon as Harper-Brown saw him he left them and walked to an empty pair of seats in the quietest corner. Sporting prints and photographs of various trophies and cups being presented to beaming, self-satisfied people filled the walls. The atmosphere of self-assurance and superiority was almost palpable, and Fenwick understood why Harper-Brown prized his membership so highly.

'Chief Inspector.' The ACC gestured for Fenwick to sit down. 'What can I get you to drink?'

'Whisky and water, thank you, sir, no ice.'

The ACC returned with a glass of whisky, and water in a little jug. There was ice in the glass.

'Cheers.'

'Cheers.'

There was an uncomfortable silence, in which both men sipped their drinks and Fenwick tried not to grimace. Harper-Brown spoke first.

'I asked to meet you here because I wanted to make sure that we had an appropriate opportunity to discuss progress on the case without unnecessary interruptions.'

'Well, things are starting to come together, sir. The circumstances surrounding Fish's murder suggest a motive beyond a straightforward mugging gone wrong. It still looks more like a case of a contract killing, and the connection with Amanda Bennett's death is being actively pursued.'

The ACC was not pleased.

'Both the Wainright-Smiths remain under twenty-four-hour watch, and when Mr Yarrell, the finance director, became perturbed about our finding papers at Fish's house, we offered him police protection.'

'You don't need to remind me who Neil Yarrell is, Fenwick; we regularly share a round. And you should have approached me before you offered him protection. Really!'

'Yes, sir.' It had been a deliberately calculated move, and Fenwick had had no intention of checking with the ACC in advance, he knew what the answer would have been. He had offered Yarrell protection to see his reaction and had enjoyed hearing the shock of the offer for once disturb the man's practised calm.

'Now, what's all this about the delays you experienced in receiving the full PM report on Graham Wainwright?'

It never ceased to amaze Fenwick how well informed the ACC was. He explained about Pendlebury's illness and confirmed that he wouldn't be making a formal complaint although the matter had obviously been logged. Harper-Brown sniffed, a dry, disapproving sound, that suggested that Fenwick had exercised his judgement in a way with which he didn't agree, but that it was beneath him to comment. He took a sip of his drink and changed the subject.

'Still, I'm very pleased with the progress DI Blite has made. He really has taken the case forward.'

Fenwick took a swallow of his drink in order to mask his anger. Blite hadn't called him since early in the morning, despite the fact that he had left two messages for him to do so. Yet it appeared that he had found the time to brief the ACC.

'It must have been sheer inspiration that made him research the share-holders of Wainwright Enterprises like that, real detective work.'

'Indeed.' There was no way that Fenwick was going to let Harper-Brown know that he was completely in the dark.

'He had to probe behind those structures in Jersey – great work that – and to make the connection to James FitzGerald was brilliant.' The ACC lowered his voice confidentially. 'I never trusted that man. Between you and me, I opposed his membership here, but Neil Yarrell talked me round. I knew I was right.'

'How large was the shareholding again, sir? I've forgotten.'

'No, you've not forgotten. They don't know yet. The trust structure is very complicated and will take quite a bit of unravelling. They only traced FitzGerald because his name appears in some of the paperwork – it's the only one. Still, I'm sure more will come out now. How was the trip to London?'

Fenwick told the ACC about his day, his anger at Blite making him less than subtle. When he drew breath and glanced at Harper-Brown's face he was glad that they were in such a public place. He watched it first turn purple, then white with suppressed rage. He continued quickly.

'As soon as Commander Cator said that the papers were suspicious, I knew that you would have urged me to cooperate fully, sir, so I did. I realised that you respected Cator, because you sent me to his seminar last month, so you would be comfortable with his close involvement. I do hope I did the right thing, sir.'

Fenwick's quiet voice had a rare hint of supplication in it that threw the ACC off guard. He was being offered a clear choice: to bawl Fenwick out, which would make him feel better but would result in loss of face because the papers had already been handed over in an action that clearly counter-manded his express instructions; or to pretend that he agreed with, had even implicitly encouraged, Fenwick's show of initiative that had led to Cator's involvement, by invitation, in a case that was outside his jurisdiction. He took a large gulp of his drink through livid lips.

'I can see that you think you took an understandable decision in the circumstances, Chief Inspector, but next time, call me. There is a fine line between initiative and insubordination, and you can be sure that I know precisely where it is drawn, particularly where you are concerned.' He locked eyes with Fenwick, and the look they exchanged expressed a complete and mutual understanding of what had just taken place.

Fenwick drained his whisky. It was far too diluted by stale melt-water to be palatable, but he thought that leaving it would have been interpreted as a further insult, and that was the last thing he needed. He made to stand up, but the ACC put out a hand to stop him.

'If there is evidence of a money-laundering operation in Harlden, Fenwick, I must be kept fully advised. We are in dangerous territory. The men who may be implicated are all highly respectable citizens, some of the most influential in the county. I don't know how this alleged arrangement was set up, but if you are right, there is no knowing how far the corruption might have reached. Legitimate businessmen could have been drawn in without any knowledge of what was really happening. Investment opportunities in local businesses come up all the time; ten thousand pounds here, fifty thousand there.'

The ACC looked around and muttered, almost to himself, 'It would be so easy. Alan Wainwright, his son, his nephew, Jeremy Kemp, Neil Yarrell, Frederick Doggett, even James FitzGerald, they all are or were members. So easy to meet casually during a round, or even in the bar. No one would remark on it.' A fresh thought occurred to him. 'What about Neil Yarrell and

James FitzGerald's alibis for Fish and Graham Wainwright's murders?'

'Not watertight, sir.'

'I would like the daily reports continued without fail. And if you find new evidence that implicates these people, call me, any time. I need to know at once.' He looked Fenwick directly in the eye. 'Make no mistake, Chief Inspector, you are already walking a tightrope over a very murky swamp, and if you fall, you will fall alone. This constabulary will neither be implicated in a cover-up nor will it wreck the lives of innocent people. That responsibility lies in your hands, Fenwick. If it's too much for you, say so now and I will transfer the investigation to other officers. If you choose to remain the senior investigating officer in charge, be very sure that you know what you are doing.'

Fenwick shook his head in amazement. Harper-Brown knew Fenwick could not give up the case without damaging his career irretrievably, but this way the ACC would always be able to claim that he had counselled Fenwick to cede responsibility to a more senior officer but had been persuaded to let him remain in charge. If anything went wrong, Fenwick would fall and the ACC would be protected from anything worse than a reprimand.

'I'll stay on the case.' Fenwick couldn't bring himself to acknowledge the ACC's superiority by adding 'sir', but Harper-Brown clearly didn't care. He had the answer he had expected.

On his way back to Harlden, Fenwick called the incident room manager, who told him excitedly about how one of the researchers had spotted a link between James FitzGerald and Wainwright's. FitzGerald had an eleven-year-old conviction for tax evasion – not something that would appear on the police computers, but it had received some publicity at the time in the local press. In a spare hour, he had been trawling the Internet, looking for connections with any of the names Fenwick had listed, and found the article. The undeclared income related to a trust owning Wainwright shares. Fenwick asked to be put through to the officer and congratulated him on a great show of initiative.

As he broke the connection, his mobile phone rang again. It was DI Blite. Before Fenwick could say anything, the inspector jumped in.

'At last! I've been trying you all day, sir. You must have been in an area with bad reception.'

Fenwick said nothing. He had received calls throughout his time in London, and there were no messages. As Blite started to tell him about 'his' big break, Fenwick cut him off.

'Yes, I know, Inspector. The ACC mentioned it and I have already congratulated the officer involved. What else has happened today?'

There was no other news of substance and Fenwick broke the connection with a curt goodnight.

Nightingale drove back to Harlden with Sergeant Gould in an extraordinary state of excitement that wasn't dampened even by the realisation that she still had a pile of records searches on Sally Wainwright-Smith to work through on her return. After two days of combing through every corner of Amanda Bennett's house, she had found tape number 10, which now lay sealed and dated in an evidence wallet in Gould's jacket pocket. Nightingale could sense his enthusiasm – and relief – as he drove recklessly through the rush-hour traffic.

When they reached the station, Gould left to have the tape entered as evidence before they played it in front of witnesses. Nightingale parked the car, then raced to the incident room. The Superintendent was there, as were Cooper and the office manager. Fenwick was apparently going straight from London to meet the ACC, so a decision had been made to hear the tape in his absence. Gould used a gloved finger to slot the tape gently into the machine, and pressed 'play'. The voice of the dead man filled the room.

As last words went, they would not have been memorable had it not been for the manner of his death, but they moved Nightingale nevertheless. She knew that Fish's body was lying chilled beyond corruption, eviscerated and roughly sewn back together, and to listen to his voice made her think of warm lips, air breathed from lungs through a throat that she could hear now being cleared and then remoistened.

'*My name is Arthur Lawrence Fish. Today's date is the twentieth of April; it is four o'clock. I am the financial controller of Wainwright Enterprises.*' A crackling silence followed, as if his few words had brought home to him the reality of his position, then he started speaking again. '*In my house at number one Greenside, Harlden, there is a concealed room. The access to it is through my bedroom wardrobe. In the room are papers, complete financial records, that prove Wainwright Enterprises has been involved in irregular financial transactions for as long as I have worked there, which is over twenty-five years. I don't know why I'm doing this . . .*' He had obviously started talking to himself, perhaps forgetting that he was still recording. '*If anybody ever hears this . . . But then I'll be dead anyway!*' Another sound; perhaps he had blown his nose. '*I want to make it absolutely clear that my wife and family have no knowledge of my involvement in Wainwright's corruption. The policy that pays for my wife's care is legitimate and the house is in her name. Not a penny of dirty money ever went into it – I saved all that – so it belongs to her and then to our children. They're good kids, they deserve it.*' The recording stopped abruptly, and when it started again after a few seconds, Arthur's voice had taken on a different quality. It was no longer scared or belligerent, just desperately sad. '*I'm leaving this tape with an old and trusted friend in case anything should happen to me. She'll see it ends up in the right hands. I'm not very good at farewells, and right now I feel stupid for even doing this, but,*' a deep breath, '*just in case, I want you to know, whoever you are, that I never hurt anybody, ever, and whatever I chose not to notice, it was because of my wife. Don't let her know about me, but please tell her that I love her, I always have.*'

The tape stopped and there was silence. They weren't eloquent words, but they were human and real. No one knew what to say, and there was a general shuffling of feet before DS Gould broke the silence.

'I'll make sure that an edited copy reaches his wife when we can release it.'

An hour later, back in the incident room, Nightingale stared at the photocopy of Sally Wainwright-Smith's marriage and birth certificates and tried to blink her tiredness away. It was nearly ten o'clock and the night duty team had arrived. The fuss over the revelations in Arthur's tape had died away, but the incident room was noisy with chatter as they settled themselves in readiness for the long night ahead. She'd set out to investigate Sally's childhood thinking it would take only a couple of hours; instead, she'd wasted a full twenty-four hours, had had to suffer Cooper's heavy-handed reminder of how important the job was, and had two pieces of paper for her pains. What was worse, they didn't make sense. According to the marriage certificate, Sally was a twenty-seven-year-old spinster, maiden name Price, born in a little village outside Harlden called Potter's Field, but the birth certificate Nightingale had managed to obtain after checking hundreds of Sallys born in the same year and month was for a Sally Bates, exactly the same date and place of birth. Something didn't make sense.

She made her way to the coffee machine on the ground floor and waited patiently behind George Wicklow, the duty sergeant. Nightingale didn't know it, but George had a soft spot for her. He looked past her Home Counties accent and the air of breeding that she didn't even know existed and saw beneath them a young policewoman of exceptional ability. And she was beautiful too, in a rarefied sort of way. She should be out with a decent boyfriend – young Nick would be good, although police relationships rarely survived – not cooped up here, exhausted and surviving on caffeine and creamer.

'What're you doing here so late?'

'Lots to do, Sarge.' Her wry grin didn't reach her eyes. She punched the 'extra-strong' button and waited the irritating fourteen seconds that, according to the sign, assured her of a fresh brew. It didn't taste any better.

'Problem?'

Nightingale was surprised. Was it so obvious?

'Trying to find out more background on a suspect, Sergeant, and I keep hitting dead ends.'

'Local or out of area?'

'Oh, a local girl, but that doesn't help.'

'Run the name past me, I might know it.' George had been with the force for over twenty-five years, after all, and had never moved from Division. Nightingale acknowledged that they would never manage to substitute *his* knowledge with a computer record, but even so she was sceptical. Then she shrugged – what was there to lose?

'OK, it's Sally Wainwright-Smith, wife of the sole heir to Alan Wainwright's fortune. According to her marriage certificate, she was born in Potter's Field twenty-seven years ago. And I've got a choice of two maiden names.'

George Wicklow had gone very still at the name of the village, but Nightingale didn't notice.

'It's either Sally Price, or Sally—'

'Bates,' he said in a flat voice.

'Yes! How did you know? You're a miracle, sir!'

But George Wicklow didn't hear her compliment. He tipped his sweet tea away as if it was suddenly too rich for his palate.

'Come to the desk.'

When he had made sure that the new constable he had left on duty was coping with the evening's usual traffic, he motioned her to sit down on one of the hard wooden chairs out of earshot of the counter.

'So, you've come across Sally Bates. My God. She's, what, mid twenties now? She was a kid of eight last time I saw her. I'm not surprised she's changed her name. And she's back here; that takes nerve.'

'Why, what's she done?'

'Not her, her father and mother. Surely you must remember the case of the Bates children? It was national news, a terrible business.'

'No, but if she was eight, that was nineteen years ago. I probably wasn't reading newspapers then.'

'Eileen and Frank Bates had three children: little Billy was nearly two; Sarah was about six months, I think; and Sally was eight. Except that nobody knew they had three children; the neighbours thought it was just the one – Sally. She went to school and church like a regular kid. Parents both went to church too, very strict by all accounts, and close with money, but nothing out of the ordinary, according to the neighbours.

'Close with money, that was a laugh! My God, if only they'd known.' George wiped his damp face with a heavy hand, and Nightingale tried not to look at him with concern. 'Anyway, they lived in this big old house on the edge of the village, down the end of a muddy track backing on to farmland. Neighbours never saw Eileen Bates from one month to the next. Frank did all the shopping, and Sally walked to school, two miles, never mind the weather.

'It was something really trivial that put us on to what was happening at the Bates house. Sally was accused of stealing at school and it came out that children had been missing things for months: pocket money, gloves, a scarf, but food mainly. The head teacher asked Frank Bates to come in for a chat. She was concerned about Sally, felt she needed some counselling, but Bates wouldn't hear of it. Said he'd sort Sally out. The head teacher called Social Services and they paid a visit, choosing a time when Frank was at work – he was a mechanic, did odd jobs on the farms round about. Eileen Bates wouldn't let them in. As they were leaving, they thought they heard a mewing sound, like a cat or a small animal, but at the time they thought nothing of it. They tried to visit a few more times and then gave up; that was one of the things that was criticised most in the inquiry later.

'Sally's behaviour didn't get any better. She'd always been bright, but she started to fall behind at school. And she became so thin. I remember, when we finally interviewed her, she was a bag of bones; huge staring eyes, sores around her mouth, but a wild cat . . .'

Nightingale listened in horrified fascination, trying to match the sharp, sophisticated wife of a multi-millionaire with the scrawny eight-year-old, stealing tuck and pocket money.

'Things became worse at school. The head teacher called in Social Services again and they held a case conference. After they'd been denied access once more, we were called in. The head persuaded the parents of one of the children Sally had allegedly stolen from to press charges, in Sally's best interests.

'I went to her home during that first visit. It was mid February but there

204

was no heating on, no carpets. The furniture looked like stuff you'd find in a skip. Frank and Eileen were at home, so was Sally. She didn't say a word; neither did her mother. Frank did all the talking. We had a bit of a look around but there was nothing suspicious. Next day, Sally showed up at school with a mass of bruises on her arms and legs – said she fell downstairs. Day after that she had a black eye. We went back with Social Services. For some reason, I don't know why, I took some sandwiches and a chocolate bar with me. They were in a greaseproof bag in my coat pocket, and as soon as I went into the kitchen where Sally was with her parents, I saw that she could smell them.

'She kept staring at me and at my coat. I've never seen such raw hunger, ever. It made my blood run cold, but it also gave me an idea. Whilst my colleague interviewed the parents, I picked up my coat and walked outside. The garden was just mud and a washing line. Sure enough, little Sally followed me out like a hyena smelling blood. I took out a sandwich, and I swear the child dribbled.

' "What's going on, Sally?" I said, and I broke a corner off and made as if to eat it, God forgive me. I was desperate to feed her, she was starving, but I wanted her to talk too. She wouldn't, though, and in the end I gave in and gave her the sandwich. She wolfed down the first few mouthfuls, but then I saw that she was putting pieces of food in her skirt pocket. I gave her the bar of chocolate and she ate all but two squares.

'I tried again to get her to talk, but all she did was keep looking nervously back at the house and raising her eyes up towards its roof. I followed her gaze but there was nothing to see – a row of empty windows, one boarded up where the glass had been broken.'

Nightingale couldn't wait any longer.

'But the other children – her brother and sister?'

George shook himself and visibly drew back from a memory he'd been reliving, minute by painful minute.

'Right. Back inside, just as we were leaving, we heard a noise from above. I was up those stairs like a shot, I can tell you. Frank was right behind me, dragging me back by the leg, but Joe, my mate, pulled him off. Eileen was screaming, hitting Joe. On the landing I just slammed open doors, one after the other, till I got to the last one at the back of the house. It was locked, so I rammed it with my shoulder. Bates was on me then, shouting, "You can't do that, you can't do that. It's my house!" and trying to punch me, but then Joe had him and I just carried on until the lock broke.'

George paused, breathing heavily, and shut his eyes as if in terrible pain.

'Some memories stay with you forever, no matter what. The stench as I went in – God, it was terrible. I can't go near a baby's nappy now without feeling physically ill. The room was so dark that at first I couldn't see anything. Then I saw what I just thought was a bundle of old clothes. I didn't realise it was a child until Sally came tottering in and went up to Billy with the chocolate she'd saved. He was lying on a filthy cot mattress on the floor. She walked straight past all of us, calm as you like, and knelt down to him.'

George's voice thickened with tears.

' "There you are, Billy," she says, bright as a button, and puts the chocolate to his mouth. But the kid's so weak he can't eat it, and she looks up to me, smiles and says, "Billy's not hungry," and puts the chocolate in her own mouth.'

He couldn't go on. Nightingale stared at his face in horror.

'Was he dead?'

George Wicklow could barely manage a whisper. 'No, not quite. He died a couple of days later. We found Sarah, the baby, in a carrycot. She was dead, very obviously dead.

'Sally was put in a home, then fostered. I think the house was pulled down. Frank and Eileen Bates were charged with murder and cruelty. He was convicted on both counts. Eileen was sentenced to two years but she died in prison. Bates is still there. Life means life for him. He's going to rot there.' The absolute hatred in the sergeant's voice made the hairs rise on Nightingale's arms.

'But why did they do it?'

George shook his head. 'Who knows. When Sarah was born, Frank just decided that they couldn't afford the children. He simply stopped feeding them. For a while Eileen continued to breast-feed the baby, and either she or Sally – perhaps both – sneaked food in to Billy. But then, after the first Social Services visit, Frank locked the two younger children up and kept the key with him.'

George shook himself and made a visible effort to look more cheerful.

'But it's good that little Sally survived and has done well for herself after such a terrible start in life. You said she's a suspect, though – anything serious?'

Nightingale stared into the sergeant's face, aware she was about to deal him yet another blow.

'Murder,' she said, and briefly squeezed his arm in compassion.

Cooper and Nightingale sat uncomfortably in front of Fenwick's desk. Nightingale had called Cooper at once, and he in turn had spoken to Fenwick despite the hour; the DCI had been there within thirty minutes. Cooper crossed and uncrossed his legs in a vain attempt to stop the metal-framed visitor's chair cutting into the back of them. He was too broad for the seat and had to perch half in, half out of it. Nightingale sat primly on the edge of hers, seeming barely to rest her weight on it. She had just finished her report, and a grim silence filled the room.

'It's a wonder she turned out normal.' Cooper shook his head in amazement.

'Did she, though? How do we know?' Nightingale was sceptical. 'If you want more detail, sir, Sergeant Wicklow can tell you; he was the officer who found her brother and sister.'

Fenwick shook his head at the gruesome thought. 'Another time, perhaps. Right now I want to see Mrs Wainwright-Smith.'

'Do you want me to come, sir?'

'No thanks, Cooper. I'll go alone. And you need to go home to bed, Nightingale. You look exhausted.'

'I'm OK, sir.' But her voice belied her words, and at Fenwick's insistence she left the two men to it.

'She looks all in. What's she been up to?' asked Fenwick once she had gone.

'Well, as far as I can tell, sir, she's been working flat out for the last twenty-four hours.'

'It was worth it, Sergeant. I knew she'd find something. But I wonder about that private investigator. Is he holding out on us? He was working for Graham for several weeks, and what he told us he knew, he could have found out in a matter of days.'

Cooper scribbled in his book.

'It's on the list for tomorrow, guv. What are you going to do with this info? It's hardly relevant, is it?'

'You think not? Well, I have to disagree. The sort of disturbed childhood Sally had could lead to all sorts of dysfunctional behaviour, perhaps even brutality, though I accept that's pure supposition. Could you talk to Claire Keating? I'd like her assessment of the likely behaviour of someone who has suffered the trauma that Sally has.'

Cooper nodded and made a note in his book.

'And Sergeant, I'd like it for tomorrow morning,'

CHAPTER THIRTY-THREE

Wainwright Hall looked abandoned and desolate as sheets of spring rain swept in from the west over lawns that had grown too long and roses that were already sickly with black spot. A coach lantern gleamed fitfully as the wet wind swung it in and out of the shadow of overhanging ivy. No other lights shone from the house into the gloomy night. He had expected Sally to defer the meeting until the morning, but when he called, just before ten o'clock she had almost seemed eager to meet him.

Fenwick parked his car in front of the main entrance and took a moment to stare at the looming gothic façade from within its warm dry depths. As his eyes adjusted to the shapes of the Hall, he noticed the details of its ornamentation; battlements, gargoyles, buttresses, turrets and a mock tower fought with each other for his attention. It looked like the setting for a horror story.

Sally was dressed for the cool in an angora jumper and black jeans. It was the first time he'd seen her out of a calf-length skirt and he couldn't help noticing that she had very long legs. The house was bitterly cold.

'After Easter I don't turn the central heating on again until November. The kitchen is warm, if you don't mind talking in there.'

As they walked through the cold mausoleum of the great hall, a sudden harsh gust of wind struck the westerly side of the house, making windows rattle and the chimneys moan. It was not a comfortable sound, and as Fenwick gazed up the grand staircase into the dark of the galleried landing above, he reassessed the nerves of the woman in front of him. She was prepared to stay here on her own during the long days her husband was away; it wasn't something he thought many women would choose to do.

The kitchen was warmer, neat and tidy. A pile of sewing lay on the scrubbed pine table and a large saucepan bubbled on the top of the Aga, but he noticed a discreet bottle of gin tucked behind a crock of bread.

'I'm making stock from the weekend lamb joint,' she explained unnecessarily. 'Alex loves my soups.'

'Does he know of your affair with his uncle?'

He'd expected shock, a gasp, something, but she simply said, cool as a cat:

'What do you think? Tea, Chief Inspector?' She regarded him calmly, her pale green eyes large and unblinking, pupils huge in the soft light. 'You've been listening to Millie Willett. Well, you shouldn't.' Her tone hardened. 'She's an interfering, jealous old woman with too much imagination and time on her hands.'

For an instant Fenwick saw within Sally a vindictive, authoritarian woman, capable of throwing ageing long-serving employees out of their tied cottage and into a high-rise flat. Then the image was gone. She made their tea with small, efficient movements. It was obvious that she regarded this kitchen as hers, not her help's, and something of this thought must have shown in Fenwick's face, for she said suddenly:

'You're surprised to find me at home in my own kitchen?'

'No, not really. Just curious.'

'A lot of money passes through a kitchen, Chief Inspector. And a lot of waste.' She uttered the last word as if it were a sin and calmly counted out four digestive biscuits on to a flower-patterned tea plate.

There was an unnatural silence in the wake of this remark. Fenwick regarded her ritual with new insight; that compulsion to control food and never to waste a bite had taken on a new significance, and he was overcome by an unwelcome pity. She sensed his change in mood and looked confused.

'You wanted to speak to me. About what?'

She went to fuss with the saucepan on the Aga, and Fenwick waited patiently until she had turned to look at him again. He wanted to see her reaction to his new knowledge. He spoke softly, unthreateningly, but even so his words had an instant impact.

'Mrs Wainwright-Smith, why didn't you tell us that your real maiden name was Sally Bates?'

She said nothing, simply stared at him open-mouthed in shock as she sank into a nearby chair.

'There is nothing to be ashamed of and it would have been helpful for us to know, rather than discover it ourselves.'

'How did you find out?' The disbelief in her voice was audible, as if her question would discover simply that he had made a lucky guess.

'Routine enquiries. It was inevitable that we would uncover your past. Is your husband aware of your childhood?'

'No, of course not. Nor do I want him to know, do you hear me?' Her voice had taken on an edge of anger and Fenwick waited in silence for it to pass. When she was calmer, he continued.

'Why did you change your name?'

'Wouldn't you, with parents like that?'

'What did you do after they were arrested?'

'I went into care. What business is that of yours?'

He ignored her question and moved on. Behind her on the stove, the stock bubbled over in the pot. The sound penetrated her distracted mind and she stood up to move the pan to a cooler position on the Aga. When she turned around again, there was a new look of calculation in her eyes.

'Why exactly were you digging into my past, Chief Inspector?'

'People have a habit of dying around you, Mrs Wainwright-Smith; that makes us curious.'

She said nothing and went back to stirring the pan, a look of intense concentration on her face. Fenwick watched her back, the rise and fall of the muscles in her narrow shoulders. She had the poise and hidden strength of a ballerina, and for a moment he doubted his judgement of her. But then she turned around and looked him in the eyes, and all doubts fled. The hair rose on the back of his neck and along his forearms. There was no doubting the insolent acknowledgement that lurked behind the expression in her eyes.

'I think you will find, Chief Inspector, that the few people of my acquaintance who have died recently have been the victims of a series of unfortunate tragedies. In none of the deaths have I been implicated in any way.'

'Not even in those of Arthur Fish and Amanda Bennett?' At the mention of the prostitute's name her expression hardened, and Fenwick was sure that a flash of concern appeared briefly in her eyes, but her words were calm enough.

'You really are clutching at straws now. Is that the best you can do?' She smiled confidently, taunting him with her knowledge that he had no real evidence against her.

'Don't play with me, Mrs Wainwright-Smith, it doesn't work. I may not have all the evidence I need right now, but it is starting to accumulate, and it will only be a matter of time before I have enough to charge you. Don't trouble yourself. I'll let myself out.'

When she was alone again in the kitchen, Sally checked the heat under the stock and returned the four untouched biscuits to their airtight container. Her movements were studied and deliberate. Then she poured herself a large gin and small tonic and made her way slowly to the little office to the side of the entrance hall. She logged on to her computer and called up details of her joint account with Alexander, then the private savings account she still held and about which he knew nothing.

She stared at the numbers on the screen until they blurred into a grey haze. Looking at them normally gave her a sense of security, but today it wasn't working. She took a small brown bottle of pills from her bag and swallowed two with her gin and tonic as the computer shut down. The drug worked almost instantly with the alcohol and she started to feel the intensity of calm that was the ironic gift of medication. Sometimes, when she couldn't bear this cotton-wool wrapper, she'd chase the pill with some amphetamines, riding a roller-coaster of toxic emotions until she came back down to earth empty and uncaring. She could never remember exactly what she had done when the drugs were at their peak, but she saw that as a benefit.

She left her study and shambled to the top of the stairs, along the landing and up the spiral staircase of the tower that dominated the north side of the house. Right at the top, in a low room under the eaves, she had made herself a den. There was a mattress on the floor and an old blanket for when the weather was icy. The windows were boarded up, and what little light there was came from an unshaded forty-watt bulb. She threw herself down on to the mattress and hugged the blanket to her chest. When her control finally went, despite the anti-depressants, it was terrible. She wept and cried; she screamed at the beams in the roof and clawed at her arms until they were red and spots of blood started from the long scratches. Her cries rose to a shriek and then a terrible, awful wail that went on and on until she could finally cry no more.

She lay there on her back, arms flung out to the sides, without moving, until slowly her reason returned to her. She staggered to her feet and had to lean against a wall until her head stopped spinning. Then slowly, clutching at the rickety wooden handrail, she clawed her way back down to the lower landing and along to her bedroom, where she locked the door behind her.

Her sleeping tablets were in a little brown bottle by the bed. She swallowed half a pill with one gulp of water before falling on to the bed fully clothed. The ceiling started to sway in and out as she drifted into the semi-consciousness that would sometimes last for hours before she fell asleep. Her mind was a void in which sparks of emotion flickered, flared and died unborn. As she drifted finally towards sleep, the glimmer of a solution came to her, as she had known it would. She closed her eyes as she felt darkness descend and folded her arms tight across her chest in a pathetic attempt to ward off her nightmares.

CHAPTER THIRTY-FOUR

Fenwick parked his car with practised economy in the prison visitors' car park. Visiting hours were over and it was almost empty. He noticed the security cameras and was glad. It was the sort of spot that invited petty crime and hooliganism despite the barriers.

He had asked Nightingale to come with him, leaving Cooper behind at Division to track down more people who had known Sally. Now that they knew who she was, he was hopeful of finally filling the gaps in her history. It was one of the reasons he was here.

'Sir?'

'Hmm, what?'

'Shall we go in, sir?'

'Yes. Come on.'

They hurried across the waterlogged tarmac, both huddled inside waterproof coats. May was proving an unseasonably cold, storm-tossed month. In the car park, stunted trees had been whipped bare of new leaves, and there was a hint of frost in the evening air.

Their warrant cards were checked carefully, but they were still searched before being let through the electronically controlled iron gates, which clanged shut behind them before an identical pair, fifteen feet ahead, clicked open. The prison guard beyond directed them to a private interview room at the end of a silent white corridor. Nightingale was already finding it claustrophobic. What must it feel like to be locked up in here for life? The smell was institutional, stale, with a trace of chemicals that didn't conceal the taint of hundreds of bodies held in close confinement. It gave her a headache, and she longed for the interview to be over.

Frank Bates was shown into the room, with a guard close behind. The prisoner stared intently at Nightingale without blinking. Fenwick turned to the guard.

'It's all right, please leave.'

'I have instructions to stay, sir, for your own safety. It's the regulations.' He pointed to a sign on the wall. 'Unless you sign a disclaimer, sir.' He passed over a pre-printed form, which Fenwick signed without a second thought. Nightingale tried not to let her nervousness show.

'Ridiculous what these privatised firms insist on now,' Fenwick muttered as he handed the form back.

When the guard had left, Fenwick turned to study Bates, who for his part kept his eyes firmly on the woman police constable. Fenwick considered him for a long moment, then spoke with a quiet authority that made the prisoner blink for the first time.

'Constable, go and stand by the door, please. You can take notes from there. Mr Bates, eyes front, now. Thank you. We're here to talk about your daughter, Sally. When did you last see her?'

'You got any cigarettes?'

Fenwick removed two unopened packets from his jacket pocket and placed them firmly on his side of the table that separated him from the prisoner. Bates was a big man, muscles slack now from lack of exercise and his jowls heavier than they would have been eighteen years ago, but still there was a sense of power about him and a latent menace that showed in his pale blue eyes. He regarded Fenwick with dislike. It was obvious that he resented the policeman's power over him, symbolised by his control of the cigarettes.

Fenwick could see him weighing up whether to pick up a packet or not. If he reached over and Fenwick moved them away, he would lose face. If he was allowed to hold on to them, Fenwick's power in turn would be diminished. Fenwick was curious to see what the prisoner would do, but after a while he grew bored of the game and replaced the cigarettes in his jacket. Bates' eyes darkened and his shoulders tensed.

'They're yours when you've talked and not before, and there are some phone cards as well if you tell us everything we need to know.'

Bates nodded imperceptibly.

'Haven't seen her since I came in here – eighteen years ago.' He had a deep voice that matched his big frame.

'Do you know what's happened to her in that time?'

The pale eyes moved sideways to Nightingale by the door and back to Fenwick. He knew something, and he was trying to calculate its value.

'What's the little bitch been up to now, then?'

'What had she been up to before?'

'Enough. She was always trouble, that one.'

Fenwick waited for Bates to continue, making it clear that he wouldn't be volunteering anything more.

'I've heard a bit from church visitors, now and then. Said she married well. No surprises there; she was bound to, cunning little—'

'Who visits you from the church?'

'Mrs O'Brien, First Presbyterian on Charlotte Road. She's visited for twelve years now. Brings me stuff and tells me the news. She's the one that's spoken most about Sally. No one else does, not now.'

Fenwick tossed over one of the packets of cigarettes, and a few seconds later a box of matches. Bates lit one straight away, drawing the smoke deep into his lungs and half closing his eyes. When he opened them again, he was smiling.

'She's a sly one, is Sally. When she was put in care she had everyone dancing attendance on her: the doctors and psychologists, the care workers and Social Services. They were so eager to remove the "scars" – I think that's what they called them. My lawyer told me all about it, Miss Llewelyn. She thought I'd be concerned.' He let out a short, coughing laugh and shook his head in wonder at the stupidity of some people. 'They didn't need to worry about her. No, sir. She was a survivor, was our little Sally. They never asked

213

that, did they? How she survived when the others ... Well, they never asked.'

'But I'm asking now. How *did* she survive?'

Bates looked at Fenwick and then at his opened packet of cigarettes, obviously calculating.

'She was useful. Had a way about her. She could lift things and no one'd notice, and she listened in at church so I'd know when people were away for the weekend, say, or on holiday. I'd know when to go round. She was a clever little thing.'

'She helped you steal?'

'That and more. Pretty little thing, was our Sally. Eight years old, perfect as a picture. There were a few old gents in the church that took a fancy to her. All innocent, of course – that is, until she got to know them. I had to coach her at first, a few home lessons like, but she soon got the hang of it, quite enjoyed it really. So did they, until I showed up . . .'

'So you were a blackmailer as well as a thief and a murderer?'

Bates' chair scraped back against the concrete floor as he stood up, ready to lunge at Fenwick where he sat calmly less than three feet away.

'Sit down. Let's not pretend you're actually going to do anything to me. You may be in for life, but there's always the chance of parole. And your privileges – pity to lose those. One word from me and they'd be gone, and you know it.'

Nightingale stared in horrified fascination at the vein that pulsed in Bates' huge forehead above his bulging eyes. She could see the tension in his legs, ready to leap forward, his hands already curled into fists, but Fenwick just stared at him coolly, apparently unmoved.

Eventually Bates sat down, unable to meet the policeman's eyes.

'So you weren't surprised that Sally survived going into care? How long was she in a home?'

'You'd need to check with Mrs O'Brien – one, two years, perhaps. She was fostered soon after.'

'Do you know anything about her foster family?'

'*Families*. She had four or five before she was sixteen. Don't know what happened to her next, but I heard she got a scholarship to college or some such. Then nothing until last year, when Mrs O'Brien told me she was back in the area.'

'And you've not seen her in all that time?' Fenwick reflected that it was unlikely that Sally had wanted to see her father again, but he needed to be sure.

Bates looked at him, eyes heavy with irony but without a trace of grief or even regret.

'No, nor would I want to. She's on her own now.'

It was said with an air of finality. Fenwick slid the second packet of cigarettes over and signalled to Nightingale to summon the guard.

'What about the phone cards?'

'Not for that little story, Bates. I'll see what Mrs O'Brien has to say. If it's interesting enough, I'll give them to her to bring in to you.'

The prisoner was led out to be escorted back to his cell. Nightingale heard a heavy door open and clang shut and let out a huge sigh. She hadn't even been aware that she was holding her breath. Fenwick stood up slowly and stared at the chair Bates had been sitting in moments before.

'I have never been able to understand what it is in a man that turns casual cruelty to evil. He abused and prostituted his daughter, and starved her brother and baby sister to death. Yet there he sat, the same as you and me. He gets up each morning, washes, shaves, and dresses. What does he think about when he looks at himself in the mirror? Does he have any comprehension of the awfulness of what he's done, of what he is? Does he care? What is it that makes a man so?'

'You said it, sir; he's evil.'

'But *why*?'

'Why not, sir? Evil is as real as good, perhaps even more so as it doesn't require self-control. It thrives on licentiousness and brings immediate rewards. Why should we be surprised to discover it so often lying behind the crimes we have to face?'

The bitter anger of her words shocked Fenwick and he looked at her in amazement. The hard fury in her eyes as she stared at the empty chair worried him. Whatever had happened to convince her of the reality of evil? And what would that belief do to her as she grew older? Of one thing he was sure: it was a very dangerous conviction to find in a police officer. It would encourage a belief in justice as a means as well as an end, and excuse any route to retribution. He would have to watch her, carefully. He encouraged her out into the gloomy car park.

CHAPTER THIRTY-FIVE

'So how much do I owe you?'

'Twenty-five quid for the parts, Dad.'

'But what about your labour?' Cooper was already grateful that his son had given up his Saturday afternoon to fix his ageing Rover and had no intention of taking further advantage of the lad.

'No, forget it. I wasn't doing anything, and it's useful to work on older engines like this. We don't see many in the workshop any more. You really should—'

'Buy Mum a new one. I know, but she's settled into this one. You know how she gets. Here's forty quid . . . No, go on, take it, you're still doing me a favour.'

It tickled him to see Lee working so well. He'd really found his niche in their local garage, and the owner had nothing but praise for his son, which warmed Cooper's heart.

'I've got a question for you. What do you know of Donald Glass, runs D and G Motors on the A24?' Cooper had come across a mention of Glass in the Social Services file they now had on Sally Bates, and had recognised the name of the self-made businessman.

Lee screwed up his face into a sneer.

'Not much. We get a few of his exes into the garage – customers and girlfriends. They're full of complaints about Don. He's a bit of a cheapskate and his work leaves something to be desired. Why?'

'His name's cropped up, that's all. He's not done anything wrong that we know of, but he knew someone who might've done.'

Cooper thought of Nightingale's detailed research into Sally's background thanks to her meetings with Mrs O'Brien. The children's home, her social workers, her many foster homes, and then, at age sixteen, her decision to live with Donald Glass before moving on again, they didn't yet know where or to whom. The foster families had all remembered Sally as a difficult child who was inclined to level accusations of sexual assault if she didn't get her own way. Social Services had finally given up maintaining her file shortly after she had moved in with Glass, and Fenwick expected Cooper to close the missing link as quickly as possible. So far, there was no hint in Sally's past of any criminal violence, but Fenwick had asked for a full search against the county's records just in case. He was still convinced she was capable of murder. Cooper was becoming worried at his preoccupation and wanted to close the file on Sally as quickly as possible. An interview with Glass would help him do that. He came out of his reverie to hear his son still talking to him. 'Well if you need to see him, come down to the Bird in Hand tonight, he's always there on a Saturday.'

'You going, then? I might join you.'

'Yup! I can stand a round now, can't I!'

Donald Glass stood with his back to the large inglenook fireplace, pint jug held at a precarious angle down by his thigh. He had a beer belly, and a nasty scar that ran from his receding hairline down his cheek to the start of a double chin. He looked considerably older than his thirty-seven years. He was holding court, Cooper decided; that was the only way to describe it. Together with a group of four cronies, he blocked the heat from the large blaze and left fellow drinkers shivering in draughty corners.

Having taken a good look at Glass, Cooper decided he'd choose another moment to question him about Sally. He'd have a quick drink with the lad and his mates, just to be sociable, and leave. Lee, though, had other ideas.

'Don!' he called out cheerily, cutting across the fireside group's chatter and oblivious to their glares. 'Got a moment for my dad? He'd like a word.'

'Got a problem with his motor you can't fix, huh? Always happy to share my expert advice, but not here, and not in my own time.'

Lee grinned; he had no time for Don Glass and couldn't care less about his opinion.

'No, he's a copper. Wants a word with you.'

Gee, thanks, thought Cooper as he squared his shoulders, picked up his pint and made his way over to the now hostile group around Don.

'Evening,' he said in a quiet conversational tone. He didn't look like a policeman at first glance. Portly, perspiring and wearing his customary tweed jacket, he could have been mistaken for a beef farmer looking to share a moan about the latest auction prices. But there was something about his eyes, a hint of authority that made people look twice once he was up close. That was exactly what Donald Glass did now. A smart remark died on his lips, though he still didn't have any patience with a man who'd invade his pub and disturb his private life.

'Urgent, is it? Can't it wait till tomorrow?'

'I'm here, so are you, and you'd be helping us if we could talk now.'

'What about?' There was a tension about Glass that told Cooper, an old hand at understanding human nature – particularly criminal nature – that he probably had something to worry about.

'I'd rather have a word in private . . .'

Glass shook his head, and Cooper knew that this time he was heading towards a smart remark, so he forestalled him.

'It's about Sally Bates.'

Glass blanched and automatically stroked his long facial scar. Then he grinned, an expression full of malice.

'Well, well. There's a name from the past. You've taken your time to catch up with her. If I can help put that little bitch away . . . Come on. Over there, they're just leaving, we can grab their table.'

Cooper and Glass settled themselves either side of a worn beer barrel that was masquerading as a table and took a moment to size each other up. Cooper pulled out his notebook; this was official business. After a brief nod,

Glass started talking without preamble.

'She gave me this,' he pointed to the long, angry scar on his face, 'and it was lucky that I moved fast or it would've been my neck. I threw her out and never saw her again.'

'When was this?'

'Over ten years ago. What's she done, then, the murderous little bitch? Topped someone properly this time?'

Cooper ignored the question, but his stomach clenched as he realised the relevance of Glass's words.

'How long did she live with you?'

'Nine months, during which she thieved nearly ten thousand quid off me – there's always a fair bit of cash in my business. That's what the fight was about. I caught her red-handed one day.'

'Why didn't you report all this to the police?'

Glass looked away, out of the window, studying a car as it backed into a narrow space between a Mercedes and a Ford. Cooper waited patiently for an answer to his question, although he suspected it was going to be a lie.

'She cleared off. Money was already gone, and she would only have accused me of worse. There was no point dragging you lot in, and anyway, I thought she wouldn't dare come back. Looks like I misjudged her. Must be a big prize that's drawn her here again. Even a cat has only nine lives, and I reckon she must be about out of hers.'

'Why?'

'Well, her father nearly killed her, didn't he, for a start.'

'She *told* you about her childhood?' Cooper was amazed.

'That she'd been abused? Sure, that was all part of the turn-on about Sally: poor little innocent kid – she looked young for sixteen – with a wicked sex drive she couldn't control and the need for some sort of father figure. And I don't mind admitting that I fell for it, hook, line and sinker.'

'So that's one life. Where did the other eight go?'

'The children's homes and the foster families – she went through a stack of them. It was enough to make you weep, the treatment she'd had, and she played the part brilliantly. God,' he stroked the long scar absently, 'but she was the hottest bit of skirt I've ever had.'

Cooper had only just returned home from his brief trip to the pub when DS Gould called him from the station.

'Bob, sorry to call you at home, but I thought you'd want to know that Blitey has had a break. He's found someone who reckons they saw Graham Wainwright with a woman on the morning he died. I've called the DCI and he's on his way in now, if you want to join us.'

Cooper was in the incident room with Gould, Blite and Nightingale within half an hour, but Fenwick had called to say he would be on his way as soon as he had found a baby-sitter. He arrived ten minutes later, apologetic and in an incipient bad mood.

'I'm sorry, the children's nanny went off for a day's holiday this morning and her replacement doesn't start until tomorrow, so I had to find a baby-sitter at short notice.' He turned to Blite. 'Tell me what you have, Inspector.'

'I went to interview Shirley Kennedy, one of the part-time helpers at

Wainwright Hall. For some reason we hadn't interviewed her before – I think we missed it because of the search of the Hall.'

Fenwick nodded at Blite to continue, hiding his concern. Graham had been murdered nearly a week ago. This was sloppy. These things sometimes happened, but not on his cases.

'She has a brother, Nigel. He's seventeen and a bit simple. They live with their parents in a cottage on the edge of the estate. Nigel spends most of his time in the woods and scrub near the river. He's got a thing about water birds, apparently.'

Now he had Fenwick's full attention.

'On the morning Graham Wainwright died, Nigel was down by the river as usual and he saw a couple under the beech tree. It was hard to get him to talk. He's got a mental age of about nine or ten, and what he saw had confused and frightened him.' He pulled out his notebook.

'He says: *I saw a man and a woman. They were . . . sort of arguing together. They were making a lot of noise. I didn't do nothing, honest. I didn't want to look but they were so noisy. I was in a tree. They didn't see me but I saw them. They stopped shouting and the man gets up but then the lady drags him back. I was scared. I ran away but I fell in the river.*'

'Can he identify them?'

'I showed him pictures of everybody, all the dinner guests and Graham Wainwright. He picked out Sally Wainwright-Smith without hesitation, called her his "princess" and said he'd seen her before, but he was confused over the man. Seems he didn't really look at his face. He thinks it was Graham but he couldn't be sure.'

'Probably not good enough for court, but more than enough to confirm what we've suspected all along. Sally has been lying about the morning Graham died.'

'There's something else as well. Shirley was up at the Hall on the Thursday. Normally she's not allowed to touch any of the leftovers. However, that night she said that Alexander was so tired he started to fall asleep at the dinner table, didn't even finish his main course and left more than half of a decent bottle of claret. Normally it would be recorked for the next day, but "the missus", as she calls Sally, insisted she take it home with her, said it would spoil.

'It really shocked Shirley because she says Sally's usually so mean, but that didn't stop her taking it home. Her dad had some as soon as she got in, two glasses while he watched the snooker. She said he was asleep within twenty minutes. They could barely get him to bed and he woke at noon the next day with a terrible headache.'

'So Wainwright-Smith might have been drugged?'

'We'll know soon enough, sir. Shirley's dad makes his own wine and he'd kept the bottle to use later. Hadn't even washed it. Forensic have already sent it to toxicology.'

'Well done, Inspector.' It still wasn't conclusive proof of Sally's guilt, and everything they had so far was circumstantial. Still, it would be enough to try to shock her into a confession, and this time he would have Blite drag her down to the station. Not tonight, though. They needed to find an identification officer to arrange an identity parade, and that would take time. She wasn't a flight risk, so it would wait until morning.

He looked at the expectant faces of the four officers at the heart of his team. They were starting to believe in his theory now, and he could tell that they were hungry to find clear proof of Sally's guilt beyond the circumstantial information they had collected so far.

'Tomorrow morning, nice and early, you are going to bring Sally in for questioning. Take a couple of uniformed officers and confront her with this witness statement.'

Blite nodded enthusiastically. He knew that she was unlikely to break, even with this latest news, but hard interviewing was a particular skill of his, and he relished the idea of practice.

'In the meantime, I want you all to think hard about how she could be linked to the deaths of Fish and Amanda Bennett. We still have no idea. Work every single connection you can think of.'

'Perhaps the Fish and Bennett cases aren't connected, sir.' Cooper voiced his thoughts cautiously, very aware that Fenwick didn't agree with him and that Blite was hanging on every word. But his boss encouraged him to continue.

'Well, sir, we suspect that Wainwright is a cover company for a money-laundering operation. When their MD dies, Alexander takes over. Suppose Fish threatens him with going to the police? He had a fortune in his safe, and who knows, he might even have been blackmailing Alexander's uncle before him.'

Fenwick didn't argue, but he didn't look convinced either.

'It's a possibility, Sergeant, I'll give you that.'

'But you don't agree.'

'Not really. I doubt very much that someone connected with the Wainwright operations would risk a murder being associated with the company so soon after Alan's death, no matter how difficult Arthur had become.'

He clapped Cooper on the back and decided to send the team home. The next day was going to be crucial to break the case, and he wanted them as fresh as possible. Overnight he was going to think hard about whether he had enough evidence to obtain a warrant for Sally's arrest. With any other suspect he would have been confident of the Superintendent's backing, but with this one he felt he needed more. Once they had the identification in the bag, not even the ACC would dare to object. He didn't notice that Nightingale merely walked as far as the coffee machine. By the time she returned to the incident room and had logged on to their master database, he was well on his way home to relieve his baby-sitter.

PART FOUR

To-night it doth inherit
The vasty hall of death.

Matthew Arnold

CHAPTER THIRTY-SIX

Thursday morning dawned clear and bright. The sudden change in the weather brought a promise of warmth that did nothing to soften DI Blite's mood as he prepared for his interview with Sally Wainwright-Smith. Fenwick had called a meeting with Quinlan and Harper-Brown that morning in the hope of persuading them to authorise Sally's arrest. It hadn't worked. A decision had been taken, against Blite and Fenwick's recommendations, that they still had insufficient grounds to arrest her although Fenwick had pushed the point almost to argument with the ACC. It had been a rare and uncomfortable moment for Blite. He wanted a conviction and now agreed completely with Fenwick that Sally was their prime suspect, but inevitably they had run into fierce resistance when they had briefed the ACC and the Superintendent.

By mutual agreement Fenwick and Blite had said nothing about their now shared suspicions about Alan Wainwright's suicide, and made no mention of Fish's murder. They had concentrated entirely on Graham's death, and outlined their initial summary of evidence with growing confidence. Fenwick had listed the case against Sally: a fifteen-million-pound motive; no alibi for the time of the murder; her fingerprints on the vegetable box recovered from the kitchen at the Hall; her treatment of the body once she had been left alone by Jeremy Kemp; her inexplicable hysterics; her pestering of both Fenwick and Blite during their investigations with queries and concerns about Jenny – classic 'guilty' behaviour.

Blite left until last the discovery of an eye-witness who might have seen Graham and Sally together under the beech tree on the morning of his death, and had presented it as his final trump card. Unfortunately the ACC had pressed him hard on the details and he had had to admit that yes, the boy was retarded, and yes, he couldn't be sure that the man was Graham, although he had insisted it was someone very like him.

'It's not good enough, Inspector, and I'm very disappointed to have you deliver a stream of coincidence and conjecture as if it were firm evidence. No, I will not authorise you to arrest her, and I'm sure Superintendent Quinlan agrees with me.'

The Superintendent had little option but to concur, although he had considerable sympathy with his officers and supported their conclusion. Sally Wainwright-Smith had become the obvious suspect, not least because she had had both motive and opportunity to commit the crime; but her arrest would be high profile, and if she didn't break under questioning they would have to release her again, because they didn't have enough to hold her.

'I agree, sir. However, her behaviour is sufficiently erratic for there to be a chance that she might confess if questioned in the right way, or at least reveal more information for us to work on. I recommend that she be brought in for questioning at the station but not arrested.'

The ACC had regarded Quinlan with obvious surprise.

'Very well. So you believe she's guilty as well?'

'Yes, sir, I do.'

'The whole team does, sir. No other suspect, with the possible exception of her husband, has the same combination of motive and opportunity.'

The ACC's face hardened at the very mention of Alexander, and he frowned at Fenwick for making the suggestion.

'I see. Notwithstanding, you are to follow procedures to the letter. The Wainwrights have money and influence, and under *no* circumstances do I want to hear even the hint of a complaint against us. Understood?' He glared at Fenwick as he spoke, despite the fact that it would be Blite who conducted the interrogation.

'Understood, sir.'

In the corridor outside Harper-Brown's office, Blite and Fenwick experienced a rare moment of shared frustration at the ACC's overly cautious approach. Blite murmured under his breath, 'Arse-licker,' which the Superintendent, appearing suddenly behind them, overheard but chose to ignore.

In the tiny lift that they shared down to the ground floor Quinlan suddenly remarked: 'He wants a conviction just as much as you do, but he has to balance so much else. None of us can do our job effectively if we have no resources or if the local political environment becomes difficult. The Assistant Chief Constable manages that for us, and whether you like it or not, the Wainwrights have been the most influential family in this county for years. He's right to make us doubly sure.'

Fenwick's head agreed with Superintendent Quinlan's logic, but in his heart he saw the ACC's behaviour as sycophantic and career-serving. He heard himself say, 'So there is one law for the rich and another for the poor, then!' and immediately regretted it.

Superintendent Quinlan looked at him in exasperation.

'I have a high regard for your detective work, Fenwick, so I'll choose to ignore that remark. But careers are built on more than great police work, remember that.'

Fenwick had agreed tactics with Blite for the interview with Sally. Blite would go and collect her from the Hall with DC Nightingale, whilst the Chief Inspector visited her husband at his office to share all they knew about her background, in case Sally tried to appeal to him when Blite arrived. Claire Keating would join Blite at the station to sit in on the interview.

Now Blite checked his watch; it was well past the hour, so Fenwick should already be with Alexander. As he waited for Sally to answer the door, he stared at the stone gargoyles that guarded the forbidding oak and fashioned his face into a grimace of reply. This was a terrible place. Even on a bright morning, the granite stonework seemed to absorb the sunlight and cast the house into gloom. The gardens were starting to show signs of neglect, and the windows were grimy where soot from the chimneys had settled in long streaks.

Sally opened the door herself. She was dressed in a black polo-neck sweater and designer jeans and from a distance would have passed for a teenager. But there were new signs of strain in her face. Dark circles had formed under her eyes and her skin had lost its wonderful lustre. Her jumper smelt of stale cigarette smoke, and Blite thought he could smell alcohol behind the disguise of fresh mouthwash.

'Your men are still searching the grounds, Inspector. I think they are in the woods – I've a four-wheel-drive car if you need a lift out there.'

'I haven't come to talk to the team, Mrs Wainwright-Smith. We need to interview you again and we'd like to do it at the station. If you'd come with us, please . . .'

'Why?'

'We need to question you in connection with the death of Graham Wainwright.'

'You've already done that.'

'Further matters have come to light since then that we need to talk to you about.'

'What?'

'We can go into that at the station.'

'Can Alex be with me?'

'I'm afraid not, but you are entitled to have a solicitor with you, should you wish.'

The severity of his tone made her blanch, but she said nothing and turned back into the entrance hall, leaving Blite and Nightingale on the threshold. They heard her voice demanding to be put through to Jeremy Kemp. She explained what was happening and then called out:

'Inspector, Mr Kemp wants to talk to you.'

Blite stepped inside and took the receiver from her.

'DI Blite here, Mr Kemp.'

'Is this strictly necessary?'

'At this stage, sir, we are simply *requesting* that Mrs Wainwright-Smith comes to the station. If she refuses, we may have to consider alternatives that I'm trying to avoid.'

'I see. Let me speak to her again.'

Within minutes, Sally had joined Blite in the marked police car he had chosen to use to collect her from the Hall. Jeremy Kemp was waiting for them at the station, together with Claire Keating, the police psychiatrist. As soon as they were in the interview room with the tape running and necessary introductions and cautions made, Blite confronted Sally with the news that she had been seen with Graham on the morning of his death at the place where his body had been discovered. She denied it, and Blite asked whether she would therefore be happy to participate in an identity parade. Jeremy Kemp intervened.

'Are you sure this is required, Inspector?'

'Your client can refuse to participate, but after her assurance that she did not meet Graham on the day he died, a jury might find it rather odd that she chose not to clear our suspicions when given the chance.'

The casual mention of the word 'jury' silenced them both. Sally went white, Jeremy Kemp pink. She asked for a cigarette, then a coffee, but when she went to take a tablet from a small brown bottle of pills, Blite asked her to pass the bottle over.

'What are these?'

'My medication.' Her voice was hard, but with a slight quaver in it that gave her away.

'I'd rather you didn't take one just now.'

'My client is entitled to her prescription, Inspector.'

'Not if it impairs her ability to answer my questions with a clear mind, and they are only antidepressants after all.'

'I need them!' Sally's voice was a squeal of indignation as she fumbled to take the bottle from Blite.

'Calm down, Sally, it's OK. Don't let him get to you.' Kemp's voice was soothing, as if he was trying to pacify a skittish horse.

Claire Keating watched the play of conflicting emotions cross Sally's face: surprise, fear, anger, cunning; she saw them all before they were extinguished behind an insolent look that she was more used to seeing on the faces of juvenile delinquents. Sally took a deep breath, then another, and smoothed her hair back into place.

'You're right, of course. It's just that this is all so ridiculous.'

'So you deny that you met Graham Wainwright on the morning of his death?'

'Yes.'

'Despite that fact that you were seen with him on the morning of his death? And *his* fingerprints were found on a box of fruit and vegetables delivered to the Hall on the morning he died?'

They both looked at him in silence. Sally's face was expressionless, but her eyes darted away from Blite's. She studied the scuffed floor of the interview room, obviously trying to control her emotions. Kemp's complexion had become bright red. He turned to her with an expression of intense concern.

'You don't need to say anything, Sally, remember that.'

'Mr Kemp is right, Mrs Wainwright-Smith, but remember, juries have their own way of interpreting silence.'

She shook her head at Kemp dismissively and looked up at Blite again with a show of defiance.

'This signifies nothing, Inspector. Whoever claims to have seen me with Graham is lying, and I don't know how his fingerprints found their way on to the box, and I suspect you don't either.'

Blite ignored her answer, asking instead:

'Tell me about Donald Glass.'

The change of subject threw her and baffled Kemp. Blite let the silence develop, then said:

'We interviewed him this week about your attack on him. You've got a nasty temper. He said you nearly killed him, and he has the scar to prove it.'

'I have nothing further to say.'

'Things don't look too good, Mrs Wainwright-Smith. Wouldn't it be better to tell us everything, get it all out in the open?'

'You heard my client; she has nothing further to say.' Kemp was trying to sound calm, but it was obvious just by looking at him that he was struggling and out of his depth.

226

'I want to go home.' Sally rose to her feet without waiting for an answer, quite the lady of the manor giving an instruction to her chauffeur.

'I have further questions, Sally.' The informal use of her first name punctured her hauteur. 'Please sit down.'

After a brief pause she obeyed. The tape was still running.

'I have nothing further to say,' she repeated.

'So be it, but I have.'

At first Blite tried to shock her by anouncing that an identity parade was being arranged. When that didn't work he kept up a continuous stream of questions, ranging from who benefited from Graham's death to Sally's lie to Shirley and Irene on the day Graham had died. He kept his tone neutral throughout so that he could never be accused of intimidation. Although she said nothing, he knew that her silence during his statement of all the evidence they had collected against her would sound damning in court. Claire watched Sally intently, but although Blite's monotonous repetition of the case against her might serve his purposes, it did little to probe beneath the surface of Sally's denial.

At the end of three hours Blite let them go, obviously frustrated that he had failed to break Sally's defences despite her nervousness. He told her to make herself available for the identity parade that was being organised either for later that day or for the following morning and to let them know where they could contact her if she left the Hall. As soon as they had gone, he turned to Claire and Nightingale and swore.

'That was a bloody waste of time. Did you get anything out of it?'

He didn't believe in the use of police psychiatrists and regarded Claire with barely concealed contempt. She was used to worse and answered him evenly.

'Not a lot; she said very little. She's very defensive and nervous. There are strong emotions there under the surface that she was having trouble controlling at the beginning of the interview, but then she seemed to shut down somehow. I'm not sure how sustainable that is. She has to be in control, that's obvious, and when she's not, she is far more vulnerable and unpredictable.

'My recommendation would be to bring her in for questioning without notice at least a couple of times more. Let me know when. I have appointments from noon but could be free at four o'clock or six. Early tomorrow morning is good for me too.'

'I'll think about it.' Blite's rude dismissal was like water off a duck's back to Claire, which irritated him even further, and as soon as she had gone he started criticising her contribution and complaining that their case was starting to fall apart. His implied criticism of Fenwick annoyed Nightingale, but she was smart enough to let it go.

'The identity parade will help, sir.'

'Don't hold your breath, Constable. I've had retards as witnesses before.' He didn't notice Nightingale wince at his choice of words. 'They're a gift to the defence, believe me. Still, it's all we have left at the moment.'

Wainwright-Smith had aged and had lost weight since Fenwick had last seen him, on the morning after Graham's murder, and the toughness he had suspected existed behind the deceptively bland exterior was less well concealed. He decided to come straight to the point.

'There is no easy way to begin the conversation we are about to have, Mr Wainwright-Smith.'

The blood drained from Alexander's face in shock at his choice of words, and Fenwick wondered whether he too suspected his wife of the crimes against his family.

'I'm going to tell you a story, Alexander. It's the story of a young girl of eight, what life throws at her – and what she becomes. You'd do well to listen.'

'If it's about Sally, Chief Inspector, I know most of it. She told me before we were married.'

Fenwick recalled his conversation with Sally in the kitchen of Wainwright Hall. She had lied to him again, then, but he still needed to be sure that Alexander knew the full truth.

He told him of Sally's childhood: the beatings she'd survived from the day she was born; the sexual abuse and the casual way in which her father had shared a girl of eight years old with his friends. He spoke in a matter-of-fact voice, simply stating the facts, with no elaboration.

Fenwick extended the story to talk of a brother and sister being born and the increasingly violent abuse towards them. Wainwright-Smith listened, at first with indifference and then in horror.

'She didn't tell me she had a brother or a sister. I thought she was an only child, like me.'

'She is now. Let me tell you what happened. Despite this appalling background, Sally survived. She was smart, streetwise. She stole to survive and to please her father; she mopped up the blood and tidied the kitchen when her father returned from the pub in one of his rages; she pleased his friends. But at eight, her life changed for ever.'

'Why are you telling me this now?'

'You need to know. Please listen.'

Fenwick could recall every detail of the police and Social Services reports that he'd read only days before. He described the systematic starvation of the three children; how Frank Bates became more and more violent as they weakened until he grew careless enough to leave marks on the little girl that the teachers saw at school. And he described the social worker's visit, which produced no action.

'The girl survived on stolen food. At every opportunity she would take sweets, fruit, anything from her classmates' bags. She shop-lifted, she ate two school meals and she tried to bring food home for her brother in case she could feed him in secret.' At the mention of the food Alexander covered his mouth with a hand, but he didn't interrupt. 'Her father discovered her attempts to feed them, so he locked the other children in an upstairs room where he couldn't hear their cries. He beat his daughter so badly that she had to stay at home, and he tied her to a radiator in the kitchen, where she slept on the floor next to the dog's basket. But the school were worried and they kept ringing her mother.

'The mother was powerless to go against her husband's wishes, but she told him that the social worker had tried to visit again and they decided to send their daughter back to school. She hadn't eaten for over a week and she had chronic diarrhoea from drinking the dog's water. It was obvious within hours that something was wrong, and the headmistress found a way to call in the police.'

Fenwick described the visit, how George Wicklow had bribed the child with food, and how, just as they were leaving, they had heard a noise from upstairs.

'The little boy and the baby died. The girl – she was eight at the time – was taken into care. Her father was charged and convicted of murder and her mother found guilty of being an accomplice.'

'Dear God, poor Sally. She never told me, but it explains so much: her compulsive hoarding of food; her scrimping and saving even now we're rich; her mood swings; her rages. Poor little kid. I hope that bastard died in prison.'

It was said with an intensity of hatred that surprised Fenwick. There were hidden emotions in this man and a depth of thought and calculation that would be easy to underestimate. He watched now as another thought struck Alexander and a look of revulsion crossed his face.

'He's not out of prison, is he?'

'No, he's in a high-security unit and is likely to remain there for the rest of his life.'

'How could he do it? Have you seen him? What did he say; could he explain?'

'No, his sort of psychopath rarely can. But I haven't finished my story yet. There's more.'

He described the foster homes, further abuse, Sally's own degenerate behaviour that led to her being taken back into care. From Alexander's comments, it was obvious that he had been told some of the story but not all of it.

'She left the children's home at sixteen, found a lover here locally, stole from him and tried to kill him.'

Alexander started to protest, but Fenwick interrupted him.

'It's *true*, Alexander. Sergeant Cooper's spoken to him, and seen his scar. She left the area soon afterwards. We don't know where but we think she might have lived on the streets or worked as a prostitute.'

'Prostitution! That's new, but if it's true I could understand it. She had to survive somehow. I wish she'd told me, but she probably coped by putting it all behind her and focusing on the future, *our* future.'

'Mr Wainwright-Smith! For heaven's sake, can't you see it yet? I've spelt it out for you – the woman you think you know and love is a fabrication. She was conditioned to please and manipulate men from the time she could walk! Your wife is not a normal woman; she's the creation of an evil, sick-minded man and a mother so weak as to be nonexistent. I've talked to the police psychologists and they've profiled someone with her background for me. Here, I'll read you some of it.'

Fenwick carefully removed a typed report from the brown envelope and turned to the second page.

'This is the bit that's written in the sort of English we can understand. Listen. *A subject of child abuse of this extreme nature could have grown up with a grossly distorted set of beliefs and values and low self-esteem which will manifest itself in compensating behaviours, and will inevitably have some sort of personality disorder. She will despise herself because she is a woman, like her mother, but may act with a confidence and conviction that will fool even those close to her. She will instinctively adapt to whoever is the most authoritative or powerful person around her (usually male), whom she will seek both to please and control. Given the sexual nature of her abuse, she will probably use sex as her main means of control. It will mean nothing to her physically, although she will be well practised in giving a performance – of pleasure or pain – as demanded or expected by her lover, as she did for her father, uncles and their friends. Her feelings towards the authoritarian males in her life will be a complex mixture of hatred and desire to be "loved" by them. She could also be submissive and easily directed by someone once they assume a position of power over her.*

'*"Love" will also be a complex concept for her because she knew none in childhood. It will instead be the provision of whatever she desired most as a child; attention usually, but in this case food and other physical indulgences. The ability to act within a framework of control will be crucial to her sense of balance and she will exert considerable energy to manage all aspects of her environment. Absence of this control will be more than usually destabilising and could trigger extreme reactions.*

'*She will have a number of compulsive behaviours, react in ways others find strange or even heartless and will have an erratic reaction to stress. You have asked for a comment on the potential for violence and, in my opinion, it could be high, particularly when sexual relationships fail to deliver what she needs. She was abused, beaten and starved as a child and could be capable of extreme cruelty herself.*'

Alexander slumped forward, his face cradled in his hands, as Fenwick read on. When the policeman stopped talking, there was a long silence before he could bring himself to speak.

'I have to accept what you've said about her past.' Alexander's voice was low but controlled. 'However, I don't agree that she's the person your psychologist has described.'

'Did *you* kill Graham Wainwright?'

'No! Of course not. Is that what this is all about, shocking me into a confession? Really, Fenwick, you're too—'

'I'm not accusing you, but someone did kill your cousin with a degree of cunning and forethought that suggests premeditation. Your wife does not have an alibi for the morning he died; she made sure that she was left with the body when it was discovered. She wrecked the crime scene and actually lied about her whereabouts on the morning he was killed. And as for motives, only you and she appear to have one.'

'Oh, come on! For God's sake, she's my *wife*.'

'Who will inherit everything should you die. Am I right?'

'Are you suggesting that I'm next? That's absurd!'

'I didn't say that; you inferred it. What I am telling you is that your wife is our main suspect for the murder of Graham Wainwright, and she is being questioned right now.'

Alexander shot to his feet and went to the phone.

'She needs a lawyer.'

'I'm sure she's had the opportunity to call Jeremy Kemp.'

'No, I mean a decent criminal lawyer. Just give me a moment. There's someone at the club who'll know how to find the right man.'

Fenwick let him make the call, conscious that any complaint would waste time he could ill afford. As soon as Alexander was off the phone, he continued with the second purpose of his visit: testing Alexander's reaction to his wife's suspected affair with his uncle.

'There's something else we need to discuss. It's important. It concerns your wife and Alan Wainwright.'

Alexander looked at him in confusion, but the bizarre sentence had recaptured his attention.

'We have been told that your wife was having an affair with your uncle before he died. Is this true?'

He had expected shock, anger or denial, but instead Alexander walked away slowly and stared out of one of the huge picture windows.

'I've heard rumours but nothing to substantiate them. Do you have proof?'

'No.'

'My uncle's long dead and buried, Chief Inspector. This is old history – even supposing it's true. And it doesn't make her a murderess.'

'No, but she was seen with Graham on the morning he died. We have an eye-witness.'

Fenwick stared at Alexander's broad back and waited for some sort of response, but the man said nothing.

'You're taking the news about your wife with remarkable calm, Mr Wainwright-Smith.'

'What other option do I have?'

Wainwright-Smith's reaction felt wrong to Fenwick, it was just too controlled, and it made him wonder how much of Sally's past the man had actually known about. Sally had lied to him about it, saying that she had told her husband nothing, but perhaps Alexander was lying too about the extent of his previous knowledge. What if he had known all about her past, including even her affair with his uncle? Supposing he had tacitly encouraged its continuation? Alexander was a major beneficiary of his uncle's will and had been his heir apparent within the business. Perhaps he had been happy to pay a high price to secure his legacy.

The expression on Fenwick's face didn't alter, but he considered the man before him with a new suspicion.

'We have to interview your wife quite intensively over the next few days, and whilst I appreciate that you will want to arrange the very best legal counsel for her, I would ask that you give us room to do our job.'

'That was an unnecessary remark, Chief Inspector. Of course you must do your duty, as I must do mine towards my wife. But if your tactics become heavy-handed in any way, you can be sure that I shall intervene.'

Fenwick nodded his understanding and rose to leave. Before he reached the door, Wainwright-Smith called out to him.

'By the way, we are going to seek an injunction for the return of the papers you retrieved from Arthur Fish's house, and I expect us to succeed.'

Fenwick merely turned and smiled, confident that Miles Cator would by now have enough evidence to use in order to prevent their return. He knew who he expected to win.

CHAPTER THIRTY-SEVEN

The Hall was in darkness when Alexander eventually returned home. He hadn't hurried despite the fact that, since his meeting with Fenwick, he had been unable to do any work. Instead he had spent the time considering how to handle the very real police threat, and most particularly what he should do about Sally. If she had reacted badly to the day, she could be in any mood now, from almost catatonic to violent, but whatever state she was in, he would need to talk to her and explain why he had to go away.

He found her in the kitchen, dozing in front of the Aga, a half-drunk gin bottle on the kitchen table next to two empty crisp packets. Her supper, he was sure.

'Sally!' He called to her from several yards away.

'Huh. What?'

'It's me, Sal. I'm back.' He used his friendly father voice, which worked in most circumstances.

'You're late. There's no dinner, I put it in the freezer.'

Relief filled him; she wasn't yet drunk. Her tolerance for alcohol had increased in line with the amount she drank, and as long as she hadn't taken any tranquillisers, he would be able to have a decent conversation with her.

'That's fine, I ate at the office. We need to talk, about the police.'

'I didn't tell them, Alex, I promise I didn't.'

'What didn't you tell them?'

'About Graham. They asked me lots of questions and I was so confused – sometimes I thought they were talking about Graham, then they'd throw in a question about the will. They were all over the place, but I didn't say a word.'

'Good girl. You're not to worry, because I've found you the very best criminal lawyer in the country. He's coming here to see you tomorrow morning. His name's Michael Ebutt and he's going to look after you. He's already called the police to confirm the interview for tomorrow lunchtime, and he'll meet you there.'

'I want you to look after me. I want us to go away. I've sort of packed already.' There were tears in her voice, and he went over and put his arms around her. This was better than violence and a mood he knew how to manage. He had to make the most of it while it lasted.

'We can't do that, you know we can't. Remember, it's very important that we continue to behave just like normal; we've been all through this before. You do what you need to do and I'll do what I must do. Soon, when Graham's estate is settled, we'll be very rich and we'll be able to go and live on our island together, just like we've always wanted.'

'I've gone off the idea of an island.'

'You always said you'd feel safe on one.'

'Not any more – you can get trapped on an island. I want a big motor yacht. I can sail and we can trade in the Boston Whaler for something serious. No one can find you at sea. We can hide forever and visit all the islands we like.'

Alexander smothered a sigh and said brightly: 'A big boat it is, then. Now, let's talk about what you must do next, because the police will come back, you know.'

'OK.' She sounded too docile, and he turned her face so that he could look into her eyes and make sure that she was concentrating. The look of utter fatigue and confusion he saw there made his stomach turn over. She was exhausted and in turmoil, which meant that she would be very close to the edge of her precious control. At that moment she reminded him so much of his mother that he could have struck her. She was meant to be strong-willed, capable, determined. She couldn't crack up now, not when they were so close. He summoned up his deepest reserves, laid down over a lifetime of subtle manipulation and dissembling.

'We need to talk about the next few days. Now, what are you *not* going to do?'

'Talk.'

'Good girl, that's the right answer. You've always been good at keeping secrets, so you go on keeping them.' He bent and kissed her smooth forehead, wrinkling his nose at the smell of stale cigarette smoke in her hair. 'And when the police tell you what they've found out, you just deny it or say nothing, all right?'

'Yes.' Her voice was tiny, like a child's. 'But I think they know quite a lot anyway.'

'Like what?'

'About Graham, about Daddy and what he did, even about Donald – I told you about him, how he attacked me. How do they *know* these things?'

'They're policemen; it's their job to find out things, but they're also human beings, just like us, so don't think they are invincible.'

'They didn't ask me about Uncle Alan, though.'

'That's good, but don't be surprised if they do.' He recalled his conversation with Fenwick and decided he'd better tell her. 'They know about your relationship with him; they told me so.'

Two dangerous spot of colour appeared on her cheeks.

'I hate them, bastards, every fucking one of them.' She dug her fingernails into his wrist so that he had to prise them out before she drew blood. 'Did they say anything about the other thing?'

He had coaxed her away from this once before, and realised with a sinking heart that he would have to do so again.

'There is nothing else.'

'But there is, I told you. The night he died, I—'

'Sally,' there was a note of warning in his voice, 'stop it. Remember the coroner's verdict. Alan killed himself. He's dead, and nothing remains of him now but ash. Say nothing and it will all go away. History has already written its record of his life and death; don't change it.'

'But sometimes at night I dream of him in the car, looking at me, and he's still alive!'

'Enough!' He slapped the back of her hand sharply and she stopped talking at once. 'Forget your dreams, forget everything about the old man. He's gone forever.' There was such anger in his tone that she was quiet at once.

'Yes, Alex.'

'I have to go away for a few days – no, don't look like that – just to keep focused on the company whilst you concentrate on saying nothing. We've come through before, Sally, and we can do it again. I won't be very far away. Just don't panic.'

She nodded and tried to set her mouth in a determined line. Something of the old Sally returned and he breathed a sigh of relief. She was a chameleon. Her personality was so contorted, her behaviours so extreme that he never knew which Sally would greet him when he returned home. But as long as she could keep control in the police interviews, they would be all right. Ebutt was apparently an amazing lawyer, and all Sally needed to do was to say nothing.

'Of course we can do it. But when you're not here, Alex, sometimes things are so difficult, and I think things . . . Well, you know what I think about. You're so good for me. You understand me and forgive me when I'm wicked.'

'You know I always forgive you. Come on, let's go to bed right now, together, in my room, like the old days.'

Alex made himself breakfast before dawn and tidied away the gin bottle, in case the police arrived early. Since Irene and Shirley had left the Hall had gradually become more faded and grubby, but Sally – once so house-proud – seemed not to notice. Thinking of Irene, he went over to the phone book and found her number, writing it down carefully on a scrap of paper before he left.

Alex wouldn't be going far, and he certainly wasn't going into hiding, but it was better to have some distance between himself and Sally right now, for both their sakes. After he'd gone, Sally drove herself to Harlden Park, where she stayed for most of the morning, watching children play on the swings and trying not to think of her next interview with the police. By late morning she had smoked twenty-five cigarettes and she was dying for a drink. If she walked quickly, there would be time to find a wine bar in the centre of town and have a drink or two before one o'clock. As she turned westwards and walked slowly uphill, the thoughts she had managed to keep at bay all morning crowded in on her.

She felt as if she was balancing precariously on a tightrope, and far below her lay a swamp populated by sucking, flesh-eating animals. The support behind her was the memory of her father, a rigid, upright figure who had dominated her childhood and whose voice she still heard in her dreams. Ahead of her stood Alex; firm, unbending, sure. He had taken her in, loved her, supported her and forgiven her when others might so easily have stood in judgement. Her past and future life stretched between them, silvery thin and delicate, strung taut with the tension of her existence.

Alex had told her to be strong and silent, and she would be, not least because it was easier to say nothing. If she once started to talk, who knew where it would take her? She had a lifetime of words stacked up inside her, unspoken and jumbled together into a confusion of memories and fantasies so strong that she sometimes had difficulty deciding what was truth and what had actually happened. The words were just one of the bundles she carried with her on her precarious journey that stretched out between the only two real men in her life.

To maintain her balance she needed to hold on to her self-control; it was what Alex expected, yet it remained her most difficult challenge. Below her in the swamp, monsters snapped at her. They were the creatures of her nightmares: sticky tongues in panting faces, all with the same bestial lust in their eyes, the same lust that she saw reflected in the expressions of men all around her, every day. They were predators all. An image of James FitzGerald suddenly ambushed her. He was a hard and dangerous man, one of nature's natural predators and a hunter whom she viewed with a blend of fear and careful respect. She had a well-developed sixth sense that recognised power and danger in others, and she felt it strongly in him. He was an unknown and unpredictable element in her universe, and one that she would prefer to avoid.

As if the thought of him had somehow conjured him up, she heard heavy, hurrying footsteps behind her and turned to see FitzGerald bearing down on her.

'I thought I saw you go by. This is a stroke of luck, it saves me a journey.'

'Hello, James. I'm very busy, what do you want?'

'Now that's no way to treat an old friend!' His tone was one of mock annoyance, but Sally's stomach contracted painfully.

'What's the matter, Sally? You've gone pale.'

'I'm fine, just in a hurry.' She stopped abruptly and turned to him, determined to show no fear.

'What is it you want?'

FitzGerald looked about at the shoppers and strollers who bustled around them in the pedestrianised area.

'It's a little bit public here, don't you think? Let's go up Castle Hill. It's only a few minutes away.'

Castle Hill was an area of lawn and walkways that rose up steeply behind the High Street. A wrought-iron kissing gate guarded the path to its summit, on which stood the lovingly restored remains of the castle that had once dominated the valley around Harlden. Thick, close-cropped green grass covered the whole hill, except for the few paths, and urbanised rabbits huddled in bunches wherever early-lunching office workers had left a space.

It was a typical English spring day; sunshine with the threat of sudden showers and enough of a wind to keep coats on people's backs, but the hill was busy, clearly busier than FitzGerald had expected. He muttered under his breath as she walked silently beside him, and they had reached the top before they found a place private enough for the conversation he clearly wanted to have. They walked into the shadows of the twelfth-century keep walls, which rose open to the sky. FitzGerald leant back confidently against the stones and smiled slowly at Sally. She stared back, saying nothing, but a cold dread of the inevitable grew inside her that she recognised from childhood and her father's late-night return from the pub.

'You never did ask me how I came to have those photographs of you and Alan.'

FitzGerald spoke with a mock innocence that put Sally on immediate alert. She still said nothing.

'I've had you watched, Sally, on and off since you appeared as Alex's surprise fiancée. I never did trust the coroner's verdict on Alan's death. It was nothing I had planned, so I looked to the next most obvious culprits: you, Alexander and Graham.'

Sally's stomach was knotted so tightly now that she could taste bile in her throat. A group of three office girls walked into the hollow keep, chatty, pretty and cold in the shadow of the stone walls. The wind gusted through empty windows and the gaping archway where the grand entrance doors had once stood, impregnable. The girls looked about them, shivered collectively and left. FitzGerald waited until he was sure that they were out of earshot. He was about fifteen feet away from where Sally stood in a slanted patch of sunshine that made her hair gleam like a beacon in the gloomy keep.

'I didn't think it was worth having you followed all the time, which was an error of judgement on my part. I had one man cover you, Alex and Graham, because I didn't want my interest too widely known. Consequently I don't know where you were when Arthur Fish and Amanda Bennett died, but I can be absolutely sure that Alex wasn't involved.

'Similarly I wasn't having you followed on the day Graham died.' He paused and scrutinised her face for the faintest change of expression. There was none, so he abandoned his nonchalant slouch against the wall and walked over to her. She stared resolutely over his shoulder, tall enough in her high heels to be almost at eye level. He put a single finger under her chin and tilted her head upwards and around until she could no longer avoid his gaze.

'As I said, I wasn't having you followed on the day Graham died,' he smiled into her wide eyes, 'but I did have someone following him.' His smile grew into a snarl that exposed his sharp canines and he dropped his hand. There was no mistaking the menace in his eyes now. 'Would you like to see the photographs he took? I have a spare set here. The man I used is very good – well you know that, you've seen his work before. I'll give you one thing, Sally, you're ingenious. I don't know how you persuaded him to join you for a breakfast picnic – and in such a remote location. You're amazing.'

She remained silent, remembering Alex's words. Under no circumstances was she going to reveal to the evil man in front of her that it had been remarkably easy to arrange her meeting with Graham. She had simply refused to go to his hotel, and he had been so determined to confront her that he had agreed to her meeting place. She'd waited for him in the early morning, having caught the bus into the nearby village first. It had been stupid to bother with the fruit and vegetable order; even more careless to ask him to collect it as she waited, head scarf pulled forward, in the passenger seat of his car. But it had reassured Graham, that little touch of domesticity, and he had been visibly more relaxed after he had returned to the car. She had despised him for his weakness.

'Here, you'll like this one.' FitzGerald handed her a glossy black-and-white photograph of the beech tree, with two figures beneath it. It had been

237

taken with a powerful telephoto lens from some distance, and the faces were less than the size of her fingernail. However, she had no doubt that with modern equipment it would be abundantly clear who it was in the picture.

'Why haven't you taken this to the police? I'm sure they'd be interested.'

'Oh, they'd be more than interested, particularly in this one.' He handed her another. 'That really was very ingenious, Sally, but it still must have been very hard work. I decided that these would be of more use to me than to the police. This way, you and your hard-working but stubborn husband will have to behave. Wainwright's is very important to me, and to my business partners, and it must be run smoothly, just as it was by dear old Alan. If I went to the police with these they would immediately meddle in our affairs – and anyway, with the photographs in my back pocket, your independent-minded husband will have to behave.

'Whether you tell him what I've got or simply use your influence, I frankly don't give a shit; I just want him to be good. Understood?

He squeezed her wrist hard, and she began to feel her self-control ebbing away. She made as if to leave.

'Don't. That would be dumb, Sally, and you know it.'

'I don't want to see any more.' Her voice was barely a whisper.

'That's fine, you don't have to, but you do need to know that I have these. And you needn't worry about the photographer; he's worked for me for years and has seen worse – though not much worse, come to think of it.'

'What do you want?'

'I told you: complete and assured control of Wainwright's and, of course, a small contribution to my pension fund.'

'How much?'

'Three million pounds.'

'What!' The figure appalled her.

'It's a fraction of what you and Alexander have inherited, and it's much better than losing it all.'

'Don't you have enough already?'

'Ah, well, no, it's impossible to have enough, surely *you* realise that. I want more.'

'But three million! How can I get that much together?'

'You'll think of something. I don't need it all at once. A few hundred thousand up front to show we have an understanding, and then the rest over the next year or so. I know you'll be able to do it – how is up to you.'

A teacher and a group of children stormed into the keep, bombarding the old stones with high-pitched laughter and corresponding calls for quiet. The teacher saw Sally and FitzGerald standing together and mistook their meeting for a lovers' tryst, the blush of embarrassment showing bright in her cheeks.

FitzGerald held on to Sally's forearm in a grip that was not to be denied and walked her out of earshot, smiling benignly at the teacher, who promptly blushed again and shooed the children outside.

'How long do I have to think about it?'

'You don't. It's non-negotiable, Sally. All you need to do is work out how you'll pay me. As I say, the first instalment should be easy to raise and I expect to see that within the week. Liquidate some of the trust fund; it should be easy.'

'Graham's estate isn't settled yet.'

'But Alan's is, and I know exactly how much he left you. As for Graham's, as soon as the letters of administration are granted, you can liquidate his assets and pay me the balance.'

Sally seemed to capitulate suddenly. Her shoulders slumped and her head drooped.

'I might need some help to realise the money.'

He doubted that. Knowing Sally, there was bound to be a fortune in cash stashed away in the Hall.

'Jeremy Kemp can help. I'll let him know that you may call, but it is essential he knows nothing about the money coming to me. That's our little secret.' He gave her wrist a squeeze as a reminder of the alternative.

'I'll talk to Jeremy, and as soon as I've worked it out, I'll call you and we can agree how you receive the money.'

'Splendid!' He sounded almost avuncular, delighted. 'I knew you'd be a sensible girl. Come on, I'll buy you a drink.'

'No thanks, I need to think. You go on down. We'd best not be seen together anyway.' She sounded low, defeated.

'Very well.' He planted a moist kiss on her cheek and ignored her shudder. 'Well done!' he said, as if she had just passed a difficult test, and then waved as he strutted off down the path.

Sally watched him go, her eyes as cold and empty as the windows of the keep. Her mouth jerked, then twisted. She bit her lip and chewed at the skin until it was raw. When FitzGerald reached the bottom of the hill, he turned and blew her a silent kiss from the shadow of the gate. Seconds later he had disappeared back up the High Street. As soon as she was sure he had truly gone, Sally threw back her head and let out a terrible wail. Her cry bounced off the walls, rising higher and louder with every echo. It seemed to go on forever.

Below the keep, on the grass, the children looked up from their drawings, wide-eyed and scared, and then carefully crayoned in the ghost they expected to appear any minute from above the walls of the ruined castle.

CHAPTER THIRTY-EIGHT

Whilst Sally prowled in Harlden Park, her solicitor, Michael Ebutt, started to earn his extortionate retainer. At precisely nine thirty, his customary time to commence the day's work, he opened the file on his latest high-profile client. Had anybody been studying his face in an attempt to discern how serious was the case against her, they would have noticed a deep frown line form between his immaculately groomed eyebrows, then the corners of his mouth turn down into the margins of his closely trimmed beard. By ten o'clock they could have been forgiven for deducing, from the expression on his face, that Sally's predicament was bleak. But at 10.14 precisely, his clouded demeanour cleared and a sudden, triumphant smile broke out before being smothered again in an expression of grim satisfaction.

Fenwick was in his office, rereading the latest reports of the interview with Sally the previous day and checking on the preparations for the identity parade, which had been arranged for lunchtime, when his secretary interrupted to tell him that Mrs Wainwright-Smith's lawyer was on the phone. He decided to take the call and was momentarily surprised to hear Ebutt's name. He had a national reputation and was regarded by police forces throughout the country as a fearsome criminal lawyer. This was the first time that Fenwick had ever spoken to him.

'Chief Inspector, I have been retained by Mr Wainwright-Smith to represent his wife, and within half an hour of reading your supposed evidence against her, I can see at once why you haven't dared to arrest her. You simply don't have a case!'

Fenwick was surprised that the man had called to tell him this over the phone when he could have taken the opportunity of expressing his opinion face-to-face later in the day. It seemed an odd tactic for such an experienced practitioner, but the reason became clear within seconds.

'I suggest you cancel this intended identity parade today, or I shall be forced to advise my clients to allege harassment by you and your team.'

If Ebutt was trying to annoy Fenwick, then he had failed, but he had made the policeman curious to know what weakness it was about the case that made him so confident, and Fenwick asked him to explain.

'I understand that the method you say was used to murder Mr Graham Wainwright was ligature strangulation, after which he was strung up in an attempt to make it look like suicide by hanging.' Fenwick said nothing, and after a pause Ebutt was forced to continue. 'Perhaps you can tell me, then, Chief Inspector, how a young woman of one hundred and eight pounds managed to lift the dead weight of a man weighing ten and a half stone, balance him whilst she attached a noose to his neck and then run around to the other side of the tree and tie the rope to a branch on the far side?'

Fenwick felt the blood drain from his face. He had specifically asked Blite to test whether hanging as a means of killing would stand up, and he had been told, categorically, yes. And Blite had known Sally was their prime suspect. He had relied on Blite's judgement as SIO, and he had let him down. Ebutt was talking again, and he forced himself to concentrate.

'Until you can answer my question, I strongly suggest that you suspend all further interviews with my client. And before you compound your mistake by suggesting that she was working with someone else – say her husband – I must tell you that I have this morning received a statement from one of the helpers at the Hall that confirms he was in his room, fast asleep, all morning. She has kindly provided us with the times at which she had to enter his bedroom, and I can assure you that they mean he has a robust alibi.'

Fenwick remembered Irene's eyes, how he had identified her immediately as a casual breaker of the law. He wondered how much she had been offered to change her story. There was only one way for Fenwick to manage a man like Ebutt if he wanted to keep in control of this investigation: firmly, and with complete confidence. Ignoring the questions and doubts that were now crowding his mind, he toughened his tone into one of polite insistence that brooked no denial.

'On the contrary, we will still expect her to be at the station at one o'clock for further questioning and to attend the identity parade. I suggest we suspend further conversation until then, Mr Ebutt.'

As soon as he was off the phone, he called in Blite and Cooper and explained the problem. Both men looked ashen, and he could see Blite already thinking how he would move the potential blame from his own shoulders and on to Fenwick's. He forestalled any prospect of blame-throwing by moving at once to concentrate their minds on solving the problem instead.

'We need to consider two options: she was either working with an accomplice who helped her lynch Graham's body after he was dead or unconscious. Or two, she was working alone and somehow did manage to string the body up. Cooper, I want a reconstruction. Talk to George Wicklow; see if between the two of you you can find a tree of similar proportions to the beech on the Wainwright estate. It shouldn't be too difficult, given the number of woods we have in the county. And Inspector, you continue to prepare for the interview and talk to the identification officer about the parade. Despite what Ebutt said, as far as Sally is concerned we're going to continue as if nothing has happened. This is a technical difficulty, understood?'

Blite looked uncomfortable.

'Shouldn't we tell the Superintendent and the ACC?'

'They'll be receiving my report this evening as usual, and until then I don't think *any of us* need trouble them. Understood?'

Both men left, and Fenwick forced himself to go back to the papers he had been studying before the phone call. There was nothing he could do until the reconstruction started, and in the meantime, he was determined to check every last possible avenue for a connection between Sally and Arthur Fish.

'Are you sure this tree is a match to the old beech, Cooper?'

'As close as we could get, sir. This branch here is within three inches of the height off the ground, and there are roots over there that we can attach the rope to.'

Cooper had spent an hour finding a suitable tree, and then a further twenty minutes persuading an irascible farmer to allow them the use of his field. It was obvious that the man didn't hold with having the police on his property, and his mood hadn't been improved by the fact that he had been interrupted in the middle of a delicate manoeuvre to lift the engine block out of an old tractor. He had agreed eventually, wisely deciding that Sergeant Cooper was a man to keep on side.

Now they had an hour and ten minutes before Sally was due at the station for her next interview, and the tension in the team was making them all short-tempered. Nightingale had assembled what they would need for the reconstruction: a long sandbag the same weight as Graham Wainwright's dead body, a rope and a stool. Fenwick had decided to attend, as well as Blite and Cooper, leaving Nightingale the only junior officer present. She was fractionally taller than Sally but almost the same weight, so much of the physical work was going to be hers.

'We need to time all this. Inspector, you keep a record.'

'What do you want me to do, sir?'

'Watch, Sergeant; make notes and feed back your conclusions at the end.'

The first challenge was for Nightingale to knot a noose, and she made heavy weather of it. After fifteen minutes Cooper took over, and they all agreed that Sally could have brought the rope, ready prepared, to the scene, so they would start the count all over again. It was 12.13 p.m.

By 12.18, Nightingale had attached the noose to the sand bag, creating a floppy 'head', and had managed to drag the weight of it ten feet to lie underneath the branch. She was sweating and panting with exertion, and both Fenwick and Blite were looking worried. They watched as she positioned the stool and took a deep breath before throwing the free end of the rope up and over the branch. She was successful the first time, and by 12.24 had secured the loose end to a far root. The next part of the reconstruction was the most challenging; she had to pull the body upright and over the branch. For ten long, exhausting minutes she struggled alone, but the weight wouldn't budge. They called the station and had them postpone both interview and identity parade by an hour. Fenwick wanted them all confident of Sally's guilt, Blite most of all, before their first encounter with Ebutt.

'Sergeant, act as the accomplice; go and lift the bag up so that it creates slack in the rope.'

Cooper tried to do as he was asked, but at the end of a further fifteen minutes, all he and Nightingale had succeeded in doing was to haul the body upright so that its weight rested against Cooper. It was ten to one, and Fenwick ordered a break. Nightingale and Cooper sank gratefully to the ground. Blite lit a cigarette and kept repeating, 'Shit, shit, shit' under his breath.

Fenwick walked away from them, trying to ignore Blite's carping in the background. He needed to think. So much of the evidence pointed towards

Sally as the murderess, but now it looked as if it had been physically impossible for her to lift the body, even with help.

He replayed the details of the case in his mind, walking distractedly far away from his team. He was wearing wellington boots, but the field and track were so muddy that he had already wrecked his trousers with splashes of mud.

'Oi! Watch yourself!' An angry voice broke his concentration and he looked up to find himself in the middle of one of the farmer's yards. A combine harvester was being overhauled by a farm mechanic to his left, whilst the farmer and one of his labourers were repositioning a repaired engine into an old tractor. He had almost walked right under their block and tackle, and pulled back quickly, aware of the weight of gleaming metal swinging a mere foot away from his head.

'Sorry.'

'Daft bugger.'

Fenwick ignored the man's justified remark and turned back towards the track that led to the field and their doomed reconstruction. He was opening the gate before the full significance of what he had seen finally hit him. He ran back towards the yard, his excitement making him fresh and sure-footed despite the slime beneath his boots.

'Well, this is a cock-up on a grand scale, isn't it?' Blite's tone implied that it was anybody's fault but his, and Cooper had to bite his tongue to prevent himself from reminding the inspector that *he* was the SIO on the case after all. 'He should have realised from the beginning that it was physically impossible for her to lift the dead weight of a man's body. Thank God we didn't arrest her, is all I can say.'

Cooper and Nightingale looked at each other in shared misery. They still had absolute faith in DCI Fenwick, despite their failure during the past hour. Both of them had laboured to breaking point to prove him right, so much so that small blood vessels had broken in Cooper's cheeks and Nightingale was quite concerned for him. There was nothing they could think of to say in reply to Blite's criticisms, so by tacit agreement they wandered off further into the field to commiserate with each other in silence. Nightingale was trying to identify something that they might have missed which could explain everything when she heard a shout from behind her.

'Back to work! Come on, you lot, we have to be back in Harlden by one-forty-five. Hurry up!'

They turned as one to see Fenwick striding purposefully towards the tree, closely followed by a farm worker. His obvious confidence and determination lifted Nightingale's spirits. She saw a slow grin form on Cooper's face and heard him mutter:

'The old bugger's done it again, I'll wager! What is it this time?'

'Right, listen up, the gentleman with the package over there is Pete. He has kindly agreed to help us with our experiment.'

A look of nervous confusion crossed the man's face, but he held his silence and merely nodded a greeting to the three police officers, who were staring at him with open curiosity.

'Off you go, Pete.'

The man walked over to the branch and stood on the stool, then secured a wide canvas strap with a metal hook attached to it around the branch and buckled it tight. Next he took a block and tackle from the bag he had been carrying and attached it to the hook. He spent a few minutes straightening the links in the chain that ran through it and then tied a loop of rope from the chain and around the sandbag. He stepped down from the stool and pulled on the chain; the ratchet jerked up about six inches. Another pull and it rose a further foot in the air, the block in the pulley preventing the chain from sliding back between pulls. The sandbag was vertical and swinging free of the ground within two minutes. Fenwick went over to the rope where it had been tied to a root and pulled up the slack until it was taut. Pete released his rope from around the sandbag and they watched in silence as it turned very, very slowly in the air.

The grin on Cooper's face was in danger of splitting it in two, but it disappeared in an instant as Blite spoke.

'So the murderer was a farm mechanic who knows how to work a pulley system. Well, that narrows the field, doesn't it?' He didn't even try to hide his sarcasm.

Pete went pale; he hadn't reckoned on becoming an immediate suspect. Nightingale gave the man a reassuring smile that made him blush, and spoke quietly.

'Sally's father was a farm mechanic, Inspector. She must have seen him at work many a time.'

'And remembered how to rig a block and tackle system from when she was eight years old!'

'It's possible, yes; and remember that when she lived on the coast she sailed regularly. There are plenty of winches and pulley systems on a boat. Anyway, there's an easy way to find out.'

'Which is, Constable?'

'Let me try it. I've just watched Pete once. If I can do it, I don't see why Sally couldn't if she saw her father at work all the time.'

Fenwick nodded his approval. He went and untied the rope, allowing the bag to fall, and Pete passed her the block and tackle. Nightingale repeated every one of his steps methodically, not rushing but with no hesitation either. She made it look simple and straightforward. Cooper timed her. The dead weight of the sandbag eventually started to move, and although it was obvious that it took her more effort than it had Pete, she finally managed to lift it clear of the ground. As she tied off the rope, Cooper called out:

'Twelve minutes exactly.'

Nightingale nodded with fierce satisfaction and looked up at Fenwick. He met her eye and she saw the approval there that warmed her as nothing else could. DI Blite remained silent. Fenwick thanked Pete for his help and sent him back to the yard.

'Inspector, I want the outhouses and old farm buildings on the Wainwright estate searched again. And make sure your warrant is water-tight. You know what your team is looking for. Have the exact position of the impressions we found on the ground under the tree plotted against the rope marks, and have the branch rechecked for signs of other abrasions where the pulley might have been. I will interview Sally and oversee the identification parade.'

In effect, Blite was dismissed to his duties. Fenwick wouldn't forget how he had behaved, and they both knew it.

Ebutt and Sally were waiting for him in an interview room at the station. If either of them noticed his dishevelled state, they said nothing. Fenwick waited for Claire Keating to join them, then turned on the tape recorder and started the interview with the usual formalities. As soon as he had finished speaking, Ebutt replied.

'My client has decided to say nothing, Chief Inspector.'

'Naturally I respect her right to remain silent, but the question I'm about to ask has nothing to do with the alleged crime.'

'So why are you asking it?'

'Because Mrs Wainwright-Smith's childhood may be relevant to this case and I would like to make sure we have as full an understanding of it as possible.'

The lawyer and Sally put their heads together and there was a whispered exchange.

'Very well, but my client may cease to respond at any time.'

'Understood. Now, Sally, tell me about your father. What job did he do?'

'He was a mechanic.' Sally's voice was a dull monotone. Fenwick wondered if she was mildly sedated and was angry that her solicitor had allowed it to happen. On the other hand, it might help him.

'What sort of mechanic?'

'He worked on farms mainly, with tractors and harvesters, bailers, that sort of thing.'

'Did he always go to the farms or did he bring work home?'

'Both. Sometimes, if he wanted to stay around home for a while, he'd drive a tractor home. That was for maintenance or for when he had to do something complicated. He had a workshop at the back of the house, you see.'

'Yes, I do. Tell me, did you ever help him with his work?'

'Yes, always. He said I had nimble fingers so I'd have to do all the fiddly bits. I was good at it.'

'I expect you were, but how on earth could an eight-year-old girl reach inside a tractor engine and find the right parts?'

'Oh, it was easy. My dad would lift the engine out of the machine and work on it on his bench.'

'He must have been very strong.'

'He used a hoist, silly, and to put it back.'

The blood drained from Ebutt's face at her words, but it was already too late; the tape was running. He recovered almost at once and said with a smoothness that Fenwick could only admire:

'I can't see that this is of any material help, Chief Inspector.'

But Fenwick already had what he needed, and he excused himself to go and find out whether the parade was to take place or not. He was back within ten minutes.

'I'm sorry to have kept you waiting. The identification officer has postponed the parade for today as over half the volunteers have left because of the delay. He'll try to rearrange it for tomorrow, if you could both make yourselves available. He is waiting for you outside to agree a time.'

Once they had left, Cooper switched off the tape recorder.

'Well done, sir. That was just what we needed.'

'Thanks, Sergeant, but I bet we still don't have enough to persuade the ACC that we can arrest her. You handle the writing-up of the reconstruction this morning and whatever Inspector Blite's team discover on the estate.'

'DC Nightingale did some digging on James FitzGerald, sir, as you requested.'

'And what was the result?'

'Basically, he's very rich and well connected, far more so than could be explained by his financial business alone.'

'What about the check against HOLMES or the PCN?'

'They're running that this afternoon.'

'What's Nightingale up to now?'

'Trying to find the private investigator hired by Graham Wainwright. He's disappeared, so we still don't know whether he's been holding out on us. She's found out where he lives and the landlady thinks he went off on holiday, so Nightingale's checking with the travel agents.'

'Good. Whilst we've got this lull, I'm going to go home and spend some time with the children. Call me if anything breaks.'

Sally was silent during her taxi ride back to the Hall. The effects of the pill she had taken were wearing off and she could feel an intense anger threatening to overwhelm her again. She missed Alex, and she wondered whether he would be angry with her for speaking to the police. The pill she'd taken just before the interview had fuddled her, and even now she couldn't quite remember what she had said. Something about her father and his job, she thought. When Alex called that evening as he had promised, she would have to tell him about FitzGerald's attempted blackmail and he'd be furious. They both knew now, thanks to Jeremy Kemp's blabbing tongue, that FitzGerald was a very dangerous man, associated with organised crime throughout the south-east of England. Precisely how, Kemp hadn't told her, not even when she had promised to have sex with him in exchange for the information, so she and Alex had been left to speculate. She had guessed that it could involve either drugs or prostitution – perhaps both. It seemed unfair that FitzGerald was choosing to blackmail her when he must already have all the money he needed, and part of her was tempted simply to say no to see whether he would carry out his threat. One thing was for sure: they wouldn't pay him. A blackmailer was never satisfied, and all that talk of 'settling up' over the coming years filled Sally with dread. The thought of FitzGerald having a neverending hold over her was unbearable. She would need to come up with another way of dealing with him.

There were police cars parked in front of the Hall when she arrived home, and her heart sank. She paid the taxi-driver quickly, without giving him a tip, and ran towards the sound of voices coming from the stable block at the rear. The police were just leaving, led by that odious man Blite. She disliked him intensely but he didn't worry her as much as Fenwick did. Those were such odd questions today. Why on earth had he been asking them?

One of the police officers behind Blite was carrying a large plastic sack.

'What are you taking away?'

'Possible evidence, madam. We have a fresh warrant, and I have a receipt, here.'

'What is it?' Sally regarded the sack with dread. As the officer carrying it passed her, he tripped on the edge of the path and the contents clanked. She recognised the sound, saw the weight and size of the bundle and realised suddenly what it contained. Now she understood why Fenwick had been asking such banal questions. Sally looked at Blite with horror and felt sick as he gave her a slow smile.

'I think Chief Inspector Fenwick is going to be very pleased with today's work. You can be sure we'll be in touch, and soon. Good afternoon.'

Sally ran back to the house and closed and bolted the door behind her. Her hand shook as she poured out the gin she now kept in the kitchen into a mug that was draining by the sink. She took several long swallows and felt the hammering of her heart start to slow. Then she poured more gin into the mug and sat down heavily in the chair beside the Aga to think. She had made another mistake and now she would have to put it right or Alex was going to be very, very angry. The thought of it made her shrink back in her chair as she slowly drained the contents of the mug.

CHAPTER THIRTY-NINE

As Fenwick steered his car carefully through the wooden gateway, two eager faces pressed up against the hall window. He didn't have to make himself smile as he swung the driver's door closed and locked the car. There was a slap-crunch of slippered feet on gravel and then a thud into the back of his knees as Bess clasped his legs. Then a second shock as Christopher lurched into them both.

'Daddy!' High-pitched shrieks of sheer delight buffeted him and he was overwhelmed yet again by the simple miracle of their love for him. He found himself laughing as they clung on, one on either leg. 'You're home early!'

'Careful, you'll have me over. Gotcha!' His great arms swooped down and lifted them both up to dangle on either side of his waist, their legs kicking behind him, arms flailing about to the front. The shrieks of laughter intensified as he staggered crablike past his car and towards the front door. They were getting heavier, both of them. Even delicate little Chris was gaining weight at last.

'They've just had their tea, don't make them sick.' Wendy was smiling, pleased to see him home early for once.

As he lurched into the hall and deposited both children in a jumbled heap on the carpet, he saw her glance at her watch.

'Do you want to go out?'

'I haven't washed up yet and the kitchen's a real mess; we were painting.'

It was typical of Wendy. They would have eaten their tea in the midst of organised chaos as she tried, as always, to do too many things at once.

'No problem. You go on out. We can cope.'

'Well, there's a film on that Tony was keen to see this week. If I go now I'll still be back for ten, as always.' She was putting on her coat even as she spoke.

She never was. Wendy was habitually late for everything, but that was her only failing and she was great with his children.

Fenwick stopped any more protest and ushered her out of the door, shivering in a sudden chill blast of air from outside.

'You're cold, Daddy! Come by the fire and get warm.' Bess's commanding little hand dragged him into the sitting room, where a cheerful fire was spitting and sparking behind a fireguard.

'New wood,' explained Bess knowingly. 'Next time, Daddy, you'll need to buy us seasoned logs.'

'Yes, ma'am. Now tell me about school today – both of you.'

Delighted to have their father as an audience, they chatted on, Chris for once holding his full share of the conversation. It gladdened Fenwick's heart to see the six-year-old so happy and normal when a year before he had been close to putting him in a special school because he'd been so traumatised by Monique's illness.

'What's the matter, Daddy?' Chris sounded concerned, and Fenwick realised his preoccupation must have shown.

'Nothing, sorry. Say that last bit again while I go and make myself a cup of tea.'

The kitchen looked like a battle zone. Red, orange and green paint splattered the floor and units, which fortunately had been protected with thick sheets of old newspaper.

'What's this?' Fenwick held up a piece of black paper on to which thick stripes of paint had been brushed with obvious enthusiasm.

'It's a bonfire.' Chris was half proud, half indignant.

'Of course it is. And this bit here?' Fenwick pointed to some random splodges in the top corners.

'Sparks, but I've got to do the glitter next. Look.'

Sure enough, a pot of paste and five thin phials of multicoloured glitter stood ready.

'How do you do that?'

Christopher's mouth dropped open and horror filled his eyes.

'Don't *you* know?'

Fenwick realised that knowing how to make glittery blobs had become the next of his son's neverending tests of his omniscience.

'Yes, I do, but I wondered whether you did.'

Chris shook his head. Bess looked up from her own picture and shook hers.

'I don't know, Daddy.'

'I'll just make my tea and get changed, then I'll come and help.'

By the time he was in jeans and sweatshirt, with a strong cup of English breakfast tea to fortify him. Fenwick found himself equal to the glitter challenge. He and Chris blobbed the glue on top of the paint, then scattered the tiny particles freely all over the paper. It looked magnificent. Their only problem was that they'd forgotten Bess's painting. Hers was neatly drawn, the fire showing precise flames and sticks, and most of the paint had stayed within the pencil lines. All she lacked now was sparkle to finish it off. But there wasn't any. All five tubes were empty, their contents extravagantly spread over the floor and table, save for the perfect star bursts on Chris's paper. Fenwick's heart twisted painfully as he saw his elder child's eyes fill with tears. He and Chris had just become so carried away. He put Chris's picture to one side, then took Bess's and started to dab the glue on very carefully.

'Do you want to do this?'

A big shrug and a sullen 'There's no point. All the glitter's gone.'

'There'll be some, don't worry.'

Bess and Chris both looked at him in astonishment, and Bess even condescended to dab some glue on to her picture herself. When it was ready, Fenwick gave it to her to hold, moved all the brushes, paints and

249

sticks to one end of the table and carefully folded the newspaper that had covered it into a stiff V shape. The glitter cascaded into an iridescent funnel in the middle.

'Put the painting down on the table.'

Bess did as she was told, and with arms fully extended, Fenwick salted the picture liberally until the last flicker of glitter had been absorbed by the globlets of glue. Perfect.

He enjoyed being the hero of the hour, every precious second of it. Even when they realised that glitter had gone everywhere and their baths took double time and Chris ended up with some in his eyes, he loved it. When the children were tucked up in bed asleep, he showered and changed again and put the oven on for a pizza. Then he remembered his vow to eat more vegetables and found tomatoes and onions for a salad and some peas as well. He was just clearing the last pea from his plate when the phone rang.

'Sir? It's Cooper. DS Gould has had a result. One of the teenagers on the train down to Brighton with Fish has positively identified the woman Francis Fielding met when he arrived. It was Sally Wainwright-Smith.'

'You're joking! Is she sure?'

'Positive. She says she bumped into Sally, who called her a "stupid bitch". She remembers her clearly. The girl was arrested for causing a breach of the peace this afternoon, and offered to identify the woman in the hope that Brighton would go easy on her.'

'Is it strong enough to hold up in court?'

'Gould thinks so; he's spoken with her directly.'

'What's his theory as to why Sally was meeting Fielding?'

'He thinks it was she who hired Fielding to kill Fish. Money wouldn't be a problem, but he can't think of a motive.'

'Perhaps Fish threatened her right to the Wainwright fortune in some way – it's the reason we think she killed Graham, after all.'

'Possibly. I'll put it to him. Anyway, he's found a new lease of life, and Brighton Division has suddenly turned very cooperative. Confirming a link between Sally and Fielding has finally convinced them that perhaps Fish's murder is connected with Amanda Bennett's. He's going to stay down in Brighton all night if necessary to find out more.'

'Excellent. Have him call me on my mobile at any time if something else breaks.'

Fenwick was frustrated now that he couldn't go back to work at once; he would have to wait until Wendy returned at ten. The rest of the evening stretched out ahead of him like a prison sentence. At quarter past eight the phone rang again; it was Cooper, telling him that they had found reference to James FitzGerald on HOLMES. He was an associate of a career criminal, Benjamin Harris, who was known to be behind a string of crime syndicates headquartered on Brighton. Fenwick then risked a call to Miles Cator's office number. The Commander was still hard at work, and Fenwick explained FitzGerald's connection to Harris.

'So you're saying that Wainwright's could be laundering money for Benjamin Harris! Well, that would be highly significant. This is a timely call, Chief Inspector. We're due in court tomorrow to defend an action by Wainwright's for the return of the Fish papers, and this will strengthen our case enormously, although I'm irritated that my own team hasn't already made the connection. I'll have them run the names of all shareholders and officers of the company against HOLMES, PCN and every other index at our disposal.'

'Do you think there's sufficient evidence to warrant a full-scale investigation into Wainwright's, sir?'

'We've had these papers less than a week, Chief Inspector, so that's a tough call, but my initial assessment is yes, they have a lot of questions to answer. This looks like turning into something very significant.'

Both the children were long in bed and Fenwick was trying to read a very worthy book on criminal psychology when his mobile phone buzzed softly. To his surprise it was DI Blite.

'Yes, Inspector?'

'I wanted to run my plans for tomorrow past you, Chief Inspector.' There was a new respect in the man's tone that surprised Fenwick, but he was realistic enough to realise that it wouldn't last.

'I'm bringing Sally in for questioning again at nine o'clock, and Claire Keating is going to join us. If possible she's also going to meet with her separately, provided Sally's lawyer agrees. What did the ACC say when you reported back to him today?'

'Not a lot. He wants us to get a move on with both the identity parades – for Shirley's brother and the girl who says she saw Sally meeting Fielding – so that this is sorted one way or another. I think that he believes a positive ID will make it much easier for him to justify an arrest, particularly if we find her fingerprints on that block and tackle you recovered *and* trace evidence on it that links it to the scene. It will be our first unbroken chain of evidence.'

'There's no chance of an arrest tonight?'

'Now that Ebutt is involved he's become even more cautious. Whenever I try to push him, he just keeps reminding me about the wrecked crime scene when Graham was found, and the weakness of the initial PM. He says that we've given the defence, and I quote: "enough gifts" for one case and he wants the rest of it watertight. You can try if you like . . .'

'No, Chief Inspector, I agree with you – it would be pointless. We just need to have the identifications confirmed as a top priority and continue to watch her in the meantime. Meanwhile, could you let Cooper know that I'm stuck here until ten o'clock at the earliest. It anyone's spare, can he have them send over the latest reports for me to read?'

No sooner had he broken the connection than the phone rang again, and a computerised voice told him that he had a new message. It was Cooper, and Fenwick could hear the excitement in his voice despite the flatness of the recording.

'Nightingale has traced Beck, the private detective, and he was holding out on us. She's recovered his full file. It provides us with conclusive proof that Sally was in Brighton before she turned up at Harlden. Nightingale's bringing it over right now – I thought you'd want to see it straight away.'

Nightingale crunched over Fenwick's gravel drive as he unlocked his front

251

door. He had obviously been waiting for her and she could sense his impatience right away. What she'd found out was the final missing link in the chain connecting Sally to Amanda Bennett's murder.

'Come on in and get warm. I've just made coffee. Would you like some?'

The embers of a fire glowed behind the fireguard in the sitting room. Kindling and a few lumps of coal soon brought the blaze to life. Nightingale looked around the room, remembering her other visits to the house. The year before, she and Cooper had sat in the cheerful garden sipping wine that the sergeant had called cat's pee after they'd left, but which she had recognised as a decent Chablis. The memory of that summer morning over a year before was piercing in its clarity and brought a sudden lump to her throat that made her feel foolish.

Nightingale tried not to let her curiosity show as she surreptitiously glanced around the room. It wasn't elegant, you could never call it that, and today signs of his children were everywhere; in photographs, a colouring book tucked down behind a cushion, and a stack of Disney videos beside the TV. But there was something about the room that called to her and made her heart ache. There was a faint smell of home baking, fresh flowers stood in a heavy crystal vase on a shelf, safely out of harm's way, and some of the children's paintings were propped up on the mantelpiece.

With a start she realised that they were birthday cards. Next to these were two more. With the pretence of going to warm her hands she walked over so that she could study their greetings. One was a traditional boating scene and inside she could just glimpse the words 'love Mother'. The other had a black and white photograph of the Keystone Cops on it, their car falling apart and with a white balloon stuck on to the front: 'It's your birthday – call for back up' It was from someone called Wendy and she recalled the young woman she'd met before. She wondered again just exactly who she was.

Fenwick returned to the room carrying a tray of coffee. He let her serve herself whilst he rummaged in a walnut cupboard and brought out a whisky bottle and glasses.

'It's a cold night. Would you like a small glass? I know you're driving but a sip won't hurt.'

She hadn't eaten since breakfast, but the idea of a drink with Fenwick was compelling.

'Thank you, sir.' She sat down on a sofa opposite the fire and removed a huge file from her bag. 'You were right, that private investigator hadn't told us everything. I was waiting for him when he landed at Gatwick today and we went straight to his flat. Look at these.'

Fenwick came and sat beside her on the settee so that they could look through the papers together. Nightingale was acutely conscious of the heat of him, and of his leg, barely an inch from her own thigh. She sipped the whisky and felt warmth spread inside her.

'So what's this?'

'It's his whole file on Sally's background, sir, all one hundred and fifteen pages of it. These are copies; the originals have already been logged. It appears that Mrs Wainwright-Smith has something of a chequered past. He found nothing on her before the age of seventeen, so he knew little of her childhood. But apart from that, he's found out virtually everything about her. And he told Graham.

'He had a team of two investigators working on this for six weeks, with unlimited funding from Graham Wainwright so he was able to dig deep. This is her police record.' She handed Fenwick a thick file that he could tell at once was authentic. 'She was arrested for soliciting aged seventeen and two months, and for actual bodily harm two years later, following an affray in Brighton town centre.'

'Brighton!' Fenwick couldn't help himself.

'Exactly. She escaped a custodial sentence on both occasions. After the second conviction, she was ordered to do one hundred hours of community work. She spent it in a council-run old people's home: gardening, cleaning, doing refurbishment. By the end of her time there she was trusted enough to be sent on shopping errands, and as an additional carer on excursions. Beck tracked down the matron of the home who was full of praise for her, called her a reformed character; except that she wasn't. The following year she used her experience to get a job at another old people's home, far more up-market this time, and in the course of the next few months two of the residents, both old men, died leaving her a small legacy. The first one was five hundred pounds, the next, one thousand five hundred pounds and a small boat. This didn't go down too well with the owners of the home and she moved to another one. Within six months she was engaged to a retired army Major, aged seventy-five. Just before they were due to be married he died in a car accident. Sally was driving and escaped with a broken arm. He ended up going through the windscreen. He left her twenty-two thousand pounds and a house in Wittering.'

'Were there suspicions at the time?'

'None at all. Eyebrows had been raised when the Major had announced his engagement, but car accidents happen, and there were no unusual circumstances. And, of course, she had been injured herself.'

'What did she do next?'

'This is the really surprising part; she went to college. She did a course in business administration and then, at the age of twenty-two, she found a job as office administrator for a local charity.'

'So she *was* a reformed character.'

'On the face of it yes, but Beck, the private investigator, is unconvinced. Whilst she was at college, he's fairly sure that she returned to prostitution. Don't ask me how, but he found the building society where she had a savings account and it *increased* from the twenty-thousand she had been given by the Major to over thirty-five thousand whilst she was studying, apparently without a job! And later she had a series of wealthy boyfriends, all much older than she was, and she was somehow able to afford to move from the house in Wittering to rent a cottage on the outskirts of Midhurst by the time she was twenty-five.

'She joined local societies – cooking, flower-arranging, the choir, drama – and continued to work for charity. By this time she was describing herself as the orphaned only child of wealthy parents who'd lived north of London. A year later she met the Wainwrights at a musical function in Harlden, and married Alexander within twelve weeks. Three months later, her husband's uncle died and she jointly inherited an estate worth fifteen million.'

'And who is the beneficiary under Alexander's will?'

'According to Beck, it's Sally Wainwright-Smith.'

There was a silence in the room, broken only by a soft crackle from the fire. Fenwick gathered the papers together and returned them to their files.

'Why didn't Beck hand all this over, Nightingale?'

'He said he was scared stiff following Graham's death. That might be true, but I wonder whether the thought of those millions had tempted him with the idea of blackmail. He's coming in to make a statement tomorrow afternoon.'

'It's the final piece. She probably knew Amanda Bennett from her time in Brighton.'

'I was looking through the arrest reports for anything on Amanda anyway, whilst I was waiting to find Beck, sir. I'll go back to them tonight. With these dates, I'll be able to concentrate on the time we know she was there. And Fish?'

'I don't know, perhaps Amanda told Fish about Sally's past and he tried to blackmail her with it, or even to expose her. We know there was no love lost between them. You've done a good job, Nightingale, yet again.' His praise brought the colour to her cheeks and he smiled to see it. 'You'd best be getting back. I'm going to come in tonight, as soon as the nanny's home.'

'I'll let Sergeant Cooper know, sir. Thank you for the whisky and coffee.'

She closed the front door behind her, and walked on shaky legs to her car. There was a tremor in her hands as she tried to insert the key in the ignition, and it took several seconds. Her thoughts were in turmoil. She knew now what had been happening to her, and cursed herself for her stupidity. She'd broken her engagement; had no interest in any other man since her fiancé had gone; pined in Brighton, and had been dumb enough to put it down to a miserable working environment. She had craved his attention, yet put it down to professional pride. What a stupid, stupid idiot she had been. How could she have been so blind to the emotion that had been building inside her?

As soon as she was sure that she was out of sight of his house, she pulled the car over on to the verge and rested her forehead on the steering wheel. It was hopeless, he was barely aware of her. And he was her boss, for heaven's sake, so professional that the very idea of a relationship with a colleague would be anathema to him.

As the cold of the night chilled the heat inside her, she told herself sternly that she would just have to resign herself to the impossibility of anything developing between them. Her feelings for him – which she surely couldn't deny any longer – were doomed to be unrequited, and she would just have to get used to the idea. She shook herself and squared her shoulders, a look of clenched determination on her face.

'Grow up,' she said out loud, 'this heartsick nonsense is worthy of a teenager, not a grown woman.' She nodded her head firmly in agreement, sure that she was in control of her emotions once again. She turned the key in the ignition, and, without warning, burst into tears.

Wendy returned at ten thirty, full of apologies for being late, and Fenwick explained that he had a case that was developing fast and he might be away all night. She promised to give the children his love in the morning if he wasn't there for breakfast.

CHAPTER FORTY

It was an unusually quiet night in Harlden. No road traffic accidents, an absence of post-pub brawls and not one domestic disturbance. The veneer of calm in the reception area of the police station was deceptive, though, because in the incident room two floors above, a team of a dozen officers was frantically reviewing every single report, file and piece of evidence associated with the Wainwright and Fish cases. Cooper had called in every officer on the case and set them to work rereading all the files. The sight of Chief Inspector Fenwick arriving shortly before eleven o'clock merely added to the tension. He called Cooper and Blite to his office and handed them mugs of coffee he had made himself.

'What have you got?'

'Nothing, sir,' the two officers answered in unison.

'There has to be a link. We know for certain that Fish visited Amanda Bennett on the night they both died, and he gave her the tape to hide. But why on earth did Sally want Fish dead so badly that she'd risk paying someone like Fielding to kill him? He must have had a hold on her, or threatened to expose her. Yet I can't believe he had the guts.'

Cooper blanched visibly at Fenwick's choice of words.

'Amanda knew her killer, the neighbours confirmed that.'

'Good point, Inspector. So if we can prove that Sally met Amanda whilst they were both prostitutes in Brighton, it would improve our chances of making a case against her.'

'Except, sir, that the tape we recovered from Amanda's didn't mention Sally in any way. It was all about criminal activities at Wainwright's. Perhaps Fish was killed to shut him up about the company, and it had nothing to do with Sally.'

'Perhaps, Inspector. But we have a confirmed sighting of her with Francis Fielding on the night of the murders. Supposing Fish knew about her background and had threatened to expose her – or even attempted to blackmail her. He wouldn't have known about her instability and history of violence. He would have expected her to react to a threat of public humiliation like any rational human being.

'No, my money's still on Sally as the person behind the killings of both Fish and Bennett. I can't believe that Fish would have been murdered so openly and so soon after Alan Wainwright's death by anyone associated with the money-laundering we think's going on at Wainwright's. It's brought too much police attention on the company.'

'*If* Sally knew Amanda as well, sir,' Cooper didn't fully believe the DCI's theory but he was willing to go along with it, particularly in front of Blite, 'she could have assumed that Amanda had either already been told about her by Fish or that she would make a connection once Fish was dead.'

'Good point. We need to prove that a connection existed between Amanda and Sally, and then we can link her to all the murders. Have Sergeant Gould check Amanda's arrest reports again. Find out who the arresting officers were; we need to talk to them.'

Blite left the room and Cooper rose to go.

'Stay a moment. I want to talk about Alexander. Is he in on all this? He knew about Sally's past, yet he married her, and he's the major beneficiary, after all.'

'You think it's a conspiracy between the two of them?' Cooper had difficulty in keeping disbelief from his voice.

'Not quite, no. Let's just say a happy coincidence for him. What if he started to realise that she has a capacity for violence and sexual manipulation? Does he try to limit it or direct it? Supposing that he encouraged her seduction of his uncle because of his desire to progress within the family firm? Then he sees that there is even more potential – an inheritance. His mother died penniless, leaving him nothing, largely because his uncle spent years disinheriting her from every vestige of the family fortune. Alex feels he's been neglected and ill-treated. Enter Sally, the perfect little temptress of older men, and suddenly life has new possibilities.'

'This is all conjecture, and even if it were true, sir, it stops a long way short of murder.'

'Yes but supposing Sally *doesn't* stop. We know that she has a history of violence. She was arrested for it in Brighton, and she nearly killed Donald Glass. She knew death as a child; she watched her father systematically beat and starve her brother and sister. Perhaps death has a different significance for her.'

'You mean she's a psychopath?'

'That's a word that's often used because we just can't believe the evil that lurks inside us, Sergeant, but every now and then I think it does apply. For someone with no moral judgement or self-control, and scarce understanding of what they are doing when they kill, perhaps. And yes, I think that could be Sally. It's essential we have Claire assess her formally tomorrow. And as for her husband, we know from the officers still tailing him that he hasn't been home for a few days, which is very odd behaviour.'

There was a hesitant tap on the door and Nightingale walked in. Even Fenwick noticed how deathly pale she looked, and Sergeant Cooper insisted that she sat down.

'We have cross-checked Bennett's arrest reports with those of Sally Price,' she said. 'Amanda Bennett was arrested three times. The first two were for soliciting, the third for living off immoral earnings. That's the one she went to jail for.

'On the night of her first arrest, three other prostitutes were picked up at the same time, including one Sally Price. No charges were brought against either woman.' The silence in the room was so intense that they all heard Sergeant Cooper's empty stomach gurgle, but all ignored it. 'On the night of her third arrest, six customers from Bennett's brothel were also taken into custody, although charges against most of them were later dropped. One of the customers was Arthur Lawrence Fish, resident of Harlden.'

'So Amanda Bennett knew them both and Fish could have known Sally. He might even have been a client. My God!'

'Yes, sir, and Amanda knew her killer; her neighbour was certain of that.'

'Who was the officer in charge on the night that Amanda and Arthur Fish were arrested?'

'Inspector Black, Brighton Division Vice. He's retired now. Sergeant Gould called him earlier this evening, but he said he couldn't remember the case.'

'I'm going to see Black tomorrow – let Sergeant Gould know. And you can tell the team upstairs to go home and rest; we have the connection we need.'

'What are you going to do, sir?'

'Work on my report to the ACC and Superintendent Quinlan. As soon as Sally's formally identified tomorrow, I want her arrested without delay, so the paperwork needs to be ready.'

'I'll help if you like.' Cooper did his best to smother a yawn.

'No, I'm fine. You'll both need your wits about you tomorrow, so get a few hours' sleep while you can.'

Fenwick took a further hour to finish his report. Then he found an empty, clean cell in the detention block, which had remained unnaturally silent throughout the night, and slept until the custody sergeant shook him awake with a cup of coffee at seven thirty the following morning.

CHAPTER FORTY-ONE

Wendy was buttoning Chris's coat and checking that he had his latest project in his bag when the phone rang. Fenwick explained that it was going to be a busy day and asked her to bring a fresh shirt round to the police station for him on her way to the school. She was already running late, so she cursed under her breath as she found a freshly laundered white shirt in his wardrobe and ran with it to the car, where the children were already huddled in the back.

Sally was awake, dressed and fully alert when Ebutt called for her at nine o'clock. She had resisted the idea of both drink and pills, and her mind ached with a dreadful clarity. She had spent over an hour on the phone to Alex the night before. He was staying in a hotel right next to the office and had insisted that he had to stay away, despite her pleading. He had again cautioned her to silence with the police. She hadn't told him about the block and tackle they had removed from the estate; she knew he would be very angry that she had kept such potentially incriminating evidence rather than throwing it away in some distant builder's skip. He was concerned, though, about the identity parade, and the thought of it made her shiver.

Inspector Blite started the tape recorder and began to repeat his questions. That Keating woman was with him again. After about twenty minutes, in which Sally had successfully resisted the temptation to give in and correct some of the Inspector's more stupid assumptions, the woman stood up and moved her chair to sit next to the policeman. He nodded to her and she spoke for the first time.

'Sally, my name is Claire Keating and I'm a psychiatrist. The police have asked me to talk to you. Would either you or your solicitor mind?'

Her lawyer had no objection, but Sally was confused. Was she allowed to talk to this woman or not? Alex hadn't told her how to handle questions that didn't come from the police.

'I'm not going to ask you about the allegations the police are making against you. I only want to get to know you a little better.'

'All right.'

The woman asked a lot of meaningless questions about her childhood, which Sally answered with ease. This was just like talking to the social workers all those years ago, and she slipped into the role of traumatised child with ease. As the subject matter became more recent, she was surprised at how much this woman Keating knew about her past, and she became more guarded in her answers. Whilst they changed the tape, the woman asked for tea and biscuits for them all, reminding Sally of how hungry she was. When the biscuits arrived she ate three, one after another, and couldn't concentrate until the plate was empty.

'Would you like something else to eat?'

'Can I?'

'Of course – anything you like, within reason.'

'A bacon sandwich – with tomato sauce?'

'No problem, I'm sure the Inspector will arrange it.'

Sally enjoyed the look of displeasure on the policeman's face as he went out to fetch her late breakfast, and gave the woman opposite her first smile. As soon as he returned, the tape was switched on and they started again.

Claire wanted to talk about Alex this time – how they had met, what she called their 'whirlwind romance'. They seemed harmless enough questions. She was curious to know what he looked like; was he handsome?

'Sort of. He's tall and strong-looking. He's always clean and smart.'

'Is he clever?'

'Oh yes, and hard-working.'

'He sounds perfect! Who fell in love with whom first, do you think?'

'Oh, Alex with me; he was very persistent, always taking me out for meals and buying me presents.'

'What sort of presents?'

'Clothes mainly, even shoes. He had great taste for a man – he knew exactly what I should look like.'

'So he was a fashionable dresser himself, then?'

'Alex? Never, but he made sure I was.'

'Tell me about your relationship now.'

'What about it?'

'Are you close to each other – forever talking on the phone when you're apart, that sort of thing?'

Sally looked away from the woman's friendly eyes.

'Sometimes, but he's very busy and I don't like to trouble him at work.'

'I have to ask you this, Sally: did you marry him for his money?'

The unexpectedness of the question shocked her and she wasn't sure how to answer it. Sometimes she wondered whether what she felt for Alex was this love thing that everyone seemed so besotted with. Whether it was or not, she both needed and feared him just as she had once needed and feared her father. Claire Keating was still waiting for an answer.

'That's none of your business.'

The woman didn't seem put off by the answer and kept on asking apparently meaningless questions. At the end of an hour, Sally's lawyer called the interview to a close. Before they left, the policeman went to confirm the time of the identification parade. Sally could see that he was annoyed at her continued silence in the face of his questions, whilst she had happily talked to the woman.

'Wait here!' he said rudely. 'I'm going to find out how quickly we can do the parade, arrest you, lock you up and bring this fiasco to an end. Once you're in custody you won't be such a smart aleck!'

It was the first time that the possibility of being locked up had entered her mind, and Sally froze in horror.

Claire saw the expression on Sally's face as she leapt to her feet.

'Sally, are you OK? Sally?'

'Mrs Wainwright-Smith? Please sit down! Stop that!' Blite turned to Claire Keating. 'Why is she screaming like that?'

'I think it's a panic attack. We need to calm her down, stop her hyperventilating. Put your hand in front of her nose and mouth.'

'I'm not putting my hand anywhere near her!'

Claire picked up the paper bag that the bacon sandwich had been delivered in and, grabbing Sally around the shoulders, forced it over her nose and mouth. Within minutes she had swung from acute agitation to semi-collapse.

'Take her to her doctor before she goes home,' Claire advised the solicitor as he escorted his zombie-like client from the room.

'Is she mad?' Blite was worried that his suspected murderess might be able to plead insanity.

'I couldn't say based on one interview, but that was simply a classic panic attack.'

'Will she be fit enough for the identity parade at one? The ACC is insistent that we can't arrest her without one.'

'It depends whether the doctor decides to sedate her, but I'd say it's doubtful.'

Blite swore, and Claire left him to make a decision as to whether to postpone the parade a second time. She needed to think carefully about her report for Fenwick; it was going to be a difficult one to write.

Wendy dropped the children at school with strict instructions to wait for her in the playground as always until she came to collect them at three o'clock. She watched them skip off into their classrooms before getting back into the car. She had a busy day ahead of her: letters to write and her own washing to do, as well as the breakfast debris to clear away. With luck it should be possible to pick up her dry cleaning, complete the weekly shopping, take the Renault for a wash at the garage and still be back at school in the afternoon in plenty of time.

Detective Chief Inspector Ian Black had retired to a bungalow on cliffs overlooking the Channel. Fenwick found him busily engaged in tending his acre and a half of garden, adding mulch to a raised bed of azaleas, which bloomed with an almost tropical abandon. He saw Fenwick's admiring glance and started talking with enthusiasm.

'It's a constant battle, trying to grow ericaceous plants on this cliff. Feel that wind! If the lime doesn't leach through and kill them, the gales do. I lose at least one each year. I'm Ian Black, by the way; you must be Andrew Fenwick.' He removed a gardening glove and shook hands.

A look crossed Black's face which Fenwick found difficult to interpret; caution or envy, it was hard to tell.

'Come on back to the patio and have some tea. Margaret's at the WI, so you'll have to make do with my brew, I'm afraid.'

They sipped their tea in a silence which both men appeared reluctant to break. Eventually Fenwick put his cup down.

'You spoke to one of my officers, DS Gould, last night. He was asking you whether you recalled Amanda Bennett's arrest.'

'It was a long time ago, Chief Inspector, and as I told your colleague, I don't recall that particular incident. If you've come all the way down here to jog my memory, I'm afraid you've had a wasted journey.'

Again Fenwick detected a strange defensiveness which seemed out of character. Black was known to have been a solid, dependable officer and it was surprising that he was giving the impression of having something to hide. Fenwick decided to approach him obliquely.

'How long were you in Vice?'

'Four years.'

'Were you in charge whilst you were there?'

'No, I was an ordinary inspector. I was only made up to chief just before I left; late in life compared with you fellas now, I know.' It was said with an edge of bitterness. 'DCI Harris was the boss. He retired years ago and died the winter before last.'

'It must have been great back then to have a few magistrates still intent on imprisonment; I can't tell you how frustrating it is now. All that work, for what?' Fenwick shook his head in mock disgust, hoping that Black would respond. He did, talking at length about the old days, enjoying reminiscences with a younger officer who was showing him respect.

Fenwick let him ramble and expand on his comparison of old policing methods with new. When he eventually paused for breath, Fenwick took up the theme.

'I tell you something else they don't value enough these days, and that's informants. The number of times I've been able to close a case because of the right piece of information at the right time! Yet it's looked down on now.'

Black nodded vigorously in agreement. 'Some of the best arrests of my career followed a good tip-off.'

Fenwick encouraged him gently back to his time in Vice, until he was halfway through a story about one of the best informants he'd ever had, a young slip of a thing. Fenwick thought of Sally. With her dominant survival instinct and lack of morals, she would make a perfect snitch. He played a hunch; what had he to lose?

'Would that be Sally Bates? Or was she Price by then?'

'Yes, Sally Price. Only about seventeen, but always reliable.'

Fenwick pursued the idea he had been carrying since he'd arrived.

'Grassing on Amanda Bennett's house was big-time even for her, though, way up from the usual bits and pieces.'

'Yes, but she had to deliver or we were going to push the magistrate for a custodial sentence; she had no choice.'

Fenwick let the words settle gently into the silence. He sipped the last of his tea and heard a clock chime two in the distance. Black turned to him and shook his head.

'You bastard.'

'You asked for it. Why did you pretend not to remember the Bennett case?'

Black sighed, a long, hollow sound of defeat.

'Misplaced loyalty, I suppose. Harris was a good policeman even though his methods were a bit near the edge. He ran Sally, but the Amanda Bennett

262

thing was a bit too rich even for him. Sally gave us Amanda but we wanted whoever was behind her. We knew that someone was backing her with a lot of money and connections. The way the house was set up, the clientele, all very classy. Harris was about to retire, and this was his swansong.

'We raided the place one Thursday night, almost exactly ten years ago. There were eight clients in the place, and nine girls plus Amanda.'

'Was Sally there?'

'Not that night. She called in with flu and stayed away. The youngest there was fourteen; she was with a man who ran a local chain of printing shops. I remember him because his ex-wife still goes to the WI with mine. Then there were two patrons tied up in separate bedrooms. One was having his bottom beaten as we walked in, but that was mild compared with the other bloke. I can never look at a bag of pegs now without thinking of him.'

An alarm bell went off in Fenwick's head, but he let Black carry on talking.

'The rest were just your usuals. We took all their details and were about to run them down to Division to be charged when the phone rang. It was for Harris. I don't know who it was or what was said, but when he came back his face was black. I've never seen a man so close to a seizure. He told us to take the girls on ahead, that he'd sort the men out with one of the other officers on the scene.

'I thought nothing of it at the time, but later, when I was reading the reports that had been filed, I noticed that apparently only six clients were on the premises at the time of the raid. Two had disappeared. Someone had pulled strings to save their embarrassment.

'We never did catch the backers. Amanda Bennett wouldn't talk. She did her eighteen months and came out and into private practice, as you might say.'

'Did you see any of the clients' faces?'

'Oh yes. I untied two of them! I'm not likely to forget that.'

Fenwick took a photograph out of his pocket and passed it to Black.

'I know it was ten years ago, but take a look at this, imagine him ten years younger. Could he be one of them?'

Black took the picture with a look of scepticism that changed to incredulity.

'Good God! How could you possibly have known that! Yes, this is the weirdo who was having his bottom spanked by a girl in leathers. Who is he?'

'He *was* a Mr Arthur Fish. He was murdered three weeks ago, and I think we finally know the reason why.'

Black raised his eyebrows and sighed as he looked across his beautiful garden to the white horses in the sea beyond.

'There's no such thing as the past, you know, Chief Inspector. The legacy of what you've done lives on in the present, shaping everything. I should have known that I couldn't escape it.'

He rose to shake Fenwick's hand and show him out.

CHAPTER FORTY-TWO

Sally was taken back to the Hall by her solicitor, who insisted on calling her doctor. As soon as he had gone, she rang the surgery to cancel the visit and poured herself a drink. She was calm again now but needed to think. Inspector Blite had postponed the identity parade for a further twenty-four hours, and she had decided that under no circumstances would she subject herself to it. His casual reference to being locked up had shattered her confidence, and memories of her brother and sister shut away in that stinking room crowded her mind. With a shudder she realised that if James FitzGerald ever realised that the police were already building a case against her, he might simply send them the pictures anyway and abandon the idea of blackmail as too risky. Either way, Alex had been adamant when she'd spoken to him that they should resist paying him one penny. He hadn't gone so far as to tell Sally how to deal with FitzGerald, but the hint had been there in his unfinished sentences.

She knew that he was hoping she would find a way of handling this, but without him ever having to know the details, just like her father had once done. He had coached her, reprimanded her and praised her, and she had always been a fast learner. Alex was kinder; he didn't beat her and he knew that she wasn't as fearless as she pretended to be, but nevertheless, he had his expectations. It was clear to her now that James FitzGerald would have to go; precisely how she wasn't sure, but an idea would come to her. And she had to avoid the police, particularly Fenwick. Inspector Blite was persistent but he was simply a bully and she knew how to deal with him. Provided she could avoid his identity parade he wouldn't be a problem. Fenwick was a different matter. He was clever and he didn't trust her. His absence from the interview today didn't fool her; he would be plotting somewhere.

Sally dropped her forehead on to the palm of her hand and started rocking slowly, forwards and back. Then she balled her fist and beat out a rhythm on her temple, softly at first, then harder and harder. The walls of the kitchen billowed in and out and her head whirled. She needed another drink. Both Irene and Shirley had handed in their notice, and apart from a momentary spurt of anger, she didn't care. Let them, stupid bitches! There were more where they came from, and in the meantime she could live with the dust and a few cobwebs. The first gin and tonic went down quickly, the second a little more slowly. She was just trying to decide whether or not to have a third when the phone rang. She lunged for it, tripped, spilt her drink and dropped her glass. She let it lie on the carpet and dragged her eyes away from the spreading damp patch long enough to find and raise the handset.

'Alex!' Her voice was breathy, almost panicking.

'No, this is DCI Fenwick, Mrs Wainwright-Smith.'

Her *bête noire*. How she hated this man. It was as if her fear of him had somehow conjured him up. 'Yes, Chief Inspector?'

'I wanted to let you know that when you come in again later today, I will be interviewing you afterwards about Amanda Bennett's death.'

Sally felt the tonic rush up into the back of her throat. For a moment all thought and all cunning left her. She sensed defeat, and the idea of it was momentarily so compelling that she sank down exhausted, already beaten, into a chair. Then the thought of prison filled her and she rallied. He was trying to bait her, and it wouldn't work.

'I've told you before, I don't know her. Please stop pestering me.'

'Of course, I wouldn't dream of doing that, but given that we now have a witness who will testify to your having known her, I thought it was only fair to warn you.'

How could he? They were all dead, she had made sure of that. It was a bluff and one she was prepared to call.

'I'm very busy, Chief Inspector, and also a little bored of your games. I don't know what you're talking about.'

'I've spoken to a member of the police team who made the arrests ten years ago, Sally. He remembers you well.'

'I wasn't there.'

There was a heavy pause, and she could hear the interference on his mobile phone. He was trying to weigh up whether she had made an admission or not. Sally started beating her head with her fist again. This wasn't fair, it wasn't right. What had she ever done to make this man hound her like this?

'I have nothing to say.' She needed time now more than anything else. He was the enemy and she needed to think how to handle him. She spoke abruptly, 'I have to go,' and replaced the receiver before he could reply.

She glanced at her watch; it was nearly two thirty. She needed to get away, and to do that she needed money. The small Swiss bank into which she had transferred the cash she and Alex had inherited would be shut by now. She poured herself another gin and tonic and gulped it down in one.

Her mind was racing, and the gin surging through her blood gave her a heady sense of euphoria one moment and absolute depression the next. She had to think, but her mind whirled. She needed to get away, from Fenwick, from FitzGerald, from England! If she could only reach Brighton she would be able to use the boat. It was only seventeen foot long, but they'd crossed the Channel in it before, and she could sail single-handed if need be.

Sally found her handbag and her prescription for antidepressants. She wasn't meant to take more than three a day, and she'd already had two. She poured herself another gin, with less tonic this time, and swallowed another pill. For long seconds she simply rested her head back against a soft cushion, her eyes shut. An incredible weariness closed around her, but if she gave in to sleep, all would be lost.

She needed to think. There was money in her old savings account, squirrelled away over the past twelve years, starting with the ten thousand pounds she had stolen from Glass. To that had been added various legacies from dying old men and every spare penny of her earnings as a prostitute in

Brighton. There was over sixty-five thousand pounds in her account now, including the proceeds from the sale of the house she had inherited in Wittering. She knew the bank branch's number off by heart. It was in Brighton, and she'd been a customer from the time she had arrived there. She was put through to the manager.

'I need to make a cash withdrawal, immediately.'

'For how much?'

'The whole balance, in cash.'

'That would normally take at least three days to arrange.'

'I don't have three days!' Wild thoughts cascaded through her mind as she improvised. 'Look, you don't understand, my father's been taken seriously ill in Africa and they won't treat him unless I can pay them in cash. I'm flying there tomorrow and I need the money!'

'I'm so sorry, please calm down. We could wire the money; give us the details of the hospital's bank there, and I'll arrange it as soon as I have your instructions in writing.'

'You don't understand.' Sally didn't have to fake the sound of tears in her voice. 'They want cash. I have to take cash.'

'Could you hold?'

Sally waited, listening to the automatic phone system play 'Greensleeves' and gradually calming down. When the manager returned, full of apologies for keeping her waiting whilst he'd contacted his regional office, she had an alternative proposal ready.

'I can visit the branch in person tomorrow and bring a letter of authorisation with me.'

'Normally we require three days' notice.'

'I know, but this is an emergency.'

The manager had already agreed with his regional boss that he could make the cash available. Sally had been saving consistently in modest amounts for over ten years, and nothing in her profile was suspicious. If he hurried he would have just enough time to order the exceptional cash she would need.

'Very well, Miss Price. Are you sure you'll be safe carrying such a large amount of cash around?'

'Oh yes. I'll be safe.'

Sally leant back in her chair with a deep sigh. In twenty-four hours she would have enough money to escape. Now all she had to do was consider how to avoid Fenwick and deal with FitzGerald before she left. She needed to find a way of distracting Fenwick so that she could sort out FitzGerald and travel to Brighton to collect her money. All she had to do now was work out how.

'Chief Inspector? It's Claire Keating.' Fenwick had called the psychiatrist from his car, eager to hear her assessment of Sally. 'I haven't finished writing my report yet, but your message said it was urgent.'

Fenwick pulled over into a lay-by so that he could concentrate on the call. He explained to her that they now had a confirmed link between Sally and Arthur Fish and Amanda Bennett. He had already called Blite to tell him to arrest Sally based on this latest evidence, notwithstanding the lack of an identity parade. If the ACC hadn't been so lily-livered he would already have done so with complete confidence, irrespective of who she was. He hoped that the inspector was already on his way to the Hall.

'A connection doesn't prove guilt, Claire, but if we can charge her we'll be able to work on her whilst she's in custody. I need some input from you so that I know how to handle the questioning.'

'She is a very complex character, Andrew. In the course of two hours I saw evidence of several different personality disorders, as well as witnessing a full-scale panic attack just before she left.'

'She seemed perfectly all right when I spoke to her just now.'

'Did she? That's interesting. She was disturbed enough for Inspector Blite to postpone his identity parade again.'

'She was being manipulative, I'm sure of it.'

'Well, that's consistent with my preliminary diagnosis. She exhibits clearly defined symptoms from a number of Cluster B personality disorders; those are the abnormal types of people who have an overly dramatic and emotional personality and who can seem extremely selfish, lacking in self-control and manipulative.

'Sally has very shallow and rapidly changing emotions; she uses sex as a tool for control or reward and is utterly self-centred. At the same time she displays a need to be the centre of attention – that's a classic diagnosis of histrionic personality disorder, but I think her condition goes way beyond that. You and your team have described severe psychotic episodes, extreme reactions to stress and a tendency towards violence that suggests she could also have characteristics of an antisocial personality. She's capable of holding a deep grudge, she trusts virtually no one, she's amoral, has no sense of remorse and scant regard for the truth. Her attack on Donald Glass shows that she can be spontaneously aggressive, and I sense – but I don't know – that she could be capable of reckless and impulsive behaviour.'

'If she's fickle, shallow and unstable, why has her relationship with her husband lasted so long?'

'They've been together less than six months, but even so, that's longer than many relationships last for someone with a severely histrionic personality. Typically she would want to manipulate and control him whilst looking to him for reassurance and adulation. If he's smart enough to make her think she's in charge, then their relationship would achieve some sort of balance. But I think his control over her may run deeper than that. She has a curious dependency on him that isn't associated with any Cluster B disorders. I think it must have its roots in her childhood abuse. Her father dominated her totally and destroyed any chance she ever had of natural development. She was forced to be sexually active at such a young age that her childhood stopped. Somewhere inside her is a child still desperate for approval and guidance.'

'Could that personality co-exist with the other disorders?'

'I think it does.'

'Is she dangerous?'

'Yes. She doesn't respect normal social conventions and her capacity for aggression and lack of remorse make her potentially very dangerous indeed, particularly when she perceives she's being threatened. That would prompt highly erratic and violent behaviour against the supposed attacker.'

'Sufficient to kill them?'

'I'd need more time with her before confirming that formally, but off the record, yes, she's quite capable of murder.'

Sally paced the great hall as she ran through her plan again. She only needed to stay out of police custody for twenty-four hours, then she would be able to collect her personal savings and take the boat across the Channel. Within days she would disappear in the vastness of continental Europe, with enough money to hide until she had established a new identity and could start life over again.

She had re-created herself before, but her ambition then had been limited by adolescence. Now she knew how to live and behave like a millionairess and she could set her sights accordingly. Even if Alex stayed in England for a while, there were bound to be suitable single men holidaying somewhere, and she would be able to trap a few before her money ran out. To her surprise, the thought didn't warm her as completely as it once would have done, and she realised with a rare sense of fear that she was becoming dependent on Alex.

She brushed the unwelcome thought away and concentrated on what she would have to do to remain free for one more day. Her immediate problem was Fenwick; he simply wouldn't leave her alone, and he had to be dealt with. She had to work out a way to distract him for long enough to deal with FitzGerald and make her escape, yet he seemed untouchable. There was no obvious way to reach him. She stared fixedly at the table in front of her as she tried to concentrate. The local newspaper was still lying there from the week before, a thin rag, full of car wrecks, burglaries and school competitions. A sudden memory returned to her, and she scrambled for the paper, smoothing its wrinkled pages back into some semblance of order. She had seen his name in here, somewhere. Where was it?

Sally flicked through the pages until she found the photograph with its caption that had somehow lodged in her subconscious. It showed a group of five children proudly holding their recorders, and there in the middle was a pretty dark-haired girl with enormous eyes, gazing confidently at the photographer. The caption beneath the photograph identified her as Bess Fenwick, seven, from Harlden Primary. She had to be the Chief Inspector's daughter. It was common knowledge that he had children, and his was such an unusual name.

Her instincts screamed at her that the only way to attack the man was through his child. She checked her watch: two forty. With luck and light traffic she could be at Harlden Primary in fifteen minutes. What she would do then, she had no idea, but coming between Fenwick and his daughter would undoubtedly be a way to slow him down. She snatched up her car keys and ran out of the Hall, forgetting to lock the front door. What did it matter? From tomorrow night it would mean nothing to her. She felt a strange pang at the idea of leaving its comfort behind after so short a time, but then the thought of freedom and a new beginning filled her and she jumped into the car without a backward glance.

Her driving was crazy, erratic. Three strong gins mixed with almost her whole day's allowance of antidepressants was playing havoc with her coordination, but her thoughts raced forward. It was as if her consciousness was somehow too big for her body now, driven by her intense hatred for Fenwick and the need for action to keep thoughts of captivity away. A cock pheasant strutted out into the road and she swerved across to hit it full on, feeling an immense surge of pleasure as the thump jarred her hands on the wheel and blood splattered the front of her car. Auburn feathers flew up and lodged under the windscreen wipers. She stared at their richness, fascinated, until the blare of a horn from an oncoming car caused her to correct her steering and swerve back on to her side of the road.

She found the primary school easily, as if guided there by some external force. The playground in front was deserted, and for an awful moment she thought she had missed the daily exodus. Then she noticed a line of waiting cars and realised that she was just in time.

A bell rang within the school building and as if on cue the drivers left their cars. They were nearly all, but not exclusively, women and they queued up obediently at the school gates waiting for their offspring. There was a peculiar familiarity among the group assembled by the gates, and she realised that if she ventured from her car she would immediately be recognised as the intruder she was, so she waited.

The children came out of the school in several waves, class after class rushing to the narrow gateway en masse, then breaking and filing through. Each child or group was snapped up at once by the waiting adults, and Sally stared with fascination at the picture of care and protection before her. She had never known that parents could be like this, and a weird, sickening pain encircled her heart. She opened her handbag and found her bottle of pills. She took one, dry-swallowing it with difficulty, and closed her eyes as it took effect. She felt better at once, optimistic and with renewed energy. As she replaced the bottle in her bag, she saw the warrant card she had stolen from that policewoman at the Hall. It had been a natural reaction to an opportunity that had presented itself unasked for. She took the card out and stared at it. She had forgotten that she had it, but noticing it now was almost like an omen.

Sally found a Polo mint in her bag and sucked on it thoughtfully. So far, she had no clear idea why she was here; it just seemed the right place to be. She could follow the child home, perhaps, and find out where it lived. Or they might go to a park or the shops. Her thinking was vague, but she was sure that the reason for her journey would present itself soon, and in the meantime she was enjoying the buzz of the pill and its distinctive euphoria.

Wendy was stuck in a queue at the car wash behind a Mini which, although clean now, wouldn't start. Surely the driver had realised that old Minis and damp didn't mix! There were two other cars behind her waiting for their turn, nose to tail. It was nearly three and she tried, but rarely succeeded, to be at the school before the children came out, even though Bess and Chris were always among the last to leave and always waited for her obediently. The school was only a few minutes away, so if only this idiot up ahead would do the decent thing and push his car out of the way, she would be fine.

* * *

269

Bess waited for Chris in the playground if the weather was fine, or by the big school doors if it was raining. Today it was very windy but dry, and she was tapping her sandalled foot impatiently as she waited for her younger brother. He was always one of the last.

Here he was now, ambling out, daydreaming. She called to him.

'Chris, over here!'

He looked up, grinned and trotted over. Most of the other children had gone already; only a few stragglers remained.

'Come on, Wendy'll be here soon.' She grabbed her brother's hand and started to stride off purposefully towards the gates. She was almost there when she stopped suddenly.

'Chris, your shoe bag; where is it? You know you're not meant to leave anything behind. Go and get it. Go on, hurry up!'

Chris trotted dutifully towards the school building without looking back. There was no arguing with his sister, so he might as well do what she said. He found his shoe bag hanging on his peg and slung it over his shoulder. Then he noticed that someone had left a Mars bar on the bench and he wrestled with his conscience for a moment before turning his back on it and leaving the building once again.

The playground was deserted. All the grown-ups had gone and he was the only child left. He called out his sister's name, softly at first, then louder. There was no reply. He ran over to the climbing frames and swings, but she wasn't there. Then he ran back again towards the gates. There was the sound of a car turning the corner at the end of the road too fast, and he thought he recognised the engine. He waited hopefully. The car screeched to a stop, a door slammed shut and Wendy rushed into the playground.

'Chris! Thank goodness. I'm so sorry I'm late, but I'm here now. Where's your sister?'

Chris stared at Wendy's worried face and started to cry.

CHAPTER FORTY-THREE

Fenwick returned to the station with high hopes of finding Sally in custody, only to be told by Blite that he had thought it best to check with the ACC before arresting her. Surprise, surprise, Harper-Brown had insisted on a court warrant, and the application Fenwick had drafted the night before had assumed a successful identification parade.

'As you're the one who interviewed Black, sir, I thought I'd better leave it until you returned.'

Fenwick was furious and ordered Blite out of his office before he said something he would regret. He was just finishing the revised application when his secretary put Wendy's call through. He knew at once from the tone of her voice that something was terribly wrong, and his heart constricted in his chest. Wendy was almost in tears.

'It's Bess, she wasn't in the playground when I went to pick them up from school. I drove home slowly with Chris, exactly the way she would have walked, but there was no sign of her and she isn't here either.' There was a rising note of panic in her voice, and Fenwick struggled to remain calm.

'You're sure that she isn't at home?'

'No, I've searched everywhere.'

'And she hasn't gone to play with friends?'

'I've called all her best friends; she's not with any of them. Oh, Andrew, I'm so sorry. I was only two minutes late, honestly.' She had been late before and two minutes was nothing, a mere fraction of time. It was obscene that it should suddenly count for so much.

'How's Chris?'

'He's very upset. I can't get him to talk but he clearly doesn't know where Bess is.'

Fenwick's mind was racing. Bess had been missing for less than half an hour, and she was likely to be with friends somewhere, or in her own private daydream in the park, but he wasn't about to take that risk. She was normally an obedient child, and going off on her own was completely out of character. There were few privileges these days in being a senior police officer, but it was an easy decision to take advantage of his position. He told Wendy to wait in the house with Chris and offered her words of comfort he was far from believing in, then ran down the corridor to Superintendent Quinlan's office. He was in a meeting with the divisional head of traffic, but Fenwick went in anyway. The look on his face made it obvious that he had a major problem.

'My daughter's gone missing. She wasn't at the school when the nanny

271

went to pick her up, and none of her friends have seen her.'

'How long?'

'Only half an hour, but this is totally out of character. She'd *never* leave her brother or go off on her own.'

Superintendent Quinlan barely took time to think.

'I'll talk to Operations and have them set up a team; you go home, and don't worry about the Wainwright case. I'll have the others follow through with the warrant and arrest.'

The drive home was a nightmare of crawling hopefully through streets with pedestrians on the pavement and racing impatiently along empty stretches at well over the speed limit. He saw no sign of Bess.

At home, both Chris and Wendy welcomed him with tears. He picked his small son up in an enveloping hug and kissed Wendy on the top of her head.

'It's not your fault,' he whispered.

He walked out to the garden with Chris, still hugging him.

'Ssh, it's OK, don't cry. Everything will be all right soon,' but Chris's sobs grew louder until he was almost wailing. His father just squeezed him tight, hoping that the security of his arms would somehow infuse the child with some of his own strength. Wendy brought him a cup of tea and sat on a nearby bench, staring forlornly at the ground between her feet. There was nothing she could say.

Fenwick took one of his arms from around his son long enough to drink some tea, then wrapped it back in a tight hug. After some time Chris's sobs reduced to snuffles and then he was silent. Fenwick remembered how badly affected he had been by his mother's long illness and eventual committal; within his simple toddler's brain Chris had assumed all the guilt and responsibility, leaving lasting scars that made him a vulnerable child even now. Fenwick had to find the right words to stop him being damaged again.

'It's not your fault, Chris. You're a good boy, a very special boy, and Daddy loves you.'

His words brought more tears, but they were softer this time and subsided sooner. The three of them sat in an empty silence for a long time, until the wind made it too cold to stay outside. Fenwick called all of Bess's friends again without success while Wendy made some sandwiches and Fenwick watched in amazement as his son ate his whole plateful and drank a glass of orange juice without a word of protest. He could barely manage a mouthful of his own, but he kept forcing the food down, too aware that he could be up all night. Until Chris was asleep in bed, though, there was no way he could leave him to go and search for Bess. In the meantime, the little boy needed as much normal routine as possible.

After tea, Fenwick took Chris into the sitting room to watch television, stroking his hair as the meaningless cartoons paraded in front of them. He had received three updates, two from the operations centre and one from Superintendent Quinlan himself. They had interviewed all the teachers at the school, and most of Bess's classmates. No one could recall anything unusual. The last time Bess had been seen was whilst she waited patiently in the playground for her brother at the end of the day. Now it was past seven o'clock and the light was starting to fade. Fenwick tried to keep from his mind the terrible thought that she had been abducted by concentrating on Chris and his needs.

He couldn't shake off the compulsive desire to be out searching for Bess, and recalled the faces of other fathers he had seen trying to cope with the awful wait until they discovered their child's fate. He shivered, and the movement disturbed Chris.

'Has Bess gone to be with Mummy, Daddy?'

Fenwick held his breath and let it out slowly, not wanting to scare the boy with his reaction to those awful words.

'No, Chris, Bess is likely to be home soon.'

It was as if he hadn't spoken.

'Because if she has, I'd like to go too. I miss Mummy, Daddy. I miss her a lot.'

'I know, Chris, I do too, but I need you to be here with me.'

Chris turned and stared at his father with huge grey eyes filled with a look of wonder.

'Do you, Daddy?'

The idea seemed extraordinary to the child, and he shook his head in wonder as he turned contentedly back to the video he was watching.

'Daddy needs *me*,' he said to himself in a satisfied little whisper, and snuggled further back against his father's chest with a little sigh.

Fenwick had to tilt his head back to look at the ceiling in order to prevent the tears in his eyes from dropping. He sniffed and managed to blink them back under control. His son's fragility always surprised him; he had so little confidence and self-esteem that it frightened him. He would have to remember to make his love for Chris and his pride in his achievements more obvious. He dropped a kiss on the top of the little boy's head. Fenwick was feeling increasingly torn apart. He wanted to be out searching for Bess, but he knew that Chris needed him. As soon as he'd put him to bed he would go out, leaving him in Wendy's care.

A call came through from Operations just as Fenwick finished tucking Chris up for the night. They had both avoided looking at Bess's bed on the other side of the room, and by the time he had said his last good night to Chris, Fenwick could barely stand straight. The weight of fear and pain that was on him now was unbearable. Memories of Bess ran continuously in his mind, to be cruelly interspersed with more grisly images from past cases: children killed accidentally in a playground fall, or drowned in a neighbour's unfenced pond; of a car wreck he had attended when still in uniform which wiped out a whole family; of a child's murder, the body hidden in a roll of carpet on waste ground less than fifty yards from her home.

He could hear Wendy's muffled tears. He didn't blame her, but she obviously blamed herself. What was two minutes after all? Nobody could be criticised for the fact that it wasn't safe to leave a child alone for a moment. He groped his way downstairs to the kitchen to take the call.

'The Superintendent asked us to let you know as soon as anything develops, sir.'

Fenwick felt a familiar knot tighten in his chest.

'Yes?'

'We've found a witness in one of the houses next to the school who saw Bess getting into a car with a young woman.'

It was no longer supposition; he could not pretend that Bess had been playing somewhere on her own and had slipped and banged her head. He had to face reality now that she had been abducted. His fingers tightened on the receiver.

'Any details?'

'Very few. The car was a pale blue or silver, "racy" was the word the witness used, but she knows little about cars so she couldn't even guess at the make. We're taking pictures round for her to look at. She didn't see the registration number.'

'And the woman?'

Fenwick already hated this stranger with an intensity that frightened him.

'She can't remember a lot other than that she was smartly dressed. Above average height, wearing expensive black shoes. That's it. She didn't see her face.'

'And Bess?' His voice nearly cracked as he said his daughter's name. 'How did she seem?'

'Fine. She was holding the woman's hand and walking beside her normally. The witness was most insistent that nothing seemed out of the ordinary.'

They always were, thought Fenwick, otherwise how could they explain away the guilt of watching a child go off like that? The officer from Operations was still talking, and he tried to concentrate on his words and not on the image of Bess getting into that stranger's car. Why had she done it?

'Sir, are you still there? They'll be round straight away to attach taps to the phone, in case there is a ransom demand.'

'I'm going out now to join the search, but the nanny will be here.' He broke the connection.

The telephone rang again immediately. It was his boss, calling to find out how he was.

'I'm all right, sir. I just want to be doing more. Where are the search teams concentrated?'

'There are six external teams.' The Superintendent wouldn't give him the locations at first, too aware that the very names themselves would conjure up previous searches for missing children, some with terrible ends. 'We have to consider that you've been targeted deliberately by someone with a grudge. DS Cooper and a team are going through closed cases to identify possible suspects . . .'

'There'll be a lot of those.'

'. . . Who are still at liberty to organise an abduction; there will be fewer of those. And you're not to worry about the Wainwright case. Blite has the surveillance of James FitzGerald under control and he will arrest Sally Wainwright-Smith first thing in the morning.'

Fenwick hadn't given the case any thought since he had heard that Bess had disappeared, and was dumbfounded by the Superintendent's misjudgement of him. He wondered whether he should feel flattered or appalled.

Before the Superintendent said goodbye, Fenwick asked him to contact the Edinburgh police to check his mother's progress in her journey to Sussex. They were driving her down at his request. As he rang off, Fenwick rubbed his forehead with his hands and found that he was bathed in sweat.

His stomach clenched suddenly and he rushed to the downstairs bathroom. Heaving over the sink, he watched through watery eyes as a thin dribble of greenish bile splashed the enamel. He threw water on to his face and sucked drips from his palm into his coated mouth. Once, twice, he retched and washed face, mouth and hands in the freezing water. Eventually he could think again and forced himself to be calm.

He felt hollow. Ever since his wife's illness had slowly taken her from the heart of his family, despite all his physical and mental effort to prevent it, he had been suspicious of the idea of hope. Now he could feel the start of that terrible desperation again, and he knew that he had to be active or face the prospect of madness in the hours ahead. He left to join the searchers.

Nightingale sat across from Sergeant Cooper and opened another case file. Superintendent Quinlan had taken them both off the Wainwright investigation, which he had left in DI Blite's capable care, and had them searching through Fenwick's old cases, looking for anyone who might hold a grudge and who wasn't in prison. She was concentrating on the computerised files and Cooper on the ones that remained on paper; both were sick to the stomach and worked in utter silence.

The whole incident room was quiet, except for the sporadic tapping of keys or the faint rustle as another page was turned. Behind her, the door opened as someone delivered yet another report on the Wainwright case for the researchers to add to their growing databases.

'It's Dr Keating's report. She rushed it through for the Chief Inspector.'

The words wrecked Nightingale's concentration and she cursed their speaker under her breath for no good reason. Cooper heard her, looked up and saw the misery on her face.

'Well, lass, it's nearly midnight, and I'm in need of sustenance, which means that you should be too. Why don't you go and get us some grub?' He pressed some money hard into her hand. 'And make sure you get something yourself; you're as thin as a rake.'

Nightingale descended the silent stairs to the canteen on the lower ground floor in search of the food machine that had been installed as one of the ACC's many economies. The canteen was empty and in semi-darkness, waiting for the early morning shift, which wasn't due in for another six hours. As she pressed the sticky buttons and forced coins into the slot, she found herself thinking of Fenwick and his agony. He was facing this completely alone. She realised that she wanted to be with him, simply to give him the comfort of her presence. She could share some of his grief; help him when his fear turned to anger; comfort him in the dark hours of waiting that stretched ahead. In her imagination she could feel the weight of his exhausted head on her shoulder, and sudden tears came to her eyes. She spoke suddenly into the silence.

'Why am I thinking like this? Why do I feel like this about him? It's just not like me!'

The word shocked her back into silence. Whenever possible, she tried not to think of her father, and anyway, Fenwick must be years younger than that. Yet the thought, once spoken, wouldn't go away, and Nightingale realised that within it lay the seeds of truth. He was so much the father she had always wanted. That Bess should have been snatched away from such love was unthinkable. The little girl must be terrified, and Nightingale's heart ached for her.

She balanced the coffees and cakes in a cardboard box and carried them back upstairs without spills. Cooper was where she had left him, head down, reading perhaps his thirtieth case file that night.

'The Chief Inspector's just rung.'

Nightingale struggled to keep her breathing level.

'He's visited every one of the search areas – nothing's been found – and now he's going home. He wants us to send Claire Keating's report over, and copies of the transcripts from every one of our interviews with Sally and Alexander Wainwright-Smith.'

'I'll do it!'

'I thought you would, but you can drink your coffee and eat your cake while you're making the copies. Don't look at me like that. You eat up, and that's an order!'

Fenwick sent Wendy back to her flat upstairs as soon as he arrived home. He couldn't face the idea of her company, and he needed to think. As he had driven from one search area to the next, each one as unproductive and hopeless as the last, he had forced himself for the first time to concentrate on the case like a policeman rather than a father. By the time he had reached the deserted playground in front of the school, he had almost succeeded, but then the sight of the gates, locked and cordoned off with police tape, had brought the awfulness of the reality back to him. Bess was not at home in bed whilst he went in search of some poor man's missing child. He had to face the fact that she was the victim of a crime he hoped desperately was only an abduction, and that made him a victim too.

In the solitary silence of his home once again, he tried to force his mind to return to its earlier analysis and the key question – why had Bess been abducted? There were two choices – she was either a random victim or someone had a motive for her disappearance.

If it was random, that meant he could do nothing, so he forced the logical part of his mind to focus on motive. Who would benefit from her disappearance? He pulled out paper and pen from his desk drawer and stared at the blank page as he let his subconscious work. At midnight he had called Sergeant Cooper with his instructions, and now he waited, trying to keep the demons of speculation away.

It took Nightingale half an hour to find and copy all the papers Fenwick had asked for, and less than ten minutes to drive to his home.

His house would be quiet; she knew that the music he loved would be no distraction whilst his mind was in turmoil. Some work, perhaps reading these papers, would help him. She parked behind his car and swivelled her long, trousered legs elegantly to climb out. She pressed the bell in the shadows of the darkened porch.

Fenwick heard the doorbell and rushed to answer it, experiencing as he did so a painful twist of emotions. Despite the craziness of the idea, part of him insisted that it would be Bess, home at last. Then another image filled his mind; it could be a police officer, some old friend, come to tell him that they had found her, dead and cold. Hope and fear fought within him for supremacy. He saw the single tall outline through the hall window and fear triumphed. He opened the door.

Nightingale was shocked by his haggard appearance. His hair was a mess where he had obviously been running his hands through it, and she resisted an inexplicable urge to smooth it down for him.

He stared back at her with eyes so shadowed and full of anguish that she could feel sympathetic tears start in her own. For a flicker of a second, their souls seemed to touch: '*I am in so much pain*' his seemed to say; '*I know, that's why I'm here*', hers replied. Then she blinked her tears away unshed and the moment was gone.

'I've brought those papers, sir,' she said in a voice shaky but determined.

'Thank you.' His voice was barely a whisper. He reached out to take them from her where she stood on the threshold, and to her dismay she felt herself hang on to them. He noticed the tug of resistance and looked up, confused for a moment. Indecision, so rare in him, flashed across his face. He hesitated for a further second.

'Can I stay and help you through them, sir? There's an awful lot.'

In that delicate moment she felt the balance of such power as there was between them swing in her favour.

'Come in.'

She remembered the hall from her previous visits, and an unexpected memory of Bess in her nightdress ambushed her thoughts. Again those wretched tears were threatening; why *couldn't* she control herself tonight of all nights?

His study was cool and smelt of him: the sharp animal tang of his anxious sweat, a vague residual hint of aftershave applied in happier hours, and the earthy scent of old leather from the books that lined the walls.

'What are we looking for, sir?'

'Evidence.' He spoke brusquely, but she understood. 'I've developed a theory as to why Bess has been taken. Who benefits from her abduction, Nightingale?'

'*Benefits*?' His choice of word appalled her.

'It's a crime; we have to think of motive.'

Nightingale realised suddenly why he had asked for the files she still carried.

'You think Bess's disappearance is somehow connected with the Wainwright case? But why?'

'I was going to arrest Sally Wainwright today. Within hours, my daughter has disappeared.'

'But Inspector Blite will arrest her anyway.'

'Possibly, but he's taken her in for questioning and an identity parade twice now, with zero results – she's still at large.'

'That can't last; she must realise that it's only a matter of time.'

'You're assuming that she's rational, but I know that she isn't.'

He took the latest Keating report from the top of the file and read it swiftly, nodding to himself with satisfaction.

'Think about it. She's used to controlling every man in her life, she has done ever since she was a child; even her father. Whilst he was exploiting her, she learnt how to manage him in order to limit his violence towards her. And in every situation in her life since then, including each foster family and children's home she stayed in, she has come out on top. It's how and why she survived.'

'But she's never tried to control you.'

'She's tried, but it hasn't worked. As soon as I appeared on the scene I became the most dominant male in her life. I have her fate in my hands; the power of search, even of arrest. She would have been desperate trying to think of a way to control me.'

Nightingale felt sick.

'If you believe this, why haven't you gone to the Hall?'

She hadn't meant to accuse him, but her tone of voice was hard and flat as a result of her struggle for emotional control. To her dismay she saw him flinch.

'You think I don't want to? So far this is all supposition. I have no evidence that Sally might have taken Bess. If she hasn't and I go bursting in there, it will be a perfect gift for her defence, but if she *has* and I handle this without backup, I could risk Bess's life.'

Nightingale was awed by the strength of his professionalism and willpower.

'I need to persuade the Superintendent to back me on this. We'll need experts, a crack team, and the ACC will hate the fact that it's the Wainwrights. I can't afford to get this one wrong, Nightingale.'

'But to abduct a child . . .'

'I agree, it seems extreme, but what option would she have? Think about it. She's already committed murder, and the police are closing in, making connections she thought we would never uncover. And as a diversion it's working – look at what it's done to the investigation already. If you think about it, Sally's the obvious suspect. And with her husband away, she's free to do what she likes.'

Nightingale said nothing. He had clearly worked it all out. He took a pen and marked up key passages of Claire Keating's report and then of the interviews with Sally and her husband.

'I think we have enough here. Come on, Nightingale, you can drive me to the station. Give me five minutes to tell Wendy I'm going.'

As she waited, Nightingale covered her face briefly with her hands. Seeing him in his agony, alone, isolated, in pain, she could not deny her feelings for him. This wasn't some crush or a fixation on some authority-figure. This was painfully real. She heard his low voice on the stairs, explaining to Wendy that his mother was on her way down from Scotland and should arrive within a few hours, and removed her hands. Nightingale composed herself and swallowed the hard lump in her throat. A clock chimed one, and with a start, she realised that, although she had only been in the house for ten minutes.

'Right, let's go. We'll take your car.'

During the cold drive back to the station, Nightingale dared to voice some of her doubts.

'How did Sally plan an abduction? Surely she'd realise that the children had a nanny?'

'She probably disregarded her. Remember that her own mother was powerless to protect *her* children. Women don't count in Sally's world.'

'Where would she hold her?'

Fenwick shook his head. 'I don't know, but the estate is huge . . . There's the tower at the Hall; that's self-contained. Sally's brother and sister were locked away upstairs, remember, and not discovered until it was too late.'

'Why don't we simply go and ask her a few questions?'

'It's one o'clock in the morning, and think how Sally could behave if approached the wrong way. She *is* a murderess, you know.'

By the time they reached the outskirts of Harlden, Nightingale was as convinced as Fenwick that Sally had motive and opportunity to abduct Bess. Fenwick called Quinlan from the car and he agreed to contact the ACC immediately for approval, and secure the team they would need.

CHAPTER FORTY-FOUR

Sally paced the length of the landing in agitation, pausing to stop on each turn at the oak door that blocked off the spiral staircase to the tower. The hammering and yelling was just audible, and she was amazed at the determination and stamina of the little girl. She hadn't reckoned on her being quite so strong.

A rare yet strangely familiar feeling stirred within her. For no reason she suddenly remembered her baby brother being born; how for a few days life had been wonderful. She and her mother, in the hospital together, watching a beautiful little doll-like child cry and wave his perfect fingers in the air. Then they had gone home and . . . Tears choked her throat; she could barely breathe. The past was a dead zone, not worth the energy of thought. Sally hardened her heart and walked downstairs. Within a few hours it would all be over; she had it all planned and it was really very simple. By abducting the child she was sure that she would have diverted police attention for long enough to deal with FitzGerald once and for all, and then make good her escape before they came for her again.

FitzGerald would arrive soon. She would kill him, then set fire to the Hall and leave for Brighton. Simple. She had made sure that there were plenty of inflammable materials about, mostly left over from the refurbishment and decorating work. It was spread throughout the upper bedrooms, and in the kitchen and library she had already lit kerosene stoves that she could overturn as she left. All the internal doors were wedged wide, and there were upper windows open sufficient to make sure that there would be a strong through-draft. Alex would be furious at first, but he would understand her need to conceal her crime. And anyway, if she couldn't have the Hall, why should he?

The Hall and all it stood for was no longer of any interest to her. If she stayed she would be arrested and charged with murder. The only assets she could rely on now were those that she and Alex had offshore, beyond the power of the authorities to freeze them. There was enough money in her savings account for her to live quietly on the Continent for a few months, after which Alex would either join her or she would start her life again somewhere else. She had it all planned.

She refused to think about the child. It was an unfortunate pawn, stupid enough to believe her story, that she was a policewoman come to fetch her and take her to her father.

The grandfather clock in the entrance hall downstairs chimed one o'clock; FitzGerald was late. The thought of him twisted her face into a scowl. Her

280

survival had depended since infancy on her ability to manipulate those around her. They had all been men, without exception, and Sally had grown up to regard other women as mere obstacles to be worked with or around. And her tactics had proved very successful. She was married to a multi-millionaire, with enough money in her own name to guarantee her freedom. She would be able to travel the world, building her own wealth, beautiful, unassailable, discarding lovers as she used and then tired of them, perhaps even with Alex trotting dog-like at her heels. She had successfully managed to disappear before, and had no doubt that she could do so again – provided that she silenced FitzGerald.

Whilst he and his secrets lived, she could not enjoy any of her success; therefore, he had to die. The clock struck a quarter past. He must be on his way by now. She checked that her handbag contained her passport, credit cards and account book. Her suitcase was already in her car with jewels, clothes and ready cash. In a few hours she would be on the south coast and the police would have no idea where to start their search.

Sally walked across the hall to the pretty sitting room where a fire blazed fiercely in the grate. Three days' worth of newspapers and some highly inflammable dress fabrics had been folded neatly in one of the armchairs; more fuel for her fire. The gun was hidden behind the back of a large cushion on the sofa. All she had to do was slide her hand down casually as she was talking to FitzGerald, pull it out, aim and press the trigger. He would be dead within seconds and then she could turn the heat on under the oil, light the candles, start her other fires and leave. Thinking of the gun, she reached for her long evening gloves and pulled them on. She was wearing an evening dress, diamonds and her best watch. More sensible clothes were ready in the back of her car to change into. This way, she had reasoned, she would not look suspicious and might even distract FitzGerald.

She looked out of the window and saw the distant sweep of headlights as a car turned off the road and into the long driveway to the Hall. Perfect.

CHAPTER FORTY-FIVE

FitzGerald drove at the speed limit all the way to Wainwright Hall. It wasn't far, and he needed time to think. He was going to be late because it had taken him longer than he'd expected to shake off the police tail they had put on him. He didn't trust Sally Wainwright-Smith, and he had proof that she was capable of murder. Yet here he was, calmly driving to meet her in the early hours of the morning, on his own. His left hand fumbled in the glove compartment where he normally left his gun, and his fingers eventually closed around its cool metal. If she tried anything, he'd be ready.

She still had no idea that he knew who she was and what she had been. It was ironic that one of Amanda's little whores should end up married to the managing director of Wainwright's, the legitimate company that had laundered money for over twenty-five years. Ironic but not entirely unlikely. Many of the senior management at Wainwright's had been encouraged into liaisons with women that Amanda had saved for them. It had become an expected perk and had meant that he always had enough information to keep them in line should their consciences ever trouble them.

Was that how Sally had first learnt of the Wainwright fortune and gained a sense of the money that was available if only she could smarten up her act and redefine her past? He shook his head as he drove steadily through darkened country lanes. No, Sally was ruthless and cunning, but he doubted the bitch was capable of that degree of planning. Of course, she had turned herself legitimate; a few of the brighter, tougher girls always managed to do that. It must have been a lucky break for her to hook Alan. He'd always had a peculiar sexual appetite, one that would be hard to satisfy in a normal relationship. Sally must have come as a great relief to him. And once she'd come so close to his fortune, the smell of money would be sufficient aphrodisiac for her to play her part well.

When he reached the ornate wrought-iron gates that stood open at the entrance to the drive to Wainwright Hall, FitzGerald slowed to a gentle stop. She had said on the phone that she had the first instalment ready, which came as no surprise. It wasn't like Sally to be in possession of a fortune and not have at least some of it accessible. He could imagine her sitting up at nights, counting it and growing excited. There was no doubt in his mind that the only thing in life Sally really loved was the security of money, which was why he had been so sure she would have plenty to hand in the safe at the Hall.

Once he had the first instalment of his money, he could start to make arrangements for a more luxurious and earlier retirement than he had envisaged being possible. At the right moment sometime in the future, he would find a way of ensuring that the police received all the surveillance photographs he had of Sally and Graham Wainwright on the morning of Graham's death. She'd end up in prison and Alex would be able to go on running the family firm that so successfully channelled the money he and others in the West Sussex criminal community made into legitimate investments.

Gravel crunched under his tyres as he approached the house. In the fitful moonlight on this windy May night, it looked like something out of a horror movie. On the ground floor a single light was burning to the left of the massive front doors, in what he knew to be the sitting room. Up above, all the bedroom lights were on, slicing into the dark from uncurtained windows. The shadow of the grey stone tower stretched out to meet him, elongated by the gargoyles on its roof, which reached out like grasping fingers over the bone-white gravel. They were everywhere, these gaping stone monstrosities, concave ribcages, folded bat-like wings, taloned claws holding heraldic shields. He slowed to a stop and stepped out into the chill of the night.

Sally opened the door before he could knock, and stood back to let him pass. She was dressed in a midnight-blue evening gown with a halter top that had been cut low between her breasts and left her back bare. She had ridiculously high stiletto shoes on, which raised her to his height. Her skin shone like marble and the diamonds caught the low light and sparkled like raindrops as she breathed. He was reminded for an instant of a graveside stone angel, and he shuddered involuntarily at the image. She had swept her pale blonde hair up into a smooth pleat, leaving her long neck clear for its heavy wreath of cut stones. The woman before him could not be described as angelic, yet there was such an aura of death about her tonight that the air resonated with it and his fantasy image held. The contrast with the street whore Amanda had rescued could not be more absolute.

'James, thank you for coming at such an ungodly hour. Go on through to the sitting room and warm yourself by the fire.'

'I'm not cold and I don't want to stay. Just give me the money and I'll go.'

He noticed her eyes narrow at his refusal to go through, and he became aware of a peculiar tension about her, as if she was waiting for something to happen. Instinctively, he looked around the entrance hall and into the dark of the two passages that led to the grand hall and staircase behind. Without meaning to, he took a few steps towards the right-hand passage, his hand lying loosely on the gun in his pocket.

'Where's Alex?'

'Away. Where are you going?'

He ignored her and took a few more paces, curious to find out what her reaction would be.

'I asked where you were going. There's nothing there and it's better we talk in the sitting room.'

Why was she so nervous when she could be as poised as a cat? Intrigued, he walked on and had reached the passage before she caught up with him and grasped his arm. He looked down at her in surprise and watched as she struggled to control her expression and form a smile.

'Really, you know, you are the most unusual man. Here I am trying to encourage you into a comfortable chair in the warm, and you go prowling off into the dark.'

'I'm curious by nature, dear; you of all people should know that. But you're right, it is dark down here. Aren't you scared all by yourself?' He was pushing her deliberately, wanting to test her mood.

She laughed, a little silvery giggle that irritated him.

'Oh, you are sweet. Yes, sometimes it's a little spooky, but I'm used to it.'

'Just the same, as I'm here, I'll take a quick look around to make sure everything's all right.'

The hall clock chimed the three-quarter hour and he noticed Sally frown at the passing of time.

'You don't need to. Everything's securely locked up and I'm OK.'

'I wouldn't want you worried in any way,' he said with a rare smile that obviously confused her. He lifted her hand away from his arm, found switches and waited a moment as light flooded the great hall and galleried landing above. He didn't doubt that the house was secure, nor did he have the slightest concern for her safety, but he was determined to unsettle her.

He climbed the grand wooden staircase, conscious of her eyes on him as he reached the half-landing and paused, deciding whether to go left or right. He turned to his right and mounted the next flight to the main landing. She was at his side in a moment.

'I don't know, James, I really don't, but if you are going to insist on a patrol of my house, the least I can do is accompany you.'

She chatted on, her voice overloud in the silence of the house. He walked into every bedroom one by one and checked the walk-in cupboards and en-suite bathrooms. He didn't notice that all the doors had been wedged open until he was leaving the third bedroom and had to kick the door stop out of the way to close the door behind him. Sally saw his surprised frown.

'I'm airing all the rooms. There's such a smell of glue and paint left over from the decorators that I can't shift it.'

He didn't reply, but carried on his steady checks of the fifteen bedrooms and seven bathrooms. Then he walked up to the next floor and checked each of the attic bedrooms, whilst Sally waited with growing impatience on the landing below still talking about nothing in a penetrating voice that was getting on his nerves. Without her by his side, he paused to stare out of the windows into the moonlit grounds below. The wind was buffeting the trees that bordered the drive, casting weird, constantly changing shadows. He thought he saw a shape move in the dark pool beneath an oak tree, but when he looked again there was nothing there. He worried for a moment about the police, and then dismissed the idea.

In the next room he looked out again, and this time he was almost sure he saw a movement away to his right in the shadow thrown by the east wing of the house. He felt the skin between his shoulder blades crawl as he waited for the motion to come again. It didn't, and he left to return downstairs feeling discomfited.

Something about her manner tonight had put him on alert and he felt the need to be extra cautious.

'Satisfied?'

'You're right, it stinks of paint and paste up there, but it's no wonder with all the materials your decorators left behind. It's a fire hazard apart from anything else.'

She shivered and he realised that she'd been standing there in the chill of an unheated house in a backless dress.

He started to walk back down the stairs. Then:

'What was that?'

'What?'

'That thumping? I heard a noise, definitely. It was coming from the tower.'

'Don't be silly. There's only us here. It must have been the wind in the roof. Come on.'

She linked her arm through his.

'Are you sure you don't want me to check? There! I heard it again, a knocking, I'm sure of it.'

'All I can hear is the wind and the call of a glass of whisky in front of the fire.'

She shivered again, melodramatically, and FitzGerald reluctantly turned his back on the tower and went with her down to the great hall.

'Let's get on with it, I want my money?'

'Ah yes, that money.'

Sally laughed, but the silver had run out of it, leaving a hollow, mirthless sound he distrusted even more.

The moon was nearing the western horizon as Nightingale drove Fenwick down the centre of a deserted road at nearly ninety miles an hour, judging each bump and bend as if she were in a race. The team was to rendezvous at 0200 hours in the woods half a mile east of the main gates to the Hall. Firearms had been authorised. The Superintendent had approved Fenwick's involvement, realising that the only way he would be able to stop him attending would be to lock him up.

She risked a glance at the clock on the dashboard; one fifty. They were almost there, and Nightingale killed the headlights, barely slowing as their eyes adjusted to the semi-darkness. The copse loomed in front of them and she swung in and slowed down. There was a patch of dense cover to one side, and she pulled into it.

Fenwick was surprised to see so many officers. A dozen were gathered around the man who had been put in charge of the investigation into Bess's abduction. His name was Boyd, and he was attached to a specialist team at the Met which handled high-profile and sensitive abductions. He appeared competent and alert, and Fenwick relaxed infinitesimally for the first time in ten hours.

'Chief Inspector.' Boyd offered his hand and then pulled Fenwick into the centre of the briefing. 'We need to know as much as possible about the layout of the Hall and where Sally Wainwright-Smith might be holding your daughter, if indeed she is there. Inspector Blite has already given us a full briefing, but you may be able to help us on details.' He spoke in a low, confident voice tinged with a Yorkshire accent.

Fenwick described the layout of the Hall; the kitchens and work rooms at the back, the front hall with sitting room to the left, small study to the right and twin passages leading through to the great hall, flanked by dining room and library. He could recall every detail of the large staircase that led from it, dividing in two to reach the galleried landing above. In the north corner of the first landing there was a spiral staircase leading to the tower which was blocked by a stout oak door from the landing, with a further one at the top of the stairs.

Fenwick managed to keep his voice calm and dispassionate, with no trace of fear, but he had to pause and take a deep breath to maintain his tone as he concluded.

'If Bess is there, my guess is that she would have her in the tower. There are plenty of outbuildings and some estate cottages, but there would always be the risk that Bess might escape from those. The tower is secure and remote from any visitors but still right under Sally's nose.'

A radio squawked into life and Boyd was called to receive a message from Superintendent Quinlan in the operations centre, leaving Fenwick a prisoner of his own thoughts again. His whole body was charged with a sickening mixture of adrenaline and overwhelming fear. He so distrusted the idea of hope that he refused to let it take root within him. He had a superstitious dread of wanting something so much, believing that the strength of his desire alone could turn the balance of probability against him. Even so, he found that he was offering up to God ludicrous bargains of good works, personal sacrifice, church attendance and baptism for the children, if only He would let Bess be returned to him unharmed. He had worked through his mental offerings to the point of presenting his own life in exchange for hers when Boyd returned to the group.

'Does the name FitzGerald mean anything to you?'

Fenwick nodded and turned to look for Nightingale, whom he thought of as the team's expert on FitzGerald. She was hovering at the edge of the tight knot of officers and he beckoned her over to hear what Boyd had to say.

'Apparently FitzGerald left his home an hour ago, spent fifteen minutes losing the tail you had put on him and has driven off somewhere. The report came through to the operations centre some time ago, but they've only just considered it potentially significant. Is it?'

Fenwick answered as Nightingale nodded her head thoughtfully.

'It might be. There's a confirmed connection between FitzGerald and Wainwright Enterprises.'

One of the men in the group spoke up.

'What car does he drive, sir?'

Nightingale answered for Fenwick.

'A brand new silver-grey Mercedes, top of the range.'

'A car matching that description has passed here since we've been waiting, I'd say less than ten minutes ago. We were the first group to arrive and I saw it myself.'

Boyd frowned with concern.

'That changes things significantly. We have to assume now that whoever is at the Hall is awake, so we can't rely on the element of surprise. As soon as the men I've already sent to the Hall call in, we'll have a better understanding of our options.'

The men he had sent called within minutes. They reported lights on all over the upper floors of the Hall and both front and back doors securely locked. They also confirmed that a silver-grey Mercedes was parked in the front drive.

'Is he in on it, do you think?' Boyd looked to both Fenwick and Nightingale for guidance, but they couldn't help him. FitzGerald being at the Hall with Sally was a complication no one had expected.

'We have to assume he's potentially hostile,' Boyd decided. 'I think we need a distraction. Sergeant Amos, you take your team and circle the Hall. On my cue you will close and enter silently from the south, west and east. Aim for total silence until you are inside. As soon as you have access, your goal is to reach and secure the tower, stairs and exits and then move to search all other potential hiding places.

'Chief Inspector Fenwick, you and I will approach from the main entrance to the north. Your female officer can come with us; it'll make us look less threatening. I'll be armed but I'll stay behind you two so that she doesn't see a strange face. The rest of you,' four officers looked up, two men and two women, 'I want you in the shadow of the front north side of the house to support our entry. Set your watches. The time now is . . . two-oh-three on my mark. Chief Inspector Fenwick will be knocking on that door at two fifteen exactly and you will enter the house as he does so. Any questions?'

There were none, and the two groups of officers disappeared into the night, leaving Fenwick, Boyd and Nightingale alone. Boyd checked the velcro and tape fastenings of his bulletproof vest and buttoned his jacket over it. Fenwick became aware of their vulnerability. They would be walking right up to the front door, in plain view, protected only by their vests. He and Nightingale were unarmed; they would have to rely on Boyd's reactions. He thought of his last desperate plea to a God he had found that he suddenly believed in, and felt a strangely peaceful resignation grow within him. Just let Bess be safe, he thought; that was all that mattered.

'Coffee?' Nightingale was passing him a mug, and Fenwick realised suddenly that she was still here. In a previous investigation Nightingale had risked her life for a woman he had asked her to protect and had almost been killed. He would not ask that of her again. He took the mug from her and turned to speak to Boyd, but he was busy listening to reports from his teams. Fenwick turned back to Nightingale.

'After we gain access to the Hall, I want you to stay back.'

'Sir! I'd rather be up front with you, and I'm supposed to make us look less threatening, remember.'

'Don't argue. You'll be in view but I do *not* expect you to come into the Hall until it's safe. Understood?'

She started to protest again but instead bit down on her lip and nodded, not meeting his eyes. Fenwick was suddenly reminded of Bess. That was exactly how she looked when he made her do something against her will, and the fleeting resemblance made him even more determined that Nightingale should remain safe.

Boyd glanced at his watch.

'Time to go. We'll take my car. Constable, you drive. We have six minutes. When we reach the bottom of the drive, put the lights on so that they can see us coming. We're the diversion.'

They climbed into the car, Fenwick and Boyd in the back seat, Nightingale in front. There was no conversation as they made their way to Wainwright Hall.

Sally led FitzGerald into the brightly lit sitting room and directed him towards an easy chair to the left of the fireplace. FitzGerald ignored the invitation and remained standing with his back to the fire, looking out over the sofa and towards the window beyond. The curtains were wide open.

'Now, that drink.'

'I don't need a drink. Just give me the money.'

Sally poured herself a drink anyway. FitzGerald watched her profile as she did so and was disturbed by the smile on her face. She was thoroughly enjoying herself, as if there was a joke that only she knew about. His right hand slipped into his trouser pocket and found the handle of his gun.

'You always need to be in control, don't you, James?' Sally had turned to face the fire; her long bare back was towards the window, the drink in her left hand as she leant her weight on her right where it rested along the back of the sofa.

'It's very late. Let's just get on with it.'

It was as if he hadn't spoken.

'All the men I've known in my life have wanted to control me. It's a thing you all have in common, a sign of deep insecurity, I think.'

'Sally!' FitzGerald sounded exasperated.

'Men like you nearly destroyed me once and I'm not going to let it happen again. I've known a lot of violent men in my life, but none as bad as you, with your network of thugs and watchers, and your superiority. You are a very, very dangerous man and I can't allow you to destroy me.'

Her right hand slid behind the cushions on the sofa and pulled back again in a smooth, practised movement.

FitzGerald watched Sally's gloved hand come up holding the gun as if in slow motion. His fingers tightened around his own weapon and he jumped to his left even as she fired. He felt the whistle of the bullet as it went past his ear, and then he was firing his own gun, a rapid double pressure on the trigger with the muzzle pointing at mid height, aiming for a body shot.

But Sally had ducked down behind the sofa and his shots missed. Then she fired again and he felt as if he had been punched hard in the shoulder. His hand went numb and he dropped the gun. Then he heard another shot, as if from a distance, and a pain flared in his chest, so hot and tight that it seemed to choke the air out of him. He fell to the ground and sensed the feeling in his body fade away.

Sally looked down at FitzGerald lying unmoving before her, and then glanced casually at her watch. It was only ten past two, but she had a lot to do before she left. He was lying less than two yards from the fire, and it didn't matter whether he was dead or alive so long as the flames reached him quickly.

She threw her gun into the fire and picked up the newspapers and yards of material that she had waiting and trailed them from the upholstered furniture to the fire. Within five minutes there would be enough smoke and fumes in here to make sure that he was dead. She would still have plenty of time to unlock and open the lower tower door to provide better access for the fire. The one at the top of the staircase was bolted anyway. Then she would put a match to the methylated spirits, paint and old decorator's cloths on the top floor. She laid the materials into the fire and left the room without a backward glance.

The sensation of choking and drowning gradually returned FitzGerald to consciousness, and he raised his head, lungs heaving and painful. All he could see were flames surrounding him, leaping from the fireplace on to chair covers, across antique carpets to the curtains. Sparks flew through the air and he watched one land on his trouser leg, blaze briefly and snuff out for lack of immediate fuel.

He tried to stand, but his head swam and the pain in his chest was so intense that he collapsed again into a slumped crouch. The heat against his legs was painful now, and he tried desperately to move away from it. He managed to raise himself on to his good shoulder and inch away from the fire that was already blazing brightly on the hearthrug.

He noted a smear of bright arterial blood on the carpet as he managed to crawl another few inches then collapsed again. The fumes were so thick now that he choked unless he kept his nose and mouth inches from the floor. He could just make out the shape of the open doorway about five feet away, and the tiles of the hall beyond. If only he could keep moving, he might still make it.

He struggled to lift his weight again but his arm buckled. A great tongue of flame suddenly shot up from the curtains and he watched in horror as the ceiling started to bubble, smoke and then catch fire. The painted plaster acted like kindling, and when he opened his eyes next he could see holes appearing and flames leaping up through them to the floor above. With a last awful effort FitzGerald raised his chest off the floor again and started to drag himself towards the doorway. Inch by inch he crossed the floor. At the edge of his vision he could see the varnish on the floorboards blister, and the backs of his hands glowed bright red then black as the heat scorched his skin.

There was a deafening crash and a large section of ceiling collapsed on to the chairs and sofa, which immediately exploded into flame. A piece of smouldering furniture from the floor above landed on FitzGerald's legs, pinning him to the floor. Thick black choking smoke boiled towards him, and he stared in agony at the last terrible few feet that remained between him and the open door to safety. He tried to cry out for help, but the boiling air burnt his lungs and he collapsed at last back into unconsciousness.

They had just reached the iron gates to the Hall when Boyd suddenly put his hand to his ear and then slapped it down hard on the driver's seat in front.

'Enter at will from all sides. Repeat, enter at will immediately. Maximum discretion, armed suspect on premises.'

His skin was pallid in the moonlight as he turned towards Fenwick's appalled face.

'They've heard shots from inside. Drive as fast as you can, Constable. Go!'

Fenwick's whole body cried out for action, but he had to wait as the powerful car lurched forward, splattering gravel. He stared at the lights that blazed from every window of the Hall. It was obvious that the doors were shut fast and the lower windows had security grilles on them, preventing access. Fenwick watched as one man scaled the lower wall, climbing nimbly through an open window on the first floor. He disappeared inside and his colleagues soon followed.

Beside him he heard Boyd maintain a steady stream of instructions to his team, but Fenwick ignored the words, his whole body searching the windows for the tiny silhouette that might be Bess. There was the sound of breaking glass, and a hungry tongue of flame flowered suddenly from a downstairs window.

'Oh my God, it's on fire!' Fenwick watched in horror as the flames took hold. His daughter was in there somewhere; he had to reach her!

Nightingale saw the fire and reached automatically for the car radio. It was tuned in to the operations centre, and as they reached the front of the Hall, Fenwick heard her calm voice call for fire support, ambulance and backup.

He was out of the car before Boyd and was about to climb to the first floor when he heard bolts being drawn back and the front door was opened by one of the team who had braved the fire to search downstairs.

Fenwick saw two officers dragging a man's body from the seat of the fire to his left and then trying to shut the door on it, but they were beaten back by the flames.

'Get him out of here!' Fenwick heard Boyd's voice but assumed he was talking about the injured man. He raced past the officers, down the passageway, through the great hall and up the staircase beyond. His only thought was to find Bess before the fire claimed the rest of the Hall.

He heard someone breathing hard behind him and turned to see Nightingale by his side. Before he could order her outside, she grabbed his arm and pointed up to the galleried landing above where wisps of smoke trailed from one of the bedrooms.

'She's set the whole house on fire!'

'Get help! Find Boyd.'

Nightingale stumbled back to the entrance hall, where Boyd was now directing the operation personally.

'The Chief Inspector's on the upper floor – he thinks his daughter is in the tower.'

'My team will help him.' He looked at the unarmed junior officer in front of him. It was bad enough having to worry about Fenwick; the last thing he needed was amateur help.

'We've got this covered. You go outside and search the outbuildings in case she's there.'

Nightingale started to protest, then nodded reluctantly. There was no time to waste in argument.

Fenwick sprinted along the landing towards the spiral stairs that led to the tower. His spirits rose at the sight of the first door standing open. Three of

Boyd's men were swinging a ram against the second door with a power that shook the hinges. He watched for a long, agonising minute as they strained and pushed at the door. Nothing seemed to happen; then, with a tearing sound, the lock pulled away from the wood and the door swung open. Fenwick pushed past and raced up the spiral staircase.

He found Bess huddled inside. He hugged her, raining kisses on the top of her head, then a waft of smoke from below recalled him to his senses. He lifted her in his arms, cradling her head in case they should fall.

'Pass the lass to me, sir. Easy now.'

Hands came to take her away, but he clung on to her.

'I'm all right, let me through, we're all right now.'

As he walked outside, Fenwick could hear the distant sirens of ambulances and fire tenders nearing the scene. Bess was silent as he held her close, but he could feel her breath on his cheek and the strength of her tight little arms around his neck. He knew that she would be all right now. He sat down on the gravel away from the blazing house and waited patiently until the second ambulance drew up and he could follow the paramedics and Bess inside.

They laid his daughter down on a stretcher but she sat up again at once and held out her arms towards her father. He held her on his knee as one of the medics took her pulse, listened to her chest through a stethoscope and shone a bright light into her eyes.

'She seems fine; lungs are as clear as a bell.'

'I'm thirsty, Daddy, and I haven't had my tea.'

The three grown men in the back of the ambulance stared at her in amazement then burst out laughing. Bess looked at them in confusion and they stopped at once. Someone passed her a carton of orange juice and she drank it down thirstily, followed by an egg sandwich from someone else's lunch box. Fenwick's mobile phone rang, and he answered it one-handed. It was his mother, calling from the police car that was escorting her to Harlden. She was on the bypass less than five minutes away.

As he told her the good news, Fenwick thought quickly. Bess was physically all right, eating heartily and showing no signs of shock. She would need to be questioned by a specialist about the abduction, but that could wait until the morning. Right now what she needed more than anything else was her family around her and a good night's sleep.

The fact that she was alive and well hadn't reduced Fenwick's intense anger towards Sally Wainwright-Smith. She was out there somewhere and he was consumed by a compulsion to find her. He told his mother to ask the police driver to come straight to Wainwright Hall. As soon as she arrived, he was going to rejoin the hunt.

CHAPTER FORTY-SIX

Sally watched the sudden arrival of the police from the upper landing, where she had just lit the last of her many fires. There was a sound of breaking glass from the floor below and her heart somersaulted up into her throat, but the burst of adrenaline that came with it was as welcome as an old friend. There were footsteps on the floor below, pounding across to the tower and down the main staircase to the ground floor. Sally realised that she was still wearing her evening dress and those ridiculous gloves and shoes.

She knocked the last lighted candle on to its side, and watched briefly as the flame found the wallpaper and glue she had left to feed it. Then she removed her high-heeled shoes and padded over to the south-east side of the house, where there was a metal fire escape leading down to the kitchen roof. Her car was parked in the stable block on the opposite side of the yard from the kitchen, no more than fifty feet away. If she could climb down unseen, there was a chance that she would be able to reach it and escape using the track that ran through the woods.

She opened the small window that led out on to the ladder, then, with her left wrist threaded through the ankle straps of her sandals, climbed out into the chilly darkness. Her bare foot found a metal rung and her toes curled around it. She was easily forty feet above the ground, but the bulk of the Hall protected her from the wind that was gusting strongly from the west.

She eased her body down a few rungs at a time until she was no more than a few feet above the kitchen roof. She was just coiling herself to jump on to it when she froze. A single police officer, preceded by the bouncing light of a torch, was walking from the kitchen door out towards the stables. Her car was in the outhouse in the furthest corner, opposite the large archway that led on to the track that ran through the kitchen garden and out to the woods.

Her feet touched the rough asphalt of the kitchen roof and she walked across it, as light on her feet as a cat. There was a ten-foot drop to the ground on to gravel, but she jumped down with confidence and dropped straight away into a crouch, barely making a noise. In her mind she was a child again, escaping from the house in the early morning to steal the neighbours' milk and anything else that they had been stupid enough to leave out for her searching little fingers.

There was a wide yard to cover between the kitchen and the stables, and although there was little moon left in the sky, the lights from the Hall illuminated the gravel in a patchwork of yellow, grey and black. She had no choice but to risk the crossing. The bobbing firefly of torchlight in the stables was making its way steadily towards her car and she had no time left to work her way around slowly. She waited until the officer left one building and entered the next before dashing across the open expanse, her bare back and billowing skirt catching the light of the flames like some menacing gargoyle brought to earth.

Nightingale tried to put thoughts of Bess and Fenwick out of her mind, but she could hear sirens in the distance and the smell of smoke pervaded the yard. She flashed her torch into yet another empty corner of an abandoned stable. It was difficult for her to orientate herself inside the pitch blackness of each building. Heavy cloud was being blown in by westerly winds, obliterating the moon and stars. The Hall was behind her, and she seemed to be in some sort of stable block, long abandoned. She bitterly resented being this far away from the action, but she knew that she would be a liability, and an unshakeable sense of duty prevented her from doing anything but a thorough job.

The sound of a car engine misfiring then starting with a roar broke the silence of the yard. Nightingale ran outside, banging her foot hard against an old boot scraper as she did so. She ignored the shock of pain and swung round to find the source of the noise. Twin main-beam headlights cut through the night, dazzling her, and she ran towards them, almost blinded. She could just discern a pale face behind the wheel, and then the driver found first gear and the vehicle lurched forward. Nightingale twisted sharply to her right in an attempt to get out of its path as the vehicle came straight towards her. She almost made it, but slipped in the mud of the yard and fell to her knees. The nearside wing smashed into her shoulder and sent her sprawling into the wall of the stable. She put her hand out to break her fall and felt her wrist crack, just before her head crashed heavily into the brickwork. There was a vicious light behind her eyes and then a blackness so absolute she felt herself suffocating in its depths as consciousness ebbed away.

A car drew up to the front of the Hall, and Fenwick watched with relief as his mother climbed out of the back seat with the stiffness inevitable after a high-speed seven-hour journey. He handed her his now sleeping daughter, kissed her cheek briefly and told the driver to take them both home. Then he turned at once to find Boyd. He was standing with his men in the yard at the back of the Hall, watching helplessly as flames engulfed the roof of the building, fanned by the strong winds that were gusting around them. As Fenwick walked up, Boyd turned and spoke to him.

'If she's still in there, Chief Inspector, she's dead.'

Fenwick shook his head. He would have known if Sally was dead. Somehow she had escaped; he was convinced of it.

'Are you sure she's not hiding on the estate?'

'Half my team have left to check the cottages, and your constable searched the outbuildings earlier.'

At the mention of Nightingale's name, Fenwick felt his heart shrinking. He looked around. She wasn't with the group.

'Give me your torch.'

'What?' Boyd looked at him stupidly.

'Give me your torch!' Fenwick snatched it from him and ran towards the

293

stable block, a terrible fear growing inside him. It was his own life he'd pledged in return for Bess's; nobody else's. The din of the blaze and attendant firemen dwindled as he turned into the square stable yard.

'Nightingale!' He shouted out her name as he searched the first building. There were footsteps in the yard outside as Boyd sent men to join the search. He heard a shout: 'Over here!'

Two of Boyd's team were bending over a motionless figure lying on the muddied straw.

'Sweet Jesus, no,' Fenwick whispered to himself, feeling a terrible sickness.

He joined them and crouched down, shining his torch on to the bone-white face of the woman who lay on her side, half curled into a ball. A huge bruise was already showing on the side of her face, and blood trickled from her nose.

'Get an ambulance here now!' His voice was harsh, full of anger and hatred.

Nightingale didn't seem to be breathing, and he reached out and felt at the base of her jaw for a pulse. There was the faintest beat, and he pressed harder, just to be sure, letting his hand linger on the smooth skin as if in comfort.

Then he felt the ground shudder, and two medics with a stretcher rushed into the yard. He stood back to let them reach her and watched as they strapped a collar around her neck and lifted her carefully on to the stretcher.

'Will she be all right?'

'No idea. She's obviously taken a heavy blow all down her left side, so who knows what internal injuries there are, and with a head injury like this there's no way of telling until she's been looked at properly.'

Fenwick watched them take her away in the ambulance that his daughter hadn't needed, and tried to rationalise the guilt he felt growing within him. He couldn't and his thoughts would lead to madness. He focused his anger on Sally.

He examined the yard with new eyes; Sally must have had a car hidden out here. There were fresh scratches on one of the wooden gate posts, and traces of silver paint glinted in the light from his torch. Fenwick knew in his gut that she had come this way.

'Her escape route,' he said simply, and Boyd nodded, even as he shouted fresh instructions to his team. Four of them clambered into a sturdy four-wheel-drive car and raced off, bouncing painfully along the track. Another brought a large Ordnance Survey map over and they quickly traced the route they believed Sally must have taken.

'It comes out three miles to the south, here.' Fenwick pointed to an edge of woodland on the map. 'Just a mile away from the main A23. Once she hits that, she could go north to London or south to the coast and we'll lose her.'

'We don't know how long she's been gone but it can't be more than twenty minutes, and it will have taken her a good ten to fifteen minutes at least to clear the woods. We may only be five minutes, maximum ten, behind her.'

'I'll have road blocks set up on all the main roads and scramble the helicopters. Trouble is, there are so many minor roads, she could be anywhere . . . Chief Inspector! Where are you going?'

Fenwick was racing back towards the Hall and called to Boyd over his shoulder.

'You've got this end covered; I'm going to speak to her husband. He may know where she's gone. I'll keep in touch through Operations.'

As he ran to find a car he could commandeer, Fenwick called Cooper in the operations centre.

'I need to speak to Wainwright-Smith, now. Find the officer who's been talking to him and have him call me back at once on my mobile.'

Fenwick drove the strange car efficiently, delighted to feel the power of a two-litre engine surge when he put his foot down. At the entrance gates he paused – right or left, north or south: should he wait or guess? He turned south. She had spent more than five years on the south coast and he was willing to bet that she was heading for familiar territory.

CHAPTER FORTY-SEVEN

His mobile phone rang and he snatched it up quickly. Cooper was on the other end of the line, calling from the station.

'I've spoken to Wainwright-Smith and he's going to call you direct, but he says his wife's contacted him. She's on her way to a harbour just outside Peacehaven, about nine miles east of Brighton. I've let Operations know, and the Superintendent has already briefed Brighton Division.'

'Where in Peacehaven?'

'At Halingford Harbour. Wainwright-Smith says they have a motor boat there. Apparently she plans to hide overnight, collect money from a private account and then take the boat over to France tomorrow.'

'I'm on my way there right now. Get details to Boyd.'

He broke the connection, eager to keep the phone free for Alexander, and pressed the accelerator pedal to the floor. Wind buffeted the car and he realised he was heading into a rising storm. Angry gusts were stripping new leaves off trees and snapping older branches that couldn't bend to their sudden force. Five miles beyond Harlden, an old pine branch lay across the road and he had to brake sharply. He was drawing away from it when Wainwright-Smith finally reached him.

'Chief Inspector, she's just called me again and she's changed her plan. She almost got caught in one of your road blocks and it spooked her. She's cut across country.'

'Which route?'

'Towards Lewes, I think, but that's not the point. She's going to leave the country tonight. She's asked me to join her – in fact, she thinks I'm already on my way.'

'Surely she's not thinking of sailing on a night like this? It must be blowing force six or more.'

'More, I think, but she's a competent sailor. One of her sugar daddies owned a launch down there and paid her to go sailing with him.'

Fenwick, driving at over seventy along the empty A23, now turned with a squeal of rubber on to the A27 that skirted north of Brighton. Sally was probably only a few miles ahead on the empty, orange-lit road. It was nearly three thirty in the morning, but he felt as alert as if he'd just had a good night's sleep.

'Where are you supposed to meet her?'

'At Salingford Harbour. It's two miles west of Peacehaven, little more than a cobb with a slipway into the water. We have our boat there.'

'Did you say *Salingford*? My sergeant thinks you said Halingford.'

'Good Lord, no. That's miles away.'

Fenwick's phone emitted a series of high-pitched bleeps. His battery was running low, not surprising given his usage of it that night.

Alexander heard it. 'Don't worry, I'll call him straight back. I have his number.'

'What time is she expecting you?'

'Between four and four fifteen. Chief Inspector?'

A sudden pleading in Wainwright-Smith's tone immediately alerted Fenwick.

'What?'

'She told me what she's done.'

'Which is?'

'How she killed Graham, the abduction of your daughter, and about shooting FitzGerald tonight.'

'Nothing about murdering your uncle?'

There was a pause, then Wainwright-Smith said simply, 'No.'

Fenwick suspected that he was lying, but realised that that was one crime they would never be able to prove now.

'Why are you telling me all this?'

'I thought you ought to know!' Wainwright-Smith sounded surprised. 'It won't affect her defence. With the lawyers I can hire, you won't get a conviction. I've already received advice that we have grounds for pleading not guilty on the grounds of diminished responsibility.'

Fenwick could feel his anger, present from the moment he had been told that his daughter had disappeared, growing in intensity. His chest, neck and face felt white hot and he was gripping the wheel so hard his fingers ached.

'My job is to apprehend her, not try her, sir – so why don't you give this a rest.' He could hear his voice tight, hard, barely polite, and bit his tongue. His phone was wedged so tightly between his jaw and his shoulder that his neck muscles suddenly went into spasm. He asked Wainwright-Smith to repeat directions to the harbour and was glad when the battery finally gave out for he was no longer able to trust himself to speak.

For the next ten minutes he concentrated on nothing but the route ahead. He was driving on a minor road across the South Downs which descended into the silent village of Rottingdean. At the coast he turned left, through Saltdean, then was forced to cut his speed as he searched on his right for the road that would take him down to the harbour where Sally was waiting for her husband. He switched off his engine and lights and tried to called the Harlden operations centre. It was 04.08 by his watch; plenty of time had passed for Brighton Division to assemble a team and arrest Sally as she waited for her husband. His phone was dead but there was a call box not far ahead so he walked over and dialled the enquiries centre. He asked to be put through to Cooper.

'What's happening, Sergeant? I'm at the rendezvous and there's no one else here.'

'They are, sir! Brighton's mobilised a full team and Inspector Boyd's just joined them. Problem is, there's no sign of Sally Wainwright-Smith.'

A horrible idea occurred to Fenwick.

'Which harbour, Cooper?'

'Halingford, about two miles east of Peacehaven.'

'She's at *Salingford*, not Halingford; that's seven miles away. Alexander Wainwright-Smith was supposed to call you. Get the team over here right now!'

'Are you sure she's there, sir?'

'I don't have eye contact but she's not where you are, and I've just followed Wainwright-Smith's exact directions, so yes, I am sure. Hurry them up or she'll start to panic. She's expecting her husband by quarter past.'

'I'll put you on to Inspector Boyd – hold on.'

There was a pause, then the familiar Yorkshire voice.

'We're sending half the team over, sir, and the coastguard is alerted too, but can you go and make visual contact? I don't want to send the whole lot in case we miss her.'

'OK. I'll try and call you back within the next five minutes.'

It was 04.12 as he opened the door of the phone box. It was caught at once by the force of the wind. Each gust smelt of salt and rotting seaweed. It stung his exposed face and brought tears to his eyes as he stumbled down the unlit path to the sea.

Sally waited in the lee of an abandoned chandler's stall, clutching the ignition key for the boat tightly in her hand. The harbour was empty except for half a dozen boats, which bobbed in the chop that found its way in despite the encircling sea wall. Tonight there were white horses even within its sheltering arms, and she hoped they would be able to put off the start of their journey until the weather had improved.

Sally looked at her watch, started to worry and then remembered that Alex had said he might be late. She would wait until five o'clock and then return to her car. She looked down at her feet as if to check that her suitcase was still there. It contained every single item of value that she owned. Of course there were millions in their joint offshore account, but this was hers, absolutely and in her own name. There was ten thousand pounds in cash that she had taken from the Hall safe that afternoon, the family diamonds and her Patek Philippe watch. On top were the few clothes she could fit in, plus toiletries and shoes. She had chosen a stout aluminium case in which to carry her worldly possessions. It was heavy but water-proof, and the sight of it at her feet filled her with an extraordinary feeling of security.

Fenwick stumbled over a stone that had rolled into the single-lane road that wound down to the shore, and paused for a full minute to let his eyes adjust to the dark. There were a few houses around but they were in darkness, and thick scudding clouds covered the moon. As he waited he thought about the mix-up of names – Halingford instead of Salingford. It was a crazy mistake to have happened, particularly as it was Operations procedure to spell out the names letter by letter.

The more he thought about it, the more certain he became that it was no mistake. Wainwright-Smith had sent the full operations team to the wrong location, yet directed Fenwick with minute care to another one. If Sally was here, then Fenwick had been set up to meet her on his own. Why? He hunched down and crept along the narrow roadway. About thirty metres from the shore, the screening hedgerow petered out and he could see the beach ahead. Even in the pitch black the waves shone with an eerie phosphorescence as they crashed and broke on the shingle. To his right was the tiny harbour, with an electric storm lantern hanging from a post by the gate to the boat-owners' moorings. At first he thought the place was deserted, but then the lantern swung in a wide arc and he caught site of a figure huddling in the shelter of a small hut. It was Sally.

He felt a surge of adrenaline. She was less than a hundred and fifty metres away; he could reach her within half a minute. Part of him wanted to rush out and grab her immediately, but then he remembered that she could be armed, and that he had deliberately been sent out here alone and without backup for a reason he couldn't fathom.

Before returning to the phone box to call Boyd, he took a moment to scan the scene. The coast here was long and featureless, marked only by the faint line of surf on the shore. To his left as he faced the sea he could see a few lights shining still in the centre of Peacehaven two miles away; otherwise, there was nothing but blackness. He was edging back towards his car when he noticed that one of the far lights seemed to be moving towards him, then another and another. As they came closer, he realised that they were the headlights of oncoming cars; it was Boyle's team. Any moment now Sally would notice the sudden traffic and wonder at its significance. He hesitated only for a second before deciding what he needed to do.

Sally was scanning the western road, desperate to spot the lights from Alex's car, and at first she ignored the cars to the east, but it was strange to see three cars driving together this late at night, and she watched them come closer with growing apprehension. The wind was screaming around the hut and she could hear nothing else, which made their steady advance almost predatory. She held a hand up to her eyes to shade them from the rain and peered into the distance, then a movement closer to her caught her attention and she swung round to face the landward road with its scattering of houses. She saw a tall figure enter the harbour and then start towards her. At first she thought it must be Alex and she almost cried out, but then stopped herself. Something was wrong.

Alex had said he would be carrying a torch and that he'd flash their signal of three dots – 'S' for Sally – to let her know all was well. This man walked with his hands in his pockets, head bent, and there was something wrong in that walk. This man was too tall. This man wasn't Alex.

She realised in a sudden panic that this could be a trap. Alex had been taken somehow and this man had been sent in his place to capture her. She had left her gun to burn at the Hall. Unarmed, alone, there was no way she could fight him. He was still well over a hundred yards away, neither running nor ambling. If she moved quickly enough she could yet reach her boat. It was her only chance.

To her right, the chill black sea thrashed against the harbour wall. Ahead of her, away in the distance, her boat strained against its mooring, eager to escape. She picked up her case and ran towards it. The wind was ice cold, stronger now than it had been all day, and she could see white horses form and dissolve into foam in front of her. Her feet touched the wet stone of the lower wall and she was struck at once by the sea spray flung up into her face. She heard the man cry out her name and ran even faster. It *was* Fenwick! The weight of her case slowed her down, but it was her only lifeline and she couldn't leave it behind.

She heard another shout behind her as she reached the boat. She turned on the petrol as a matter of habit but the night was so dark now that she could barely see the controls. By the flickering flame of her lighter she pushed the key into the ignition. She turned it, and the engine spluttered then grudgingly coughed into life.

Fenwick looked along the harbour-wall, disappearing into the darkness. He could see Sally crouched in the cockpit of the sturdy sea-going boat but couldn't believe she would be foolhardy enough to try and leave the tiny harbour and head out to sea. Waves were crashing over the top of the stout stone wall, leaving the rough concrete blocks and seaweed-covered rocks awash with spray.

He called out: 'Stop! Halt! Police!' but there was a sudden white swirl of foam and he watched as she yanked the mooring line free.

'Sally, for God's sake! Come back! You'll never make it!'

He couldn't tell whether his words reached her over the noise of the wind and engine, but she carried on relentlessly driving the boat towards the stormy waters at the harbour mouth. The protective wall was a long curving arm of stones and concrete blocks about five feet wide and twelve high with a flat, roughly finished walkway along the top. Fenwick started to run along its slippery cobbles and was drenched within seconds by the relentless pounding of the waves. Twice he was knocked off his feet as spray crashed over him, and he had to cling on to the slimy rocks to prevent himself from sliding into the water. Sally was close enough to see now, white-faced, wide-eyed, determined.

He watched helplessly as the small boat fought through the churning mass of water swirling around the rocks that marked the end of the harbour wall. At times the force of the sea was so strong that she appeared to go backwards, but eventually the nose of the boat crept forward.

'Sally! Don't do it. Come back!'

She turned to face him as if his words had reached her, and in the faint glow cast by the harbour light he was sure that he saw her smile and shake her head. He was almost at the end of the wall now. The waves here were higher and stronger than they were closer to land, and he could barely retain his balance, but he was still desperate to try and stop Sally from rushing headlong into almost certain death. Her boat seemed tiny in the waves, and even with its powerful motor he could see that she was already in trouble.

Behind him there was a sudden sweep of headlights. He looked back; the rest of the team had arrived. When he turned around again he had lost his night vision and stumbled on the rocks as a solid wall of water almost pitched him head first into the churning maelstrom at the foot of the sea wall. He landed heavily on his knees, felt the right one creak and crack as his old injury took the strain badly, and put out his hands to prevent himself falling. Sharp rocks lacerated his palms but there was no pain as he clung desperately the top of the wall.

At first Sally had felt confident of her ability to handle the boat. She had driven it many times and it was in good condition with a strong engine. She had thrown her suitcase into the bottom of the cockpit and eased smoothly away, but as soon as she came out from the protection of the wall, her perspective was shattered. Waves buffeted the craft and the wind was so strong that its noise drowned out thought; she found it hard to correct the boat's course to avoid it being swamped, and it shipped inches of water within minutes. She felt even more tiny and exposed now as she moved beyond the protecting wall and out to sea, but the thought of returning to face Fenwick and certain imprisonment filled her with horror.

The boat bounced and jumped in the waves, as light as a cork, and she had to apply the throttle just to keep it steady. She could feel the pull of a strong undertow and saw the sea churn as it was sucked through the harbour mouth. Wind and spray stung her face, almost blinding her. The power of the waves even this close to the shore was awesome, and she was suddenly afraid. She decided on impulse to turn the boat around and return to the harbour. Anything was better than facing the storm alone at sea.

As she manoeuvred the boat a fierce gust tossed the bow up and round as if it had been made of paper. A following wave crashed into the side, knocking her off balance. For a frantic moment she lay in the bottom of the boat in three inches of water, looking up at the waves above her. They seemed to tower over the side. When she stood up, their height diminished, yet their threat did not. She wrenched the wheel around again fighting the force of the waves.

Ahead of her the violence of the sea, whipped up by storm-force winds, was being funnelled into a ten-metre gap between the arms of the harbour wall. She would have to run its gauntlet.

As he clung on to the sea wall, unable to stand because of the force of the wind and breaking waves, Fenwick watched the boat falter as Sally tried to turn it back through the waves. For long seconds she fought their strength but then a wave crashed over her stern and the small craft spun like a top. The undertow caught it and inexorably dragged it towards the churning water out to sea beyond the harbour mouth. He was momentarily close enough to see the terror in Sally's eyes as she fought for control of the craft. She struggled to keep it steady and opened the engine to full throttle to pull back into the harbour. For a moment he thought she had succeeded, then a huge weight of water crashed over the bow and the wheel was jerked from her hands with enough force to knock her off her feet. He heard a faint cry of terror, high-pitched and childlike, and any hatred he had towards her evaporated even before the sound died. He was overcome by pity and an instinctive urge to save her.

There were two life belts on a post at the extreme end of the wall. Crouching to prevent himself from being knocked off balance and into the sea, he threw one as far as he could, watching its stout nylon rope snake out into the air before being blown back inland. It fell far short of where she lay in the bottom of the boat, holding on to her silvery case as if it could somehow save her life. He stood up to his full height and cast the rope again.

It bounced into the water mere metres away. He dragged it back and was about to throw for the third time when he sensed a huge pressure of air and turned to see a black wall of water rolling in on them both from the open sea.

Sally felt a tipping sensation, as if the boat was coming down on top of her. As she held the suitcase tightly to her chest, she looked up at the side of the boat above her, and beyond that at the mountain of water that was slowly falling on top of her. Then the boat was no longer beneath her and she felt the sea surround her body. Her legs kicked out instinctively, but her arms still held on to her suitcase as if it would somehow buoy her up and keep her afloat. At first, the airtight case floated easily in the choppy waves. Then, it slowly filled with water and started to sink. The undertow sucked greedily at her legs as another wave washed over her, and suddenly that was all there was: the night, the water and her money. She looked up, eyes and mouth wide, as the waters closed over her head. She thought she saw a hand stretching out for her, brushing her fair hair as it floated back up towards the surface, but she couldn't reach it and sank down and away, holding her suitcase tight, until finally her eyes closed.

Fenwick felt his legs lifted off the rocks by the wave as it carried him over the edge of the harbour wall and down beneath the surface of the sea at the harbour mouth. The waves caught him at once, greedy and powerful, and started to suck him out into the Channel. He surfaced once and gulped a desperate lungful of air before yet another wave filled his nose and mouth with scalding salt water. His lungs were burning and his legs ached with the effort of kicking against the current. With one superhuman effort he strained up to the surface again and took another breath, arms beating the water in a vain effort to stay above the deadly suction of the undertow. It was hopeless; it was too strong. The weight of the waves conspired with the drag of the current to suck him under, and he went down for the final time, eyes wide.

An orange nylon rope shone like a beacon in the water in front of him. He lunged for it, feeling its coarse slipperiness burn his fingers, and pull away. He reached again and caught it. With burning muscles he pulled against it until his head was back above water. He rested his cheek against the ridiculous polystyrene ring, too exhausted to do more, arms and legs numbed by the cold. He could see men on the wall now, waving to him, calling him in, but it was impossible for him to move. He was caught like a fish on a line between the power of the current and the anchored rope. They were only ten feet away but it might as well have been a mile. They couldn't reach him and he was stuck fast, with waves beating his hands and arms in a constant deadly rhythm. He realised that unless they did something he was going to die, within sight of land, within a stone's throw of help, and the pointlessness of it all filled him with a fury so strong it flooded his useless arms with renewed strength. He clung on and willed them to drag him in, but he had no strength left other than a desperate desire to hang on, fuelled by the thought of his family and the irony of dying like this. He felt the suction lessen. Then there were rocks under his toes and he was able to wedge his left foot into a crevice and push his body forward through the water.

Torchlight swung through the night above his head and a hand reached out for him, so close that he could see the fingernails thick with grime from the rocks. He made one last enormous effort to close the gap and at last, felt strong arms reach down to lift him up and wrap a coarse blanket around him.

CHAPTER FORTY-EIGHT

Fenwick woke up for the second time in a small private room in an anonymous hospital. He knew, in an entirely abstract way, that had been here for three days, since the night that Sally Wainwright-Smith had died, her body swept out to sea and still unrecovered. The doctors had stitched his hands and put his knee back together, and today he would be allowed home, under strict instructions to keep all weight off his leg for a further three weeks. Instructions he was already determined to ignore, because as soon as he saw his children he was going to hold them until it hurt too much to go on.

But it wasn't that longed-for thought that made him close his eyes; it was the continuing confusion in his mind surrounding Alexander Wainwright-Smith. Ever since he had first regained consciousness he had been obsessed with thoughts of the man. How could he ever have thought him an innocent dupe? He should have realised that Alexander would never allow Sally to act against his wishes. He had inherited more than the Wainwright millions. He had his grandfather's savage domination and his uncle's obsessive need to control everything around him.

After hours of thinking, Fenwick was convinced that Alexander was implicated in the planning of all the Wainwright deaths, and that Sally was simply his weapon of choice. He also realised that he would never be able to prove it. Sally was dead.

He was still puzzled by what had happened on the night of Sally's death; why had Alexander sent him to meet her alone? Fenwick was convinced that he had been set up, even though Boyd had accepted an explanation from Wainwright-Smith that it had been the result of a simple mistake. What possible motive impelled a man to isolate his wife at a hopeless and dangerous rendezvous – for Alexander could surely have persuaded her to wait somewhere else – and then send the father of the child she had just abducted and tried to burn to death to meet her on his own?

Had Wainwright-Smith expected him to kill his wife? The thought shocked and appalled him. Surely the man realised that Fenwick would be compelled to seek justice before revenge? Then it occurred to him that perhaps Alexander had expected him to behave as he would have done himself; a common mistake. Fenwick rubbed his forehead with a bandaged hand, trying to dispel the headache that still lingered from that terrible night. If he had been sent to kill Sally, then Wainwright-Smith had judged him ill . . . and yet his wife *had* died. Fenwick sat bolt upright in bed, startling the orderly who had come in to deliver his morning coffee. She backed out quickly, leaving Fenwick staring blankly at the opposite wall with a look of horror on his face. It wasn't Fenwick whom Wainwright-Smith had manipulated that terrible night but his own wife! He had driven Sally to attempt an escape she could never have accomplished against a trained team of officers intent on her capture.

How often had Alexander set the stage and then sat back, perhaps miles away, to wait for his wife's psychotic yet malleable behaviour to deliver for him the rewards that had before been just beyond his reach? He had his inheritance, had rid himself of a dangerous wife, and was free at last of FitzGerald's inside control of the family firm. He may have lost the Hall to the fire but he had enough left to have made all his plotting worthwhile. Unless Miles Cator and his team found enough evidence to close the business for money-laundering, Alexander would literally get away with murder: his uncle's death, Fish's, his cousin's, now finally his wife's.

It was as if his thoughts of the Commander had conjured him up. Miles Cator breezed into Fenwick's room unannounced carrying a bunch of grapes wrapped in a brown paper bag. The man looked tired but he smiled when he saw that the patient was awake.

'I came to say thank you, Chief Inspector. I'm glad to hear that you're making a full recovery.'

'Thank you?' Fenwick's mouth was dry and his voice came out harshly.

'Yes, for the Wainwright case. It's a gem. With the papers you gave us, and particularly Arthur Fish's little brown book, we have more than enough information to open a formal inquiry. I'm going to seek a court order today for the suspension of trading across the whole business, and then the Fraud Squad will go in along with the rest of my team, Customs and Excise and the Inland Revenue. That's why I'm here in Sussex, finalising the arrangements. We'll be in there for months, but at the end of it I'm confident we'll have exposed one of the biggest and most carefully concealed money-laundering operations the UK has ever seen. You deserve most of the credit for this and I'm going to make sure that you get it, even though I'm sure there will be plenty of others wanting more than their fair share!' He didn't need to mention who he meant, and Fenwick enjoyed his knowing grin.

Cator shook Fenwick's bandaged hand with care and left the grapes on his bedside table before bidding him a cheerful farewell.

Fenwick dropped his head into his hands, not in despair but with a huge sense of relief. Thank God for Arthur Fish. To Wainwright-Smith he must still seem a minor casualty of his wife's paranoid psychosis, but in reality Fish was his nemesis. By his death he might eventually bring down the Wainwright empire after over a century of totalitarian and utterly selfish dominance. He didn't know whether Wainwright-Smith knew of the extent of the corruption beneath the skin of his family firm, and he didn't care. The reality was that everything for which the man had manipulated, married and murdered was going to vanish tomorrow, vaporised thanks to Arthur Fish's little brown book. To his amazement Fenwick found yet again that he did believe in God – an Old Testament vengeful and jealous God Who from time to time would mete out justice beyond the wit of man.

He felt empty but calm with this realisation, and gradually the pain of his knee returned him to reality. His coffee had grown cold but he drank it anyway and was dozing despite the caffeine when his next guest arrived. He was glad his eyes were closed; it meant that he could regain control of his emotions before he opened them and looked his visitor in the eye.

'I won't stay long but I had to come to say thank you. You tried to save her, despite everything; you cared enough to want her to live, and I'm incredibly grateful to you.'

Fenwick shook his head gently as if to clear the haze of sleep from his mind, and Alexander mistook the gesture.

'No, I'm so glad you tried, particularly knowing what she'd done. It means that even you, you of all people, thought she was worth saving.' With his heightened sense of awareness, Fenwick could hear the artificiality of Wainwright-Smith's voice, and wondered how often he had practised that heart-broken yet grateful tone.

He couldn't think of anything to say. He felt physically sick at the man's hypocrisy, and only the thought of the court order kept a look of loathing from his eyes.

'There *was* good in her, you know, there really was. If she hadn't had such a terrible childhood she'd have been a wonderful person, I know it.'

Alexander sounded close to tears and Fenwick looked at him afresh. He had rarely encountered true wickedness. He had seen stupidity, greed, hate, and even love in excess, with all its terrible consequences, but wickedness was rare. Sally had been wicked, either born that way or nurtured into evil, but what was it that had made her husband so?

'I'm very tired.'

'Of course, I'll go.' Wainwright-Smith gave him a superficially sympathetic smile and left.

Fenwick rested his head back against his pillow, and watched his unwelcome guest depart. Within twenty-four hours Alexander's whole world would fall apart; his bank accounts frozen, his reputation left in tatters and his influence bankrupt. It couldn't happen to a better person. He never wanted to see the man again.

Half an hour later, the ward sister walked in, brisk and cool.

'The doctor says you can go any time you like now, Chief Inspector. Shall I get your clothes out for you?'

'No, I can manage.'

'Well, I'll bring the wheelchair round in fifteen minutes.'

'For the last time, Sister, I do not need a wheelchair.' They had been arguing this point since early morning.

'Your injuries are not to be taken lightly. If you don't convalesce properly it will have very serious consequences, particularly for a man of your age.'

There was no point arguing with her.

'Tell me, Sister, is DC Nightingale still in here?'

'Yes, she's in the room at the far end of the ward, but she'll be out soon. Another day or two at most will see her right. *And* she'll have put on some weight before she goes!'

Fenwick didn't doubt it if the sister had anything to do with it. As soon as she'd left, he washed, shaved and dressed quickly, ignoring the deep ache in his muscles and the pain in his right knee that made him hobble on his crutches. He was determined to be gone before she returned. He picked up the grapes and put them in his pocket, then walked painfully down the corridor.

Nightingale was lying propped up on pillows, reading a book, her face pale except where the bruising had dyed it purple and yellow.

'Hello. I brought you some grapes.'

At the sound of his voice she looked up, startled, and her hand flew to cover the contusions on her cheek. When she answered, her voice was brittle and high-pitched.

'Thank you, that's very thoughtful. They've let you out?'

'Yes, this morning.'

'And you've had time to buy grapes already?'

She really was going to be an excellent police officer.

'Well, no, someone brought them for me and I thought you deserved them more.'

She smiled, relaxed and confident.

'It's still a kind thought. Come in, sit down. I need to talk to you.'

'If you're sure it won't tire you.'

She shook her head, still smiling. 'I'm fine. They're worrying too much.'

'Still, you need to build up your strength. I want you back fighting fit.'

There was an awkward pause. He had just reminded them both of who he was and therefore the nature of their relationship. The smile slowly faded from her face.

'Don't worry, sir, I'll be back soon.' She looked away and there was a small silence, then she blinked and looked him firmly in the eyes again. 'I do need to talk to you, about the Wainwright case.'

Fenwick suppressed a laugh; she really was impossible.

'It's closed, by which I mean there won't be a trial for the murders. The investigation into the money-laundering will go on, but that's not our affair, thank goodness.'

'No, it's the murders I want to talk about. I've been thinking. I'm not sure we should close the case like that.'

'Not again! I seem to recall that this is the second time that you've tried to persuade me to reopen a Wainwright case. Sally's dead, so is James FitzGerald. They were the criminals; two separate and devious people intent on manipulating Wainwright's for their own purposes.'

'Let's ignore them, sir. I'm talking about Alexander Wainwright-Smith. What makes you think that Sally was working alone? Do you really think she could have orchestrated the whole thing by herself? This took stealth and planning, starting with the death of Alexander's uncle.'

'I think Alexander is the real beneficiary of all this – he has his money, control of the family business and freedom at last from a psychopathic wife. He can do what he likes with his life now. Supposing he knew her background, married her and manipulated her into committing these crimes . . .'

Fenwick managed to cover his look of admiration by bending to help himself to some of his gift of grapes. She was right, of course she was, and some day he might just tell her so. But not today.

'No, Nightingale, this has to stop. It's all supposition and the result of having too much time on your hands.'

'So you think she was working alone?' Nightingale looked glum and Fenwick attributed it to her disappointment at his lack of interest in the theory.

'I think, Nightingale,' he soft-punched her good shoulder, suddenly very aware of the bandage on the other one, 'that the case is closed, and you should concentrate simply on getting better.'

Nightingale looked at him, frowned, then grinned suddenly.

'Just testing,' she said, and laughed as he threw a grape at her head.